THE
LOST SHEEP

STERLING R. WALKER

The Lost Sheep
©2013 Sterling R. Walker

Cover by Jessica Bartlett and Nathaniel Walker
Model: Kelly Furr

Disclaimer: All characters appearing in this work are
fictitious. Any resemblance to real persons living or dead
is purely coincidental.

Printed in the United States of America

ISBN 13: 978-0990019015
ISBN 10: 0990019012

PART I
SHRINKING

ONE
OVERHEARD

"SHIMA, GET BLAZE or Lorina on the com for me."

Heshima Oryang hesitated at the com control board, her long brown fingers hovering over the keypad. "But . . . Danae"—Shima still wasn't used to addressing Captain Shepherd by her first name—"did you not tell them they could have three days for their honeymoon?"

"We can't afford to delay the lift another day." Although Danae's voice was filtered through the ship's speakers, Shima could still detect the tension in her tone. "I can't explain it—it's just a gut feeling."

Shima was well-acquainted with the captain's gut feelings. "I will put it through to your office." She tapped in the code for Blaze's ship-to-shore com but left the speaker open on her console.

"This is Smith." The engineer's drawl sounded composed, although Shima could hear some muttered complaints in the background from his bride Lorina Murphy.

"Blaze, I want you and Lorina to check out of your inn and meet me at the beauty salon across the street," Danae began without preamble. "We have a lot of work to do if we're going to lift tonight."

"Tonight, Captain?"

"We lift at midnight. Sorry to cut the honeymoon short."

There was a moment's hesitation. "I understand, Captain."

"See you in fifteen minutes. Shepherd out." Shima watched the light wink out on Blaze's connection. "I know you're listening, Shima, so meet me at the airlock."

Shima was embarrassed to be caught eavesdropping, but she knew the captain understood her insatiable need to keep track of every detail aboard the *Ishmael*. She shrugged it off as a minor infraction. "Yes, Captain—I mean, Danae."

She descended the ladder to the entryway, where Danae Shepherd was waiting for her at the open airlock. Shima hadn't seen her since yesterday. She tried not to gawk at the captain's startling transformation. Her short brown hair had been dyed jet black, along with her eyebrows, and her fair skin was tanned like she had spent weeks in the sun. Danae was also wearing brown contact lenses, disguising her prominent blue eyes.

"What do you think?" Danae slipped on a pair of dark sunglasses. "Do you think Acheron would recognize me?"

"I would not recognize you." Shima tried to keep a neutral expression on her face. She was also unaccustomed to seeing the captain in casual attire. "What are you wearing?"

"The new uniform."

Shima noted the white letters embroidered on the breast pocket of Danae's red, pink, and orange tropical print shirt. "*Alex's Legacy?*"

Danae turned to the round doorway of the airlock. "I'm changing the name of the ship."

Shima suddenly had a hundred questions but couldn't seem to vocalize a single one. She decided to say nothing, preferring to listen and observe.

She followed the captain down the temporary staircase to the sandy soil. The two women walked across the field of knee-high tropical grasses toward a large white Victorian-style house facing the main road. The field had once produced sugarcane but hadn't been farmed since Danae Shepherd's mother died two years ago. Shima glanced over at the huge, abandoned sugar processing plant, which stood out like a sore thumb on the lush open plain. There were green hills in the distance, and a few coconut palm trees dotted the landscape. It was a beautiful and private setting for an orphanage.

The orphanage. Shima felt a flutter of fear. *I cannot believe she wants me to be in charge of The Lost Sheep.* She had tried to envision what the job would be like, but it was overwhelming. Although the new social worker Gordon Grey had placed many of the orphans in families all over Maui, there were seventy-seven children still in need of homes. And The Lost Sheep was understaffed. Shima would need to hire several more childcare workers and a cook. The thought of conducting interviews with people older and more experienced made her anxious. Her stomach had been in knots ever since Danae announced her promotion a week ago.

I am too young to be given such huge responsibilities. Shima longed to stay on board the *Ishmael* where the routine was comfortable and familiar. *But Danae trusts me. I am her right hand, as she said. I must be strong and do this—for her. She is my mentor, my best friend—my family.* Her mind felt crowded with the myriad of details demanding her attention. She forced herself to focus on the here and now.

Groups of children representing many different nationalities were playing soccer on the large mowed field near the house under the watchful eyes of Olivia Grey, the orphanage's new live-in childcare supervisor. As Shima and Danae reached the house, they discovered some of the younger children sprawled on the front lawn, finger painting under the direction of Elizabeth Murphy, Lorina's mother.

Danae leaned over one child's colorful masterpiece and watched him add fire to his volcano. "Where did you find the paper, Beth?"

"Niyati found it in an antique roll-top desk in one of the upstairs bedrooms."

Shima noted the presence of Blaze and Lorina's adopted Indian daughter. Five-year-old Niyati stayed close by her grandmother, following Beth around the yard as she checked on each child's progress. "Where did you find the paint, Ms. Murphy?"

"Call me Beth, please." She tucked a strand of strawberry-gray hair behind her ear. "It's pudding! I made several batches of chocolate and vanilla and added food coloring. When they're done painting, they can lick their hands clean."

"Good idea!" Danae smiled and nudged Shima. "Do we have her on the payroll as an art teacher?"

"Assistant cook and childcare worker," Shima said.

"Well, let's make her a teacher and double her pay!"

Shima couldn't hold back a chuckle. "Double what pay, Captain? She refused to be on the payroll."

"Free room and board is good enough for me!" Beth laughed. "I'm living in paradise with my daughter and granddaughter! It doesn't get any better than this!"

Shima didn't want to point out the fact that Lorina and Niyati would be heading back to Mars Station aboard the *Ishmael*. "When do the O'Briens need to go to the airport?"

"Tomorrow morning," Beth said. "They wanted to say goodbye to the newlyweds and spend one more afternoon at the beach."

"Are there no beaches in Delaware?" Shima tried to recall her limited knowledge of Earth geography. "Is it not on the Atlantic Ocean?"

Beth snorted. "If you don't mind the chemical soup in the water and the stench of dead fish washed up all over the sand. The only way I'd visit Rehoboth Beach is in a pressure suit."

Danae tugged on Shima's sleeve. "We need to go." She nodded to Beth and climbed into the driver's seat of the fifteen-passenger mint-green solar van parked in the driveway.

Shima climbed in next to Danae and stared out the window as the captain drove the five kilometers into the quiet town of Lahaina, Maui. Along the way, they passed coconut palms and an occasional weather-beaten house or business.

"It's beautiful here, isn't it?" Danae asked. "The people have been friendly and helpful."

"You are trying to cheer me up." Shima kept her nose pressed to the window.

"Yes, I am. I know how you feel, Shima. I didn't think I was ready to captain the ship after my father died. I wish I didn't have to ask you to stay and supervise the orphanage."

"I know. We have spoken of this many times. You said, 'There is no one else I can trust with this.'" Shima sighed. "If I were you, I would make the same decision."

"I'll be back as soon as I can." Danae parked in front of the Whalesong Bed and Breakfast Inn on Front Street.

"I made enough money from the sale of my mother's diamond earrings for the return trip. I *will* be back."

"I know you will. I trust you." Shima managed a weak smile. "Just try not to come back with another bullet hole."

Danae seemed lost in thought for a moment as she scratched her left side, which had been reconstructed from synthflesh from the bottom of her ribcage down to her hipbone. She was also missing the kidney on that side, although novice medic Jake O'Brien had assured her it could be replaced by a more qualified surgeon—when, or *if,* she felt like going under the knife again.

The captain turned to Shima and mustered a half smile. "I promise, no more shootouts."

"Good."

The two women climbed out of the van and crossed the broken pavement to the beauty salon. Blaze and Lorina were waiting out on the sidewalk, holding hands, their overnight bags by their feet. Their mouths dropped open when they caught sight of Danae.

"Is that you, Captain?" Lorina asked. "Why did you change your appearance?"

Danae took off her sunglasses. "This is how we're going to return to Mars Station without walking right into Acheron's waiting arms. I hope you had a nice honeymoon. Sorry to cut it short, but we have a lot of work to do before we lift."

Blaze and Lorina exchanged a mystified look but nodded in unison to Danae.

"We're ready, Captain," Blaze said. "Tell us what we need to do."

"I'll explain everything to you when we go over to the courthouse to change the ship's registry. I need your

DNA imprint on the records, Blaze. I'm listing you as captain."

"Wh-what?" he stammered, but Danae didn't give him time to ask questions.

"You won't need to change your appearance since you already have dark hair and brown eyes. With your Native American ancestry, you could easily pass for a Hawaiian, but your lovely Irish bride"—she turned to Lorina—"will need a makeover."

Lorina clutched Blaze's arm. "Why do I have to—?"

"Because Acheron would recognize you. Don't worry; it won't be permanent." Danae gestured to the door of the beauty salon. "Nalani is waiting for you. I already paid her yesterday for your transformation."

Lorina shot Blaze an anguished look, but he leaned down and kissed her on the forehead. "I'll love you no matter what you look like."

As Lorina turned to walk into the salon, Shima noted Blaze's wistful gaze. He stared after her until the screen door closed.

Shima and Danae exchanged a sympathetic glance.

"Just put your bags in the van, Blaze, and we'll walk to the town hall." Danae pointed down the street. "It's just two blocks that way. Grey already told me which clerk I need to see."

Blaze nodded. "I guess he knows his way around the town hall pretty well by now."

"He finalized six adoptions yesterday," Shima said.

"At this rate, you won't have any children left at the orphanage, madam director." Blaze grinned at Shima as he tossed the bags into the back of the van.

"That's the general idea," Danae said.

Twenty minutes later, Shima was pressing her right thumb to the ID lock on a datapad. When she lifted her thumb, the Asian clerk standing across the counter from her turned the wafer-thin screen around and read the results. He confirmed her DNA from the Earth's database. "Heshima Oryang of Kampala, Uganda."

Shima nodded.

"And now the captain?" Blaze pressed his thumb to the same lock, and the clerk studied the results. "Robert Smith of Tulsa, Oklahoma." He scribbled on the datapad with a stylus for a minute before turning to Danae.

"Let me verify the new information. Merchant ship *Alex's Legacy,* registered on this date in Lahaina, Maui?"

Danae nodded.

"New transmission number: 9857490?"

"Sounds fine."

"Owner: H Oryang. Are you sure you just want her initial on the records?"

"That's right." The captain nodded, impatient.

Shima felt weak in the knees. "Are you sure you want to give the *Ishmael*—I mean, *Alex's Legacy*—to me?" she whispered in Danae's ear.

Danae whispered back, "If anything happens to me, I want you to have the ship."

Shima felt like she was going to cry. "Nothing is going to happen to you. You are going to come back from Mars in one piece. You promised."

"I'll make sure she keeps that promise." Blaze placed a hand on Shima's thin shoulder, giving her a gentle squeeze of reassurance.

"Can we continue?" The clerk frowned at the interruption. "Captain: RJ Smith."

"That's me." Blaze nodded.

The clerk offered them a different datapad and stylus. "I need the owner's signature here and the captain's here." He pointed to the spaces on the screen. When

Shima and Blaze finished signing and pressing their thumbs to the ID lock for authentication, he said, "That'll be ten thousand dollars for the registry, and I'll need an additional three thousand for your port taxes."

"We aren't docked at a spaceport," Blaze said.

The clerk shrugged. "Makes no difference. All spacecraft on Maui pay port taxes no matter where they're parked."

"Just pay the man, Captain."

It took Shima a moment to realize Danae was speaking to Blaze. He obediently held out his left hand and slid the edge of his black thumbnail through a slot on the proffered datapad. "This will empty the account, Cap—I mean, ma'am."

"I know, but don't worry about it. Our finances are in good shape."

The clerk gave Danae a puzzled look. "The registry is complete. You're free to go."

Shima still felt dazed as they walked out of the dark Lahaina Town Hall into the bright sunshine.

"If I'm the captain, Captain, what are we supposed to call you?" Blaze asked.

Danae shrugged. "We'll figure that out before we dock. Let's get back to the ship."

They walked the two blocks back to the van.

Blaze glanced over at the beauty salon across the street. "What about Lorina?"

"I'll send Vipul to pick her up in an hour. The tanning process takes a long time." As Danae slid into the driver's seat, she glanced with approval at Blaze. "I'm glad to see you already have a tan."

Blaze folded his lanky two-meters-tall frame into the passenger-side seat. "Two days in the sun is all it takes. It's my Osage ancestry, like you said, Captain."

"You are a natural tan, like me." Shima climbed into the middle of the first back seat. "Only you are more like cinnamon and I am dark chocolate."

Danae said, "I'm sort of beige."

"No, more like toasted almond." Shima laughed.

"You're makin' me hungry," Blaze said. "What do the others look like?"

"Ting came out kind of dark." The captain chuckled, stopping for the single traffic light on Front Street. "He could pass for Vipul's younger brother."

"Vipul's *evil* younger brother," Shima muttered, her good mood disappearing at the mention of Ting's name. She noted Blaze's gaping jaw. "Sorry."

Blaze laughed. "Yes, Ting has a way of bringin' out the best in all of us. So what does Jake look like?"

Danae grinned. "You'll have to see him with your own eyes. His mother didn't recognize him."

"I guess that's good since he's wanted by Acheron for practicin' medicine without a license."

"I hope Acheron doesn't recognize *me*," Danae said. "Since I'm wanted for murder."

"Shootin' a predator like Thanatos in self-defense shouldn't be considered murder, Captain," Blaze said.

"I don't think you'll convince the police chief of my innocence." Danae snorted. "Not since I shot *him* in the shoulder."

"You should have aimed higher."

Now it was Danae's turn to look stunned. "Did I hear you right, Shima?"

"That monster abducted my niece and sold her into slavery, along with thousands of other children. I feel nothing but contempt for him. I wish I could go with you! I would make him tell us what he did with Zuri."

Danae frowned. "Are you turning vigilante on me?"

"Sorry!" Shima exchanged a troubled glance with Blaze. "I do not mean to sound so angry."

"It's fine," Blaze said. "Let it out, Shima. We're all friends here."

"We're family." Danae glanced at Shima in the rearview mirror. "I might bring more homeless children back from Mars Station. I know I can depend on you to have everything organized at The Lost Sheep."

"Yes, but I *will* go with you when you search for Zuri."

The captain bit her lip. "We'll talk about that when the *Ishmael*—I mean, *Alex's Legacy*—returns to Maui."

Shima nodded and leaned her head back against the seat. *Not so smooth, Shima. You must be calm and patient, like a responsible leader. You must be more like Danae.* She resolved to keep a better rein on her emotions.

The van pulled into the last driveway at the end of Lahainaluna Road. Shima glanced at the freshly painted sign in front of the house. *The Lost Sheep.* It was a fitting name for an orphanage founded by a woman named Shepherd.

I guess I am also a lost sheep, Shima thought, recalling the fateful day seven years ago on Mars Station when Danae took a frightened, grieving, sixteen-year-old orphan aboard the *Ishmael.* Shima had been a member of the crew, and an unofficial member of Danae's family, ever since.

Do not think about being separated from Danae, Shima advised herself. *Focus on what needs to be done.*

As Blaze climbed out of the van, he was greeted with a leg-hug from Niyati. "*Baba!*"

"Hey, Niyati!" He scooped his daughter up and flipped her over, holding her upside down by her ankles.

Niyati shrieked with laughter. "Down, *baba!*"

Blaze flipped her right-side up and set her back on her feet. "Did you miss us?"

"Where *amma*?" the child demanded, glancing around as Shima and Danae exited the vehicle.

"Getting a haircut," Shima said. "She will be home soon."

At the word *haircut*, Niyati reached up and touched her own black hair, which was cut in a chin-length bob. "*Amma* cut hair."

"Yes, she knows how to give good haircuts, but someone else has to cut hers." Blaze reached into a duffel bag in the back of van and pulled out a dark-haired baby doll dressed in a blue muumuu. "She wanted to make sure you got this."

Niyati shrieked again with delight and grabbed the toy from Blaze, hugging it to her thin chest. "Tenk you, *baba!*"

"Hey, Blaze, welcome back." Jake O'Brien crossed the large front porch and jumped off the side, onto the driveway.

Shima found Blaze's reaction amusing. The engineer shut his gaping mouth with an audible *click*. "Jake?"

The medic shook his hand. "Kind of startling, isn't it?"

Blaze nodded. "There's no way Acheron'll recognize you. You look like the lead singer for a Latino band."

Jake ran a tanned finger across his new tapered sideburns and thin goatee. "Maybe I should call myself Juan."

"Not a bad idea." Danae came around to their side of the van. "We'll need to falsify the ship's crew roster for the port master."

"How can we do that?" Shima asked.

"We just need to find some volunteers willing to let us use their names and traces of their DNA," Danae said.

"But isn't falsifying IDs a felony?" Jake asked.

"Well, compared to murder, or practicing medicine without a license . . ." Danae raised her eyebrows at Jake.

The medic laughed. "Yes, I see what you mean. Just add it to the list of charges."

Blaze glanced down at Niyati, who was clinging to his left leg as if it were a tree trunk. "Speakin' of new names, how many people have you hired since the weddin', Captain?"

"Just one—Phailin Kim. She'll be the cook aboard the *Ishmael*." Danae sighed and rolled her eyes. "I mean *Alex's Legacy*. Shima will have to hire the rest of the orphanage staff."

"Lucky me," Shima muttered.

"How was the honeymoon?" Jake raised his newly blackened eyebrows at Blaze.

Shima almost laughed at the flush spreading across Blaze's cheeks. "I'd love to chat, but I have to get to the ship and make sure the new solar engines are ready to go."

"And Jake has to finishing stocking the infirmary, don't you?" Danae shot him a stern look.

"Yes, ma'am." Jake grinned. "Come on, Blaze. I'll walk you over."

"I will go with you," Shima said. "I want to see how Phailin is managing in the galley."

"Right, just a sec." Blaze went down on one knee and spoke to Niyati. "I have to work now. Can you stay here at the house and wait for *amma* to get back?"

"Yes, *baba*." She smiled at him with a mouth full of artificial baby teeth—her decayed originals had been extracted.

"Good girl."

Shima could see Blaze was turning out to be a good father. He watched Niyati race to the front door before picking up the duffel bags and crossing the lawn toward the ship with Jake.

Shima had to jog a few paces before falling into step between the two men. She felt comfortable with both the easy-going engineer and the temperamental medtech. They had been through a lot together, and she felt a pang of sadness to realize she wouldn't be working with them anymore.

Blaze's new mother-in-law Beth Murphy waved to them from across the field where she was refereeing a game of kickball.

The engineer returned the wave. "What do I call her, Jake? Mom?"

Jake grinned. "I think she'd like that."

Shima noticed Blaze's downcast expression and recalled that his own mother committed suicide when he was only eight years old. "I think it would be nice to have a mother again," she murmured to him so Jake wouldn't overhear.

Blaze cast her an appreciative glance.

Shima changed the subject. "I cannot get used to calling the *Ishmael Alex's Legacy*." She glanced ahead at their destination—the renamed and repurposed ship.

From the exterior, it looked like a giant silver bird. The bridge, infirmary, and galley comprised the oval-shaped head with the decorative glass beak of the helm window jutting out the front. The wings consisted of two levels of passenger and crew cabins with a lounge on the tip of each wing. Right where the belly would be located was the airlock and entryway, and the engines stuck out the back like a tail. It was a one-of-a-kind design.

"Even with all the carefully orchestrated changes, how's the captain going to disguise the ship? Acheron will recognize it as the *Ishmael*," Jake said.

"Have you ever seen a ship once it is docked at a spaceport?" Shima asked.

"Only if you look out the lounge window and see what's docked next door." Jake shook his head. "Outside the ship, all you see is the airlock."

Shima nodded. "Exactly."

"But the port master'll recognize the ship," Blaze said. "Won't he alert Acheron? We didn't exactly leave the station under ideal circumstances."

Jake grimaced. "That's an understatement. I'm sure he's got a nice hologram of the ship right next to his monitor."

"No, the port master has a limited view of the spaceport from the exterior of the station," Shima explained. "The satellite orbiting Mars is outdated and used mainly for audio communication."

"What about surveillance at the airlocks?" Jake asked.

"I read an article in the *Martian Chronicles* about the flaws in spaceport security," Shima said. "The airlock holo-cams, like the rest of the station's equipment, are poorly maintained, due to budget cuts.

"Ships often damage the holo-cams during landings. Ting once mentioned"—the edges of her mouth turned down when she spoke the pilot's name—"that he damaged many holo-cams when he had less experience at the helm.

"The article reported that at least half of the spaceport's holo-cams are not working. With four kilometers of airlocks on fourteen levels, there are about two hundred ships docked, landing, or departing every day. Captain Shepherd believes the port master does not have the time or the resources to get a visual on each one. He will request a copy of the ship's schematics, which we will alter with Lorina's assistance.

"Captain Shepherd is planning to request permission to dock with the merchant ships on Level 14. She hopes the port master will be watching for a passenger ship to dock at a lower level. If we are lucky, the *Alex* will be assigned an airlock without a working holo-cam."

"So you and the captain are trusting the accuracy of one news article and gambling that the port master doesn't catch sight of the ship on surveillance?" Jake shook his head in disbelief. "That's crazy. We have a fifty-fifty chance of being assigned an airlock with a broken holo-cam? Sounds like we need a whole lot of luck to dock without being recognized. And what about holo-cams in the access corridors? I'm sure those are all working."

Shima frowned at Jake before turning to the staircase which led up to the open airlock. "That is why we have also disguised ourselves—so we will not be recognized. And I do not hear any better ideas coming from you." She ascended the stairs without waiting for them to follow.

As Shima stepped into the entryway, she paused and listened to Jake and Blaze's whispered conversation on the ground.

"What happened to our angelic Shima?" Jake asked.

"Don't take it personally," Blaze said. "I think she's just upset about bein' left behind."

"Maybe, but I think she's really mad at Ting too."

"Yes, I noticed some of that on the ride back from town. What did he say to her?"

Jake didn't bother to whisper. "What else? He made a new prediction. He felt it was his duty to inform her of some imminent catastrophe, which would be her fault as the orphanage director."

"What's wrong with that idiot?" Shima had never heard Blaze get angry. "Doesn't she have enough stress to deal with? I'm so tempted to punch his lights out."

"I guess you'd better take a number because I'm first in line. I still don't know what disaster he predicted for Lorina, but it was horrible enough to make her cry."

"What? He told her one of his premonitions? She didn't mention it to me. When did this happen?"

"The first day here when you were laid up in the infirmary. She'd just come back from checking the house with Ting. I've never seen her so upset."

Blaze's tone was arctic. "I think I'll have a word with the clairvoyant cynic as soon as I see him."

"I'd love to stand here and think of ways to torture Ting, but I've got work to do."

"Yes, me too."

Shima heard them ascending the stairs and ducked into the open doorway of the starboard elevator. Her mind was so busy processing what she'd overheard, she almost forgot her reason for boarding *Alex's Legacy*.

Reaching the top level, she turned left and followed the short hallway to the galley. The dining room was empty except for the eight square stainless-steel tables, each with four stainless-steel chairs bolted to the floor. Shima walked over to the long counter which separated the kitchen and dining areas. "Phailin?"

A soprano voice called out, "I'm in the pantry."

Shima walked around the counter into the kitchen and found the new cook struggling to reach the top shelf of the stocked walk-in. "You need to use the android. Its purpose is to assist you."

Phailin came down off her tiptoes and turned to Shima with a dimpled grin. She was a beautiful Asian woman in her mid-twenties with a quick smile and an hourglass figure. Shima felt like a skinny boy compared to the cook. She noted with approval Phailin's Hawaiian-print *Alex's Legacy* shirt and blue jeans uniform.

Phailin looked up again at the elusive shelf. "There weren't any androids on my last ship. Where is it? Could you show me how to use it?"

"Over here." Shima led the way over to the huge kitchen sink and reached into the cabinet beneath it, where the android was recharging in its storage niche. It resembled a bald, chalk-colored department store mannequin. She flipped the switch on the back of its neck to turn it on. It climbed out from under the sink and straightened to its full height of one and a half meters.

Phailin studied the faceless mechanical with a suspicious frown. "How does it work?"

"Just tell it what you need."

"Get me the can of tomato juice on the top shelf of the pantry."

The android's movements were stiff, but it moved fast as it walked to the pantry with Phailin right on its heels. It raised one claw-like arm, which extended like a telescope up to the high shelf. The claw grasped the can and, a moment later, placed it in the cook's waiting hands.

Phailin nodded with approval. "What else can it do?"

"Any task. Just be specific with your directions."

"Can it cook?"

"Not really. It can stir oatmeal and make sandwiches. It does a good job filling plates and cups for the passengers. I think you will find it useful."

"Does it have a name?"

Shima pursed her lips, trying not to smile. "No. It is just an android."

"Can I call it Charlie?"

Shima shrugged. "If you wish. If you have things under control here, I should check the water tanks."

"Right. Thanks."

Shima stopped by her cabin on the third level to do something she put off for several days—packing. Although she owned little, she would need to vacate her cabin for potential passengers. She studied the contents of her tiny closet and realized she had a problem. She didn't have anything to wear except the navy-blue *Ishmael* uniforms and a few off-duty T-shirts and jeans. *Nothing that would look appropriate for an orphanage director,* she thought. *And when do I have time or credits to shop for clothing?*

She decided to recycle the old uniforms, since she wouldn't need them anymore. She took them off the hangers and fed them into the recycle chute, where they would be broken down and processed into new fabric which would be sewn into sheets for the ship. Shima slipped on jeans and a T-shirt before tossing the rest of her clothing into a plastic storage crate on her bed.

She paused to study her reflection in the mirror. Her neat shoulder-length cornrows looked dry, so she took a minute to apply hair gel to her scalp. Her full lips were chapped, so she applied lip balm. Her big brown eyes reflected sadness, but she couldn't do anything to fix them.

Only time will ease the pain, she thought, glancing at a framed hologram on her dresser of a blond young man in an *Ishmael* uniform. It showed him at the airlock, waiting to help a family board. He had a warm toothy smile. The mischievous green eyes behind the silver-framed glasses twinkled for the camera.

Shima felt hot tears begin to sting her eyes. *I must keep busy.* She snatched up the frame and placed it in the box on top of her clothing. The rest of her belongings found their way into the box—hair accessories, a few pieces of jewelry, four books, and a child's drawing of a house Shima once called home. The crayon sketch had been made by her young niece, Zuri Oketta, who'd been abducted from Mars Station seven years ago and sold as a slave, along with hundreds of other homeless children. The drawing was the only tangible connection Shima had to her family in Uganda. Kampala's population had been decimated by starvation and cholera shortly after Shima and Zuri arrived on Mars.

The tears threatened to well up again. *Keep busy.* Shima blinked them away and wrapped the framed drawing in a T-shirt.

All her worldly possessions fit into the one box. Shima closed the lid and carried the box to the starboard lift. She descended to the entryway and left the box on the floor near the airlock because she still had one more task to complete.

She climbed the ladder down to the lowest deck, the basement. In the corridor, she tiptoed past the open doorway to the engine room so she wouldn't distract Blaze from his work. She walked down to the end of the narrow hallway where the cold storage/brig was located, right next to the ship's water tanks.

Shima pressed her thumb to the ID lock next to the doorframe, waited for the door to slide open, and stepped inside the small narrow room. Two five hundred-liter tanks and a refrigerator-size water treatment unit between them took up most of the space.

One tank contained fresh water and the other contained used water from the ship's showers, sinks, and dishwashers. The used water would be treated and recycled into the fresh tank as needed.

She checked the gauge on each tank to verify it was full. Although she knew Danae had arranged to have the fresh tank filled, she still felt a compulsive need to check behind the captain, *since she has had so much on her mind lately.*

She also took a moment to check the control panel for the solid-waste containment tank, which was beneath the floor of the small room. It reported the septic system was empty and functioning normally.

As Shima stepped out of the tank room, she heard angry voices coming from the engine room. Although she didn't intend to eavesdrop, the loud words carried down the corridor.

Lorina Murphy was shouting, "You're not going to Mars without me! I can't believe you're bringing this up again!"

Blaze was trying to keep his voice down. "I wish I didn't have to bring this up again, but we haven't settled anythin'."

"I'm going. There, it's settled!"

The engineer sounded exasperated. "Would you please listen to me for a minute? And please lower your voice."

"I didn't plan to spend our entire honeymoon arguing!"

"I don't want to argue, either."

"Well, what does it look like we're doing, *Robert?*"

Blaze hesitated. "Lorina, I'm not askin' you to stay because I don't want us to be together—that's the last thing I'd ever want. I'm askin' you to stay because it's gonna be *dangerous.*"

"Kirsten Sorensen is my friend! I worked with her at the juvenile shelter for six months! I have to do something to help her!"

"But Captain Shepherd doesn't even have a plan for this rescue—if that's what it is. There's so much we don't know from Dr. Sorensen's transmission. He and Kirsten might both be in jail. As soon as the *Alex* docks at Mars Station, Acheron's probably gonna arrest the entire crew."

"And I'm a member of this crew! Acheron's not going to recognize us—look at me! I'm browner than Niyati!"

"So you look like her birth mother. It's fine, and it's only temporary." Blaze was pleading now. "Please just calm down and listen. You know how much I love you, don't you?"

Shima flushed. *That was definitely not for my ears.* There was no way to exit the basement without being seen by the newlyweds.

Blaze continued, "I just wanna keep you safe. You know what we're up against with Acheron. I can't help feelin' like this'll be a one-way mission."

"Do you have so little faith in *me?* Do you think I became a helpless, fragile female when I said I do?"

"Of course not, I—"

"You don't think I can take care of myself? Don't you remember I broke your nose the first time we met?" There was a trace of humor in her scathing tone.

"How could I forget? It was only three weeks ago."

"Do you remember what I said when Acheron was waving a loaded gun in my face? I'm not afraid of him.

We're in this together, so you can drop the cavalier act. I'm going."

"But —"

"No buts. I'm going."

There was a long pause.

"Good, I'm glad that's settled," Lorina said.

"Not yet." Blaze cleared his throat. "We still have to discuss what to do with Niyati."

"We're taking her with us, of course!"

"We can't—for the same reason I didn't want you to go. It's too dangerous."

"I'm not leaving my daughter behind!"

"She's my daughter too. My name is on the adoption decree right next to yours. Don't I get a say in how we raise her?"

"You're not attached to her like I am! I can't bear the thought of being separated from her!"

"You managed fine for the past two days."

"That's because she was just five kilometers away! I spoke to her on the com twice a day! Leaving her here while we travel to Mars Station is a completely different situation!"

"She's only five. Think of her safety. You don't want to put her in any danger, do you?"

"She'll be safe aboard the ship!"

"Then someone will always have to be on board to look after her. Did you think of that?"

Lorina seemed to have no response for this remark.

"Captain Shepherd will need us all dirtside on the station. Maybe she'll keep Ting on board, but do you trust *him* to watch Niyati?"

Lorina floundered for a rebuttal. "But if we leave her behind, she'll feel abandoned. It could really damage her emotionally. She was already abandoned once by her birthparents."

"So you're sayin' you want to stay on Maui with her?"

"No, that's not what I'm saying!" Lorina's voice cracked. "I have to think about this! I can't make a decision right now!"

"We have to decide right now. We lift tonight. Look," Blaze was trying to sound soothing, "Niyati likes your mother. Beth wants to stay and work at the orphanage, so you know she'll be happy to take care of her granddaughter while we're gone."

"Mom hasn't decided how long she plans to stay. You're assuming too much."

"If your mom doesn't stay, you know Shima will take good care of her."

I hope your confidence in me is not misplaced, Shima thought.

"How long do you think we'll be gone?" There was defeat in Lorina's tone.

Shima arched her eyebrows. *The woman who never loses an argument is giving up? Perhaps she is not as stubborn as Jake claims.*

"Three days there, three days back, maybe a week to locate and make arrangements for the Sorensens. Let's say two weeks—three, at the most."

"Maybe forever if Acheron gets his hands on us."

"I won't let that happen. Trust me."

"I do. You know I do. I don't like the idea of leaving her behind, but you're right, we can't risk her safety."

Shima was relieved to hear the door to the engine room slide shut. She made her escape to the ladder without Blaze or Lorina realizing she overheard their argument. *I cannot concern myself with ship's matters any longer,* she decided, *I must focus on the work that needs to be done at the orphanage.*

THE LOST SHEEP

She retrieved her box at the airlock, descended to the ground, and started toward the house.

TWO
PREMONITIONS

THE PREMONITIONS WERE becoming a nightly routine. They were more detailed and accurate than ever before, and Marco Ting couldn't figure out why. *Maybe it's the tequila I bought on Titan.* He glanced at the two-liter bottle on the dresser and noticed the liquor level was just above the neon-green worm in the bottom. Marco knew the tequila wasn't the reason, but he often speculated about his so-called talent when he was recovering from a hangover.

He sat up in bed and winced at the pounding headache. He ran a hand through his thinning hair, down the back of his aching neck, down to the med patches on his bare left shoulder. One was an antidepressant, prescribed for him by the *Ishmael*'s former medtech. The other patch was for his erratic thyroid. Both patches needed to be replaced.

Marco frowned at the thought of approaching Jake O'Brien for new prescriptions. *He's not even a real doctor!* He found a third patch on his bedside table and pressed it to the skin behind his right ear. The relief was quick as the headache faded. *Thank you, Dr. Martschenko, for keeping me well stocked.*

The word *doctor* stirred up some painful memories. Marco glanced over at the hologram perched next to his bottle of tequila. The scowling face of his father, Dr. Qiu Ting, stared back at him. *He's not a doctor, either, just a PhD in history.* Marco wasn't sure why he kept the grim reminder of his painful childhood, although the hologram did make a handy target when he felt like venting his frustrations at someone who couldn't argue back.

Marco wished he had a hologram of his archaeologist mother, who died during a research sabbatical to Xi'an, near the beginning of the war, but his father hadn't kept any memories of Hong Xia. Dr. Ting had blamed his fourteen-year-old son for his wife's untimely death. Marco understood the reasoning behind this unreasonable position: his father was embarrassed to have a son people considered *feng dian*—crazy. With his wife gone, the senior Ting didn't have anyone around to prevent him from taking out his frustrations on his son, yet the Chinese culture expected Marco to show his father respect in public, which he did, grudgingly. What went on in the Tings' private life was another matter. Their daily arguments grew more heated as Marco got older.

The parting of the ways was inevitable. Marco was accepted to Beijing Flight School when he was eighteen. His father was more than willing to pay his tuition, just to get him out of the apartment. After graduation, Marco hired on with the *Ishmael,* way back when the ship was called *Danae's Dream.* He had been the *Ishmael*'s helmsman for ten years now, preferring the solitude of space to the crowds of dirtside.

Throughout his painful adolescence, Marco managed to grow a thick skin. He became an expert at pushing people away, particularly with the acerbic vocabulary he inherited from his father. He found it ironic the old man kept himself immersed in the past while his son couldn't stop seeing the future.

Most of the premonitions came to him while he slept. Alcohol seemed to dull the effects, but the visions never went away. Sometimes the premonitions came to him in the daytime, in the form of feelings—*bad vibes*, for lack of a better term. These were more difficult to interpret. People, places, even the weather forecast could give Marco bad vibes. It was hard not to be a pessimist when he always knew something bad was about to happen.

He knew how much the other crewmembers wanted him to keep his premonitions to himself, but he felt it was his duty to warn them. *How can they keep ignoring me after I was right about Ganymede, and about the crazy steward who assaulted Shima, and about Shepherd killing someone? How can they keep dismissing my warnings when they're so accurate? I'd want to know if something terrible was going to happen to me.*

The captain had ordered him not to tell her any more of his premonitions. The foolish woman preferred not to know what she was running into, no matter how dangerous the situation. His recent vision of their return to Mars Station had been disturbing, but he obeyed Shepherd's strict orders and kept his mouth shut.

However, that didn't stop him from annoying the rest of the crew with his words of wisdom. *Someday they'll take me seriously and show me the respect I deserve.*

Marco pushed aside the tangled covers and climbed out of bed. He walked into the head, where he hooked up his breathing tube, stepped into the tiny shower stall, and enjoyed the ultrasonic pulses of ice-cold water for eight repeat cycles. Refreshed and shivering, he donned his ridiculous new uniform of blue jeans and a Hawaiian-print shirt, monogrammed with *Alex's Legacy* over the right breast pocket.

Glancing in the mirror above the sink, he frowned at his complexion, which had been temporarily dyed to a chocolate brown. Captain Shepherd told him he looked Indian, like the new navigator Vipul Ganguli, but Marco thought he looked like an idiot who'd been dipped in brown paint. *Even with sunglasses, this is never going to work. Acheron will recognize us.* Marco noted his bloodshot eyes. He applied some eye-drops to his almond-shaped orbs and brushed his teeth.

A glance at the time made him chuckle. It was 1530. There were only two bars in Lahaina, but he managed to talk his way into the seedy back rooms of both establishments. Marco knew his late-night vices were taking a toll on his health, but he didn't care. He was only thirty-two, but determined to die happy.

Trouble was *xi'*—happiness—still eluded him.

Didn't Shepherd say something about lifting off at midnight? I suppose I'd better see if the helm is in order. Though he preferred the privacy of his cabin to any other place on the ship, the bridge felt comfortable, especially if no one else on the crew was around. Marco left his cabin and ascended the ladder to the top deck.

Although the empty bridge was enticing, he couldn't ignore the hollow rumblings of his stomach. He took a detour to the galley, to the area known as the crew's mess, which contained an entire wall of labeled drawers. Marco opened drawers at random, searching for something to tide him over until dinner. He was tired of bananas and pineapple, so the fruit drawer went untouched. He found a bagel in the bakery drawer and took a big bite.

Marco found the coffee dispenser empty and grumbled to himself with impatience as he touched the refill button. He had just opened the cup drawer when he heard an unfamiliar feminine voice behind him.

"Can I help you find something?"

Marco spun around with a retort already poised on his lips, but he took one look at the speaker and found himself overcome by a fit of coughing as the bagel lodged in his throat.

"Are you all right?" The woman hurried to his side and pounded him on the back. "Do I need to do the Heimlich?"

He shook his head and tried to get the coughing under control. She snatched a bottle of water out of the beverage drawer, opened it, and attempted to pour some into his mouth. Marco sputtered as she soaked his face and shirt. In the deluge, he managed to swallow a mouthful and wash the bagel down. He took the bottle away from her and leaned against the counter to catch his breath.

Despite the fact that he was dripping wet and humiliated, he tried to keep the sarcasm out of his tone. He smiled at his would-be rescuer. "Thank you, but I don't need any help, Miss—?"

"Kim. Phailin Kim." She placed the palms of her hands together and brought them up to her chin, bowing slightly toward him in a respectful Thai gesture he recognized as a *wai*. "I'm sorry, Mister—?"

"Ting. Marco." He reached for some napkins and began to blot the front of his shirt. "That's all right. I know you were just trying to help."

"My first day," Phailin said with an embarrassed shrug.

Marco quit fussing with his shirt and gave her his full attention. She was the most beautiful Asian woman he ever set eyes on with her creamy taupe complexion, large brown eyes, and shoulder-length, straight black hair that shimmered like silk. He stifled a gulp as he noted her incredible figure and forced himself to focus on her face.

"Well, you must be a good cook if Captain Shepherd hired you."

The comment earned him a dazzling smile, as he hoped. Phailin had some attractive dimples. "Thank you, Mr. Ting."

"Please call me Marco. You said your name is Kim? But you don't look Korean."

He noted the sudden spark of anger in her eyes. "I didn't mean to offend you—" It was the first time Marco tried *not* to offend someone.

"I consider myself Thai-American," she said. "I grew up on Kauai, raised by my Thai mother—after my Korean father left us to bomb villages in Russia."

Marco made a sympathetic noise. "We're all victims of the war in some way."

Phailin nodded, the scowl replaced with a smile. "What's your position on the ship, Marco?" She moved over to the crew's mess and began to mop up the counter with a dishtowel. She drew a hot cup of coffee from the dispenser and offered it to him. "You must be freezing."

"I'm the helmsman." He thanked her for the coffee with what he hoped was a charming smile. "It's fine, I'll just change my shirt."

Phailin glanced down at the soggy towel in her hand. "I should get back to work."

Marco wanted her to stay, so he tried to keep the conversation going. "You know how to cook Thai food, I hope?"

She nodded. "And Korean."

"Mmm, kimchi and panang curry?"

"Yes, but never at the same meal." She laughed as she turned and headed back to the kitchen. "I'll see you at dinnertime, Marco," she said over her shoulder.

Marco was too flustered to think of anything else to say except, "Nice meeting you, Phailin." He burned his tongue on the coffee as he watched her skintight jeans disappear into the kitchen. *My compliments on the new crew selection, Captain.*

The helm kept his attention for the next three hours as he ran scans on each of the ship's systems. After their near-fatal landing, he worried about the decelerator and the newly repaired hull on the basement level. He also had no idea if the new solar engines were working. He only had Blaze's word that they were ready.

Rookie engineer. Marco found a glass-cleaning cloth and wiped off the oval-shaped helm window. The blue Maui sky outside was enticing, but one look at the field full of frolicking children was enough to stifle his desire to leave the ship.

Ting didn't like children. He didn't particularly like adults, either, but he avoided children whenever possible. *Shepherd said something about bringing back more homeless brats from Mars Station.* He frowned, thinking hard. *Maybe I should take Murphy's advice and quit. I could sign on with a bigger ship for twice the pay.*

It was a tempting idea, but Marco knew he would never find a more secure position again. *I'd get fired the minute I opened my mouth.*

He appreciated the fact that he could behave as badly as he wanted and not get fired. Ishmael Thompson, the former captain of the ship, had written a special agreement into his employment contract. Danae

Shepherd, Thompson's daughter, had been a witness to the agreement. As Thompson's heir, she had a legal obligation to uphold the contract.

The terms of the agreement were simple. Marco once saved Thompson's life, so the helmsman was to remain on the employee payroll for as long as wanted. Although Shepherd threatened to fire him many times since taking over the captaincy after Thompson's mysterious death, Marco knew she would never oppose her father's wishes.

But it wasn't just the agreement that kept him aboard. For years Marco felt a sense of loyalty to the crew, but the Zenithian Flu changed everything. Less than a week out of Ganymede, half the crew was dead from the virus, including the engineer Giovanni Medici.

Vanni had been his only friend. They were kindred spirits, risk-takers, reckless. The engineer loved to gamble, he was a magnet for women, and he could drink someone twice his size under the table. Marco admired him and grew to love him like a brother.

He still couldn't believe Vanni was gone.

He shut his eyes, remembering their last conversation on Ganymede Station two months ago.

"Vanni, I don't think you should go dirtside with the others. I've got a bad feeling about The Black Hole."

His friend had been in a restless mood that day. "I don't want to hear about your bad feelings right now, Ting. I'm hungry, and I haven't been dirtside in two weeks."

"I'm serious!" Marco grabbed Vanni's arm to prevent him from opening the airlock. "Please don't go!"

Vanni jerked his arm free. "You're like a gray cloud hanging over my head all the time, Ting. I think I can go dirtside without your babysitter services tonight." He punched the button to cycle open the airlock double doors. "Now if you'll excuse me, the others are waiting at the lift."

And he left without another word. Three days later, Vanni was dead, the first of the four to succumb to the virus. Marco wanted to help Shima move the engineer's body down to cold storage, but he had been sick himself at the time, vomiting, feverish, wondering if he would be the next to die.

Two days later, Marco recovered, along with the three crewmembers who hadn't been directly exposed to the virus. The four who'd gone to the restaurant were dead: Vanni, Captain Shepherd's husband Alex, Dr. Natasha Martschenko, and Shima's fiancé Hugh Zimmerman—the engineer, navigator, medic, and steward.

Marco was quarantined on the bridge for the remainder of the jump from Ganymede to Mars. He used the long hours to decide what to do with his life, now that his only friend was gone.

Ting shook his head, shoving aside the painful memory as he watched the children through the window. *So why do I stay where I'm not wanted?* He thought about the beautiful new cook in the galley. Phailin seemed like an excellent reason to remain on the ship.

Forget it, he advised himself. *As soon as someone mentions your dirtside interests or your fanatical predictions, Phailin won't give you a second look.* Marco's conscience began to bother him for the first time in decades.

It dawned on him that he didn't know how to act around women. He deferred to the captain's orders because she was his employer. He ignored Shima, and she did a good job of avoiding him. He despised Lorina, but figured she was Blaze's problem. He planned to avoid her as much as possible.

But now what do I do about Phailin? He scratched at one of the patches on his shoulder. *Maybe I should ask someone for advice.*

Marco laughed to himself, dismissing the idea as fast as he thought it up. It was easier to be a loner. After all, he'd had years of practice.

But he couldn't get Phailin off his mind. He couldn't decide if it was a physical attraction or if he just wanted to find a friend to fill the void Vanni left in his life. Either way, Marco wanted to make a good impression.

He tried to catch a glimpse of Phailin when he returned to the galley at dinnertime, but she never emerged from the kitchen. He took a plate of lemon beef salad from the counter and sat by himself at the corner table. Vipul, Blaze, and Jake were engaged in cheerful banter three tables away. Marco tried to ignore them as he enjoyed his spicy dinner—*with meat!* He hadn't tasted beef in six months. *I'll definitely stay on if I have meals like this to look forward to three times a day.*

Ting felt a pang of envy as he eyed the two Americans and the UK-born Indian navigator enjoying their food and their camaraderie. Toothpick-thin and graying at the temples, the soft-spoken Vipul hadn't been required to endure the humiliation of a makeover. *Neither did Blaze, and I know Acheron got a look at him in McConnell Park. Why should they be so privileged?* He stabbed a slice of cucumber with his fork and listened in on their conversation.

Vipul was saying, "Where's your lovely bride, Blaze?"

"Tryin' to convince Niyati we won't be gone long. She's not takin' it well."

"Who?" Jake asked. "Lorina or Niyati? Personally, I'm glad you're leaving her here. A starship is no place for a five-year-old."

I'd have to agree with that, Marco thought.

"Lorina's worried we're contributin' to Niyati's abandonment issues," Blaze said.

"It's only abandonment if you don't come back," Jake said.

"Anything's possible," Vipul said.

Jake groaned. "Don't get me started on the worst-case scenarios."

"We dock, we find the Sorensens, we lift off. That's the plan," Blaze said.

Jake snorted. "There's enough holes in the plan to put a Swiss cheese factory out of business."

"We had no idea how we were going to get the kids off Mars," Vipul reminded them, "but it worked out."

"Except for the nasty business of the captain shooting the CIP chief and killing Thanatos," Jake said.

"I was there, don't forget," Vipul said. "Thanatos's gun was pointed at *me*. I'm *grateful* she killed him. I wish I'd had the courage to do it myself."

Blaze whistled. "Did it just get cold in here?"

Vipul chuckled. "Sorry."

Jake whispered the next comment, but Marco overheard. "Maybe it's cold because Ting's in here."

Blaze stood abruptly and glanced over at Marco. "That reminds me. Ting, I want a word with you."

"Not here." Marco shot a nervous glance toward the kitchen. *Don't make me look like a fool in front of Phailin.*

Blaze approached his table. "Right here, right now."

Marco slipped out of his chair and started toward the galley door, but the tall engineer put out an arm to block his way. He was cornered.

"I want to hear the prediction you made to Lorina."

"And Shima," Jake piped up from his seat. "You upset both of them."

Marco wished they would keep their voices down. "I don't know what you're talking about."

Jake swore and got to his feet. "You made my cousin sob like a baby, Ting! You don't know Lorina. It takes something huge to upset her. I want to know what you predicted." He folded his arms and took a stand next to Blaze.

Marco considered his options as he glanced toward the kitchen again. Though his normal impulse would be to deny everything or lie his way out of the confrontation, he didn't want to raise his voice. There was still a slim chance Phailin was out of hearing range.

"I'm sorry if you don't like my premonitions, but you have to admit I've been right more often than I've been wrong." Marco kept his voice low, his tone reasonable.

Blaze and Jake exchanged a puzzled glance.

"Believe it or not, I'm just trying to keep this crew safe."

"How does fear-mongering and intimidation keep us safe?" Jake asked.

Marco flinched. "Didn't you ever hear the phrase 'don't kill the messenger'?"

"Maybe the messenger needs to learn a better way to deliver his messages," Blaze said.

"Or not deliver them at all?" Jake nodded. "Captain Shepherd had the right idea. She told you to keep your mouth shut, and I think you should do the same for the rest of us."

The helmsman felt his anger stirring but tried to remain calm for one last attempt at defending himself. "What if someone's life was in danger? Wouldn't you want to know so you could do something to save them?" He went for sympathy, donning a forlorn expression. "I tried to warn the crew not to go into that restaurant on Ganymede. I tried to warn them, and now they're dead."

Jake looked as if he wanted to say something vindictive, but Blaze spoke up first. "That's true. You did try to warn them." He was thoughtful for a moment before continuing. "I think the real problem is the abrasive way you share these premonitions."

Ting started to protest the abrasive remark but realized it would come across as, well, abrasive. He narrowed his eyes at Blaze. "What did you have in mind?"

Jake seemed to be thinking ahead. "What if you wrote down each premonition and gave the person in question the option of reading it or not?"

Blaze nodded. "Good idea. Then maybe you wouldn't feel the need to intimidate people."

"I don't have a need to intimidate people."

Even Vipul snorted at that remark.

Marco could feel his face getting warm. "If I agree to soften my approach, would you leave me alone?"

The engineer smiled. "That's very generous of you, Ting. You can be mature when you try."

Jake said, "Ha!" but had nothing to add.

"But I'm not lettin' you off until you tell us what you predicted for Lorina."

"And I want to know what you told Shima," Jake said.

At that moment, Phailin came around the counter from the kitchen with a tray of desserts balanced on her shoulder. "Anyone for sweet sticky rice with mango?" She studied the scene with a puzzled frown. "Marco?"

Blaze and Jake exchanged a cautious glance as they turned to face Phailin.

"We were just telling Ting to join us at our table," Jake painted on a big fake smile. "We have a lot to discuss."

"I love sticky rice." Marco slipped surreptitiously between Blaze and Jake. He took one of the plates from Phailin's tray and tried not to scowl as he sat next to Vipul. "Thank you."

The cook glanced over at the corner table. "I guess you didn't like the salad."

"It's delicious! But I didn't have a chance to finish it," Marco said as smoothly as he could manage. *There's still a chance,* he hoped.

Blaze deposited Marco's plate of salad on the table in front of him as he and Jake resumed their seats across from him and Vipul. "You were just about to tell us somethin' interestin', Ting?"

Marco glanced up at Phailin and was relieved to see her walking back to the kitchen. It was obvious she sensed the tension between the men. He wanted to call after her with something witty or gallant, but he had zero experience with charming remarks.

Blaze lowered his voice as he took a bite of mango. "What did you say to Lorina?"

Marco dropped his gaze to the table. "I told her the orphanage would be a challenge for Captain Shepherd over the next few years."

"That wouldn't make her cry," Jake said. "What are you leaving out?"

Marco was trapped. He couldn't tell them the rest. "I don't remember."

"You're lying!" Jake's right fist was halfway to Marco's nose before Blaze intervened.

"Stop!" The engineer deflected Jake's punch with an outstretched arm. "Take it easy!" Blaze lowered his voice again. "We all want to pound him, but we need to hear what he has to say first."

"I'm not going to sit here and listen to lies!" Jake's face was turning red beneath his tan. "You know what you said to her, so you'd better spit it out!"

Marco could feel his own face heating up. He was starting to shake from a combination of fear and anger. *Stay silent and take a pounding, or take a pounding* after *I tell them?* He didn't care for the limited options.

"They say confession is good for the soul," Vipul spoke up.

Marco shot the older man a withering glance.

Jake sneered. "Ting doesn't have a soul."

That remark did it for Marco; he was livid. "You want a confession, O'Brien? Here it is: I told Lorina someone close to her is going to die!"

There was instant silence at the table. The color drained from Blaze's face.

Jake appeared to be having an internal battle with his emotions, his mouth flapping silently until at last he roared, "*Who?* Which one of us is going to die? Is it me, or Blaze, or Niyati?"

"Don't you have a shred of decency?" Blaze asked. "How could you say that to her?"

"*Who is it?*" Jake shouted.

"I don't know." Marco's adrenaline was racing. He had taken on bigger men than O'Brien, and he was ready to defend himself.

"*Liar!*" Jake cleared the table with a sweep of his arm, sending plates and food flying across the galley. He reached across the table and seized Marco's collar with both hands, yanking him up from his chair. "*Tell me!*"

"I don't know!" Marco grabbed Jake's wrists and pried his grip free. "Get your hands off me!"

Jake shoved him backwards. Marco's chair seat swiveled and dumped him onto the floor. "I can't believe we have to work with a *psychopath* like you!"

Marco was on his feet. He threw himself at Jake, driving his shoulder into the medic's abdomen. The two men crashed to the floor between the tables. Marco managed to land a single punch to Jake's ribs before he felt large hands seizing his shoulders, pulling him off the medic.

"Settle down!" Blaze had Marco on his feet with his arms pinned behind his back.

On the floor, Vipul was restraining Jake, although Marco noted with satisfaction that O'Brien looked as if he was in too much pain to put up any resistance.

"Ting! O'Brien! My office—now!" Captain Shepherd was in the doorway of the galley before Marco had time to catch his breath. He caught sight of Phailin at the counter, a stunned expression on her gorgeous face.

So much for making a good impression, he thought. *It's all O'Brien's fault!*

Blaze gave him a shove toward the captain. With his arms free, Marco straightened and marched past Shepherd without making eye contact.

"He started it!" He heard Jake behind him, but the medic didn't utter a word beyond that feeble argument.

No doubt Shepherd shut him up with her infamous glare. Marco climbed the ladder down to the next level and slouched into the captain's tiny and soundproof office. O'Brien and Shepherd squeezed in behind him a few moments later. The door slid shut.

Captain Shepherd elbowed her way past Marco and took a seat at her desk. Marco tried to create some space between Jake and himself, but there was barely room for the two of them to stand. The medtech was breathing hard and leaning forward with one hand on his side.

"Do you want to tell me why you were brawling in my galley like a pair of overgrown grade school bullies?" Marco started to open his mouth, but Shepherd silenced him with a look that would have frozen lava in its tracks. "No, on second thought, I don't want to hear it."

"He—" Jake began, but she cut him off with the same look.

Marco simmered in silence and thought about what he would say when he had the chance.

"I've a good mind to throw both of you off my ship, but I'd have a difficult time lifting in six hours without a helmsman or a medic on board." Shepherd laced her fingers together under her chin and rested her elbows on the desk. "Let's shelve the drama and get to the point. I assume Ting made a prediction you didn't care for, Jake?"

O'Brien's reply was quiet. "Yes, ma'am."

With her brown contact lenses, she regarded Marco, although she continued speaking to Jake. "Are you hurt?"

"I'm fine."

"Well, you look like you're in pain. Why don't you go patch yourself up, and aren't you due dirtside to say goodbye to your family? Does your father have the transmission for Erik?"

Jake nodded. "He'll send it when they layover in Dallas early tomorrow morning."

"Good. Go. I want a word with Ting."

"Yes, Captain." The door slid open for Jake and slid shut after him.

Marco felt as if he would explode if he couldn't say something, but Shepherd didn't give him a chance to get a word in. Her message was sharp and to the point.

"I think we've reached an impasse, Ting. Shima told me why she was so upset today. Thanks to you, she's petrified she's going to make a huge mistake and something terrible is going to happen as a result. How could you tell her something like that? Can you think of one reason why I shouldn't throw you out the airlock right now?"

She gave him a vicious look. "And don't give me any garbage about the agreement in your contract! My father's been dead for eight years! This is *my* ship, and I'm tired of the problems you create with your premonitions! I can fly the *Alex* myself! I'll give you one hour to pack your cabin and get out!"

Marco felt as if his knees were going to buckle. All bravado gone, he sat down heavily in the single chair facing her desk. For the first time in his life, he didn't know what to say.

Shepherd lowered her voice. "I'll write you a letter of recommendation. With your experience, I'm sure you'll find a job right away. Do you need plane fare to the nearest spaceport?"

More than any other emotion Marco was experiencing at that moment was fear. His hands were shaking. "Permission to speak freely, Captain?"

Shepherd hesitated, her scowl deepening. "As long as you don't make any predictions, you can say whatever you want."

"The *Ishmael* is the only real home I've ever had. I don't want to leave."

"I see no other solution, Ting. None of us can work under the conditions you create. You're an expert at demoralizing the crew. After everything we've been through, you could at least *attempt* to show the other crewmembers some support." Her eyes seemed to bore right through him. "Or at least learn to keep your big mouth shut!"

Marco flinched, but didn't break eye contact. "Captain, my visions, my premonitions, have the potential to save lives—if someone would only listen to me."

Her response was unsympathetic. "I've mentioned before that most people would prefer not to know about impending doom. It's impossible to function under a cloud of fear. You have"—she struggled for a moment to find the words—"an unusual gift. But you've used it to stir up fear and dissension. I have no choice but to fire you."

"I can change!" Marco leaned forward in his chair. "Please give me another chance!"

Shepherd slammed her fist down on the desk. "You haven't changed in ten years! I'm not naïve enough to expect an overnight transformation! You're too much of a pessimist!"

Marco was desperate to convince her. "Wait, Captain. Jake—Jake gave me a good suggestion, just before he tried to break my nose!"

Danae Shepherd looked askance at him. "*What?*"

"He told me I should write down my premonitions! If someone wants to know the future, they could just read it—or not. It would be their choice! And I'd keep my mouth shut—at all times!" He noted her skeptical scowl. "I can do it, Captain! Please give me another chance!"

"Your track record isn't very convincing." Shepherd frowned and stared at the ceiling.

Marco knew he made his point, so he shut his mouth and let her think. Years of experience had taught him to be quiet when the captain needed to make a decision.

After a few minutes, Shepherd faced him again. "I must be completely out of my mind, but I need you at the helm. But I want you on the bridge or in your cabin at all times."

He nodded with relief.

"Write down your premonitions if it makes you feel better, but you are not to show them to anyone without my approval." She shook a finger at him. "In fact, I think you should avoid speaking to anyone on the crew. Not even to ask 'how's the weather?' or 'what's for dinner?' Am I making myself clear?"

Marco thought of Phailin and winced, but he nodded. "I can do that."

"Although it goes against my better judgment, I'll give you one more chance. But if you upset anyone on this crew between here and Mars, you're out. And believe me, you don't want to be dirtside on Acheron's home turf."

He felt a stirring of concern. "What do you mean, Captain? Acheron's not looking for *me*, is he?"

For a fleeting moment Shepherd appeared chagrinned, as if she said too much. But the moment passed and she dismissed him. "Just stay in your cabin until it's time to lift."

Marco stood, his mind in a whirl. He managed to thank her before leaving her office. "I'm a changed man, Captain, you'll see. I'm sincere this time."

Shepherd called after him, "This is your last chance to earn my trust, Ting, so you'd be wise to keep your mouth shut. Prove to me you have *cheng yi*, and you can keep your job—for now."

He turned away without another word, wondering where she learned the Mandarin phrase for sincerity.

THREE
PRISONER

"SORENSEN, YOU'VE GOT a visitor." The guard's voice crackled over the com.

Dr. Erik Sorensen opened his eyes to the shadowy gloom of the two-by-three meter titanium room which had been his home for the past three weeks. Prisons hadn't changed much over the centuries. It didn't matter if they were built of stone or Plexiglass, they were still miserable places to live. This one didn't even have the luxury of a barred window to the fresh air outside or a fellow prisoner in the next cell to argue with. Solitary confinement was reserved for the most dangerous and hardened criminals, but in Erik's case, the real criminal was on the outside of the cell.

Not Acheron again, Erik thought. He sat up on the thin mattress, the cot springs squeaking in protest. He was amazed the bed hadn't collapsed yet. It wasn't designed for someone his size. He scratched at the white-blond beard he was growing—not by choice—and took his time answering the guard. "Who is it?"

He touched a bruise on his left cheekbone, winced at the resulting pain, and tried to prepare himself psychologically for another round of *interrogations* by the

Central Intelligence Police chief of Mars Station. Acheron had paid Erik several visits since the CIPs arrested him right after the *Ishmael* lifted off from the station with one hundred and forty-eight homeless children aboard. The children were supposed to have boarded the slave ship *Elmina*, but Danae Shepherd's crew thwarted Acheron's plan. Erik was now paying the price for his involvement in the rescue, but he was determined not to let Acheron break his spirit.

"It's a woman," the guard answered his query.

Erik heard him unlock the door to the corridor outside his cell. A narrow slot in the center of the cell door slid aside, revealing an opening only large enough to admit a tray of food—or a pair of familiar hands.

"Hello, stranger."

"Kirsten!" Erik rushed to the door and grasped his sister's hands. He dropped to his knees so he could see her through the small slot.

"Erik! Your face!" Kirsten scrutinized what she could see of him. "Acheron's been beating you!"

The doctor shrugged, embarrassed. He was unaccustomed to Kirsten assuming the role of protector. "It's not as bad as it looks. He hasn't knocked me around for at least three days."

"How can you joke about it?" She shook her head. "You wouldn't believe the blockade I've had to navigate to get in here. Why haven't the hospital administrators bailed you out yet?"

He sighed in frustration. "Acheron's playing his usual games. He won't let them post my bail because he hasn't officially charged me with anything."

"Then he has no right to hold you!" Kirsten bristled. "I'll get you a lawyer!"

He shook his head. "Acheron's got all the lawyers and judges on his payroll. It won't do any good." He squeezed her hands and felt a stirring of hope at her presence. "Look, I know we don't have much time to talk. You've got to tell me what's going on outside. The clinic?"

Kirsten winced. "It's closed. I'm sorry. It's already been dismantled."

The doctor knew Mars Community Hospital would never keep the Outreach Clinic open without him there to run it. He had put his heart and soul into the struggling organization for three years, working by himself around the clock to help the homeless children of Mars Station. For the past seven months, unlicensed medic Jake O'Brien had been his apprentice at the clinic. Acheron could hold Erik for aiding and abetting a criminal.

"What about the shelter?" he asked.

Kirsten shrugged. "I'm keeping it open, but the kids are staying away because there's always a CIP outside the front door."

Erik nodded, trying to think of some words of comfort. Mother Teresa's Juvenile Shelter was Kirsten's lifeblood. It was the only place on the station where a homeless child could be assured a hot meal and a safe place to sleep. Lorina Murphy had volunteered there every day for the past six months, helping Kirsten run the shelter like a real home. If Acheron wanted to arrest Kirsten, he could also charge her with aiding and abetting a criminal because Lorina forged a quarantine notice to keep the CIPs out of Mother Teresa's.

"Any word from the *Ishmael?*" As soon as he said it, he realized their conversation was being recorded. He switched to their native Swedish and spoke fast. "I was forced to record a transmission for Danae. Acheron wants to lure her back to Mars, and he's using me as bait."

"I received a transmission at the shelter yesterday. It was addressed to you." Kirsten bit her lip. "I probably shouldn't tell you anything else because I know they can translate our conversation."

Erik felt his heart racing. "Was it from Danae? Is she all right? I heard she was shot leaving the station."

Kirsten nodded. "Yes, she sent it. She's fine. Jake saved her life. That's all I can tell you in here."

"I understand." Erik was relieved to hear Danae was alive. He felt as if a huge weight was lifted off his shoulders. However, the news of a transmission brought another concern to light. *If Danae sent a transmission, she must be on her way back to Mars. Acheron will arrest her the instant she sets foot on the station.*

He had another thought, this one even more frightening. "You've got to delete the transmission! I'm sorry I mentioned it! Now Acheron will come after you to find out what was on it!" The thought of his kind-hearted sister being subjected to a brutal interrogation by the CIPs made his blood run cold.

"I anticipated that, *broder*, and it's already deleted. Don't worry about me. I'm not afraid of Acheron." Her words were calm, but her face was paler than normal.

"Can you find a way to get me out of here?"

"I'm trying," Kirsten said. "I've got an appointment with someone on the city council this afternoon."

"You're the best."

"Visiting time's over." The guard tapped Kirsten on the shoulder.

Erik was reluctant to release her hands as she drew them away from the narrow opening in the door. "I love you," he said, in English.

"I love you too, Erik. I'll get you out of here, I promise."

Don't make a promise you can't keep, he thought. The slot in the door snapped shut, and he turned to face his Spartan cell. It was furnished with the single bed, a toilet, and a sink which only produced a trickle of cold water.

Acheron should be here any minute to question me about my visit. I've got to convince him to stay away from Kirsten.

He decided to pass the time by doing his twice-a-day workout. Erik exercised as much as he could in the small space. He did crunches, push-ups, yoga stretches, and ran in place. It wasn't much, but it kept him from getting soft. He knew it would be impossible to break out of Acheron's stronghold with his bare hands, although he wouldn't hesitate to put a fist in the smug police chief's face, should the opportunity present itself.

"Sorensen, Chief Acheron would like to see you."

Despite the sweat from his workout, Erik felt a chill. He stopped his push-ups, got up from the floor, and turned to face the cell door.

Hunter Acheron took his time with the DNA access panel. Erik heard the locks releasing, metal scraping metal. The door swung inward, and Acheron stepped into the cell. The door slammed shut behind him and the locks engaged. The two men faced each other across the narrow space.

"Do you want to tell me about the nice little chat you had with your sister, or do I need to use the same old method of persuasion?" The CIP chief wasn't as tall as the doctor, but he was broader through the chest and shoulders. He had pale features and a dark crew cut streaked with gray. Acheron's police uniform was jet black—*to match his soul,* Erik thought.

He took a deep breath and thought fast. This was new. Acheron usually brought two other CIPs into the cell with him to hold Erik down while the chief used his face for a punching bag. *Does he intend to take me on solo? Or does he have something more brutal in mind?*

He measured his response with care. "You recorded the conversation. What more do you need to know?"

"What was on the transmission from Shepherd?"

"I don't know," Erik fired back.

"But your sister knows, doesn't she?" Acheron's smile didn't reach his eyes.

"I'm sure a clever cop like you can find a way to hack into an interstellar receiver, if you haven't intercepted the message already."

Acheron's smile became an arrogant smirk. "I know it was transmitted from Dallas on November twelfth. I don't have a copy of the transmission yet, but I will soon. What do you know about them landing in Dallas?"

Erik's anger was stirring. "I told you I don't know where the ship landed. Dallas seems as good a site as any city on Earth."

"That would be true if the Dallas spaceport had any record of the *Ishmael*'s landing. You're a terrible liar, Sorensen."

"So are you."

Acheron narrowed his eyes. "If I thought I could get any more information out of you, I would, but I think it will be more productive to have a chat with your sister."

His last shred of self-restraint vanished, and Erik seized Acheron by the shoulders, slamming his back against the wall. "You keep your filthy hands off Kirsten!"

The CIP chief flinched beneath Erik's crushing grip on his right shoulder. The doctor knew he would still be sore from the gunshot wound, but Acheron took only a moment to recover from the attack. He delivered a hammer blow to Erik's midsection. The doctor staggered backward, gasping for breath, and Acheron punched him hard, opening up the already-bruised area of his cheekbone.

The pain was blinding. Erik braced himself for another blow, but it never came.

Acheron straightened and brushed off the front of his uniform. He wasn't even breathing hard. "You're not even a challenge, Sorensen. You're pathetic. It's hardly worth it to charge you with assaulting a police officer."

So that's why he came in alone, Erik thought, disgusted. "I gain nothing by fighting you. Some of us use our strength to *help* others." He touched his throbbing cheek and came away with blood on his fingers. "That's probably a foreign concept to a cruel *odjur* like you."

The CIP chief smiled and pressed his thumb to the ID exit lock on the door. "You can share those sentiments with your fat sister. She'll be warming the cell next to yours in fifteen minutes."

Erik was shaking with rage as Acheron slammed the door behind him. He went to the sink, dampened a corner of his towel, and pressed it to his bleeding cheek. *If only I had a way to contact Kirsten! I'd tell her to hide, tell her not go back to Mother Teresa's.*

He had looked after his sister her entire life. He sat down hard on the cot, overwhelmed with despair. *I can't protect her this time, not from Acheron.* He buried his face in the thin pillow to hide his tears from the guard.

FOUR
PUZZLE

ROSAMAR DELACRUZ PUSHED aside the pile of datapads demanding her attention on the desk. She had been elected to office only three months ago, yet she was already a month behind in work. "Orlene?"

"Councilwoman Delacruz?" Rosamar's young, first-day-on-the-job administrative assistant stuck her bleached blond head in the doorway. "More coffee?"

Rosamar stifled a groan of frustration and reminded herself to be patient with the inexperienced girl. "Please just call me Rosamar."

Orlene blushed and bobbed her head in apology. "What do you require?"

"Check to see if I have any transmissions."

"Yes, *madam*." Orlene bolted from the office.

Delacruz winced and wondered how long this assistant would last. *If I have to go back to that stupid employment center one more time . . .* she couldn't come up with a threat strong enough to finish the thought. She settled on a sigh and massaged her aching temples.

The newest Mars Station city council member sat back in her chair and put her bare feet up on her faux-mahogany desk. The gesture was unladylike, but

Rosamar didn't worry about what people thought of her. *Like this lowlife Acheron,* she thought with a snort. *Since when does the chief of police tell me what I can and cannot vote for during a council meeting?*

She ignored the warnings about Acheron from the other six council members. *Cowards,* she thought in disgust. *How can they expect to represent the people when they wet their pants around that bully?* Rosamar wasn't stupid. She recognized a dictator when she saw one. *If Acheron gives me so much as a dirty look, I'll slap him with a lawsuit.*

Rosamar was an attorney, but it wasn't something she announced during her campaign. Lawyers weren't popular on Mars Station. They were too expensive for the average person to hire. She spent twenty years in a cushy office in Connecticut, catering to the wealthy farmers who loved to haggle over land rights. Some farmers would spend a billion in legal fees just to acquire a square kilometer of untainted land from his or her neighbor. It was a cutthroat business, and Rosamar was ready to move on when the lawsuits slowed to a trickle and her marriage ended badly.

When the Mars Station Port Authority offered her a position as chief counsel, she was happy to close her office in Bridgeport and take over the legal headaches of the interstellar shipping trade. It was still a cutthroat business, but she found the clientele much more attractive than the farmers of New England. Rosamar developed a fondness for the rugged ship captains she defended.

One captain, in particular, had stolen her heart. *But that was a long time ago,* she thought, shaking her head. *He must be seventy years old and remarried by now.*

Even though she was close to retirement age, Rosamar still loved litigation. Her struggle for justice in the shipping trade had dove-tailed into concerns for the oppressed citizens of Mars Station. Mars had been her home long enough for her to feel fed up with the current government. It had been a landslide election to the city council when she replaced a retiring councilwoman. Rosamar's campaign promise to turn the Martian economy around had endeared her to the people. The reality of that promise weighed heavily on her as she struggled alone to fight a corrupt system under the reins of Acheron.

Orlene interrupted her reverie. "You have three new transmissions, *madam*," she announced over the com, "and one of them has been forwarded from your Earth transmission receiver. It's probably junk. Shall I delete it?"

Rosamar felt a chill. *From Earth? But I sold my condo in Bridgeport four years ago. Who could be trying to contact me?* "No! I want to view that one first."

"Yes, *madam*." Orlene sounded flustered, but Rosamar didn't care. She put her feet on the floor and sat straight in her chair so she could see the monitor on her desk.

At first Rosamar didn't recognize the woman's holographic image, but when she began to speak, the councilwoman muffled a gasp of surprise. "Danae?"

"This transmission is intended for attorney Rosamar Delacruz of Bridgeport, Connecticut, recorded on October twenty-sixth." The speaker appeared cool and composed, despite the fact that she was wearing Chinese red silk pajamas.

The chill Rosamar felt earlier seemed to settle into her stomach. *She looks so much like Ishmael.*

Danae Thompson continued. "Greetings, Ms. Delacruz. I hope this message finds you well. I apologize for contacting you after so many years, since we didn't part on good terms."

Oh, she's clever, Rosamar thought. *She's a real diplomat, just like her father.*

"I request you set aside any hard feelings for a moment and please hear me out. I am in a desperate situation and need a safe port to land my ship. The *Ishmael* has one hundred and forty-eight homeless children aboard."

Rosamar punched the pause key and slumped back in her chair, her emotions in a tailspin as she tried to comprehend the last few words of the transmission. *Her ship? The Ishmael?*

Her hands were shaking as she checked the transmission code on the message and compared it to the one she kept in her personal log in an old datapad in her desk. The codes were identical. The ship she had known as *Danae's Dream* was now the *Ishmael*. That could only mean one thing.

He's dead.

Rosamar wrestled with her emotions for a few minutes before composing herself enough to continue the transmission.

"—one hundred and forty-eight homeless children aboard from Mars Station."

She hit the pause button again. *Homeless children?* Her mind was racing now as she found another datapad in a bottom desk drawer. She scanned the list of articles she kept from the *Martian Chronicles* until she came to one she was searching for, dated October twenty-fourth.

Homeless Children Disappear From Station—Again?

Central Intelligence Police Headquarters on Dentist Street was swamped today with reports from

homeless individuals, claiming a number of children disappeared from McConnell Park during the night. The CIP officer in charge, who asked not to be named, refused to file any missing persons' reports when he learned that none of the individuals were related to the children in question. "They have no holograms or DNA traces to help us locate the purported missing children," the officer explained. "Chief Acheron has asked us not to get involved in this matter. He believes it is a widespread hoax, and that the people involved are trying to claim benefits they don't deserve."

A similar incident was reported back on March 11th from the director of Mother Teresa's Juvenile Shelter on Farmer Street, Kirsten Sorensen. In speaking to Ms. Sorensen by com today, she denied the reports were false. "Hundreds of children disappear from Mars Station every year. This isn't a hoax. Unless concerned citizens of Mars get involved, it will happen again. We must do more to protect the children."

CIP Chief Acheron could not be reached for comment.

I'll bet he couldn't. Rosamar set aside the datapad and turned back to Danae's frozen hologram on the screen. *So what are you doing with a bunch of homeless children on your ship, Miss Thompson?*

For several years, Rosamar had been concerned about the growing number of homeless people on the station. The corruption in the system was easy to pinpoint, starting right at the top with Acheron. But laws were difficult to change when the council votes were always six to one in favor of whatever Acheron wanted.

Rosamar wasn't afraid to fight the system, even if she had to do it alone. She was determined to make some changes so people could find jobs without resorting to the extortion of the employment centers.

I can't believe Ishmael's daughter is involved in the abduction of homeless children. She resolved to view the rest of the transmission without jumping to conclusions.

She tapped the keypad, and Danae continued. "My crew and I rescued them at great personal risk from a slave ship captain named Thanatos. Now we are wanted by the CIPs for violating several laws in our attempt to get the children off the station."

The name Thanatos jogged a memory, but Rosamar stuck to her resolution and kept her finger away from the pause button.

"I'm asking for your assistance to find a safe place to land. I don't want these children to become homeless again on Earth, nor do I want them to fall into the hands of slavers. Could you please use your political influence to help me find a port? It's crucial we don't give the CIPs our location, particularly Chief Acheron of Mars Station."

Rosamar's jaw dropped as Danae concluded the transmission. "Thank you for taking time to view this message. I hope to hear from you soon. Shepherd out."

Shepherd? Well, it's been over eight years since I set foot on Ishmael's ship, I'm sure she finally found a man desperate enough to marry her. Delacruz put her feet up again. *This transmission is almost three weeks old, so I assume she found a place to land by now. Thanatos? Why does that name sound familiar?*

"Orlene?"

"Yes, *madam?*"

"Check the *Martian Chronicles* database from the past month and see if a man named Thanatos is mentioned in any of the articles."

Orlene responded after just a few moments. "There's a Thanatos, captain of a ship called the *Elmina*, mentioned in a CIP report, dated October twenty-fourth. It says he was murdered by another ship's captain named Danae Shepherd."

"Murdered!" Rosamar couldn't believe her ears. *There must be a mistake. The Danae I remember wasn't a violent woman—although her tongue was sharp enough to cut steel.*

"Yes, *madam*, there were several witnesses. He was shot in the head at close range. Shepherd remains at large. Her ship, the *Ishmael*, escaped the station. Do you want to read the entire article?"

"No, not right now." Rosamar was already putting the pieces of the puzzle together as she reviewed the transmission again. *Thanatos was a slave ship captain, and Danae left the station with one hundred forty-eight homeless children aboard.* She glanced at the datapad in front of her with the article about the vanishing children.

Thanatos ran a slave ship? Then maybe Danae shot him while trying to rescue the children. That made perfect sense, and it fit well with her memory of Ishmael Thompson's fearless daughter.

Now she's asking for my help to avoid running into the CIPs. Rosamar pursed her lips, thinking hard. *Why does she mention Acheron by name—unless he's involved?* She nodded to herself. *I wouldn't put anything past that maggot.*

"Excuse me, *madam*," Orlene interrupted Rosamar's thoughts again, "there's a woman here to see you. She has an appointment for 4:30, but she says it's an emergency. She can't wait."

Delacruz's first impulse was to order the woman to come back at the appointed time, but she reminded herself it was her duty to represent the people of Mars Station. Sometimes duty was inconvenient. "What's her name?"

"Kirsten Sorensen, *madam.*"

Rosamar was grateful she was sitting down as she glanced at the *Chronicles* article a third time. "Send her in."

The woman who presented herself in Rosamar's office was in her mid-thirties, blonde, heavy-set, and close to tears. As Rosamar stood and offered her hand, the woman rushed forward and grasped it in both of hers.

"Councilwoman Delacruz, thank you! Thank you for taking time to see me!"

Rosamar pried her hand free. "Won't you sit down, Miss Sorensen?"

Sorensen sat in a chair facing the desk and did an admirable job of getting her emotions under control. "Please excuse the intrusion, but I had to see you right away."

"I think I know why you're here." Rosamar pushed the datapad with the article across the desk. "Something to do with homeless children disappearing from the station?"

Sorensen barely glanced at the datapad. "Yes, but the situation is more complicated than what's written here."

The councilwoman held up a manicured index finger. "Before you tell me about your emergency, let me ask you something. Do you know a woman named Danae Shepherd?"

Sorensen hesitated before nodding.

Rosamar swiveled her desk monitor around for Sorensen to view. "Replay Shepherd transmission." She studied the woman's worried face as Danae repeated her plea for a safe port.

As soon as the transmission ended, Rosamar asked, "Did you know about this, Miss Sorensen?"

"Yes, ma'am." She looked down at her hands clasped in her lap. "That's why I'm here. My brother's been arrested for helping Shepherd get the children off the station."

Rosamar pursed her lips, leaning back in her chair. "I suppose Acheron's treating him like a convicted murderer?"

Sorensen hesitated again, and then began to pour out her story. "Erik's innocent! You've got to help me get him out of jail! Acheron's been beating him, trying to force him to say where Shepherd took her ship—but Erik doesn't know! I'm afraid Acheron's going to kill him!"

The councilwoman gestured for her to slow down. "Who is your brother?"

"Dr. Erik Sorensen. He ran the Outreach Clinic at Mars Community Hospital. When Captain Shepherd met him and told him she knew about Acheron's plan to gather up the homeless children and sell them to the slaver Thanatos—"

Rosamar held up a hand to interrupt. "Wait! Are you saying *Acheron* sold the children to the slaver? You're sure about this?"

Sorensen nodded. "Acheron had his officers give the children drinks and muffins laced with sedatives. Erik tried to bring as many children as he could to the shelter the night before the CIPs were going to round up the homeless children in McConnell Park. If it wasn't for Captain Shepherd offering to take the children off the station, they would all be slaves now."

The councilwoman felt her heart pounding, but tried not to show any emotion on her face. Her thoughts were already racing ahead. *This is the answer. This is how I'm going to bring the tyrant to his knees.* "Miss Sorensen, do you have proof Acheron is behind all this?"

"There are several witnesses, including myself."

Rosamar leaned back in her chair, disappointed. "Acheron has all the judges in his back pocket. Eyewitness reports won't be enough to take him down."

Sorensen's eyes widened. "You want to take down Acheron, ma'am? How?"

Delacruz allowed herself a small smile. "I'm not sure yet. But if he's guilty of abduction and slave trade, I can do it. All I need is some proof that will hold up in interstellar court."

"Erik probably has some lab reports from the children who were drugged by the CIPs," Sorensen said.

Rosamar shook her head. "It would be dismissed as circumstantial unless we could prove the CIPs gave the sedatives to the children under Acheron's orders."

Kirsten Sorensen's shoulders slumped for a moment, but then she sat upright in her chair. "Thanatos's ship! All ship captains have to keep accurate records. I'm sure the *Elmina*'s database is filled with evidence that could convict Acheron!"

Rosamar blew out a breath, thinking hard. "*If* Thanatos recorded his cargo as humans—which seems unlikely—and *if* Acheron didn't have the *Elmina*'s database wiped clean already."

"It's worth checking." Sorensen looked hopeful.

The councilwoman nodded. "I'll find out where the *Elmina* is docked and see what I can do."

"And my brother?"

"I'll look into his case, but short of breaking him out of jail with my bare hands, I don't know if I can free him. Not until we have proof of Acheron's involvement with the slaver."

"Couldn't you find some way to protect Erik while he's in custody?" Sorensen asked. "Move him to a different location? Even a psychiatric ward would be safer than where he is now! Please, get Erik away from that monster! Please help him!" At this, she burst into tears, burying her face in her hands.

Rosamar stood and came around the desk to Sorensen's chair, placing a firm hand on the woman's shaking shoulder. "I'll go see Acheron myself right now. I'm not sure if it'll do any good. In fact, I *know* it won't do any good. But maybe Acheron will stop beating your brother if he knows a lawyer is checking up on him."

Sorensen nodded, wiped her eyes on the backs of her hands, and looked up at Rosamar. "You're a lawyer, ma'am?"

"You could say that. I have over thirty years of litigation experience. I represented the Mars Station Port Authority in the Baronowski Brothers case eight years ago."

"The space mafia? Interstellar organized crime?"

Rosamar nodded. "Liam Baronowski threatened to murder my entire family if I didn't dismiss myself from the case." She folded her arms and leaned back against the desk. "You'll be pleased to hear my family is still alive and well. My sister and her husband are enjoying retirement on Ganymede, and even my rotten ex-husband in Belize is still breathing. I know how to handle vermin. You may have given me the leverage I need to take down the station's biggest rat."

Sorensen stood slowly, her expression grave. "I just want my brother freed."

"I know. But it will take some time to gather evidence against Acheron."

"I understand. And I'm grateful for your help, Councilwoman."

"I'll keep you informed." Rosamar shook the matron's hand. "Leave your com code with Orlene."

"Thank you." Sorensen left the office.

Rosamar shoved the stack of datapads off her desk, into a drawer. She stretched and paused a moment to primp at the ornate mirror on the wall behind her chair. She fluffed her thick chestnut-brown hair, which she wore long, in defiance of traditional old lady, short curled hair-dos. She leaned closer to her reflection and smoothed the makeup around her dark brown eyes. Rosamar's olive complexion disguised the normal age lines on her face and neck. She still had a great figure for her age. She often wore low-cut blouses to emphasize her best feature.

Age is just a state of mind, was her mantra. *I can still pass for forty-five—at least from a distance.*

She slipped on her good shoes and headed out of the office.

"Orlene, cancel my appointments for the rest of the morning. I need to pay a visit to Chief Acheron. Please call his office and tell him I need to see him on an urgent matter."

"Yes, *madam.*"

Delacruz took a deep breath as she walked to the lift. She knew she would need to keep a firm rein on her temper if she wanted to pry any information out of Acheron.

She exited city hall and crossed Dentist Street to CIP headquarters. She breezed right by the main receptionist and marched down the hall to Acheron's suite.

"Councilwoman—" Acheron's uniformed police assistant was on his feet, trying to flag her down as she marched straight by his desk to the door of the chief's office.

"Is he in?" she barked.

"He's in a meeting—" the young man tried to get to the door ahead of her, but Rosamar was already on her way in without knocking. She pushed open the door to the plush office, which seemed suspiciously out of place in an otherwise utilitarian police department, and strode right up to Acheron's priceless teak desk.

Acheron was seated behind it, on the com. He gave Rosamar an irritated look. "I'll have to call you back, detective."

"I'm sorry, chief," the assistant spoke up from behind Rosamar. "I tried to stop her."

Acheron gave his underling a cold look, and the man backed out of the room, pulling the door shut behind him.

"Councilwoman Delacruz." Acheron stood. Physically, he was an imposing figure, but Rosamar wasn't intimidated by his threatening stance. She was more concerned about what was going on inside his cunning mind.

"I'm so pleased to see you." He appeared anything but pleased. "Won't you have a seat?"

"No thank you, I prefer to stand." Rosamar kept her tone even, but she couldn't help putting her hands on her hips.

"Suit yourself. What's so urgent that you needed to see me right away?" Acheron's words were polite, but Rosamar could almost see the steam rising off of him as his scowl settled into something more sinister.

"I'll make this brief. It's come to my attention that you're holding a doctor without cause and without bail. I want him released."

"If you're referring to Sorensen, there's a long list of charges against him—not that it's any of *your* concern." Acheron sneered.

Rosamar returned the sneer. "He *is* my concern because, as of this moment, I'm his attorney."

"Attorney?" Acheron laughed without smiling. "I knew there was something I didn't like about you."

"I demand to see his arrest record."

"I'm well aware that police records in the United States are open to public scrutiny." Acheron rested his meaty fists on the desk and leaned forward, his cold eyes boring into hers. "But they aren't here. I'm sure you've learned we do things differently here on Mars."

"As his attorney—"

Acheron's polite tone vanished. "Come back with a warrant if you want to see his record! He's a criminal, Delacruz! It'll be a long time before Sorensen sees the light of day! Now I'm a very busy man, and I'll thank you to *get out!*"

"I'll be back!" Rosamar drew upon her litigation skills, staring down Acheron like a hostile witness—he was definitely hostile. "And I'll have that warrant!"

"I suggest you stick to your city council business before you get yourself in real trouble!"

"*What?* What's that supposed to mean?" she snapped.

"You get in my way, and I can promise you won't be staying in that cozy office of yours for long!"

Rosamar blinked, speechless. *Did he just threaten me?* It was mafia boss Liam Baronowski all over again. Now she was really angry. *This arrogant thug has no idea who he's dealing with!*

She realized she wouldn't learn anything by returning the threat and it might endanger her life. *I'll make him think I'm afraid, then go behind his back to do some digging.*

She took a deep breath and gave him what she hoped was a scared but defiant expression. "I'll be back with that warrant."

"*Get out!*" Acheron spat the words in her face. He sat and picked up the com again, ignoring Rosamar as she stormed out of his office, struggling to contain the rage burning inside her.

She was still muttering obscenities to herself in Spanish when she marched past her assistant's desk a few minutes later. "Orlene, I need an appointment with every judge on the station. See if you can fit them all in tomorrow morning."

"Yes, *madam.*"

Rosamar sank into her desk chair and sighed. *There has to be a weak link somewhere,* she thought. *Acheron might think he rules with an iron hand, but someone in power has to be willing to stand up to him.*

All I need to do is find that someone.

FIVE
THE CHAIN

"STAY BEHIND THE line!" Gordon Grey shouted to the crowd.

The orphanage children and some of the curious locals stood back from the makeshift string fence Blaze, Vipul, and Jake erected just before boarding *Alex's Legacy* for liftoff. It was midnight, but the ship's exterior lights lit up the field like midday.

Shima kept a close eye on Beth Murphy and her granddaughter Niyati Smith, who were standing nearby, pressed close to the string barrier. Beth's face was etched with worry lines and tears rolled down Niyati's small brown face. Shima felt a pang of sympathy for them. There were no guarantees any of the crew would return from the rescue mission. Shima knew she would start to cry if she allowed herself to think about it, so she made a valiant effort to focus on the task at hand.

"Ready to lift," Danae's voice came through the com clipped to Shima's left earlobe.

She glanced around, assuring herself everyone was standing safely back from the barricade. "All clear, Captain."

The *Alex*'s tail section began to hum. The sound grew to a rumbling roar, loud enough to force all the spectators to clamp their hands over their ears. At the same time, the tail of the ship began to glow fluorescent blue, becoming brighter and brighter to match the rising pitch of the engines. As one, the crowd shut their eyes or squinted to filter the glare.

Unlike the ancient NASA shuttles still used by Earth spaceports, *Alex's Legacy* was a McConnell-class starship. Instead of wasting hundreds of liters of fuel to push off from the surface of the planet, the *Alex* would escape the Earth's gravity with McConnell's most practical invention, known in layman's terms as the Sling Launch. The ship would gain altitude as it circled the globe, increasing in speed until it broke free of the atmosphere.

The silver ship lifted slowly from the ground, the engines glowing. It hovered until it had enough altitude for a horizontal launch. Then it emitted a sound like a clap of thunder and became a streak of light climbing into the night sky.

It was out of sight in seconds.

Cheers went up from the crowd. The children laughed and applauded. Shima knew it was probably the first time any of them had seen a ship launch. She pulled out her referee's whistle and blew it until she had everyone's attention.

"It is late! I want all the children in the house! Go to bed!"

There was some good-natured grumbling from the older kids, but the younger ones were rubbing their eyes, willing to comply.

The Lost Sheep strained at the seams to accommodate the seventy-seven children who had yet to be adopted. There was room for forty-eight in the upstairs bedrooms—eight in each of the six rooms—so the twenty-nine extra kids slept on the floor of the large living room on donated sleeping bags.

Shima went from room to room, attempting to monitor the chaos. Her childcare supervisor Olivia Grey kept vigil in the four upstairs bathrooms, making sure each child brushed his or her teeth. It took a long time to get the children settled for the night. Shima felt ready to collapse when she could turn off the lights and retreat to her own room downstairs.

The large downstairs master bedroom had been converted into three smaller rooms. Two served as bedrooms for the live-in staff, and the third functioned as an infirmary for the future medic—either Jake or Dr. Sorensen.

Shima suspected the orphanage would be a work in progress for months. She had already decided Kirsten Sorensen should take her place as the orphanage director as soon as possible. *As the director of a children's homeless shelter, she is much better qualified for this responsibility. And I will* not *be left behind when Danae begins the search for Zuri.*

***

Morning came early as Shima headed to the kitchen at 6:00 a.m. to help Beth and Olivia prepare breakfast for the children. It took some effort to keep her eyes open as she cored and diced eight pineapples. She placed the huge serving bowl of fruit next to the cauldron-size pot of oatmeal Olivia prepared. The antique china in the kitchen cabinets had been replaced by a colorful assortment of unbreakable bowls, plates, and cups. None of the donated flatware matched, but Shima knew the kids didn't care. In fact, some of them still didn't know how to use forks and spoons.

Around 7:00, the early risers began to troop through the kitchen to collect their breakfasts. Since the dining room only seated sixteen, the children took their food outside to eat. Shima was grateful for the large backyard and grassy fields surrounding the house, which made it easy for the children to spend most of the day outside. The Lost Sheep, while spacious for a family home, was too small for eighty-two people. Fortunately, the children enjoyed being outside in the gorgeous Maui sunshine. About the only downside to the beautiful weather was the daily expense of replacing the sunscreen patches each child wore on the underside of his or her right arm.

As soon as they finished their oatmeal, pineapple, and mango juice, the kids began to bring their dishes back inside. The kitchen android Danae purchased was set at top speed to wash dishes after each meal. Shima made a mental note to install three stainless-steel cafeteria-sized sinks as soon as possible.

Am I a nanny or a contractor? she thought, stifling a yawn.

After eating, the kids headed upstairs to brush their teeth and comb their hair before going back outside to play. Showers were scheduled to be taken in rotations in the evenings, with each child getting a quick clean-up about every third night. Thankfully there were no more toddlers to be diapered and bathed, since they had all been adopted as soon as Grey was hired. The children who remained were old enough to manage their own hygiene, ranging in age from eight to thirteen.

Shima was grateful the number of orphans was declining as the children were adopted by Maui citizens, who were now coming from as far away as Hana to visit The Lost Sheep.

With the departure of both Jake's family and the crew of *Alex's Legacy* the night before, the staff had been reduced from fifteen to four. Shima was already beginning to feel the weight of responsibility as her to-do list grew long. Grey had suggested they advertise on Oahu for adoptions, and she thought it was a good idea, but not until she hired more help.

"Ideas for today?" She asked Beth and Olivia as the last of the children deposited their empty cups and bowls on the counter next to the sink. Because everyone had been up so late the night before, it was close to nine. *Three hours for breakfast is much too long,* Shima thought, covering another yawn.

Niyati hovered close to Beth as the women put food away and wiped down the counters. The child appeared withdrawn as she watched her grandmother's every move. When Beth sat down at the small dinette tucked away in the corner of the kitchen near a window, Niyati climbed onto her lap.

Beth and Shima exchanged a look of mutual understanding as Niyati buried her face in her grandmother's shoulder.

"Grey left at seven in our solar car. He has eight home visits scheduled for today," Olivia reported, easing into the chair across from Beth. A thin, quiet Brit with a serious demeanor and a head full of thick, bushy blond hair, Olivia Grey was a sharp contrast to her portly, bald, always cheerful, and never-stops-talking Aussie husband. "I could organize a football game and keep an eye on the kids while I assemble home study reports for him."

"I have to hire more help." Shima refilled her coffee mug for the third time. "I have some messages on the com in response to the jobs I advertised for in the *Lahaina Times*. I need to schedule interviews for today. I do not think we can manage without a full-time cook and at least two more childcare workers."

"No arguments here," Beth said. "I think the kids could use an outing. How about if I take them to the beach?"

"All of them?" Olivia asked, wide-eyed.

Beth laughed. "Yes, that does sound crazy, now that I think about it. I should spread it out over several days, take maybe twenty-five at a time. What do you think, Shima?"

"I am concerned that most of the children cannot swim, having had no opportunities to learn. I cannot swim."

"So I won't let them swim," Beth said. "I'll tell them they can only wade up to their knees, and anyone who disobeys that rule will have to sit out for an hour."

"I think it sounds manageable," Olivia said. "Grey and I have walked out to the beach a few times. It's absolutely beautiful and there are dozens of tidal pools so the kids can explore the sea life with no worries. We found sea urchins, anemones, starfish, and a few crabs."

Shima found herself wanting to visit the beach too. "I have never seen a starfish before. Maybe I could accompany you tomorrow."

Beth smiled. "We're living in paradise, Shima. We might as well enjoy it."

"I look forward to it." *Unlike the job interviews I must conduct today,* she thought with a twinge of nervousness.

As Olivia and Beth, with Niyati right on her heels, headed outside to replace sunscreen patches and organize the children into two groups—beach or soccer, Shima clipped on an earcom and took her datapad so she could make calls while she worked. First, she gave the android instructions to pack peanut butter and jelly sandwiches, apples, and bottles of water for twenty-six into a large box. Then she found the anti-grav unit, which would be needed to transport the box. She made another mental note to request portable refrigerators from anyone who asked what the orphanage needed.

Next, she called the first contact on her list while she headed upstairs and went through the children's rooms, checking each pillowcase for lice or nits as Lorina had advised.

"Hello, Miss Parker? This is Heshima Oryang of The Lost Sheep orphanage in Lahaina." Shima stripped a bed that looked suspicious.

"I am calling to see if you could come for an interview today." She stepped over a pile of Legos and decided to ignore the clothes scattered around on the floor. *They will have to be responsible for their own belongings.*

"Can you come at 10:30? Do you have the address?" Shima moved on to the next room, surveyed the mess, and decided a chore schedule for the kids would need to top her to-do list. She moved through the room, bending or standing on tiptoe to inspect each bunk.

"I will see you at 10:30. Please bring at least three letters of reference, and you will need to submit to a drug screen."

Shima winced at the woman's reply. "I am sorry, but the children's safety is my top priority, and I cannot make an exception for anyone. Goodbye." She stripped two more beds and called the next contact on her datapad.

"Hello, Mr. Ly?"

"Could you come at 10:30 for an interview?"

It took Shima an hour to return calls and inspect the children's rooms, including the messy living room strewn with sleeping bags and pillows. She realized her first interviewee would arrive in a moment and rushed to her room to change into something less shabby than the shorts and T-shirt she had on.

One glance at the contents of her small armoire, and she decided the only presentable outfit she owned was the tailored muumuu from Blaze and Lorina's wedding. Shima slipped it on, along with her sandals, and made a dash for the front door.

Passing through the kitchen, she saw the box of packed lunches and the anti-grav unit had already disappeared with Beth and the first group of kids headed to the beach, which was only a two-kilometer walk from the house. "Start making sandwiches for the rest of the children," she instructed the android.

The doorbell rang, and Shima remembered she didn't have any questions planned for her first interview. She didn't even have a suitable place to conduct the interview, given the state of the living room. She had no time to worry about any of it as she reached the front door.

"Hello and welcome, Mr. Ly."

A short, stout, mid-forties-looking Asian with a receding hairline greeted her with a polite bow. He was dressed in a pale gray suit with a Hawaiian-print tie. Shima shook his hand and made a quick decision to interview him on the front porch.

"I am Heshima Oryang, the orphanage director, but you may call me Shima."

"Call me Paul." Ly seemed friendly but nervous, which made Shima feel a little more at ease with her own sweaty palms. *He will not notice if I make a mistake—and I probably will.*

"Shall we sit out here?" Shima gestured to a pair of rocking chairs.

She fidgeted with her datapad as she sat in a rocker next to the one Paul chose. She felt foolish looking at the screen for nonexistent interview questions, but the gadget would be useful for taking notes. She got out the stylus and tried to appear organized as she began with the first question she could think of.

"Tell me about your culinary training."

Paul Ly turned out to be a rare find. He was a surviving veteran who'd spent his four years in the Air Force cooking in mess halls because he was too short to be a pilot. He had been stationed at various bases in the US, out of harm's way every time the bombs fell. After the war, he worked in several restaurants around the islands, and he liked children.

"I have three of my own," he said, his face downcast, "but they live with their mother on Oahu."

"Why are you interested in this position?" Shima asked.

"There are few restaurants on Maui that do enough business to pay the chef enough to pay his rent." Paul shrugged. "And my rent just went up."

Shima nodded. "So you think you could run a kitchen and prepare meals for eighty-two, three times a day?"

"Easily," Paul assured her.

"And that number will change," she said. "When the ship returns from Mars Station, we may have a hundred more mouths to feed."

"No problem."

Shima asked for his letters of reference. He handed over a datapad, and she read through them.

"There is a small medical clinic on Front Street in Lahaina where you can have your drug screen done. Once they call me with the results, I feel it is safe to say that you can move in and start cooking."

And I will have to move to a different room, Shima thought, embarrassed she assumed the live-in cook would be female and thus able to share her room. *I will have to bunk with Beth and Niyati in the infirmary until we can set up the library as a staff bedroom.*

Shima thanked Paul for coming as she stood and shook his hand. Glancing past him, she saw her next interviewee walking up the driveway. *No rest for the weary.*

Five hours later, Shima had interviewed thirteen potential childcare workers and wasn't convinced a single one of them wanted to be around children twenty-four/seven. Glancing at her datapad, she saw she had two more interviews scheduled for the day. She closed her eyes, trying to summon a hidden reservoir of energy.

At least we have a cook now. She gave herself a mental pep talk. *I will not have to get up so early tomorrow because Paul will have breakfast ready.*

Beth had returned with her group of damp, sandy children late in the afternoon. The kids were hosed off in the backyard—which they loved—and sent, four at a time, up to the showers. Olivia's group had spent the day playing outside, and they wanted to be hosed off too. Shima could hear the shouts and laughter from the backyard. A few kids came running past her as they circled the house, chasing each other.

The chore schedule, Shima thought. The bathrooms would be disaster areas after twenty-five showers. *And wet clothes everywhere,* she thought with a grimace. *Well, I will just have to trust Beth and Olivia to manage the chaos.*

Two slender black women dressed in identical bright pink muumuus were walking up the driveway. Shima noticed they were both limping, one favored her right leg and the other seemed to favor her left. She assumed these were her last two interviewees and wondered why one of them was early.

As they drew closer, Shima could see their faces more clearly. They were identical twins. She glanced at her datapad. *Tabitha McLeod and Abish McLeod. I was too tired to notice they have the same surname.* She stood and welcomed them as they reached the porch.

"It has been a long day, ladies. Would you mind if I interviewed you together?"

"To be honest, we were hoping you'd say that." Fortunately, they had different hairstyles, so Shima would be able to tell them apart. The one who spoke first had waist-length dreadlocks tied back into a loose ponytail. She offered her hand for Shima to shake. "I'm Tabitha McLeod."

"Abish McLeod." The other sister shook hands with Shima. She had short loose curls with auburn highlights.

Shima introduced herself and drew a third rocking chair over. "Please have a seat."

The sisters sat, all smiles, and Abish began talking before Shima could ask the first question. "When we saw you were hiring two childcare workers, we hoped we'd be able to work together."

"We're very close," Tabitha said. "We were co-joined at birth. We shared the same hip socket on this side." She patted her right leg for emphasis. "Even the best technology and synthbone can only replace so much, so we've always been a little self-conscious of our limps. We like to stick together."

"For moral support—" Abish said.

"And just because we're sisters—" Tabitha said.

"Best friends—"

"It's a twin thing. It's hard to explain."

Shima felt a little disoriented, switching her attention back and forth between them as they finished each other's sentences. "How old are you?"

"Nineteen," they answered in unison.

Shima smiled. *Youthful enthusiasm.* "Do you like children?"

"Love them!" Tabitha said.

"Experience?"

"Babysitting, mostly." Abish presented Shima with a datapad containing their letters of reference. "But willing to learn."

"Willing to be tested for drugs?" Shima asked.

"Yes," they said in the same breath.

She gave them the address of the clinic. "When they call me with your results, you can move in right away." She wondered where to put Paul Ly if the sisters could share her present room.

"If you don't mind, we'd like to live at home," Tabitha said.

Shima was disappointed. "I need to hire live-in staff."

"But we're just right across the street," Abish said.

"What?"

The twins pointed. Their house was the closest to The Lost Sheep, on the other side of Lahainaluna Road.

"Easy commute," Abish said. "We could be here any time of the day or night."

"Mom said it looked like there were so many people already living here, there would be no point squeezing in two more," Tabitha said.

"I think she's just trying to hold on to us a little longer," Abish said.

Shima found herself laughing. "I hope you two pass the drug screen. I would be a fool not to hire you!"

The sisters stood and smiled as they shook Shima's hand. "We'll go take care of that right now," Tabitha said. And they departed.

Shima sighed with relief and went into the house to check on the status of dinner.

***

The next day ran much smoother with the three new staff members. Paul had homemade granola, soy milk, and bananas ready at 7:00, and all the children had eaten by 8:00. Tabitha and Abish were upstairs supervising chores, and Shima was relieved to see the house tidy and organized before the kids went outside to play. This time Olivia took the next group of twenty-five to the beach, with Abish assisting, and Beth supervised outdoor activities, with Tabitha to assist her.

This is much more manageable, Shima thought. *Now I can concentrate on renovations to the house and visits from potential adoptive parents.* With an electrician scheduled to install the power outlets for two more washer-dryers on the back porch, she didn't have time to go to the beach. *Maybe tomorrow,* she hoped.

By 11:00, Shima had already received calls from three couples who wanted to begin the adoption process right away. She was grateful Grey would be on hand to interview two of the couples, but then he was scheduled to finalize an adoption at the courthouse.

"Our wonderful Vladimir will be leaving us today," Grey reported. "His new parents will meet me at the courthouse. You can handle one interview, Shima." He handed her a datapad. "Here's all the questions you need to ask."

She nodded. "I know I need to get used to doing interviews, but they still make me nervous."

Grey just gave her a reassuring pat on the back and went to the kitchen for some lunch.

The carpenters arrived at 11:30 to install doors to the library, and Shima divided her attention between them, the electrician, and Paul the cook, who needed an extra pair of hands to rearrange the pantry to his liking.

The prospective parents showed up promptly at 4:00, and Shima interviewed them on the porch. They were like so many of the other couples she had met or spoken to since The Lost Sheep had been established: late-thirties to early-fifties, healthy, educated, employed, and eager to be parents. They often glanced over at the field where the children were playing while Shima asked them awkward questions about their marriage and finances.

She managed to get through the interview without embarrassing anyone, including herself. "Thank you." She stood and shook their hands. "The social worker Gordon Grey will soon contact you."

That evening, Shima set up the former library as her own room. Except for a few dozen children's books, the contents of the three-by-three-meter room had been sold. Only the empty built-in bookcases remained. She suspected with the empty shelves, her room would become the depository for all things misplaced and miscellaneous, but she thought it was a small price to pay for some privacy. *I did not realize how much I enjoyed having my own cabin on the ship.*

Grey and Paul moved in the extra twin bed from her former room, and Shima fell asleep as soon as she had sheets on it.

The next day brought a whole new challenge as rain fell in torrents. *What to do with seventy-six children inside the house?* Shima appealed to her staff for ideas as the children ate breakfast in rotations of sixteen at the dining room table.

"Arts and crafts?" Beth said. "I think I have enough paper for origami. We could make some play dough for the younger kids."

"They can use the cookie cutters and garlic press with the play dough," Paul offered. "A few of them could help me bake brownies."

"Laundry," Olivia said. "Let's put those new machines to work. I'll supervise," she volunteered before Shima could ask.

"We could put on a holo-vid after lunch," Abish said, "but—"

"Hopefully the rain will stop by then," Tabitha finished.

"And we have seven couples coming to visit today," Grey said, "so it makes it easier if the kids are around for them to observe. That way they can decide if any of the rascals tug at their heartstrings." He grinned at Shima, his blue eyes twinkling. "Makes my job much easier."

"Mine too," she agreed.

With few exceptions, prospective adoptive parents brought donations for the orphanage when they came to be interviewed. Toys, toiletries, and clothes were the normal offerings, but today the gifts were unusual. There was twenty kilos of lean ground beef, a box of sunscreen patches, one hundred pairs of children's shower thongs or flip-flops, a box of impossible-to-find construction paper, six lacrosse sticks and balls, three new datapads, and an offer to build a chicken coop for twenty-five laying hens.

"Yes!" Shima was delighted with the last donation. "How soon could you start?"

The rain fell all afternoon, but The Lost Sheep managed to survive its first full day inside unscathed. When the seventh couple departed just before dinner, Grey told Shima fourteen more children were going to be adopted as soon as he could process the paperwork and home studies.

"It's great to see that people don't want to split up children who are close friends," Beth told Shima in the kitchen over a delicious dinner of meatloaf, mashed potatoes, and green beans. "One couple just melted when they saw Vida looking at a book with Luz. Neither girl can read, so they were making up a story from the illustrations. The couple told me, 'We wouldn't dream of adopting one without the other. They'd be perfect sisters.' They also want a pair of older boys, though they haven't decided which ones yet."

"Four children! That is good to hear," Shima said. "And tomorrow I have nothing important scheduled so I am going to the beach with you."

"Glad to hear it!" Beth dabbed gravy off her chin with a napkin. "You work harder than any of us, and you need a break."

Shima flushed at the compliment but silently agreed. "Now that we are fully staffed, we should schedule a rotation of half-days off."

Beth nodded, glancing at Niyati, who was sitting at the table with them, eating green beans with her fingers. "I know someone who could use some one-on-one quiet time with Grandma."

"Then you should have tomorrow afternoon off," Shima said. "We will make it a short outing to the beach this time. Abish and Tabitha can stay here and help Olivia."

***

Shima donned shorts, a T-shirt, her whistle, and a sunscreen patch. *I still need to buy some business clothes,* she reminded herself as she headed into the kitchen to check on the picnic lunch.

Paul already had the lunch box ready to go. "Have fun, Shima." He glanced up from the potato he was peeling.

"Thank you." She picked up the anti-grav remote control and put the box into motion, guiding it to the front door.

Beth, Niyati, and a group of eager kids were gathered on and around the front porch, swatting each other with their towels and laughing. The kids were clad in shorts and T-shirts, though a few lucky girls had on swimsuits, and they all wore new flip-flops. *No more bare feet,* Shima thought.

"Let's go!" Beth took Niyati's hand and led the way.

Shima brought up the rear with the box of lunches hovering along, half a meter above the ground. It felt good to be outside in the fresh air.

The grassy field soon led to a gravel road, then to an expanse of white sand. They climbed a sand dune and discovered the beach on the other side. They had it all to themselves.

There were outcroppings of huge rocks, several meters high, on the beach and in the ocean, close to the shore. Shima watched the waves crash over them. It was both mesmerizing and spectacular. Tidal pools were everywhere, just as Olivia said. The kids were drawn to them, climbing over the jagged clusters of orange-red rocks to look for sea life. Shima was extra grateful for the flip-flops when she noted how sharp the rocks were. She lowered the box onto the sand and decided to lay her towel over the top to protect the contents from the sun.

A few of the younger kids ventured to the edge of the water where the waves left lines of foam on the white sand, but Beth hovered near them, making sure no one went in far.

"Look, Miss Shima, look." Niyati scampered over and held up a tiny orange starfish.

Shima was surprised by both the starfish and the fact that Niyati was feeling secure enough to leave Beth's side. "Can I touch it?"

"Yes." Niyati put the starfish in Shima's outstretched palm.

"Where did you find it?"

"Come, I show you." Niyati seized Shima's free hand and led her over to a tidal pool. Four kids were hunched over it, fascinated by what they found in the clear, warm water.

Shima squatted next to Niyati and lost herself for a few minutes as she admired the tiny sea anemones, shells, and starfish.

Abruptly she remembered she had other children to supervise and raised her head to look around. Most of them were looking in the tidal pools, but a few were with Beth, laughing and splashing each other as the waves licked their ankles. *Maybe I should count them,* Shima thought, standing.

She came up with twenty-five but then tried to remember if Niyati was included in the original twenty-five. *Should there be twenty-six?* She chastised herself for not taking a head count before the group left the house. *I will ask Beth how many.*

She turned and looked to the spot where Beth had been standing moments ago and gasped. Panic shot through her as she raced over to the water's edge.

"Get out of the water," she ordered the few children who'd been splashing in the shallows, but were now staring, open-mouthed, at Beth out in the ocean.

Elizabeth Murphy was attempting to swim to shore with a terrified child on her back, his arms around her neck. The waves crashed against the tall, jagged rocks on either side of her, making her task treacherous as she tried to avoid being swept against them. The waves were rough, the current was strong, and she was in trouble.

Shima was paralyzed with fear. *I cannot swim! I must help her, but I cannot swim! A rope! Why did we not bring a rope with a floatation ring on it?*

Frantic, she glanced around for something to use as a rope, but there was nothing available. *Another type of rope?* She had an idea.

She looked over at the older kids at the tidal pools and blew a sharp blast on her whistle, waving to them. "Come quickly! Help me!"

About fifteen of the children sprinted over.

"Form a chain!" Shima wrapped one hand firmly around the wrist of the tallest boy, Mohammed. "Grip each other's wrists! Taller ones near the front, but I need a strong boy to be last in line as an anchor!" The kids were quick to follow her instructions, linking arms according to height with a stocky boy, Javier, bringing up the rear.

"Whatever happens, *do not let go!*" Shima headed out into the water, her heart pounding against her ribs. She tried not to let fear cloud her mind as a huge wave broke over her, almost knocking her down. She felt the powerful current trying to yank her off her feet and realized what happened to the child.

Beth was tiring, her strokes getting slower. A large wave broke over her and her passenger, tumbling them in the rough surf. Shima held her breath, watching anxiously for them to surface. When they did, they were a few meters closer to her. But then the current dragged them farther from shore again.

"Keep going!" Shima could no longer touch bottom, but she kicked her legs and managed to keep her head above water. Mohammed had no trouble staying above the waves, even without the use of his arms. He knew how to swim. *But do the others?*

Shima was frantic, torn between reaching Beth and leading too many kids into the deep water—kids who probably couldn't swim. She fought the powerful undertow and knew she couldn't allow the children to go any farther or they would be caught in it.

She stole a glance toward the beach, and her fears were confirmed—this was as far as she could go. Javier, the anchor, was up to his shins in the water, heels dug into the sand, both hands gripping the wrist of the tortured-looking girl in front of him.

"What should we do?" Shima shouted to Beth, struggling to keep her head above water. She watched, helpless, as Beth was swept closer, then out of reach again. Only a few meters separated them, but it might as well have been a kilometer.

"Next wave!" Beth pried the terrified boy off her back. "I'll send Zane toward you!"

Oh please, God, let me reach him!

The next big wave was upon them, and Beth shoved Zane onto the crest of it. Shima realized it would break on top of her, but she was able to grab his T-shirt right when the wave hit, knocking her down into the churning water, along with Mohammed and several other children in the lineup.

Do not let go! Shima held on to Zane with all her strength as she found the surface.

Mohammed was up, and he still had a firm grip on Shima's wrist. The human chain began to drag her toward the beach. Zane threw both arms around her neck and held on tight, crying, coughing, and shoving her head under water.

Shima fought the urge to push Zane away. *He is going to drown me!* But in a few moments her feet touched the sandy bottom, and she could surface, gasping for breath and worn out from the effort of fighting the waves and the undertow.

In a minute, Shima and the children were on the beach, and her sobbing passenger dropped onto the sand. The kids were trembling with fear and rubbing their aching shoulders. Some of the girls were crying.

"We need to go out again," Mohammed said, "and rescue Miss Beth."

"We do not have the strength. It is too dangerous to attempt again." Shima shook her head in despair. She couldn't risk their lives a second time with the treacherous undertow.

"Beth!" Shima was terrified as she searched the water with her eyes, praying Elizabeth Murphy would have the strength to reach the shore. Precious minutes passed, but she couldn't see anything—or anyone—in the pounding surf.

"Granma?" Niyati was by Shima's side, crying and clinging to her leg. "Where Granma?" Her voice rose to an anguished howl. "Granma!"

SIX
COMMUNICATION

THE PREMONITIONS HAD stopped. Marco thought it was just a one-time occurrence. Perhaps he was sleeping so soundly he didn't remember his dreams. But when the ship was a few hours from docking at Mars Station, he realized the entire trip had been dreamless. Three nights premonition free. It was liberating and unnerving at the same time.

Why now? What's different this time? Marco shifted his position in the pilot's seat, lost in thought. He'd spent the entire trip avoiding everyone, as Shepherd ordered, either in his cabin or at the helm. He avoided eye contact with Phailin when he went to the galley for a meal, which he always ate by himself at the corner table. *Do I need to be around other people to have impressions?*

"Velocity break in ten minutes," Captain Shepherd's voice interrupted his musings. She was seated in the navigator's chair to his left.

Marco focused on the streams of information flowing across the helm's multiple screens. All ship's systems were working fine. He adjusted his right-hand grip on the accelerator, his left hand on the decelerator. And, as always, he broke out in a sweat, wrestling with the old fear that something would go wrong.

At one minute, Shepherd began counting down.

"... three ... two ... one."

The Velocity break was smooth with Marco and Blaze working simultaneously to transition *Alex's Legacy* to normal space. The dull red glow of Mars filled the helm window.

"Switching to solar engines," Blaze reported, four decks below.

"Re-entry in five minutes," Marco said, breathing again. Re-entry was easy for Mars, compared to Earth. The turbulence would only last a few minutes.

Twenty minutes later, *Alex's Legacy* entered Mars's stratosphere unscathed.

"That's it. We're clear," he announced.

"Blaze to the bridge as soon as possible," Shepherd said. "Local time is 4:00 a.m. It's the perfect time for you to play the role of captain."

"On my way," Blaze said.

Marco hid a smile from Shepherd. It gave him some satisfaction to hear a tremor in the engineer's voice.

A few minutes later, Blaze and Shepherd were at the com control board. Marco glanced over his shoulder for a moment to see Smith in the hot seat, looking unhappy. The captain handed him a datapad and moved to stand behind him.

"Just like we practiced," she said. "The regular port master isn't going to be there this early, so we should be able to convince the sleepy underling who's taking his place that we're not the *Ishmael.*"

"Yes, Captain," Blaze muttered.

"Breathe, Blaze."

"Yes, Captain."

"Ready to transmit?"

"No, but let's do it anyway."

Marco was skeptical of the success of Shepherd's plan. He tried to pay attention to his flying as he listened to the broadcasted transmission.

"*Alex's Legacy* to Mars Station port master, requestin' permission to dock." Blaze's voice was steady, but an octave higher than normal.

"Port master to *Alex's Legacy,* please identify yourself," came the crisp reply of a woman.

"Captain RJ Smith of the merchant ship *Alex's Legacy*, based out of Maui."

"Cargo?"

"Fifty thousand kilos of sugar and four thousand kilos of salt," Blaze said.

Marco rolled his eyes, recalling the great debate over what to *import* that wouldn't raise too much suspicion. It was decided any produce such as pineapples would be inspected before they could go dirtside. And being inspected wasn't an option. Sugar seemed like a safe bluff. Maui did produce a lot of sugar.

"Have you arranged for a buyer on Mars Station, Captain Smith?" The Port Authority had strict regulations regarding imports. Shepherd knew this, which is why the elaborate ruse continued.

"No, ma'am, we're bound for Titan with this cargo."

"So why did you break jump to come here? Mars isn't on the way to Titan."

"Repairs to the Velocity engines. There was a minor malfunction durin' the jump from Earth. We need to acquire and install a specific part before we can make the long jump to Titan."

"Understood. Please submit ship's registry and crew roster."

Now we'll see just how good Murphy's forgeries really are, Marco thought.

"Transmittin'," Blaze said.

Marco glanced over his shoulder again to see the engineer sweating like a leaky faucet. He turned back to the helm, trying not to smirk.

"Received," the port master said.

The new Maui registration was authentic with H Oryang and RJ Smith listed as owner and captain, respectively, along with their DNA traces and modified holograms. The crew roster, however, was fictitious, composed of holograms and DNA traces from a few brave volunteers like Gordon and Olivia Grey. A handful of grateful adoptive parents from Lahaina had been happy to sign on as the rest of the fake crew. Their DNA traces would be verified from the Earth's database, although Marco wondered if the port master would notice the *Alex's* helmsman used to be a grocer.

The first big gamble was that the port master could come aboard the ship to take new DNA traces from each crewmember if she found anything suspicious on the registry or roster. *We'll all be in prison before sunrise,* Marco thought with a twinge of fear.

After several heart-stopping minutes, the reply came. "Acceptable. Please submit ship's schematics."

Forgery number two, Ting thought. The ship's schematics were from an actual merchant ship. *Since anyone who isn't blind can see this is a passenger ship.* He felt a knot in his stomach. *This is insane. I should've stayed on Maui.*

The port master required blueprints to make certain incoming civilian ships were unarmed and not on the CIP's Most Wanted list. The *Ishmael/Alex's Legacy* was probably at the top of that list.

"Schematics transmittin'," Blaze said.

"Received." Again the pause as she looked it over. This was the second big gamble because the port master could request an inspection of the ship if she found anything suspicious in the schematics.

The waiting was agony.

"Acceptable. Docking level preference?" was the next question.

Marco heard Shepherd exhale. *It actually worked.* His opinion of Lorina's skills rose a fraction.

"Request Level 14," Blaze said.

"Airlock 7 is available. Transmitting course coordinates."

"Received. Beginnin' approach in fifteen minutes."

"Report in when docked," was the port master's parting request.

"Understood. Smith out."

There was a moment of silence as captain and fake-captain waited to be sure the transmission link was closed before they both let out a whoop of triumph.

"It worked! I don't believe it! It worked!" Blaze pumped a fist in the air.

"Nice acting job, Captain." Shepherd was serious again. "One hurdle down. Now we have to pray the surveillance holo-cam isn't working at airlock 7. Then we have to go dirtside to find Erik."

"Good luck with that." Marco shook his head.

"Just keep your mouth shut, and land the ship!" Shepherd turned on her heel and left the bridge.

The helmsman spent the next two hours bringing the ship in to the crowded port by alternating braking and acceleration, and making minute course adjustments. The airlocks on Level 14 were spaced half a kilometer apart, yet the massive merchant ships docked at airlocks 6 and 8 hadn't left much space for even a small ship like the *Alex* to squeeze between them. Marco kept an eye on one of his monitors which estimated the distance between the other ships. It was going to be tight. *Thanks for leaving me eight meters on either side, you giant floating piles of rusty scrap metal.*

Parking in a small space between other starships was a skill which required steady hands and a lot of helm experience. Every time he brought the ship in to a spaceport, Marco felt confident his job was safe. Few people could do what he did, and Shepherd knew it.

When *Alex's Legacy* nestled up to airlock 7 and shut down the engines, it was 6:10 local time.

"I'm extending the antechamber," Vipul said, taking over the job which was normally Blaze's responsibility, at the main airlock. "Seals are matching up . . . seals are secure. We're connected."

"*Alex's Legacy* has secured dock on Level 14, airlock 7," Blaze reported on ship-to-shore com.

Now we find out if the port master got a visual of the ship, Marco thought. *Why don't we just make a public announcement, 'We're back, Acheron! Please come arrest us!'?*

"Acknowledged," the same assistant port master said. "Welcome to Mars Station."

"Thank you," Blaze said.

"Docking fees are ten thousand credits per day. Our new policy is that departing ship captains must pay the port master *in person* before being allowed to detach from the airlock. Failure to do so will result in the ship being boarded by the Central Intelligence Police and all crewmembers arrested."

"Understood. Smith out." He let out a long, low whistle. "Sounds like they've boosted the prices and the security, Captain."

"I think our last departure had something to do with that," Shepherd said from her office.

"How can we tell if the holo-cam at our airlock is working?" Jake asked from the infirmary.

Marco snorted. "Open the doors to see if Acheron's arranged a welcoming party for us. I'm sure he has an orange jumpsuit just your size, O'Brien."

"Give your tongue a rest, Ting!" Shepherd barked. "We've made it this far. Don't start spreading gloom. All crewmembers report to the bridge in five minutes."

Marco swiveled in his chair so he was facing Blaze at the com. *Another long, boring planning meeting.* He intended to contribute nothing to the discussion.

The crew of seven crowded onto the small bridge. Danae Shepherd was dressed all in black, but the others wore their ridiculous *Alex's Legacy* uniforms of bright tropical-print shirts.

All we need are some bongos and ukuleles. Maybe Phailin could be a hula dancer. Marco smiled at that thought.

"Should we change too, Captain?" Lorina eyed Shepherd's attire with a puzzled frown.

Marco thought Shepherd looked like she belonged in a street gang. He wondered if she was packing her pistol for this outing. He noticed a slight bulge in the right-hand pocket of her jacket. *Armed, and out of her mind to go dirtside.*

"No, you need to stay in uniform in case you encounter someone from the port master's office. A uniform is considered your security pass." Shepherd gave no explanation as to why she wasn't in uniform, but Marco had already figured it out.

She knows she'll probably get caught, and doesn't want Acheron to know the name of the ship. It might keep the CIPs off our backs for a few hours, but they'll figure it out soon enough.

The captain handed out earcoms and terse instructions. "Blaze and Lorina, I want you to go to

Mother Teresa's and talk to Kirsten Sorensen, assuming she's still there. Assess the situation and report back to the ship."

"Yes, Captain," Lorina said, and Blaze nodded.

"Jake and Vipul, I want you to find out where the *Elmina* is docked. You might need to ask around for information, but don't approach the port master's office. When you find the ship, assess the situation and report back here."

"Yes, Captain," they said.

"What about you, Captain?" Lorina asked. "Is someone teaming up with you to go dirtside?" She glanced at Phailin.

Shepherd shook her head. "I'm going alone. I'm the one wanted for murder, so if I run into trouble, no one else will be arrested as my accomplice."

There were loud objections from the others. Marco knew they were wasting their breath.

"Where are you planning to go, Captain?" Jake asked.

"I'm going to find out where Erik is being held."

"The transmission from Dr. Sorensen was sent to lure you into a trap!" Lorina said. "You can't just walk right into Acheron's waiting arms!"

Jake and Lorina argued with her for several minutes, trying to convince her she was taking an unnecessary risk by going alone to search for the doctor, but Shepherd wouldn't be swayed.

"Don't worry. I have a plan. I'll be careful not to attract attention." The captain's hands were on her hips. "Erik's the reason we're back, and we're not leaving the station without him."

Even Jake had the sense to shut his mouth, Marco noted with satisfaction.

"I want everyone to report in to Ting—"

"Me?" Marco protested, but Shepherd spoke over him.

"—once an hour. Ting, you and Phailin will keep track of everyone's movements and contact the others if someone fails to report in. We need vigilant communication to coordinate this rescue." She handed them both earcoms. "Do you have a problem with that?"

"No, Captain." Phailin shot Marco a challenging look.

"No, Captain," he grumbled.

"Good. You can take it in shifts, but one of you will cover the com at all times. Understood?"

"Yes, Captain." Phailin nodded and glared at Marco until he nodded too.

There was a little more deliberation as each crewmember checked the amount on his or her credit flash, slipped on sunglasses, and tested the earcoms to make sure they were set to the same frequency.

"Won't Acheron be able to trace us when we use our credit flashes?" Vipul asked.

"I don't think you have anything to worry about," the captain said. "With two million people on the station, he won't waste his resources searching the population for all of us. If he has the system programmed to watch for someone's credit flash to surface, it will be mine."

"Maybe mine too," Jake said.

"There's no other way to use money on the station, so it's a risk we'll have to take. Let's plan to meet back here in eight hours," Shepherd said. "Oh, and when we exit the airlock, don't look at the security holo-cam. It'll be on the left-hand side of the corridor, near the ceiling. Good luck."

You're going to need it, Marco thought as the five left the bridge. He waited until the sounds of their footsteps on the metal rungs of the ladder faded away before pulling up the *Alex*'s holo-cam view of the exterior of the airlock. The monitor showed no welcoming party outside in the access corridor. The crew exited the ship without incident.

He stood and gave Phailin his full attention. "Do you know how to work the com?"

She frowned at him. "This isn't my first time on a starship. How stupid do you think I am?"

"I don't think you're stupid." *I just think the rest of this crew is stupid.*

"Why have you been avoiding me?"

"Captain's orders. She doesn't want me stirring up any more trouble."

"Like the fight you had with Jake?"

Marco frowned. "Didn't the others tell you the details?"

"No, as a matter of fact, your name never came up in conversation. Are you going to tell me what the fight was about?"

"I'll take the first shift. You want to relieve me in four hours?" Marco sidestepped the question. He knew he had blown his chance at any type of romantic relationship with Phailin, but he hoped she wouldn't grow to despise him like the others.

"Will you tell me about it sometime?" Phailin persisted.

"Sure." Marco sounded glib, but he meant it. How could he lie to someone as gorgeous as Phailin Kim?

Phailin's expression was thoughtful as she turned and left the bridge.

He wondered what—or who—she was thinking about.

***

"This is Smith reporting from Mother Teresa's."

Marco sat up. He had been dozing at the com. "Go ahead."

"The shelter's closed. There's a new ID lock on the front door and a sign that says *condemned,* but Lorina says no way—the house was in good condition."

Marco was about to make a sarcastic comment, but Blaze continued. "Lorina and I spoke to the owner of the restaurant across the street. He said he saw Kirsten taken away in handcuffs by the CIPs yesterday."

So much for a rescue, Marco thought. "I guess you need to return to the ship. There's nothing else you can do unless you plan to walk straight into the police department."

Blaze ignored his advice. "Lorina and I are headin' to McConnell Park to talk to some of the homeless people there. We'll see if we can uncover any more information about the Sorensens. Smith out." He cut the connection before Marco could object.

The helmsman brought up a detailed map of Mars Station on the control board's right-hand screen and noted on it where Blaze and Lorina were headed.

About five minutes later, Vipul checked in. "Jake and I found the *Elmina.* It's docked at Level 10, airlock 39."

"Acknowledged." Marco didn't know what else to say since *good job* or *that was quick work* would sound like false praise coming from him. "What's the status?"

"There's a notice on the door that the ship was abandoned on October twenty-third when the owner died—"

With some help from the captain, Ting thought.

"—and it's now in probate, waiting for Thanatos's heir to claim it."

"Thanatos has an heir?" Marco asked.

"Yes, he has a nephew. I was unfortunate enough to meet him when he came aboard the ship a few times to talk to Thanatos. His name is Monsantos. He's quiet, but just as devious as his uncle. He managed Thanatos's restaurant dirtside, but I'm sure he was involved in the real business of slave trade."

"So someone else we should avoid. What now? Are you returning to the ship?"

"Not sure we want to do that yet. Where are the others?"

"Blaze and Lorina went to the park to talk to some homeless people. They seem to think it will help."

"Jake and I are going to check the Outreach Clinic. Maybe someone at the hospital can shed some light on Erik's arrest."

Maybe Acheron is waiting for you to show up there. Marco was convinced none of them had a gram of common sense. "Have fun."

He cut the connection and made a notation on the map over Mars Community Hospital.

"This is Shepherd." The captain's voice was difficult to hear. Marco realized she was whispering. "I'm sitting at a tramstop bench across the street from CIP headquarters on Dentist Street."

He noted that on the map. "And?"

"And I'm waiting for Acheron to leave the building so I can go in and ask if Erik is being held there."

Marco thought this was so stupid, he didn't know how to respond. *This is her plan? She must have a death wish.* "There are other entrances to the building, Captain."

"I'm aware of that, Ting. Acheron's custom solar cycle is parked right out front, so this is probably the way he'll exit. Where are the others?"

He told her and signed off. *I'll give her thirty minutes before she's recognized and arrested.*

***

"Ready for a break?" Phailin walked up behind him.

"Yes, please." Marco stood, stretched, and turned to face her. For a few moments he forgot what he wanted to say.

Phailin ignored his dumbstruck grin and stepped around him to the com control board. She studied the map. "Each of these dots represent a crewmember?"

"Yes."

"When did they last report in?"

Marco checked the time and his notes. "The Smiths, twelve minutes ago. O'Brien and Ganguli, fifty-three minutes ago—they're due to check in. Captain Shepherd has been silent for an hour and a half." He shook his head. "Considering where she was trying to do a stakeout, I wouldn't be surprised if she's sharing a jail cell next to Sorensen's right now."

"That would be terrible!" Phailin took his place at the com and typed in the code for the captain's earcom.

"I'm safe. I can't talk now." Shepherd immediately broke the connection.

"Well, she's not in jail yet," Marco conceded, "but Acheron's not stupid. He'll see through her disguise. I don't know if she's really got a plan or if she's just hoping a CIP will hand her the key to Sorensen's cell."

Phailin started to comment when a loud *ping* from the console got their attention.

"That's a transmission!" He reached in front of Phailin and entered a code on the keypad next to the left-hand screen. Only one person would have sent them an interstellar communication: Shima.

He felt a chill as he remembered his premonition to her. "It's bad news," he told Phailin.

"How do you know?"

Marco shook his head. "I'll explain later."

"We should wait for the others before opening it," Phailin said.

Ting dreaded viewing it, but his curiosity was piqued. "We should watch it now. It might be urgent news."

Phailin nodded with some reluctance, and they both focused on the screen as Marco started the transmission.

Shima looked as if she'd aged ten years. "This transmission is intended for Lorina Murphy, Jake O'Brien, and Robert Smith, but it may be viewed by all the members of the crew of the merchant ship *Alex's Legacy,* bound for Mars Station, November twelfth."

Bad news for Murphy. Make that premonitions—plural. Marco held his breath, waiting for the announcement.

There was a tremor in Shima's voice. Marco could tell she was trying to keep her emotions under control. "This news will affect everyone, but I must first direct my message to Lorina." She blinked hard. "My friend, I am sorry to tell you that your mother drowned this morning."

Ting let out his breath, along with a string of curses, and then apologized to Phailin for his language.

Shima continued. "I accept full responsibility for this tragedy. I was not prepared for a water rescue." She took a deep breath and plowed on. "Beth and I took a group of the children to the beach this morning. One of the boys, Zane, got caught in the undertow, and Beth went in after him. The current was so strong she could not swim back to the beach without assistance. The children and I linked arms and made a human chain, but it was not long enough to reach her. Beth managed to get Zane onto a wave, which brought him close enough where I could grab him. We pulled Zane to shore, but did not have the strength to go in again after your mother."

Shima paused, her voice choked with emotion as she continued with difficulty. "We have not recovered her body yet. The area is too rocky for boats, but several of our kind neighbors are watching the shoreline . . . searching for her, in case she . . . washes up."

She looked off camera and gestured for someone to join her. "Zane has something he would like to say." Shima drew a thin, dark-haired, miserable-looking child onto her lap.

"I just want to say Miss Beth was very brave to rescue me." Zane wouldn't look at the camera. "I'm sorry I didn't listen to her and went in too far. She saved my life." He concluded with, "I'm sorry, Miss Lorina, about your mom."

Zane ambled off-screen, and Niyati came on, taking his place on Shima's lap. The girl's eyes were red and puffy. She sniffled and wiped her nose on the back of her arm, as kids were prone to do.

Marco felt an unexpected pang of an emotion he hadn't experienced before—sympathy. This loss would affect everyone, the kids, the orphanage staff, the ship's crew, and especially Lorina and Jake. His two least-favorite people would be devastated by this news.

Rather than feeling smug that his premonitions to Shima and Lorina had been accurate, Marco was frustrated he hadn't been able predict all the details. A glimpse of the outcome might have enabled Shima to avoid the tragedy altogether.

A glimpse of the outcome might have saved Vanni's life, he thought.

"*Amma?*" Niyati's tear-stained face appealed to the camera. "*Amma, baba,* plez come home!"

"I am so sorry. Oryang out." The screen went blank.

Phailin and Marco were silent for a few minutes. He could sense she was really shaken by the tragedy.

She turned to him with a suspicious frown. "How did you know it was bad news?"

Marco bit his lip. "I'm not sure you want to know."

Phailin studied his face for a moment, thoughtful. "You seem to be very unpopular on this ship. I think you could use a friend. Yes, I really want to know. I can listen without judgment."

Without judgment? I hope she means it. He closed his eyes, sorted through his painful memories for a minute, and decided how much he wanted to share with Phailin.

"I started having premonitions when I was about five or six years old. At first it was just little stuff, like knowing what was in my birthday presents or seeing the answers to a test I hadn't studied for. I didn't give the visions too much thought until the day I scared old Mrs. Wong who lived next door. I told her she was going to lose her wallet at the market the next day." He snorted. "And when she did, she accused me of stealing it. My parents turned my room upside down, looking for the wallet, which I didn't have. I got in so much trouble over the whole thing that I began to realize there was something odd about seeing things before they happened.

"I didn't really have too many visions when I was in primary school." Marco frowned. "But when I hit puberty, I started having them more often, and they were about much more serious events."

He took a deep breath before venturing into a memory he tried for years to erase from his mind. "My mother was an archeologist. She took me on a summer dig when I was twelve. I told her where her students needed to search for a femur that eluded them for weeks. I think that was the first time she realized my visions weren't just my imagination. After the dig, she was always willing to listen to my premonitions and help me decide how to handle them.

"My father thought I was a freak. When I predicted he was going to be passed over for a promotion at his work because of his temper, I thought I was being helpful." He shook his head. "He refused to listen, and then he blamed me when the position went to a younger, less experienced colleague."

Marco felt a knot in his stomach as he opened his eyes and concentrated his gaze on the black thumbnail of his left hand. "When I was fourteen, I had a terrible vision—a nightmare. It was just after my mother left for Xi'an on another student dig. I begged my father to call her back, to warn her, but he said I was crazy."

He felt a gentle hand on his shoulder but couldn't look Phailin in the eye. "He never forgave me. He said I was the reason she died in that cave-in. I never forgave him for refusing to warn her. The rest of my years at home with my father were unbearable.

"After I left home for flight school, I didn't have visions for several years—nothing serious, at least—until a few months ago." He bit his lip, hesitated a moment. "I knew the crew shouldn't have gone to that restaurant on Ganymede, but I didn't know why, until it was too late."

Marco paused when Vipul checked in to inform them the Outreach Clinic was gone, but continued as soon as the navigator signed off.

"The most frustrating thing about this gift—or curse—of clairvoyance is I never see the whole picture. There's always something missing, some important detail. I didn't know the crew would all get sick from the Zenithian Flu, that Vanni and the others were going to die. I didn't know why I had a bad feeling about the new steward Shepherd hired. I didn't know who Shepherd was going to kill, or that it would be in self-defense, or that she was going to get shot too, along with Vipul. I didn't know who was going to die that was close to Murphy, or that the death was related to the premonition I had about Shima. Nothing ever fits together in my visions. It's like seeing a puzzle with some of the pieces missing." Marco shrugged, indicating he was done with the confession.

"Have you had any premonitions about me?" Phailin asked, studying his face with an intensity which made him uneasy.

Marco shook his head. "I haven't had a single impression since we left Maui. The last premonition I had was about Captain Shepherd getting arrested."

Phailin's mouth fell open. "You know she's going to be arrested? Didn't you warn her?"

"She ordered me not to tell her about any more premonitions. I didn't have much choice." He shrugged and glanced down at the map to avoid Phailin's accusing glare.

"Well, she didn't order me! I'm going to warn her! When and where does she get arrested?"

"That, I don't know," Marco said. "Just like I didn't know who was going to die, or when, or how. There's a limit to what I foresee."

Worry clouded Phailin's face as she turned back to the controls and tapped in the code for the captain's earcom.

There was no reply for several chimes. Marco was about to suggest they give up when Shepherd answered.

"Acheron has me cornered!" She sounded as if she'd been running. "Don't come after me!" And the connection was broken with a loud crackling noise.

Marco and Phailin exchanged a startled look. Hers was filled with dismay and his, resignation.

The cook tapped in the code again, but this time there was no signal.

"She destroyed her earcom so Acheron can't trace the call back to us. It looks like all my premonitions have just been fulfilled."

"What do we do now?" Phailin asked.

Marco shrugged. "I don't know what's going to happen next. Let's call the others back to the ship."

"I'll do it." Phailin made the calls. "Return to the ship. Captain Shepherd has been arrested."

Jake and Vipul made it back in record time.

"What happened?" Jake was already angry when he came through the doorway of the bridge. He directed his scowl at Marco.

The helmsman glared back at him. "We don't know."

"You were supposed to be keeping track of everyone!" Jake moved fast, crossing the bridge straight to Marco.

"Stop." Phailin stepped between them. "She didn't report in very often," she informed Jake. "And when we called her, she wouldn't tell us where she was."

"We initiated the last call," Marco directed his words at the much-calmer navigator who came in behind Jake. "She said she was cornered and not to come after her. Then she destroyed her earcom."

"What are we supposed to do now?" Jake asked.

"How should I know?" Marco made a fist as Jake pressed closer.

"You seem to know everything before it happens!" The medic tried to sidestep Phailin, but she wouldn't allow it.

"Stop!" She put a hand on each of their chests and shoved them away from each other. "Calm down! We'll figure things out when Blaze and Lorina get back." She gave Marco a piercing look he took to mean *no more fighting*.

Blaze and Lorina were on board a few minutes later, joining them on the bridge.

"What happened?" Blaze asked.

Marco described Shepherd's last communication.

"If the captain's in jail, there's no way we can get her out," Lorina said, "not with a murder charge."

"Acheron has all three of them." Blaze shook his head. "I have no idea what to do now."

Phailin cleared her throat. "There's more news. We received a transmission."

"From Shima?" Lorina guessed, her eyes widening. She clutched Blaze's arm. "Is it Niyati? Did something happen to Niyati?"

"No," Phailin assured her with a sad smile. "Niyati's fine. You need to view the transmission."

Marco felt the pang of sympathy again. He knew what it felt like to lose a mother. He gestured for Lorina to sit at the com.

Jake, Blaze, and Vipul looked on over Lorina's shoulders as the screen lit up again and played the transmission.

Marco had to turn away. He stared out the helm window at the blank wall of the spaceport exterior.

There was a collective gasp from the group. Lorina emitted a choked cry which escalated to gut-wrenching sobs. "Moooommmm! No! No! No! No! Not Mom!"

As the transmission continued, Lorina cried, "Oh, Niyati, my poor baby! Look at her, Blaze! She *needs* me!"

The bridge was quiet after the transmission ended, the silence punctuated only by Lorina's hysterical sobs. Marco continued to stare out the window, not willing to witness the grief.

"You were right," Blaze said.

Is he speaking to me? He turned around to see who Smith was addressing.

The engineer had both hands on Lorina's shaking shoulders and was leaning down, speaking quietly in her ear. "You were right, we shouldn't have left Niyati. I should've listened to you."

"It was an accident, Blaze. You had no way of knowing." Jake was leaning against the control board as if his legs could no longer support his weight. He had a vacant expression on his face. "It's not Shima's fault."

"I know it was an accident!" Lorina wailed. "Any of us would've gone in the water to save that child! . . . I just can't . . . I can't believe *she's gone!*"

Marco had heard enough drama and was anxious to head back to his cabin, but then something happened he couldn't have predicted.

Lorina stopped crying and looked straight at him, her expression changing from grief to fury. "You *knew!* You knew this was going to happen!"

She launched herself out of the chair and barreled straight at Marco before he could react. She plowed into him with a force that took his breath away, knocking him flat out on the floor. He found himself getting punched in the face several times before someone pried her off of him.

"Are you crazy?" He scrambled backward to get away from her, but his back was against the helm. He was trapped.

"You *knew* my mother was going to die, and you didn't have the *decency* to warn her!" Lorina was being restrained by both her cousin and her husband, one on each arm. "You worthless piece of scum! You *knew!*"

"I didn't know!" Marco touched his throbbing lip and came away with blood on his fingers. "I swear I didn't know who was going to die! Or when! Or where!"

"You're a *liar!*" Lorina's face turned beet red as she strained against her human leashes.

"He's telling the truth," Phailin said. "He can't see everything in his premonitions."

"Oh, and I suppose you didn't know the captain was going to get arrested!"

Marco flinched at Lorina's accusation, which seemed to enrage her even more.

"You *knew* that too!" She turned to Blaze. "Let me go! I *need* to *kill* him!"

"That's exactly why I'm not lettin' you go." The engineer was doing an admirable job of staying calm.

"She ordered me not to tell her about any more premonitions!" Marco argued. "What else was I supposed to do?"

He assumed Jake would be happy to let Lorina rip his arms off, but the medic continued to keep a firm hold on her. He seemed detached from all the excitement, emotionless. Jake was dealing with his grief much more quietly than his insane cousin. *Well, that's one good thing. If O'Brien reacted the way he normally does, the two of them would kill me.*

"So what happens now, Mr. Psychic?" Blaze said. "If you knew the captain was gonna get arrested, then you must know how we're gonna get her out of jail."

"I don't know." Marco rose to his feet, using the helm control board for support. "I haven't had a vision in days." He began to edge around them, toward the doorway.

"You're not gettin' away so fast," Blaze said. "You've got some explainin' to do."

"I think we're all too upset to talk about this right now," Phailin spoke up again. "Why don't we go to our cabins and calm down? Does anyone want something to eat? Some coffee or hot chocolate, maybe?"

Marco was grateful to have someone on his side. He didn't like being the crew's pariah. He also wished he hadn't been humiliated in front of Phailin again.

"She's right," Blaze said. "We all need time to process everythin' that's happened."

"Let's meet in the galley in one hour," Vipul said. "We can brainstorm then, and try to figure out what to do next. Wait until Marco's left the bridge before you let her go," he added to Jake and Blaze.

Marco didn't wait for them to respond. He was gone.

In his cabin, he went straight to the head and tended to his bloody lip and puffy eye. "I'm going to need some ice," he told his battered reflection. "And a bodyguard."

SEVEN
WARRANTS

COWARDS, ROSAMAR THOUGHT in disgust. *Pathetic overgrown babies. They all need to wear diapers because they wet themselves anytime they hear Acheron's name.* She stalked away from Judge White's chambers and took the lift from the eighth floor of the courthouse down to the third, where her ninth and final judge was waiting to meet with her.

Judge Forsetti's assistant had informed Rosamar she could meet with him for ten minutes during his lunch break. That was five minutes more than seven of the other judges had given her. The eighth wouldn't even agree to an appointment when Orlene let slip to his assistant that Rosamar wanted to meet with him about Acheron.

How does he do it? What's he holding over their heads? It was just as frustrating as talking to members of the city council. Once Acheron's name came into the conversation, their eyes would go wide and their mouths would go shut. Firmly shut. *What a waste of time,* she thought. *They're just puppets, and Acheron holds all the strings.*

Judge White developed a nervous tic in her left eye when Rosamar announced her reason for the visit. "All I need is a warrant to view someone's arrest record. Chief Acheron has been holding him—"

"Acheron?" White squeaked, and the corner of her watery brown eye began to twitch convulsively. "Sorry, I can't help you, Councilwoman." And she escorted Rosamar to the door before the attorney could ask why.

Rosamar approached her final meeting with trepidation. *There has to be a weak link in Acheron's chain, a chink in his armor. But what am I going to do if I can't find one?*

She entered courtroom 3A and approached the plaintiff's bench. She waited to be noticed by the young woman who was conferring with the gray-haired clerk seated just to the right of the empty judge's stand. They were the only people in the traditional walnut-finished, synthwood-paneled courtroom. Everyone else was at lunch.

Judge Forsetti's young assistant glanced over at Rosamar and nodded. "Councilwoman Delacruz, go right in. He's expecting you."

"Thank you." Rosamar walked around the judge's stand and approached the door labeled *Chambers*. She knocked and let herself in.

Judge Wei Forsetti glanced up from a bowl of noodles on the desk in front of him and waved her over. He indicated for her to take a chair as he dabbed his mouth with a napkin.

Forsetti's physical appearance indicated a diverse heritage. He was an athletic-looking man in his fifties with dark brown skin, like an African, but his round face and almond-shaped eyes were Chinese, to match his given name. Rosamar suspected that when he opened his mouth to speak, his accent would indicate yet another nationality, and she was right.

"Councilwoman?" Forsetti had an Arabic accent. He set aside his chopsticks, and stuck out a huge right hand for Rosamar to shake.

"Thank you for agreeing to meet with me, judge. I don't want your lunch to get cold, so I'll get right to the point."

"Very considerate of you."

Rosamar nodded, relieved he wasn't as standoffish as his peers. "Judge, I need a warrant. I need access to someone's arrest record."

Forsetti's thick black eyebrows went up. "Not the usual request I get from city council members."

"I'm making this request as an attorney."

The judge started to reply but got a sudden faraway look in his eyes, indicating his earcom distracted him. "I'm sorry, but I need to take this."

"Of course." Rosamar started to rise, but he gestured for her to remain seated.

"It's not confidential. I'll only be a moment."

She glanced around the judge's chambers as Forsetti carried on an animated conversation with his caller, something about an overpriced plumber and a leaky shower. She noted little in the way of décor, which, in her experience, was the way men preferred their offices. Unless the man was a collector, which Forsetti didn't appear to be—the room was practically Spartan.

A bookcase filled with the usual boring legal tomes took up the wall behind the desk. An unusual military-style plaque adorned the wall to her left, although instead of indicating a branch of armed service, it bore only the initials ISPP. The surface of Forsetti's simple synthwood desk contained a single datapad, the bowl of noodles, and a framed hologram placed at an angle where Rosamar could see the people in it.

A stern-looking man with wavy dark hair and a complexion a shade lighter than Forsetti's, was sitting on a park bench next to an attractive Chinese woman with long black hair, who was holding a tiny baby in her arms. Rosamar couldn't see the infant's face in the hologram. A beaming little boy was standing between the man and the woman. The child was a mixture of the two parents with his Chinese eyes, dark skin, and wavy dark hair.

When Forsetti said, "Sorry about the interruption," and gave Rosamar his full attention, she made an impulsive decision to try a new approach. *Maybe a little flattery would help.*

"What a lovely family, Your Honor," she said, indicating the hologram. "Is that your son?"

Forsetti's smile seemed forced. "My son-in-law. That's my daughter, Yong Min, my grandson Lincoln, and my newborn granddaughter Lia."

"Do they live here on the station?"

Forsetti got an all-too-familiar look in his eyes Rosamar had come to associate with an emotional wall going up. "No, they don't."

She gave him an understanding smile and changed the subject. "I was noticing your plaque." She glanced at the military crest. "I don't think I've ever seen one like that before. What does ISPP stand for?"

The judge's eyebrows went up again. "I'm surprised you don't know about the Interstellar Peacekeepers Patrol. After all, you're the reason it was created."

"Me?" Rosamar shook her head, baffled.

"The Patrol was organized right after the Baronowski Brothers' mafia ring was broken, thanks to you."

Her mouth fell open. "Really?"

"Yes, ISPP"—he pronounced it *isp*—"will ensure that organized crime never gets another foothold out here in the star lanes. Its main objective is to protect the stations."

"Strange that I've never heard of it before."

"Well, ISPP relies on stealth, so it's been kept out of the press." Forsetti shrugged with a bemused grin. "It also functions independent of the CIPs."

"That's wise," Rosamar said.

"And it's still a fledgling organization. There are only five ships keeping tabs on the eleven stations, plus Earth. My son-in-law, Cade York," he glanced at the hologram, "captains the flagship, the *Title of Liberty*."

Rosamar thought fast, trying to decide the best way to broach the subject of Acheron. "Has ISPP had any run-ins with slavers?"

Forsetti hesitated a moment before answering with a question of his own. "What have you heard about slavers, councilwoman?"

"I've heard homeless children often disappear from this station, and it's come to my attention they're being sold as slaves. I just thought—hoped, maybe—that ISPP was investigating."

Forsetti stared at her for a moment, his gaze unreadable. "I think you and I need to share some information. Just a moment." He tapped his left earlobe. "Josefa, I'm going to need more than ten minutes with the councilwoman. Let me know when court is reconvened."

The judge pushed aside his bowl and clasped his large hands together, resting them on the desk in front of him. "If you have information about slavers operating from Mars or any other station, I need to share what you know with ISPP."

"Of course, Your Honor."

"And you can dispense with the Your Honor nonsense. Call me Wei."

"Rosamar," she agreed, sitting up straighter. "Wei, I need the warrant for a client who's been arrested for trying to protect homeless children from a slaver."

"Why would he be arrested for trying to aid children?"

"That's a good question. You should ask the arresting officer, Chief Acheron." Rosamar hoped this wouldn't bring the conversation to a screeching halt.

Forsetti hesitated only a moment. "Why is it that whenever there's trouble on this station, Acheron's name is always behind it?"

"Because he's usually the mastermind," Rosamar said. "I'm almost afraid to ask, Wei, but I must. Does Acheron have you on his payroll?"

His sudden scowl wasn't intended for Rosamar. "Acheron was unsuccessful at bribing me, so he decided a threat would be more effective. He said my family's on his hit list. Too bad for him I don't have any family left."

Rosamar felt a chill as she focused again on the hologram. "But your daughter—?"

"Was murdered . . . on Venus Station . . . three years ago, shortly after this hologram was taken."

The councilwoman grimaced but remained silent, waiting to see if he would share more.

"Yong Min had just delivered Lia. The baby was only two weeks old. Cade was taking a two-month paternity leave, but he was called away to handle an urgent problem on the Moon Station. He thought ISPP could take care of it in just a few days and was planning to return to Venus as soon as possible. The *Title of Liberty* had just lifted, and Yong Min was walking back to the apartment, carrying Lia with Linc at her side. Their apartment was only two blocks from the spaceport."

The judge hesitated. "Linc disappeared that night, along with Lia." He struggled without success to mask the grief in his eyes. "Yong Min was found early the next morning . . . with her throat slashed."

Rosamar gasped. "No!"

"Cade has never forgiven himself for leaving her side, but Venus Station had no history of violent crime before this."

"That's horrible!" Rosamar whispered. "I'm so sorry!"

Forsetti nodded, acknowledging her sympathy. "We learned that healthy newborns are sold for millions on the black market. I have no hope of ever seeing my granddaughter again. But my grandson . . ." His heartbroken expression was gone, replaced by grim determination. "Many children disappeared from Venus Station that night. Cade and I believe Linc was abducted along with them and sold as a slave. We're both determined to find him and the monsters who took Lia and murdered Yong Min."

"I'll bet Acheron knows who they are!" Rosamar's own anger began to smolder again.

Forsetti shook his head. "Different stations."

"I have a reliable source that says Acheron is behind the slave trade here. He may know where to find your grandson."

The judge appeared thoughtful for a few moments. "Tell me more about Acheron's involvement."

Rosamar disclosed what she had learned from Danae Shepherd's transmission and Kirsten Sorensen's information. "It's all beginning to make sense to me now!"

"What is?"

"The homeless situation here. People come to Mars hoping for a better life, but they can't get jobs because of the employment centers."

Forsetti nodded. "If you don't have five thousand credits, you're out of luck."

"Thus the burgeoning homeless population, which gives Acheron a steady supply of children to sell to slavers."

"That despicable viper. I had no idea he was behind it all."

"Despicable, and clever. He has a chokehold on anyone who might stand up to him."

"Well, he doesn't have a chokehold on me. I can give you a warrant with full access to Dr. Sorensen and his records." The judge nodded. "What else do you need?"

"There's a ship called the *Elmina* I need access to. It may hold a lot of information if Acheron hasn't had its database wiped already."

Forsetti nodded. "Right, two warrants. What else?"

"We need to avoid the CIPs, for obvious reasons, so I think Captain York would be best suited to conduct this investigation. Where's his ship now? Could you send him a transmission?"

The judge nodded. "Cade keeps me informed. Last week the *Title of Liberty* was in Shanghai, checking on another lead about a factory using child slave labor. I'll record a transmission right now." Forsetti touched his earlobe again. "Josefa, could you come in, please?"

Rosamar stood and offered the judge her datapad. "I think we need to keep in close contact for a while, Wei. I'll give you my private com code."

"Private or not, Acheron's probably monitoring it."

"Then we should meet in person, someplace where we won't be overheard."

Forsetti nodded. "I like to take a walk around McConnell Park every morning around 7:30."

Rosamar snorted. "A 7:30 walk? I go running at 6:00."

Forsetti's eyebrows went up. "Then I guess I'll take up running. I'll wear a red T-shirt and start at the west gate. See you in the morning?"

"It's a date. Don't oversleep." Rosamar turned to leave the judge's chambers as his assistant came in.

"If you'll just wait in the courtroom for Josefa, I'll have the warrants on your datapad in five minutes, Councilwoman Delacruz."

"Thank you, Judge Forsetti. It's been a pleasure talking to someone with a backbone on this station."

***

Warrant in hand, Rosamar decided to try avoiding another confrontation with Acheron. Forsetti was her leverage, but only as long as he remained under the CIP chief's radar. This time she stopped at the main reception desk at CIP headquarters and asked to see Dr. Erik Sorensen.

The young black man squinted at her, suspicious. "He's in solitary. No visitors."

Rosamar handed over her datapad. "I'm not a visitor. I'm his attorney."

The CIP scowled as he read the warrant. He seemed baffled by it. Rosamar suspected he'd never seen a warrant before.

"I'll have to clear this with Chief Acheron."

She anticipated this response. "Please do," she said in her sweetest tone, "since I also have a warrant for *his* arrest if the department doesn't cooperate with me. It's come to my attention that Dr. Sorensen is being denied his right to an attorney and is being held without bail with no formal charges filed against him."

The CIP's mouth fell open. He glanced down at his monitor as if hoping for an answer to appear on the screen.

"His arrest record, please." Rosamar held out her hand for the return of her datapad. She kept a bored look on her face and waited to see if the CIP would call her bluff.

He didn't. He hesitated a moment and then downloaded a file to Rosamar's datapad. It was promptly returned to her. "Right this way, ma'am." He stood and escorted her down a hallway, through several locked doors, to the cell block.

There were three cells in the section labeled *Solitary*, and Rosamar wasn't surprised to learn they were all occupied. *Acheron would fill more cells if he had them.*

"Well, let me inside," she barked at the guard when he hesitated at the door to Sorensen's cell. The reception officer gave the guard a hasty nod, and the guard pressed his thumb to the DNA keypad. The locks disengaged, and the massive door swung inward. Rosamar stepped into the cell and waited for the door to close behind her before turning to face her new client.

Dr. Erik Sorensen seemed surprised to discover he had a visitor. *Late thirties,* she guessed, although it was difficult to tell because his hair was so pale it was almost white. He sat up on his cot and slowly got to his feet. *Huge.* Rosamar was impressed by his muscular physique.

Sorensen was clearly in pain, favoring his right leg. His scruffy blond beard did little to disguise an assortment of cuts and bruises on his face, including a black eye. He looked as if he hadn't showered in a week, but he extended his hand and offered her a polite greeting.

"Good morning—or afternoon—I have no idea what time it is or even what day it is. Since you're not a CIP, am I correct in assuming my sister Kirsten sent you?"

Rosamar shook his hand. "Yes, Dr. Sorensen, I'm Councilwoman Rosamar Delacruz, and I'm your attorney." She glanced around, but there was nowhere to sit in the tiny space, except the cot, so she just stood. "Please sit. You look like you're in pain."

Without a word of protest, Sorensen sat. "You're my lawyer." He arched his thick blond eyebrows. "That's good, but where's Kirsten?"

Rosamar was surprised by the question. "I don't know. I spoke to her yesterday."

Sorensen frowned. "So she's here."

"Here? What do you mean?"

"Here, in the cell next door. I didn't hear her brought in, but Acheron told me he would arrest Kirsten."

"On what charges?" Rosamar's contempt for Acheron went up another notch.

The doctor shrugged. "Obstruction of justice is his favorite. I think he has me for assaulting a police officer."

Rosamar glanced at the doctor's arrest record. "Aiding and abetting a criminal?"

Sorensen nodded, looking weary. "That would be for allowing a medical student to treat patients at my Outreach Clinic. It could also be for helping Danae Shepherd get the kids off the station. I think she's wanted for murder, although I understand it was self-defense."

This time Rosamar raised her eyebrows at him. "He hasn't charged you as an accessory to murder, which is a small relief. I think assaulting a police officer is going to be the hard one to beat, unless there were any witnesses."

He shook his head. "Acheron made sure there weren't any."

Rosamar frowned. "Dr. Sorensen, I'd like to discuss your case, but I assume nothing we say here will be private."

Sorensen nodded, his expression grim.

"At some point, Acheron should set bail for you."

"You would think so," his reply was bitter, "but he follows his own set of rules. Would you mind checking to see if my sister's bail has been set? There's no reason why she should be here."

Rosamar nodded. "Of course. But I suspect I'll have to get another warrant to see her."

Erik Sorensen stood with effort and shook her hand. "I appreciate the time you're taking to help us. I'm sure I can find a way to pay your fee."

Rosamar smiled. "It's *gratis*, doctor. I want to see Acheron on the inside of a cell just as much as you do." She raised her voice so the guard could hear her on surveillance. "Open up! I'm ready to leave now!"

"We'll talk soon, doctor." Rosamar stepped out into the hallway. When the door to his cell was shut, she turned to the guard. "I'd like to see Miss Sorensen in the next cell."

It was worth a try, but she wasn't surprised to be asked, "Do you have a warrant?"

She scowled at the CIP underling. "I'll be back in a few minutes."

***

Rosamar couldn't get a warrant to see Kirsten Sorensen because Judge Forsetti was tied up in court for the rest of the day.

She met him at the west gate of McConnell Park at 6:00 the next morning, as promised. He was ready to go running with her. His track shoes appeared brand new.

"Can you write while you run, Wei?" Rosamar handed him a datapad.

"You need a warrant to see Sorensen's sister?"

"How did you know?"

"I often check the lists of arrests in the *Chronicles*, although the charges are never mentioned. I'll write the warrant for you when we stop to stretch."

The judge tucked the datapad into the cargo pocket of his athletic shorts, and they started off at a jog, side by side, staying on the paved pathway to avoid the more aggressive panhandlers.

The wooded park was a refugee camp for the station's homeless. Blankets, tents, and cardboard lean-tos occupied every square meter of drought-resistant grass. The park offered its thousands of downtrodden occupants a small lake, which was a popular spot for bathing, several water fountains, and a few self-flushing toilets hidden among the shrubbery. Since it was never cold or rainy, people could sleep out in the open, although it was evident from the vacant stares on the faces of the residents that McConnell Park wasn't a comfortable place to live.

Rosamar was reminded every morning that she had to do something to ebb the tide of human misery on Mars Station.

"So Acheron's managed to shut down two vital services for the homeless in just a few weeks," Forsetti said.

Rosamar picked up the pace and was pleased Wei was able to keep up. "He's arrested two good people who were only trying to help the homeless, just because they got in his way."

"They know too much. This is his way of keeping them quiet."

"Well, they aren't going to stay locked up if I can help it!" Rosamar lowered her voice and said, "Sorry" to a thin, pitiful-looking child, maybe eight or nine years old, who stepped in front of them, his dirty hand out, his expression hopeful. She recognized his face but didn't know his name. There were so many homeless children, Rosamar knew she would become overwhelmed with guilt unless she remained emotionally detached. She'd learned from painful experience not to get attached to any particular street child.

"Sorry, I don't have anything for you today, sweetheart."

"Today?" Forsetti echoed as they skirted around the disappointed boy. "Do you give them handouts on other days?"

"Of course," Rosamar said. "Usually it's not much. I give out a bag of apples or oranges, but I'm not going to ignore them and hope they go away like the rest of the city council."

"Aren't you afraid of getting mugged?"

"No, I'm afraid of these people starving to death or getting wiped out by an epidemic like Zenithian Flu. If Acheron keeps shutting down charities, that's exactly what's going to happen. Wei, everyone in this park is homeless because of that man. With your help, I'm going to dethrone the tyrant."

"You mean, with ISPP's help," Forsetti said. "Acheron already made an appointment to see me today. I don't think it's going to be a social call."

Rosamar winced. "He knows about the warrant. I was hoping we had more time."

"Me too."

"Be careful. Don't meet with him alone, and be sure to record the conversation."

"I know," he said.

She noticed Forsetti's sentences were getting shorter because he was breathing hard. She slowed the pace.

"Thanks," he panted.

They didn't speak for the rest of the run, finishing one lap around the park. It was just under three kilometers, and Rosamar normally ran two laps, but she didn't want to give the man a heart attack on his first run. She slowed to a brisk walk until they reached the west gate. She stopped and stretched while Forsetti wrote on her datapad and pressed his thumb to the screen to authenticate his signature. Then the judge stretched while she read over what he wrote.

"This should work," she said.

Forsetti wiped the sweat from his brow. "I hope so. I might not be able to write another one for you."

"I know." She frowned, thinking hard. "Meet here tomorrow? Same time?"

"North gate this time," Forsetti said. "Let's meet at 6:30. If we're being watched, we don't want to give them a regular pattern to follow."

Rosamar nodded, gave him a smile, and headed out of the park.

An hour later, she was showered, dressed in her most intimidating black suit, and walking in the front entrance of CIP headquarters. She felt confident Acheron wouldn't be in the office this early in the morning so she should be able to get in to see her second client.

Rosamar smiled at the reception officer—a Latina this time—and said, "I'd like to see Kirsten Sorensen."

She got a scowl in return. "No one sees Sorensen without a—"

"Warrant." Rosamar slapped her datapad on the counter. "Yes, I know. Take me to see her—*pronto*."

This time the guard in solitary refused to let her in to the cell. He opened a slot in the middle of the door and announced, "Someone to see you, Sorensen."

Rosamar gave the guard a cold look before stooping down to look through the narrow opening at the former director of the only juvenile shelter on the station.

This was not the same woman who burst into the councilwoman's office two days ago, pleading with the attorney to get her brother out of jail. This was a woman whose spirit had been broken. There were bruises on her face, and a blank look in her bright blue eyes.

"I don't understand why I'm here," Sorensen said. "I didn't do anything wrong."

Rosamar glanced at her arrest record. "Acheron's holding you for aiding and abetting a criminal."

A single tear slipped down the side of Sorensen's nose. "I can't stay here, councilwoman. This place gives me nightmares of when Erik and I were homeless, as children. We slept in dumpsters to get out of the cold. This cell . . . isn't much bigger than a dumpster."

Rosamar felt a surge of indignation. "I'll get you out of here! You and your brother aren't staying in this dungeon!"

"Thank you," Sorensen whispered. "I appreciate anything you can do for us."

"Visiting time's over," the guard announced, tapping Delacruz hard on the shoulder.

"I'm not a visitor!" Rosamar snarled, whirling to face him. "I'm her lawyer! And don't you touch me again unless you'd like to be slapped with a lawsuit for police brutality!"

The CIP glowered at her. "You need to leave. Your two minutes are up."

The slot to the cell snapped shut before she could say anything more to Kirsten Sorensen. She stormed out of CIP headquarters, determined to do something to break Acheron's grip on Mars Station.

Rosamar was on the com with Forsetti as soon as she was back in her office. "How soon can ISPP get here?"

"Two days," the judge said. "Sit tight and don't do anything that might get you or me thrown in jail too."

"I know." She took a deep breath, sitting down at her desk. "I have a feeling it's only going to get worse."

And by lunchtime, things had gotten worse. Wei called her this time.

"I just checked the CIP list of arrests," he said. "There's a Danae Shepherd in custody. I'll write you another warrant before Acheron gets here for our one o'clock meeting."

***

"Hello, Danae."

Shepherd's prominent eyes were brown, to match her darkened skin, and her hair had been dyed jet-black, but Rosamar had no trouble recognizing her face. The expression of intense dislike hadn't softened over the years. She stared back at Rosamar in disbelief through the bars of the holding cell.

"What are you doing here?" The younger woman sat up on the cot and slowly got to her feet. "You told my father you were going back to your firm in Bridgeport."

"I did go back, but I only stayed long enough to close the office. My place is here, on Mars."

"How did you get past the guards?"

"For a native Martian, you don't read the *Chronicles* much, do you? Otherwise, you'd know I'm on the city council. I have some leverage around here."

"You?" Danae was incredulous. "A councilwoman? So you sold your soul to Acheron."

"You still have a bad habit of making assumptions about me. No, I'm no friend of Acheron's. I'm out to beat him at his own game."

"I don't believe you."

"You never have." Rosamar's temper flared. "When I told you I loved Ishmael, you called me a liar."

"I'm known for being accurate."

"You were wrong! I hope he never forgave you for coming between us!"

"He never gave it a second thought!" Danae fired back. "He said you were just using him!"

"Those were *your* words—not his!" She took a gulp of air and made an effort to lower her volume. "Tell me how he died."

"What?" Danae took a surprised step back from the bars.

"How did he *die?*"

The captain clenched her fists at her side and wouldn't answer.

"When did he die?" Rosamar decided a little guilt might loosen her tongue. "Since you never sent me a transmission, I've gone all these years thinking he was still alive. Ishmael was important to me. Whether you believe it or not, I think I deserve to know what happened."

Danae chewed her lip for a moment before replying. "Four months after he put you off the ship, I found him dead in his cabin. He'd been poisoned."

"*What?*" Rosamar gasped. "How?"

"I don't know. The coroner found Arsenide in his system. Someone poisoned a bottle of pomegranate juice he'd bought on the station."

"He loved pomegranate juice."

Danae nodded. "The seal on the bottle was intact before he drank a single glass. The poison would have killed him instantly. The CIPs ruled it a suicide."

"Impossible!"

"That's what I told them."

"What about the crew?"

Danae gave her a vicious look. "They loved him like a father! The CIPs investigated everyone, including the juice manufacturer. No one had a motive or an explanation, so they ruled it a suicide and closed the case. Someone murdered him. That's all I know."

Rosamar closed her eyes and tried to process what she heard. *Four months after we broke up . . . but that would have been during the Baronowski Brothers trial.*

A cold chill swept over Delacruz, and she started to tremble. She felt light-headed and nauseated, and had to lean against the cell bars to keep herself upright.

"What is it?" Danae demanded. "What's wrong?" The younger woman closed in on Rosamar and reached through the bars, seizing her collar. "You *know* something about Dad's death!"

She shook her head and tried to break free of Danae's grip. "No! It's impossible! There's no way they could've gotten to him—"

"*Who?*" Danae was almost choking Rosamar, her face contorted with rage. "If you know who killed him, *tell me!* Who was it?"

"Break it up!" A guard got to them in two strides, reached through the bars, and pried them apart, shoving Danae halfway across her cell. "You've done it now, Shepherd! You're going to solitary!"

"No!" Rosamar rubbed her neck, breathing hard. "I'm all right. She's not going to solitary. I'm her attorney. What's her bail? I'll post it."

The guard just stared at her, incredulous. "I'll have to clear this with Chief Acheron."

"Well, do it now!" She didn't take her eyes off Danae. She heard the guard leave.

The captain was shaking, staring at Rosamar with pure hatred in her eyes. "You're responsible, aren't you?" She spat out the words. "Someone killed Dad because they were trying to get to *you!*"

Rosamar shook her head. She tried to reason with Danae. "I didn't know. It was over between us months before the trial. I didn't know they'd go after Ishmael."

"*Who? Tell me!*"

"Liam Baronowski." She covered her face with her hands and discovered her cheeks were damp. "He threatened to kill my family. I never . . . for a single moment . . thought Ishmael was in any danger!"

Danae threw herself against the bars, trying to reach her again. "You didn't *think* at all! You *let* this happen!"

"No, no!" Rosamar was sobbing now. "It's not my fault!"

"It *is* your fault, Delacruz! You're responsible for his death!"

"No! I didn't know he was a target! You have to believe me!" But Rosamar couldn't believe it herself.

What have I done? She took some deep breaths, trying to calm down, but she couldn't stop crying.

Danae Shepherd took some deep breaths too. Her words dropped to a venomous whisper. "You robbed me . . . of my father. You *owe* me, Delacruz. If you really are a councilwoman, you find a way to get me out of here. And Erik and Kirsten Sorensen. You free all of us."

"I'm already trying to help the Sorensens," she managed between sobs.

"Good. Now I suggest you leave before Acheron shows up." Danae gave her a vindictive half smile. "This cell is built for two. You never know . . . he might put you in here with *me*."

Rosamar was back in her office in three minutes.

EIGHT
THANATOS'S SECRET

MARCO WAS SUMMONED to the galley for a meeting and a light meal provided by Phailin. When he walked in, he was relieved to note the absence of Lorina. He poured himself a cup of coffee and took a seat near the communal platter of sandwiches.

"Lorina's not doin' well," Blaze reported. "I had Jake give her a sedative. She's sleepin' in our cabin, and I don't think we should include her in any plans."

Vipul nodded. "I think the *Elmina* is our only solution."

Ting resented the fact that the Indian navigator had assumed the leadership role when the helmsman was the senior crewmember. However, since Marco was unpopular at the moment, Vipul did seem like the logical choice. He was senior to everyone in age.

Jake picked at his sandwich. "How's the *Elmina* our solution?"

Marco repositioned the bag of crushed ice over his throbbing eye. "Evidence. If we can get into the *Elmina*'s database, we should find plenty of evidence to convict Acheron and free the captain."

"One small problem," Blaze said. "How do we get inside the *Elmina*?"

"We could pick the ID lock," Vipul said. He was serious.

"You're the inventor, Vipul," Blaze said. "Ever figure out a way to break into an airlock?"

Marco could almost see the wheels turning in his shipmates' heads. Blaze and Vipul glanced at one another with raised eyebrows. "What? Is there a way to break into an airlock?"

"It's the same concept as breaking into a safe," Vipul said. "All we need is a way to override the DNA lock."

Ting thought the discussion had gone downhill, from utterly hopeless to completely insane. "Wouldn't it be easier to abduct Thanatos's nephew and force him to open the airlock?"

"That could be our backup plan." Vipul nodded.

Marco glanced at Phailin to gauge her reaction. She seemed to be trying hard not to smile. *Good, she thinks they're crazy too.*

Crazy or not, the two men whipped out datapads and began doing research.

"We'd have to disable the surveillance first," Blaze said.

"We'll need a forty-five degree angle laser drill to open the access panel," Vipul said. "I saw one in the spare parts workshop. Better get a ninety-degree drill too, just to be safe."

"What about ship security?" Blaze asked. "How do we disable the magnetic barricade once we're inside the antechamber?"

"Hold on a minute!" Marco got to his feet. "Have you both lost your minds? This will never work!"

"Anything's better than just sitting around, worrying." Jake pushed aside his uneaten sandwich.

"There are people moving up and down the corridors all the time, day and night. Even if you could disable the security, someone's going to notice you drilling into an airlock!"

"We could set up a diversion—" Vipul was interrupted by a loud gasp from Phailin.

"I'm getting a call!" She pointed to the earcom she was still wearing. "Who could be calling us from the station? What should I do?" She glanced at Marco for advice.

"Don't answer it!" he said. "Let's see who it is."

Everyone made a dash for the bridge, but Ting reached the com first. The caller ID was displaying the name *Rosamar Delacruz*.

"Who's that?" Blaze asked.

"I've heard that name before." Marco scratched his chin, trying to remember. "A long time ago. I think she was someone Captain Thompson knew."

"It could be Acheron, looking for us," Phailin said. "What if it's a trap?"

"What if it's just a wrong code?" Jake asked.

The com continued to chime, but they all stood there, undecided.

"Should we answer it?" Phailin persisted.

Marco shook his head. "Let's see if she leaves a message."

Delacruz didn't choose the message option. The com continued to chime.

The helmsman shut his eyes, concentrating, searching for an answer somewhere in his memory. He was terrible at recalling faces, and with his clairvoyance now dormant, he could get no impression about the call, good or bad.

Blaze spoke up. "I feel like it's safe to answer."

"How do you know?" Marco's eyes snapped open. He studied the peaceful look on Smith's face.

"It's just . . . a feelin'."

"I trust Blaze," Vipul said. "He has good instincts."

Marco stared at the two of them, incredulous. "If you're wrong, if it's really Acheron, we're all going to jail."

"Just do it," Jake said without his usual heat.

Phailin made the decision for them. She punched a button on the control board, opening the connection. "Hello?"

"Finally!" A woman's exasperated voice burst from the speakers. "Do you people want to get your captain out of jail or not?"

"Who are you?" Vipul asked.

"Rosamar Delacruz. I'm Danae's attorney—and the Sorensens'. I'm calling from a secure com I just purchased, but I don't know how long it will stay secure, so I'll talk fast."

"Captain Thompson's old girlfriend!" Marco remembered. He also remembered Shepherd and Delacruz hated each other. He overheard them arguing on several occasions. He was suspicious. *What's motivating her to help us now?*

Delacruz snorted. "Old is a matter of opinion. Now be quiet and listen. I have a warrant to access the *Elmina*. I think Acheron is coming to confront me right now, so I need a few of you to get aboard the *Elmina* and search its database before the vermin figures out what we're up to."

Marco's jaw dropped.

"We can do that." Blaze grinned. "How do we get past the airlock?"

"I have a trace of Thanatos's DNA from his CIP murder investigation file."

"How did you come by that?" Vipul asked in awe.

"I'm Danae's defense attorney, which allows me access to certain police records," Delacruz said. "And the less you know about that, the better. Acheron has ways of extracting information from people."

"Torture, you mean," Jake said. "We saw what he did to Erik."

"What do you need us to do?" Marco asked. This seemed too good to be true. *Another one of Acheron's schemes?*

"Just meet me at the *Elmina*'s airlock in one hour. I'll use the trace to let you aboard the ship and disable the security. Are any of you experienced at hacking into databases?"

Is she serious?

"I worked aboard the ship for almost a year," Vipul said. "I remember the database codes. Thanatos probably changed them after I left, but it's worth a try."

"Let's hope he didn't change them," Delacruz said. "One hour." And she severed the connection.

"This is crazy!" Marco threw his hands in the air. "How do we know this isn't a trap?"

"We don't," Blaze said, "but we've got to take the chance anyway. Like Vipul said, the *Elmina* is our only solution."

"Well, count me out! I remember Delacruz, and she and the captain had a mutual hatred for each other. I can't see why she'd offer to help get Shepherd out of jail."

"She must have a good reason," Phailin said. "Acheron's never seen me before. I could walk by the airlock first to see if anything seems suspicious."

"No, I won't let you!" Marco realized he blurted the wrong thing.

Phailin gave him a look that would've rivaled Shepherd's at her angriest. "You won't *let* me?"

"Good idea, Phailin." Vipul interrupted the power struggle. "Obviously, I need to go since I'm familiar with the ship, but I'll need an assistant." He looked at Blaze. "Someone who's skilled with computers."

Blaze nodded. "But I don't know if I should leave Lorina alone right now."

"I'll stay and keep an eye on her," Jake said. "I need to excuse myself from this excursion anyway. I'm having a hard time concentrating, so I'd just be in the way."

"Thanks, Jake." Blaze added, "I'm really sorry about your aunt. I know you were close to her."

Jake just nodded, acknowledging Blaze's sympathy, before turning to leave the bridge. "Good luck."

"Once Phailin walks by the airlock," Vipul said, "she can signal us on our coms. Delacruz lets Blaze and me onto the ship, and we try to access the database. Sounds simple, but we'll need someone to stand guard at the airlock."

"I can do that," Phailin said.

"No, I will." Marco ignored Phailin's scathing look.

"We could use both of you." Vipul interrupted again before they could start an argument.

Marco felt a jolt of fear for the first time. *What have I done? I volunteered to get myself arrested . . . just to impress a woman!* He glanced at Phailin and decided she was worth the risk.

"We've got forty-five minutes," Blaze said, nodding to Vipul. "Let's figure out what equipment we'll need."

The two men left the bridge, and Phailin turned to Marco with a half-curious, half-annoyed grin.

"I don't need a bodyguard. I've been kick-boxing since I was eight." She shook her head. "Why do men still assume women need to be protected? Chivalry is dead, Marco. Most women could mop the floor with you—and Lorina just did."

He shrugged, embarrassed. "It just slipped out." He fumbled for a plausible excuse. "But Vipul's right. It would be better for both of us to stand guard. One person standing by the airlock would look suspicious, but two people who just stopped to have a chat . . . it could work."

Phailin was unconvinced. "A chat? What are we supposed to talk about that would sound realistic?"

"Ship's business: sales transactions, the price of fuel, gossip among the crew—"

"That's not business," Phailin said.

"No, but gossip is realistic. Everyone loves to talk about who did what or who said what. We could have a long conversation about the incompetents we work with."

"We don't work with incompetents." Phailin glared at him.

"If you say so." He shut his mouth and hoped she would change the subject.

She did. "I guess we better change into our uniforms." Phailin glanced down at the apron she still had on over shorts and a faded Moon Station souvenir T-shirt.

Marco grimaced. "I hate those flowery shirts. They look idiotic."

Phailin gave him a cold look. "I *like* the shirts. I grew up on Kauai, remember? Are you saying my culture is idiotic?"

I should quit now before I get another black eye. "I'll go change." He quickly left the bridge.

***

Approximately fifty minutes after receiving Delacruz's call, Marco joined Phailin, Blaze, and Vipul in the airlock antechamber. The engineer and navigator were both dressed in nondescript work coveralls and carrying equally nondescript tool bags.

"I hope we can pass as port employees," Blaze said.

"No one will give you a second glance," Phailin said.

"Can I wear a jacket over this?" Marco pointed to his shirt. He refused to wear the ridiculous sunglasses that went with the uniform.

"No." Vipul clipped a com to his left earlobe. "Just stay calm, and we'll get through this."

"Let's go." Blaze touched the keypad and the half-meter-thick station airlock door cycled open. He stepped out into the access corridor, looking to the right to avoid the surveillance holo-cam.

Marco reluctantly followed his example, falling into step beside Phailin as they boarded the nearest lift and rode down to Level 10. The airlocks on the lower levels were spaced every hundred meters along the access corridor, so the lift deposited them across from airlock 28. They would have to walk just over a kilometer to reach airlock 39. The concrete hallway was slightly concave, to match the perimeter of the biosphere, so it was impossible to have a clear view of more than three airlocks at a time.

Marco trudged along in silence as they passed groups of spacers with the names of their ships embroidered on their crisp military-style uniforms. *Normal uniforms, not like these clown clothes we have to wear.* They also passed uniformed merchants and port employees going about their business.

"Just don't look up," Blaze said as they walked beneath another holo-cam. "Pretend to talk to each other so it doesn't look like we're avoidin' the surveillance."

Marco turned his head so he was gazing at Phailin's lovely profile. "The shirt looks a lot better on you."

"Stop staring at my chest," she muttered.

Marco suppressed a sigh with effort.

When they reached airlock 36, Vipul sent Phailin ahead to scout for them. The men stopped between airlocks 36 and 37, out of holo-cam range, and waited for her signal.

Marco watched Phailin walk away until she vanished around the curve of the corridor. Blaze and Vipul discussed mechanical things anytime someone walked by. Marco thought they were being obvious, but he pretended to listen to their conversation.

There was a tense moment when a CIP rode by on a solar scooter, patrolling the access corridors. She slowed down just long enough to look them over, her eyes lingering on the *Alex's Legacy* monogram on Marco's shirt. Despite her suspicious frown, she didn't say anything to them and she didn't stop. She revved the engine and continued down the corridor without looking back.

Marco didn't start breathing again until the CIP was out of sight.

"I think we'd better disappear before that CIP comes back," Blaze said.

"You think she's coming back?" Marco asked.

Blaze frowned. "I know she is."

Marco was feeling too nervous to challenge the engineer's fortune-teller skills. *That's supposed to be my job, rookie!*

"Delacruz isn't here." Phailin's report was in their ears. "She sent her assistant. The girl is terrified. She thinks a CIP followed her here."

"Oh great." Marco glanced at Blaze and Vipul. "Do we abort?"

Blaze shook his head, his expression determined. "CIPs or not, we've got to get aboard the *Elmina*."

Vipul agreed, and the two of them started to walk again at a brisk pace. Marco hesitated, thought of some Chinese curse words, and trotted to catch up.

Phailin was alone at airlock 39, holding something discreetly in her hand. She handed it off to Vipul without a word and turned to face Marco with a big fake smile on her face.

"Nice to see you!" The cook surprised Marco by throwing her arms around him and spinning him around in an enthusiastic hug. But when she released him, he realized she positioned him so his back was to the holo-cam. She stood facing him, smiling. Her body was positioned to block the airlock access keypad from surveillance view.

"Just talk to me like you haven't seen me in years," Phailin said, showing off her dimples for spaceport security. "They won't recognize me."

Marco resisted the urge to glance up and down the corridor to be sure no one else was in sight. He saw the airlock cycle open behind Phailin. Blaze and Vipul slipped inside and the door cycled shut.

"They're in." Marco gazed into Phailin's eyes. It was intoxicating to be close to her, but he had a feeling he would be risking another punch in the mouth if he moved any closer.

"Don't even think about it," she warned, still smiling. "You think I've never seen that look in a man's eyes?"

"You're hard to resist," he said. "Could I at least hold your hand?"

"No." Phailin pretended to laugh as a deliveryman walked by with a cartload of melons on an anti-grav unit. She waited until he was out of earshot before continuing.

"I know your type, Marco, and I'm definitely not interested in a shipboard romance. It's a bad idea for people who have to work together."

"So you're saying you *would* be interested in me if we didn't work together?"

"Are you always this conceited?"

"Not always." Marco shrugged. "Sometimes I'm just obnoxious."

Phailin didn't laugh at his lame attempt at humor.

"You know, Murphy and Smith had a shipboard romance. It worked out well for them. Captain Shepherd married her navigator. She even named the ship after him."

"Do you think I'm naïve enough to believe you're looking to settle down?" She rolled her eyes but continued to smile for the holo-cam.

Marco was thoughtful. "Well, I could be, if the right person came along."

"No thanks. I've already had my heart broken once." She faltered, the bravado fading. "And the wound hasn't quite healed yet."

"Do you want to talk about it?" Marco gave her what he hoped was a convincing glance of sympathy.

Phailin sighed. "That seems only fair since I know it was hard for you to tell me about your premonitions."

She was thoughtful for a moment, nibbling a thumbnail. "Here's my embarrassing secret: I'm easily wooed by men who say all the right things."

Marco made a mental note of that fact.

"I don't know why. Maybe I'm subconsciously searching for a man to replace the father I never had. So when he said, 'I love you, Phailin' and 'I've never met anyone like you, Phailin,' I lost all perspective. I was so gullible. He even proposed, but wouldn't commit to a wedding date." She shook her head. "He was just using me until he found a chance to trade up to someone better looking. Probably someone with money."

"I'm sorry," Marco said, and he meant it. It was difficult for him to imagine someone more beautiful than Phailin. *The jerk must have poor eyesight.*

"How long do you think it'll take them to get into the database?" Phailin seemed eager to change the subject.

"I have no idea. We might be out here for hours."

Her eyes widened for a moment as she glanced past Marco's shoulder, then she laughed as if he said something hilarious. "Trouble's coming. Would Acheron be able to recognize you?"

"Yes." He started to turn his head.

"Don't turn around." She seized his shoulders and pulled him close. "Kiss me."

"You just told me not to—" Marco's objection was interrupted by her mouth pressed against his. "Oww, my lip!"

He tried to whimper quietly as she paused long enough to whisper, "Don't let them see your face. CIPs—a whole squad."

Marco shut his eyes and did as he was told, silently cursing Lorina Murphy for ruining this incredible moment with a split lip that hurt like a dagger through his skull. His eyes began to water. He wished Phailin wouldn't press so hard on his tortured lip.

Not exactly how I imagined our first kiss, he thought in frustration, trying to act as if he were enjoying himself as he listened to the approaching footsteps.

"Why won't it open for me anymore?"

Marco recognized Acheron's angry voice directly behind him. He'd met the CIP chief several times, after spending the night in a holding cell. Marco lost count of how many times he'd been arrested on Mars Station for drunk and disorderly. *That's a habit I need to break,* he thought. A pang of remorse nagged at his conscience for the first time in years. *I've got to give up the booze.*

"It's an heir-lock, chief," a deeper voice said. "The lawyer must have changed it last week. It'll only open for my uncle's DNA or mine."

"So what are you waiting for?" Acheron snapped. "Let's get on board!"

"Who are these people?" a different voice demanded.

Marco felt a large hand on his shoulder, but he'd been expecting this. His spacer's reflexes took over as he lunged to the left before the hand could get a firm grip on him. He spun an astonished Phailin around so both their backs were to the CIPs. "Run!"

The cook needed no urging. She was like an Olympic sprinter off the starting blocks. Marco raced after her, expecting to get tackled from behind at any moment.

"Stop!"

Marco heard some footsteps in pursuit, but they stopped when Acheron shouted, "Let them run! They won't get far! Have Jones circle back and pick them up!"

Not if I can help it, he thought, trying to catch up with Phailin. "Next lift!"

There were several members of a ship's crew, wearing hideous eggplant-purple uniforms, waiting at Lift 38.

"Keep going!" Marco shouted.

He and Phailin dashed past the astonished crew, racing toward Lift 37.

Phailin touched her earcom. "Someone's coming aboard! Hide!"

Fifty meters from the lift, Marco saw the same female CIP on a scooter coming toward them from the other direction. Though she had more distance to cover to reach the lift, she had the advantage of mechanized speed.

"Marco?" Phailin slowed so suddenly, he almost plowed into her. He seized her shoulders and steered her to the right, through a door labeled *emergency exit only*.

An alarm loud enough to hurt their ears began howling the moment they pushed open the door. They hesitated on the dimly lit stairwell landing.

"She can't follow us on the stairs!" Marco shouted above the din.

Phailin turned to face him. "But she could still catch us on foot!"

He thought fast. "Let's split up! You go down, I'll go up!"

A quick nod from Phailin, and she headed down the staircase.

Marco took the stairs two at a time, his thighs aching by the time he reached Level 11. He couldn't hear any footsteps over the deafening siren, but he didn't want to take the time to stop and look over the landing to see if the CIP was below him. He decided to climb to Level 14, and hit the next staircase without breaking stride.

In hindsight, Marco realized Phailin was in much better shape than he was and could've ascended the stairs more easily. He also recalled he had nowhere else to run when he ran out of stairs. A pressure suit was required to climb out on the roof of the spaceport.

Marco had a stitch in his side and was gasping for breath when he reached Level 14. He burst through the door to the access corridor, bracing himself for a confrontation with a garrison of CIPs.

He was surprised to discover the corridor empty, but didn't take time to wonder about it as he ran the kilometer to the *Alex's Legacy*'s airlock, passing only an occasional port employee along the way. Thankfully—and miraculously—he didn't encounter any CIPs.

A sweat-soaked Phailin was waiting for him in the ship's entryway. "Just got here," she panted. "That was too close."

Marco cycled the airlock doors shut. "Too close, and now it's too late. I know that CIP saw the name of the ship on my stupid shirt. Acheron will only need five minutes to find out where we're docked."

***

"So . . . do you think we could do that again when my lip's healed?"

"No." Phailin studied Marco, her expression undecipherable. She hadn't said two words to him since emerging from her cabin, freshly showered and wearing her Moon Station T-shirt again. Marco could tell she was worried, so he didn't speculate aloud about the trouble they were in.

They sat across a galley table from each other, waiting for word from Blaze or Vipul. Marco sipped his third cup of coffee and thought about mixing it with something stronger, like the last of the tequila in his cabin.

Every fifteen minutes, Marco walked to the bridge to check the exterior airlock holo-cam. So far, so good—no CIPs. *It's just a matter of time*, he thought, returning to the galley.

After two hours of waiting, Phailin spoke up. "Do you think we should go by the *Elmina* to see what's happening?"

Marco shook his head. "Too risky. There's nothing we can do except wait."

"We could come up with a Plan B." Jake walked into the galley. He sat at the table with them. "Yes, I was listening," he said without apology, leaning back in his chair and regarding the two of them with the same detached gaze he exhibited earlier.

"Lorina's going to go ballistic when she wakes up and discovers her husband's missing." He glanced at Marco's black eye. "You might want to take cover this time."

"Getting angry doesn't solve anything." Phailin shot Marco a meaningful glance. "We need a Plan B, like you said."

"Maybe you could go by police headquarters and see who's locked up," Jake suggested to Phailin. "That way we'll know if Vipul and Blaze are still on board the *Elmina*, or if it's just the four of us left on this shrinking crew."

The word *no* formed on Marco's lips, but he caught Phailin's warning look and decided it would be safer to say nothing.

"We could call Ms. Delacruz. Maybe she could find out for us," Phailin said.

"Or you could ask me," Blaze announced from the doorway.

The other three were on their feet.

"Blaze!" Phailin gasped. "We didn't hear you come aboard!"

"What happened?" Jake demanded. "Where's Vipul?"

Blaze reached them in three strides of his extra-long legs. He was pale and sweaty. "Vipul was caught. He's probably in a cell next to the captain's by now."

Marco grimaced. "How did you get away?"

"Different hidin' places." Blaze sank into the fourth chair at the table. "Phailin, do you think I could get a drink of water?"

"Of course." She hurried over to the crew's mess as Jake and Marco resumed their seats. When Blaze had drained a bottle of water, he told them everything.

"The main database code had been changed, but Vipul tried out a few logical guesses and was able to gain access. Get this—the new password is *harvest*."

Jake growled something obscene under his breath about Thanatos.

Blaze continued. "So we got in, but the database was wiped clean."

"Oh no." Phailin groaned.

"Oh yes." Blaze nodded. "There wasn't a single scrap of information in the files. We decided to split up and search the ship. Vipul went down to the cargo holds to take holograms. Any evidence of people bein' held prisoner there could help our case. Since we still had Thanatos's DNA trace, I let myself into the captain's cabin to see if I could find anythin' useful there.

"Then Phailin sent us the warnin'." The engineer acknowledged her with a grateful nod. "We only had seconds to hide. I don't know where Vipul hid, but I climbed into Thanatos's closet and shut the door. I was sure they'd find me in such an obvious spot, but when I leaned against the back wall of the closet, it slid aside. Thanatos had a secret hidin' place. It's so secret, Monsantos doesn't know about it—since he didn't find me."

Phailin's mouth formed an attractive *O* of surprise.

"He had it installed in case of a mutiny, maybe," Jake said. "Or a raid by law enforcement—on some other station. It's probably insulated with lead-lined titanium to keep you from showing up on a scan. What was it like?"

"Like bein' inside a coffin." Blaze shuddered. "I stepped through the openin', and the panel closed behind me. It wasn't much bigger than the closet, and it was pitch dark. I wasn't sure how to get out again once the CIPs were gone, so all I could do was listen and wait.

"I think the tool bags gave us away. We left them on the bridge."

"Um, no," Phailin interrupted, lowering her eyes to the table. "I think Marco and I raised their suspicions."

Blaze and Jake glanced expectantly at her, but she just shrugged and said, "Long story. It can wait."

"I heard them searchin' the ship," Blaze continued, "because Acheron and Monsantos were yellin' a lot. I heard Vipul destroy his earcom, just like Captain Shepherd, so I knew he must've been caught.

"I stayed in the secret room until the ship was quiet. Then I waited a half hour more, just to be sure everyone was gone. When I pushed against the closet panel, it opened for me. I was about to leave Thanatos's cabin, but I had a feelin' I needed to look in his desk."

Blaze pulled an old datapad from a pocket of his coveralls and set it on the table.

"So?" Marco said. "There's probably datapads all over the ship."

"This is Thanatos's personal log." Blaze smiled for the first time. "Most of it's encrypted, but the pages in plain text contain enough information to send Acheron to prison for the rest of his miserable life."

NINE
EVIDENCE

ROSAMAR WAS WORRIED. A myriad of concerns battled for attention in her mind. She was still in her office, sitting at her desk. It was late at night.

First worry: Orlene assured her earlier in the evening that the DNA trace had been successfully delivered to Danae's crew. Then she offered her resignation, stating unsafe working conditions as her reason. Rosamar was once again without an assistant, but she considered it a minor inconvenience compared to the crisis at hand.

Second worry: Judge Wei Forsetti, her one ally, called her right after his meeting with Acheron to share some troubling news. "He knows where my grandson Linc is being held as a slave, and he said he would make sure his handlers start giving him poison so he dies a slow, painful death."

"He's lying!" Rosamar wished she could reach through the com and shake Wei. "He's a master at manipulating people! You know that! You can't believe a word he says!"

"I can't take the chance he's telling the truth. I'll have Cade contact you as soon as his ship docks. I did make a recording of the threat, as you suggested, and you can use it to help your case, but I can't do anything else for you right now. I'm sorry, Rosamar. I wish I had your courage."

So do I, she thought in frustration.

Third worry: Rosamar's own meeting with Acheron just ten minutes after Orlene left to deliver the DNA trace to Danae's crew. The CIP chief stormed into her office, spouting threats.

"Your judge is going to rescind the warrants he wrote. You can't have any more contact with Shepherd or the Sorensens." He placed his thick hands on her desk and leaned close, his expression dangerous. "I told you to mind your own business."

"I'm not afraid of you." Rosamar stared straight into Acheron's eyes without flinching. The datapad on her desk was silently taking in every word. She had set it to start recording the moment it recognized his voice.

"You should be." Acheron's smile was frigid. "I have a friend on Ganymede who says he'd be glad to take care of your sister for me."

"*What?*" Rosamar felt a tremor of fear for the first time. *Does the tyrant have that many resources?* "I don't believe you."

In response, Acheron told her things he had no right to know about Guadalupe Delacruz, including her home address and her husband's name. "My friend follows their every move. He knows their schedules, where they shop, where they like to eat, where they go to church. He knows the names and addresses of all their friends, and he's just waiting for me to say the word. Your sister is dead, Delacruz, unless you stop meddling in my business."

Rosamar had a chilling flashback to her confrontation with Danae. *Ishmael's dead because of me, because I refused to take Baronowski's threat seriously.* She couldn't make the same mistake with Lupe's life.

"I'll stop." She lowered her eyes, ashamed for uttering the cowardly words.

"Good." Acheron's triumphant sneer did little to improve his looks. "And in case you get any ideas about sneaking around behind my back, I hired someone to watch you twenty-four/seven. If he sees you step out of line, I'll know it, and your sister's dead."

Acheron didn't wait for her response. He spun on his heel and left her office, confident, she was sure, that she got the message loud and clear.

Rosamar tapped her fingernails on the desk, lost in thought. She was alone, literally and figuratively. She was David going up against Goliath, and there weren't any stones in her sling to take him down.

She thought about the homeless children in McConnell Park who approached her every morning, hoping for a handout. They were grateful if she had anything to offer them, no matter how small.

She remembered an adorable little Asian boy, maybe three years old, with only a skinny older brother, no more than six years old himself, to look after him. Rosamar had seen the two boys every day for several months. They must have watched for her every morning because they were always the first to approach her. Their "*xie xie*"s were always sincere. She began to suspect the orange or apple she gave them was the only food they had to eat all day. Her heart ached for them, and she wanted to do more to help them.

Then one morning they didn't show up at the usual spot to beg for food. Rosamar never saw them again. Three years later, the memory of their innocent little faces still haunted her. Knowing now what happened to the brothers made her blood boil. *There's going to be a lot more kids like Lincoln York if I quit now.*

Rosamar made a decision. She was going to end Acheron's reign of terror, no matter what risks she had to take. She would send a transmission to Lupe, warning her to leave Ganymede Station.

But first she had to wait for word from Danae's crew. She couldn't move forward without solid evidence that Acheron was enslaving homeless children. She needed stones for her sling.

Or a loaded gun, like Danae's, would be even better.

***

Rosamar awoke with a start. She had dozed off at her desk. She squinted at her watch. It was 1:17 a.m. Her earcom was chiming.

"Ms. Delacruz, ma'am, this is—"

"Don't say your name!" she hissed. "I know who you are."

Actually, she wasn't sure who she was speaking to. She only knew she recognized his voice. He was one of Danae's crew.

Her caller sounded surprised to receive this kind of greeting, but he was quick to recover. "I have the information you requested." He spoke slowly, choosing his words with care. Rosamar was pleased he realized her com might be tapped. "I'm assumin' you don't want me to send it over the com. How do you want me to deliver it to you?"

If only we had some kind of secret code, she thought, wracking her brain for a way to communicate a meeting place without Acheron's spy catching on.

McConnell Park. She was familiar with every feature of the park from her daily morning runs, and she thought Danae's crew knew it well enough from their work with the people who lived there.

"Ms. Delacruz?" Her caller was concerned about the extended silence.

"Sorry, I was just thinking." She had an idea. "Remind me again, where do you live?"

There was silence for a few moments. "In the basement."

Smart boy! He was the engineer, which meant he would understand her next message. "I have a friend who used to live in that basement. Maybe you know him? Joe Silver?"

"No, but he sounds like someone I'd like to meet. Does he still live on the station?"

I'm going to give this boy a big kiss when I meet him! "Unfortunately, no. He passed away April thirtieth. I attended his funeral. It was lovely. I've never seen so many flowers." She paused for a moment. "I'm sorry. You'll have to excuse me. I'm old and tend to ramble. You wanted to send me some information?"

"I guess it's not that urgent. I can drop it by your office in the mornin'. Sorry to disturb you so late, Ms. Delacruz. Have a good evenin'."

"Good night."

Her mystery caller severed the connection, but Rosamar knew there was a good chance the call had been traced back to Danae's ship. She was short on time. *If Acheron locates the* Ishmael *before I have that evidence, we'll all be in solitary before breakfast.*

***

Rosamar had never been in McConnell Park after dark. Most women would have had second thoughts about wandering through a homeless village at 4:00 in the morning, but Rosamar wasn't afraid. If anything, she felt safer being out in the open around people, instead of alone and under constant surveillance in her apartment.

Despite her confidence, she couldn't dismiss the sense of paranoia that someone was following her. She found herself glancing back over her shoulder every few minutes, but there wasn't another soul in sight. She kept her ears tuned for any sounds of pursuit and prayed her informant would be on time so they could both make a speedy exit.

She thought back over the awkward conversation with the unnamed member of Danae's crew. *The basement of the* Ishmael *is the engine room. And Josiah McConnell, the inventor of the Velocity engine, spent most of his life in a basement—an engine room.* She hoped he understood the reference to Joe Silver to mean the shiny chrome statue of McConnell which graced the center of the park named for him, surrounded by flowering thorn bushes—the flowers she mentioned at the funeral.

Was Joe Silver too obvious? She also worried he wouldn't understand the time reference, April thirtieth to mean 4:30. *He did say, "I'll see you in the morning," so he must have understood.*

Rosamar took a handlight from the pocket of her jacket and switched it on. She was dressed in her workout clothes, in case she needed to do some real running. She left the well-lit area near the east gate and walked into the darkness of the trees. She avoided the paved path and headed for the small lake, taking extra care not to step on anyone's makeshift shelter. Most of the people her light found were sound asleep, stretched out on their nests of old blankets and towels or huddled together under cardboard lean-tos.

People shouldn't have to live like this. She paused for a moment to look over a group of sleeping children, huddled together like a litter of kittens. They were all disheveled, dirty, and painfully thin.

Rosamar bit her lip. *I have to put an end to the homelessness, and the unemployment, and especially the child slave trade.*

She reached the lake and followed the shoreline to the shiny statue of McConnell, which was only three meters tall, although it appeared out of place amongst so much poverty. A lone figure was waiting near the statue, blending in with the darkness. Rosamar switched off the light when she was a few steps away from him.

"Ms. Delacruz?"

Make that a her, Rosamar thought. "Yes."

"Call for you." The woman walked away without another word.

The councilwoman turned and retraced her steps. She touched her earcom twice, and then tucked her hand into the right-hand pocket of her jacket where she'd stashed a datapad. "Download complete," said a feminine monotone voice in her earcom. She waited a moment to hear, "HD copy complete."

Leaving the datapad in her pocket, Rosamar felt around the sides of the device until she found the Holographic Digital slot at the bottom edge. She ejected the coin-size storage drive into her waiting palm. In one quick movement, she tucked the HD into the only safe place she knew to hide it: her cleavage.

Now she had two copies of what she hoped was incriminating data from the *Elmina,* but she knew she couldn't relax until she downloaded it to the mainframe in her office.

Rosamar couldn't decide if it was her imagination or if the nagging sense that she was being followed was reality. She walked faster, increasing her pace until she was jogging. Just as she reached the paved path, she heard a twig snap in the woods behind her. She glanced back over her shoulder for a split second and thought she saw a shadow move behind a tree.

She broke into a run, heading for the nearest tramstop. Now she was certain she heard footsteps on the sidewalk behind her, but she didn't risk another glance back.

A green line tram was just pulling up to the curb twenty meters from her when she sprinted through the east gate. She put on an extra burst of speed and was able to reach the tram before it pulled away.

Someone boarded the tram right after her. The trolley was deserted this early in the morning with only one old woman dozing on a back seat.

Rosamar was on edge, her heart racing as she tried to stay one step ahead of her shadow. She ran to the back and sat beside her fellow passenger. The woman awoke with a start, both hands clutching her tattered pocketbook.

"*Buenos días.*" The councilwoman kept an eye on her stalker, who took a seat right behind the android driver before she could get a look at his face. "Are you headed to work?"

The old woman relaxed after examining Rosamar's face. *I'm just another old woman to her, albeit one who's wearing overpriced workout clothes.*

"Just gettin' off," her companion said. "I clean an office buildin' at night. Are you headin' to the gym?"

"Yes, I like to get in an early workout." Rosamar's mind raced ahead as she tried to figure out how to get the evidence someplace safe, where Acheron and his innumerable minions couldn't get their hands on it.

"You look like you just came from the gym."

Rosamar wiped the sweat from her eyes. "I was running to catch the tram."

The woman adjusted her glasses and studied Rosamar's face. "You seem familiar. What is it you do?"

"I'm on the city council. Maybe you've seen a hologram of me in the *Chronicles*."

"That must be it," her seatmate agreed. "I'm Marta."

"Nice to meet you, Marta. I'm Rosamar." *How am I going to get off the tram? I'd have to walk right by him to reach the door. He could attack me right here and Marta wouldn't be able to do anything to help unless she's packing a pistol in that handbag. The stupid android tram drivers never respond to anything, so they're useless.*

And where should I get off? She wished she'd stayed in the park where it was relatively safe with so many people around. *I need a crowd.*

The spaceport is always crowded! I could go to the port master's office and ask to see the surveillance holo-vids from October twenty-third. She glanced at the silent figure still sitting on the front seat of the tram, facing forward. *I'll have to prove Danae acted in self-defense to get her out of jail—*

Oh, she thought, her enthusiasm deflating, *unless Acheron deleted the holo-vids already.* Rosamar sighed to herself. *I'm sure he took care of erasing all the evidence.*

"Well, this is my stop." Marta got to her feet. "Nice meetin' ya, Councilwoman Rosamar. Have a good day." She shuffled up the aisle and disembarked.

Delacruz realized too late she should've stuck with Marta. The moment the tram doors closed, her stalker got to his feet and turned around to face her.

It was Acheron, dressed in plainclothes.

Rosamar was too shocked to say a word. She felt her adrenaline climbing as Acheron made his way down the aisle toward her. She thought she would keel over from heart failure before he reached her. *Stay calm,* she told herself, but it didn't help.

"I believe you have something of mine." Acheron stood over her at last, his pistol in plain sight, tucked into the holster beneath his left arm.

She tried to get her breathing under control. "I don't know what you're—"

Acheron struck hard and fast, his fist connecting with the side of her head, knocking her to the floor of the tram. "Hand over the datapad!"

Rosamar's head was spinning. The entire left side of her face throbbed and there was a dull buzzing sound in her ear. She stayed down, panting hard. "I . . . don't have anything . . . of yours."

"I'm losing patience with you!" Acheron seized the back of Rosamar's collar and hauled her to her feet with one hand. With his free hand he searched her roughly, patting down her pockets until he found what he was looking for. The datapad vanished inside his jacket. He then yanked off her earcom, dropped it on the floor, and crushed it under his heel.

Acheron shoved Rosamar back into the seat so hard that her head struck the window. Her vision blurred for a moment. Shapes shifted in and out of focus.

"I told you to stop meddling in my business! You just wrote your sister's death sentence!"

"No! You can't—!"

Acheron shouted her down. "I should finish you off here and now! But there would be too many questions. Too many people would notice your absence. So I'll send that transmission to Ganymede, then I'll arrest the rest of the *Ishmael*'s crew, and that will be the end of this annoying little bump in the road."

He leaned closer, gloating. "I'm the law in this town, Delacruz. Not you, not Forsetti, just me. If you don't like it, I think you should find a new place to live. It's about time you retired anyway."

Acheron emphasized his point by seizing Rosamar's right hand and breaking her index finger as easily as snapping a toothpick.

She was still screaming from the pain when he exited the tram.

***

A long time passed before Rosamar gathered enough strength to get off the tram. Outside, the artificial light was growing brighter; it was dawn on Mars Station. Shops were opening, pedestrians began to fill the sidewalks and board the trams, and food vendors began setting up their carts, but no one gave her a second glance.

Rosamar wasn't sure where she disembarked. She blinked at the nearest street sign, not comprehending. It hurt to think.

Farmer Street. She glanced around and realized she was standing in front of the emergency room entrance to Mars Community Hospital.

The most fortuitous thing that's happened to me all week.

She glanced down at her misshapen finger, which was turning blue, and decided it would be prudent to go inside. She had almost reached the sliding doors to the ER when something off to the side caught her eye.

It was a kiosk for the *Martian Chronicles.* Rosamar approached the box, an idea taking shape in her aching head. She didn't have a datapad to download a copy of the newspaper, but she had something better. Something Acheron overlooked.

She fished the HD out of her bra with her left hand and inserted it into the slot next to the screen of the information terminal. The display offered her some choices for submitting news, so she selected *editor-in-chief* and *urgent*. She downloaded all the data from the HD. Then she retrieved the tiny disc and went through the ER doors, feeling optimistic, despite her pain.

It only took one stone to bring down Goliath.

TEN
TRAPPED

MARCO KEPT THE hood up on his jacket as he hovered outside the north gate of McConnell Park. *Hurry up, hurry up.* He was beginning to perspire as he watched for Phailin's return. She vetoed his offer to wait at the statue with her.

"It would be too conspicuous for two people to be waiting, especially if one of them is a man. It might scare her off," Phailin had explained. "Stay here," she added in that no-nonsense tone she was starting to use with him.

Marco was reluctant, but agreed. He watched her disappear into the darkness with only a tiny handlight to guide her way.

Now he was on high-alert, watching for signs of anyone conscious at this hour. His eyes were gritty from missing too much sleep. He had been awake for two days, and it was beginning to show in his sluggish reflexes. Fortunately, adrenaline and caffeine kept him coherent.

He checked his watch, which was set to the *Alex*'s military time. It was 0438. *She should be back by now.* He resisted the urge to search for her, knowing they might miss each other in the darkness. He wasn't sure where the statue of McConnell was located, but Phailin had been confident. It was obvious she had been to Mars Station before. He made a mental note to ask her about her past—the other starships she traveled aboard, the other places she visited. *The old boyfriend who broke her heart.*

A broken heart was a foreign concept to Marco. He had little experience with close relationships. His mother and best friend Giovanni Medici had been the only people he felt a real connection to, and he missed both of them more than he cared to admit. But there was something about Phailin that made him want to step outside his comfort zone and feel close to someone again. He wanted to give up his old habits, especially the self-destructive ones, and earn her respect.

He shook his head. *She would never consider someone like me. She deserves so much better.*

Ting was still feeling sorry for himself when Phailin emerged from the park, moving fast. When she reached Marco, she took his elbow and steered him toward the nearest tramstop.

"The datalink went fine, but I think someone might be following Delacruz," she said. "We need to take a random route back to the ship, in case we're being followed too."

"The original datapad is still on board the *Alex*," Marco reminded her.

"But who can we trust if Delacruz gets caught? If Acheron gets his hands on the evidence . . ."

Marco shushed her. "Don't assume the worst. I don't know a lot about Delacruz, but I do remember she's tough and tenacious, like Captain Shepherd. She'll come through for us."

He was struck by the irony of what he just uttered. The chronic pessimist was encouraging optimism and complete trust in a person he barely knew.

"I hope you're right." Phailin continued to hold on to his arm. He decided not to read too much into the gesture since they were both nervous, but he hoped it was more than just a nervous gesture.

They boarded a tram, got off after a kilometer, and transferred to one going the opposite direction before hopping onto one headed to the spaceport.

In case they were still being followed, they disembarked at Lift 25 and rode up to Level 14. Since the airlocks were half a kilometer apart on this level, it was a three-hundred-meter walk to airlock 7. Marco didn't mind the exercise because he wanted to burn off some of his nervous energy.

There was no sign of pursuit, so he breathed a mental sigh of relief. The access corridor was empty this early in the morning. There were no sounds except for their own footsteps. Phailin loosened her grip on Marco's arm; the contact felt friendlier now. He turned his head to study her profile, but she kept her gaze fixed on the corridor ahead of them. She was still tense. Marco tried to think of something reassuring to say, something that would impress her.

Before he could open his mouth, Phailin stopped short and shoved him against the corridor's interior wall. He started to protest, but she had already flattened herself against the wall next to him.

"Don't look. We have a problem."

Marco didn't look. He tapped his earcom instead. "O'Brien? Smith?"

"What's wrong? Where are you?" Blaze asked.

"Just around the bend from airlock 7. Check the monitor."

There was a pause, and then Jake said, "Monsantos is outside. He's got two CIPs with him."

"If he found us, Acheron can't be far behind," Marco said. "Any ideas?"

"What about Delacruz?" Blaze asked.

"What about her?"

"Maybe you could go to her office. Maybe she could protect you."

Maybe we're all going to jail unless Delacruz can do something fast with that evidence. Who are we supposed to call for help if we can't trust the local police?

"What's her address?" Phailin asked.

"Just a sec." Blaze looked it up and told them.

"Great. Right across the street from CIP headquarters." She gnawed on a thumbnail. "Any other ideas?"

There was a brief pause. O'Brien said, "Just stay out of sight. We'll let you know when it's safe to board the ship."

"That's not much help," Marco grumbled.

"That's all we can do right now, Ting," Jake fired back.

Phailin put a finger to her lips and pointed down the corridor the way they had come.

Before they could start retracing their steps, O'Brien shouted, "They're heading your way! Run!"

Not again! Marco seized Phailin's hand, and they sprinted for the nearest lift.

When they reached Lift 26, they discovered a sign posted across the doors. *Out of Service.*

Why don't they maintain this place? Marco thought as he and Phailin ran for Lift 25. He could already hear

Monsantos and the CIPs not far behind, their footsteps echoing along the corridor.

"How did they spot us?" Phailin panted. "How do they even know we were heading back to the ship?"

Marco glanced up at a holo-cam as they ran beneath it. "Maybe someone in the port master's office is helping them."

They reached Lift 25, and Marco smacked the button to summon it. The light came on, indicating the elevator was at Level 2.

He swore. "Next lift!" They raced for 24.

"Stairs again?" Phailin was beginning to sound panicked.

"No time." Marco could hear the CIPs and Monsantos gaining on them.

They reached Lift 24 just as the doors were opening and rushed inside. Marco wedged himself into a corner and began punching buttons, willing the doors to close fast.

"Stop! You're under arrest!"

Phailin spun around to face their pursuers. They were only fifteen meters from the lift. "We're trapped!"

Marco gestured for her to take cover in the corner opposite him, but she seemed frozen in place, unable to take her eyes off their soon-to-be captors.

"Stop them! They're getting away! *Shoot them!*"

Ting had no doubt Monsantos shouted those orders. *No, don't listen to him! Don't shoot!* He felt as if time slowed to a crawl as the lift doors moved toward each other.

"Phailin, take cover! Get away from the gap!"

She remained rooted to the spot like a deer in headlights, staring out through the rapidly narrowing space between the doors.

Almost there! It looked as if he and Phailin were going to escape arrest. Marco held his breath. *Just a few more centimeters!*

In the last moment before the gap closed, the CIPs opened fire.

Without thinking, Marco lunged, shoving Phailin clear of the opening. He felt a fleeting moment of triumph as the titanium doors finally met, muffling the sounds of the gunshots outside.

Then he heard Phailin scream as the floor rose up to meet him.

ELEVEN
FREEDOM

ERIK FELT close to losing his grip on reality. As near as he could estimate, he had been in solitary for four weeks.

Four weeks! Three bad meals a day. Eight interrogations by Acheron. Two visitors including his sister, who was now in solitary herself, and his attorney, whom he hadn't heard from in days. He had no idea what was going on outside his prison cell. *Where is Danae and her crew? Has Acheron arrested them too?*

The uncertainty and the waiting chipped away at Erik's emotional armor. He was beginning to understand what it felt like to be a psychiatric patient because he was close to becoming one himself.

And then the door to his cell opened without warning. "Sorensen, you're being released."

"What?" Erik got to his feet, taking care not to put any weight on his right leg.

"You heard me," the guard answered, impatient. "All charges against you have been dropped."

Erik hopped over to the doorway on his good leg, wondering if this was another one of Acheron's sick games. *Maybe he wants to charge me with trying to escape.*

There was a blur of orange to his left and Kirsten was throwing her arms around him. He staggered as she almost knocked him down.

"Erik!" She was laughing and crying at the same time.

"Oww! My leg!"

She released him. "Sorry. But it's over! Delacruz freed us!"

He noted the bruises on his sister's face and wished he could have five minutes alone with Acheron. He swallowed his anger for the moment, grateful just to be outside his cell.

"Lean on me." Kirsten slipped an arm around his waist. "Let's get out of here."

Erik shot the guard a questioning glance, but the CIP opened the door to the small hallway which sealed off the solitary section. The siblings limped their way down the next corridor toward freedom. Each locked door was opened for them by an expressionless CIP until they arrived at the main lobby.

"Good. You're here." Councilwoman Rosamar Delacruz was sporting an ugly-looking bruise on the left side of her face, but the rest of her appearance was polished and professional. She stood across from the reception desk where she was signing and thumb-printing a stack of datapads, one at a time, and handing them back to the flustered-looking CIP behind the counter. "Here are your clothes and personal items." She gestured to the tote bags on the floor near her feet. "You can just take them with you. There's a private tram waiting outside to take you to the spaceport."

"What?" Erik shook his head. "The spaceport?" He was confused and there were more surprises to come.

A door opened to a hallway on the opposite side of the reception desk, and Danae Shepherd walked out.

Like the Sorensens, she was dressed in an orange prison jumpsuit, but she was tan and her hair was dyed jet black.

"Danae!" Erik tried to smile, but his facial muscles hurt too much to muster more than a lopsided grin.

The captain rushed over, smiling as much as she could with a jagged cut on the left side of her mouth, no doubt a gift from Acheron. She could tell Erik was in pain and gave him a kiss on the cheek instead of a hug. "I'm so happy to see you free." She grasped Kirsten's hand. "Both of you."

Delacruz shot Shepherd a nervous glance but continued signing datapads.

"Would someone please tell me what's going on?" Erik asked.

"Yes, someone tell me too." One of Danae's crew approached the desk. The doctor had to think a moment to recall his name. *Vipul Ganguli.* He was also in a prison jumpsuit.

"How many of us did Acheron arrest?" Erik asked.

"Just four," Delacruz said. "You can read about it in the *Chronicles.*" She turned away from the desk to face them. "Now, come on, we need to get you all to the ship."

"Why?" Kirsten asked.

"We're not sure which CIPs are loyal to Acheron, so you'll be safer aboard the *Ishmael.*"

"It's *Alex's Legacy* now, the name of my ship," Danae said. The attorney gave her a curious look. "Never mind, long story."

Delacruz's tone turned somber. "I have an urgent message from Jake O'Brien." She glanced at a datapad and read it to them. "Ting was shot in the head. I did everything I could, but he's in critical condition, in a coma."

"*What?* How?" Danae gasped.

"By one of Acheron's officers." The attorney cast Danae another nervous glance. "I'm not clear on the details. You'll have to ask the young woman who was with him. I believe her name is Kim?"

"Phailin," Vipul supplied.

Delacruz began ushering the group toward the front doors of the building. "I'm sorry, but we really need to leave now."

"But we can't leave," Kirsten spoke up, giving Erik a searching look. "We're needed here. The homeless kids . ."

"Won't be homeless anymore," Delacruz finished her sentence.

"What?" Erik thought he was beginning to sound like a parrot. "I don't understand."

"I'll explain everything, but right now I need to get you all out of here. I think this area is about to get crowded."

Delacruz was right. Moments before they reached the doors, they were met by a squad of officers coming in. The CIPs were escorting two men in handcuffs, one in a black police uniform, the other in a dark green spacer's uniform with *Elmina* stitched across the right breast. Both had murderous expressions on their faces.

"You can't arrest me! I'm the chief of police! You have no authority here!" Acheron shouted at Delacruz, struggling to free himself from the clutches of the arresting officers, but they tightened their grip, holding him back.

The councilwoman kept a safe distance, but her words were razor sharp. "You're charged with the abduction of thousands of children and selling them to the slaver Thanatos. You're also charged with bribing, threatening, blackmailing, stalking, and assaulting dozens of city officials, including judges," she glared at him, "and me. Your reign as a dictator is over."

"You can't prove anything!" Acheron roared.

"I have plenty of proof, thanks to Thanatos." Delacruz held up an HD between her right thumb and splinted index finger. "You tried to erase all the evidence, but this time you overlooked something." There was vengeance in her smile. "If you're wondering what's on here, just read today's issue of the *Martian Chronicles*."

Acheron shut his mouth, but Delacruz wasn't finished.

"Judge Forsetti was happy to write a warrant for your arrest once I assured him you couldn't arrange to have his grandson murdered if you were in jail." She took a deep breath to calm herself.

"My office received calls today from fifty-eight people who are eager to testify against you, and that number keeps growing. Many of them have proof of your threats, recorded on datapads and holo-vids. You should be grateful you're in custody now." She glanced with contempt at the other man in the *Elmina* uniform. "You too, Monsantos."

"Grateful!" Acheron sputtered.

"Yes, grateful!" Delacruz snapped. "There's an angry mob in McConnell Park who'd like a few minutes with you. Shall we go over and ask them why they're so upset?"

Acheron seemed to be running out of steam, but he had one more argument. "Well, you can't release Shepherd! She's charged with murder—and shooting a police officer!"

"You were holding a child hostage!" Danae flared. "You were pointing a gun at an unarmed member of my crew!"

And he was trying to arrest Jake, Erik thought, recalling how both shocked and impressed he felt when Danae shot Acheron in the shoulder.

The doctor slipped an arm around Danae's waist on the pretense of needing her support for his leg, but he was actually trying to restrain her from going after Acheron. Her anger helped diffuse his own. *Justice will be served. There's no point in punching him now, although it would feel good.*

"Relax, Danae," Erik murmured in her ear. "It's over."

Danae glanced at him and at Kirsten, who was still supporting him on his other side. She nodded, understanding. He could feel her attempting to let go of the tension.

"You can't hurt anyone anymore," Danae told Acheron. "You or your slave-running business partners." She shot Monsantos a vicious look. "I hope you both rot in jail!"

Erik could think of a better place for them to rot, but he kept that opinion to himself.

Delacruz continued, as if nothing had interrupted her spiel. "I have witnesses from your own department, willing to testify Danae shot Thanatos to defend—"

"Me!" Vipul spoke up. "He was trying to kill me! And he would have succeeded if Captain Shepherd hadn't been there!"

"Get them out of here," Delacruz told the arresting officers. "There will be a complete investigation into the department to determine which CIPs were involved in Acheron's illegal activities."

Acheron sneered. "And who has the authority to conduct an internal investigation?"

"The Interstellar Peacekeepers Patrol," Delacruz said. "I expect them to arrive tomorrow morning."

The ex-police chief grimaced and fell silent as the officers led him and Monsantos away.

Erik had no idea who these peacekeepers were, but he was relieved to hear an outside organization would investigate the CIPs on Mars Station. There had been too much corruption in the system for too long.

Kirsten and Danae served as human crutches for Erik as the little group exited the building and boarded a small private tram waiting just outside.

Everything felt surreal to Erik. He eased himself into a seat and listened to the excited conversations between Councilwoman Delacruz and his fellow former inmates.

Danae brought them up to speed on everything that had taken place since the *Ishmael* escaped the station with the homeless kids aboard. Erik listened in awe as she touched on the major events: Jake's emergency surgery on herself and Vipul; the chaotic, challenging flight to Earth with a skeleton crew; the sugarcane-plantation inheritance from her mother; the near-fatal landing on Maui; Jake again proving his mettle by saving Blaze's life; establishing the orphanage; Blaze and Lorina's wedding; the plan to return to Mars Station; and the many hurdles they had to overcome to reach this point.

She concluded with, "I ventured out on my own to find out where you were being held." She shot Erik a curious glance, as if trying to read his mind.

"I guess you found me the hard way." He felt his face heating up, grateful she couldn't read his thoughts.

With perfect timing, Vipul changed the subject. "How did you get caught, Captain?"

Danae flashed a sheepish grin. "I was stupid and got something to eat."

"How is that stupid?" the navigator asked.

"I should have stuck with the street vendors," she said. "I went into a regular restaurant and my credit flash must have shown up on Acheron's spy network. It was a careless mistake. How about you? How did you get caught?"

"Acheron found me aboard the *Elmina*. I'm not sure how Blaze got away."

"Blaze? Is he the engineer?" Delacruz shot Danae another nervous look, which Erik thought odd, considering the Councilwoman just bawled out Acheron.

Delacruz continued. "He was the one who called me about the evidence he found on the *Elmina*. A woman handed it off to me at McConnell Park early this morning."

"That was Phailin," Vipul said.

"I would have expected Lorina to do something that brave," Danae said.

"Um, yes, about Lorina . . ." Vipul hesitated. "After hearing about Ting, I wanted to give you some time . . . but I have more bad news. . . ." He shifted his feet. "Captain, there was an accident at The Lost Sheep . . . Beth Murphy drowned, trying to rescue one of the kids."

Danae slumped back in her seat. She was silent for several minutes, her brow furrowed, her mouth pinched into a tight, thin line. She tucked her hands beneath her thighs, as if she felt cold, but Erik thought the move was to hide the fact that she was trembling.

He couldn't think of anything to say to cushion this blow for her.

When Danae spoke, her voice was husky. "Poor Shima. What a terrible thing to happen on her watch. Lorina and Jake must be devastated. And Blaze too, she was his mother-in-law."

"Blaze didn't know her well," Vipul said. "But Lorina was very upset. She attacked Ting."

Danae pursed her lips. "That doesn't surprise me. I've been tempted to punch him myself on several occasions. Did she do any damage?"

"A busted lip and a black eye."

"And now he's in a coma." Danae turned to Erik. "Please take over for Jake as the ship's medic. We need . ." she hesitated, then tried again, "*I* need your help."

Erik glanced at his sister. Kirsten appeared ready to burst into tears. "I don't know, Danae. We're still needed here. It will take time for people to find jobs and homes."

Danae turned her head before he could get a glimpse of her expression. "Well, if that's how you really feel . . ."

Kirsten spoke up, interrupting the awkward pause. "You should go, Erik. Lots of homeless kids on the station were abandoned. There will always be a need for Mother Teresa's."

Erik glanced back and forth between the two women, feeling torn.

"I could shuttle orphans from Mars to Maui, as needed." Danae turned to face him again. "We could work together to improve their lives. There are hundreds of couples on Maui who want to adopt—probably on the other islands too. The kids don't stay at The Lost Sheep for long."

"It sounds like a good plan." Kirsten sounded more confident. "Erik, we could see each other whenever the ship comes back to the station for more children."

"What about Jake?" Erik asked Danae.

Danae shook her head. "Jake's brilliant, but he needs more training—and a medical license. From the message, it sounds like Ting's coma might be too advanced for his skills."

Erik thought so too. He leaned back in his seat with a sigh. "It sounds like the decision's been made for me."

"Thank you." He could see the relief in Danae's eyes, but it was only there for a fleeting moment. Her calm expression was back in place, masking anything else she might have been thinking.

The doctor thought of a detail they'd overlooked. "What about my apartment?"

"I'll take care of it," Kirsten said. "I'll pack your things and store them at Mother Teresa's until you return."

"I guess it's settled, then." Erik hoped both women were satisfied with the arrangement. Since neither was glaring at him, he took that as a good sign.

The tram soon reached Spaceport Drive, where it came to a stop at Lift 28. Blaze Smith and an Asian young woman were waiting in front of the elevator with a wheelchair for Erik.

Danae disembarked first. Then she turned back and offered Erik a hand to help him down the steps.

He was in too much pain to decline her assistance. Once he was seated in the wheelchair, Kirsten said, "I guess this is where I need to say goodbye."

"Please come aboard," Danae said. "Have dinner with the crew. You're welcome to use one of the cabins to shower and change—and sleep, if you like."

Kirsten hesitated, looking to Erik for advice.

He nodded encouragement. "You don't have to go back to work right away, sis. You've been through a lot these past few days."

"You've been locked up for weeks," Kirsten said. "You're the one who needs some attention."

"Yes, we could all use a vacation," the councilwoman spoke up. "I'm the one who needs to say goodbye. I'm sure you young people have a lot to discuss."

Erik couldn't help noticing her hesitant glance at Danae again. "We're grateful for your assistance, Ms. Delacruz." He offered his hand for her to shake. "Thank you."

"You were very brave to help us," Blaze said, shaking her hand, as well. "We're in your debt."

"We had the same goal to save the people of Mars Station from Acheron, especially the children." Delacruz shook hands with Kirsten, Vipul, and Phailin. "I'm just glad we could help each other achieve that end. I think that by the end of the week, the city council will have voted to eliminate all of the fees at the employment centers, for both employers and applicants."

The councilwoman turned to face Danae last. The tension between the two was so heavy, Erik wished for temporary hearing loss. He noticed the others also appeared uncomfortable. They seemed intent on studying their fingernails or the tramstop sign.

"I'm sorry for the condition of your helmsman, and for the death of your staff member." Delacruz hesitated. "Your father would have been very proud of you." She stared at the splint on her finger. "I hope you have success with your orphanage."

Danae bit her lip, unable to meet Delacruz's eyes either. "Thank you for getting us out of this mess." She paused, shifting her feet. "I think Dad would've been proud of you too." Her voice dropped to a whisper. "I was wrong . . . about you. I'm sorry."

"An apology probably sounds empty coming from me, but I swear to you I would've done everything in my power to keep Ishmael safe if I'd known he was a target." Delacruz hesitated again before offering Danae her hand. "I hope you'll be able to forgive me one day."

The captain took it, shook it solemnly, but surprised everyone by throwing her arms around the attorney. The two women hugged for several moments. When they parted, Erik saw both had tears in their eyes.

"Goodbye, Rosamar."

"Goodbye, Danae."

Both women went their separate ways. Erik felt as if he witnessed something profound. He hoped Danae would explain it to him some day.

The lift deposited them on Level 14. It was just a short walk to airlock 7. Danae's eyes were already dry, her calm face fixed in place, when she pressed her thumb to the ID lock. The large round door cycled open to the antechamber of *Alex's Legacy*.

"Welcome aboard." Danae typed a code into a keypad in the antechamber, and the second door opened. She guided Erik's wheelchair into the entryway and down a short hallway to the lift.

"This might be of interest." Blaze handed Erik a datapad as everyone crowded into the elevator. "But you'll have to read it later. I think Jake could use some help right now."

Erik glanced at the front page headline of the *Martian Chronicles*.

NEW EVIDENCE LINKS CIP CHIEF ACHERON TO CHILD SLAVERY

A quick scroll down the screen told Erik the entire issue was dedicated to the evidence against Acheron. "Yes, I'll definitely read it later."

In moments, he found himself being wheeled through a doorway into a state-of-the-art infirmary. Four post-op beds filled each corner of the main room. Four doors labeled *exam*, *surgery*, *lab*, and *head*, were interspaced along the back wall.

"Erik!" The door to *surgery* slid open, and Jake poked his head out. Relief was evident in every centimeter of his tanned face.

The doctor nodded to his apprentice. "Coming." He told Danae, "I can handle it from here, thanks," and wheeled himself to Jake's side.

"I'll be back to check on you and Ting in a few hours," Danae called after him.

"Right," Erik said over his shoulder just before the door to the makeshift ICU slid shut with a soft hiss.

He took a moment to adjust to the cloying scent of antiseptic air. It was easier to breathe, indicating the increased oxygen output in the room. Erik took advantage of it by taking a deep breath to clear his mind. He took his time observing the patient stretched out on the operating table.

Marco Ting's face was unrecognizable, wrapped in a layer of bandages which shrouded his head. Only his nose and mouth were visible. He was also connected to several monitors, a urinary catheter, and two IVs.

"What's his status?" Erik held out his palm, and Jake handed him a medical scanner. He read over the information as Jake gave him a summary.

"Gunshot wound to the right frontal lobe. The bullet skimmed a furrow across his forehead, but luckily it didn't lodge there. The gash is six centimeters deep, so it only grazed the surface of the brain. I used a probe android to remove all the bone fragments and synthbone to repair his skull. He's stable, but he'd probably get better treatment at a hospital dirtside."

Erik shook his head. "He wouldn't recover any faster in a hospital. It's best not to unhook him from life support to move him. What's his GCS?"

"I estimate a ten. He's breathing on his own, but he's been unresponsive since the shooting"—Jake glanced at the clock—"twelve hours ago."

"Ten is encouraging, Jake. What about edema?"

"I applied subcutaneous cold gel to the brain before I pieced his forehead back together."

"How long did you use the gel?" Erik asked.

"Two hours."

"Any seizures?"

"No."

Erik nodded. "You've done good work here. We won't be able to do any testing for cognitive function or memory loss until he regains consciousness, but I think Ting is going to make a full recovery."

"Don't you want to examine him before you make that prognosis?"

"I can't. I have so many injuries myself, I can't even stand up without assistance."

"Are you in pain?" Jake took the scanner back and passed it in front of Erik.

"I haven't stopped hurting since Acheron locked me up four weeks ago. At least, I think it's been four weeks. What's the date?"

Jake looked askance at him. "November twentieth."

Erik shook his head. "It felt much longer than a month."

Jake studied the scanner with a concerned frown. "I need to get you onto a table and fix that Achilles."

"I'm fine for now. You need to take care of Ting."

"Ting is stable; you're not." Jake seized the handles of Erik's wheelchair and steered him next door into the examination room. "Wait a moment. I'll get Blaze to help me lift you onto the table."

"I can manage," Erik said. "I'm not a child."

Jake placed a firm hand on Erik's uninjured shoulder, keeping him seated. "I'm the doctor on this ship, doctor, and I'll make the decisions regarding your health. You will not move that leg. I'll get Blaze to help me lift you onto the table. Is that clear?"

Erik sighed in defeat. "Better get Vipul too. I probably weigh more than the three of you combined."

Jake smirked. "Blaze to the infirmary."

***

"How bad is it? Be honest, Jake."

Erik heard the familiar hum of a medical scanner as it passed near his right ear. He felt a probing finger on his back. "Ouch!"

"Did that hurt?" Jake asked with feigned innocence.

"Do that again, and I'll *show* you how much it hurt."

"I'd better give you a painkiller before I continue the exam." Jake didn't wait for a response. He didn't give Erik any warning, either.

The doctor felt a stab of pain in his left buttock. "*Onw!* Your bedside manner could use some improvement!"

"We'll wait a few minutes for that to numb you."

"Would you mind turning up the heat while we wait?" Erik asked. "I usually have clothes on when I'm in an exam room."

"And you're usually standing over the table instead of lying facedown on it. It's your turn to be the patient." Jake spoke to the room's controls, "Raise air temperature five degrees."

Erik felt his goose bumps begin to settle down as warm air wafted over him. "I'd better warn you I'm not a very patient patient."

"I'm used to that. I had to sedate Captain Shepherd a lot to get her to stay still."

Sorensen started to grin, but his facial muscles protested. "She did mention you like needles." He winced at the pain in his backside. The injection site still stung.

"Did she mention she wants you to put her kidney back and smooth out the mess I made of her reconstruction?" Jake's tone was glib, but Erik could detect the insecurity in his words.

"She said you did a fine job with both surgeries. I haven't seen her side, but I'm sure it looks as good as new."

Jake sighed, unconvinced.

Erik made a mental note to take a look at Danae's side as soon as it was convenient. "How did you manage to get Ting aboard the ship after he was shot?"

"By moving faster than the CIPs who chased him and Phailin to the elevator. They almost escaped, except for the single bullet that nicked Ting. Phailin started first aid on the lift. Blaze, Vipul, and I raced to meet her on Level 12 with a gurney. Then we raced to a different lift and brought Ting up to Level 14 before the CIPs realized we were already back on the ship. It all happened fast, maybe five minutes from gunshot to infirmary."

"I'm impressed, but I think we've stalled long enough. What's my prognosis?"

"Your left kidney is only bruised. The cracked ribs have healed. You left rotator cuff I can fix right now, along with your torn Achilles. You're a lucky man. I

185

don't see any permanent damage on this side, although I might use up my supply of arnica on all these bruises."

"Skip the arnica. I can heal the old-fashioned way— with time."

"Sorry, but I'll decide the course of treatment. If I don't give you arnica, it'll be weeks before you can move without pain."

"Danae also mentioned you're as stubborn as a mule. I don't recall seeing this sunny side of your personality at the clinic, Jake."

"I definitely haven't seen this sunny side of you."

Erik tried to laugh, but it turned into a groan. "No jokes, please, my ribs can't handle it."

"You forget I'm Irish," Jake said. "Stubbornness is a genetic trait."

"I guess I was always too busy to notice." Erik closed his eyes with relief as the throbbing aches all over his body began to fade. "Just warn me before you jab me— *owwww!*"

"Did you want me to warn you, starting now?"

"Jake!" Erik was too exhausted to chide his apprentice any longer. He managed to fall asleep before Jake finished treating him.

***

Erik awoke to the bright lights of the ship's post-op room. It took him a moment to realize he was lying flat on his back and he wasn't in pain. He assumed Jake had treated his front side while he was unconscious. Erik lifted his head from the pillow and glanced down at himself. He was relieved to find a thermal blanket covering his bare body from chin to toes.

Of course Jake wouldn't leave me lying around in the buff.

His thoughts were interrupted by a cheerful, "Good morning!" Danae Shepherd breezed into the room from the corridor. "How are you feeling?" She grinned at his startled face.

The doctor smiled and was relieved to discover the gesture didn't hurt anymore. "Hello, Danae."

"No visitors. Too early for visitors." Jake stuck his head out of the surgery/ICU. "I'm going to have to ask you to leave, Captain."

Erik had to grin as captain and medic stared each other down from opposite sides of the room, hands on hips like dueling desperados. Danae gave Jake her infamous evil eye, and Jake responded with his mulish pout.

"No one throws the captain out of her own infirmary."

"I do," Jake said.

"You have your hands full with Ting, so I'll help you take care of Erik."

"Excuse me?" Jake's bravado faltered.

Erik echoed his concern. "Don't you have a ship to run, Danae?"

"Vipul and Blaze have everything under control." She broke off the staring contest with Jake and turned back to Erik with an apologetic smile. "We're set to lift in eight hours. Kirsten and Phailin managed to locate the thirty-three abandoned kids from Kirsten's list and should have them on board soon, along with a few boxes of your clothes and personal items. The ISPP captain wants me to come aboard his warship for a meeting at 1300. He wants to be sure he has all the information he needs from me for his investigation."

She shrugged, looking weary. "I've got two hours free, and it might be the only time I get a break for at least a week."

Erik caught the hint. Out of the corner of his eye, he saw that Jake was starting to get angry. Erik didn't like being stuck in the middle of this power struggle, but he knew he had to say something before Jake went ballistic.

"Like Jake said, I'm not much company right now." He noted Danae's disappointed look and tried to smooth things over with some diplomacy. "I'm so pumped full of painkillers, I can barely finish a sentence. If you want to visit, you'll have to do most of the talking. And please don't think you're boring me if I fall asleep."

Danae shot Jake a challenging look. "Fair enough. Don't you think so, Dr. O'Brien?"

Jake scowled and stepped back inside Ting's room without another word. The door slid shut behind him.

The captain drew a chair over to Erik's bedside and sat where he could see her face. He was glad she removed the brown contact lenses and that the black hair dye was starting to fade back to her natural brown color. It was a proud and attractive face looking back at his, but he knew there was a lot of pain beneath the calm surface.

"I want you to know how bad I feel about everything you've been through these past few weeks," Danae said.

"It was my choice to stay on the station. I knew Acheron would arrest me. It's not your fault, so stop feeling guilty."

"But I feel responsible—"

"I'm not a member of your crew," Erik spoke over her. "Not yet anyway. You don't have to fix everything that's wrong with the universe." He noted her troubled frown and whispered, "I'm grateful you came back for me, but I would've understood if you didn't come back."

Danae managed a half smile. "You said you wanted to see me again."

"But you were right not to give me an answer." Erik stared up at the ceiling. "You need more time"—he struggled to find the right words —"to recover from your loss . . . losses."

Danae's smile faded. "I just need a friend right now. Didn't you tell me once that you were my friend?"

He turned his head so he could look her in the eye again. "I have to be honest with you. I want to be more than a friend." Her eyes widened, and she tried to speak over him, but he pressed on before he lost his nerve. "But you've been through so much these past few months, and I don't want to do anything to add to your pain. You understand?"

"Erik—"

"Please let me finish."

She stiffened and set her lips in a thin line, her piercing blue eyes locked onto his as she gave him a nod to continue.

"We've been through a lot together, so it's natural to feel an attraction. But I think if we act on these feelings, we might regret it."

"Is that all?" Danae whispered, her tone turning arctic. "Are you finished?"

Erik nodded, cowed by the fierce expression on her face.

"Now it's my turn. Are you a doctor?"

He hesitated, confused by the question. "Yes."

"So you understand how complex the human body is, how difficult it is to put back together sometimes?" She ran her hand down her left side for emphasis.

Erik nodded again, afraid to interrupt her.

"Yet you think human emotions are *simple*?"

"No, of course not."

"So why would you assume that someone who's experienced so much emotional pain is too fragile or too scared to handle more? You've heard the expression what doesn't kill us makes us stronger?"

Erik simply nodded.

Danae stood and leaned over him so she could look straight into his eyes. "Are *you* the one who's scared?"

Terrified, Erik thought, though he would never admit it. "No. . . I just meant . . . maybe what I should have said is . . . we shouldn't rush things."

Danae smiled. "Well, that's different. Let's not talk about fear, Erik. Let's talk about healing. Isn't that what doctors do best?"

He laughed gently, mindful of his sore ribs. "Truce. You've already worn me out, Danae."

Her features clouded with disappointment. "Then maybe I should go."

"No, don't go. Please stay and talk to me. I've been alone for weeks. I need to hear another human voice. Tell to me about yourself, about your life."

"As long as you promise to tell me your life story as soon as you're up and around," she said.

"Promise." Erik was already beginning to feel drowsy but tried to resist it. He wanted to savor this time with Danae all to himself.

"Well, you already know I was born on Mars Station and lived with my mom, who was an alcoholic . . ." She talked for an hour, hitting the major highlights of her life, including her marriage to Alex Shepherd. "I had a few flings with some of the passengers, but I was never really serious about anyone until my dad hired Alex . . ."

Erik heard about Danae's confrontations with Rosamar Delacruz, the woman who almost became her stepmother. *Now I understand the nervous looks from the attorney.*

He was listening to her account of the night she buried her husband on Maui when he gave in to the exhaustion and fell asleep.

He dreamt of Danae's smiling face. She was standing at his bedside, looking down on him. Then she began to shrink right before his eyes, growing smaller and smaller until she was the size of a child's doll. The doll-size Danae laughed in a little-girl voice and began shrinking again until she disappeared.

Erik startled awake, looking around the empty post-op room. He had an eerie sensation that someone had been standing at his bedside. *That's crazy,* he thought. *It was just a dream.*

When his heart stopped pounding, he shut his eyes and fell back to sleep.

***

"Strap down for liftoff in fifteen." Vipul's voice over the com awoke Erik. He had no idea how long he'd been asleep.

Jake emerged from the surgical room and placed the bed's padded restraints over Erik's knees and shoulders without saying a word. Erik thought the medic-in-training seemed tense.

"Something wrong, Jake?"

Jake pulled a scanner out of the breast pocket of his purple scrubs. "It's nothing. I just don't like flying."

Erik thought there was more to Jake's sullen mood than pending turbulence but didn't press him for an explanation. "How am I healing?"

"Good." Jake's attitude seemed to soften, and he held the scanner so Erik could read the results. "You should be able to get up in about eight hours."

Erik nodded. "Good, because I'm starved."

"You're not ready for Phailin's kimchi yet. I want you on bland foods until you're off the painkillers."

"I taught you well." Erik realized he forgot something important. "I didn't say goodbye to Kirsten."

Jake shrugged. "You were out cold when she came to say goodbye. She told me to tell you, 'Have enough fun on Maui for both of us.'" He moved out of Erik's line of vision. "I'm going to strap down on the bed across from you. Let me know if you feel any pain."

"Thanks, Jake." Erik shut his eyes. He felt some gentle movement as *Alex's Legacy* taxied away from the dock. It had been years since he traveled aboard a starship. Like Jake, he wasn't a fan of flying. "Hey, do you think I could get a Banspace patch before you get comfortable?"

Jake laughed. "I just put one on. You're in luck. I happen   to   have   a   new   supply."

PART II
EXPANDING

TWELVE
ARSENAL

CADE YORK SIFTED through the pile of datapads on his desk. This was the part of the job he loathed—the legal headaches. Usually he was handed a single holo-vid of witness interviews or an old CIP file with some vague information to decipher, but this case was buried in an avalanche of evidence. There were enough witness interviews to send Hunter Acheron to prison forever.

Too bad the snake has to have a fair trial first.

Fortunately, someone had already saved Cade the trouble of gathering a case against Acheron's business partner-in-crime, Thanatos. He still couldn't believe the captain of a small passenger ship shot Thanatos dead, in self-defense, with an antique Glock. He was looking forward to meeting Danae Shepherd in person to thank her for ridding the universe of the slaver.

Cade glanced at the time: 1245. He stood, stretched, and took a moment to check that his olive-green uniform was spotless.

Though ISPP was a privately funded military organization with a generous budget, its resources were insufficient to cover the eleven biosphere stations, Earth, and all the space in between. Cade needed at least fifteen more ships to police the galaxy, but he did the best he could with the five warships he'd been assigned to lead.

ISPP had been called upon many times to infiltrate corrupt businesses or governments to remove the leaders and restore order. Removing the leaders could involve abductions or assassinations, but only if lives were at stake. ISPP was, after all, a peacekeeping organization. Peaceful solutions were always Plan A. Arresting culprits or neutralizing threats was the preferred mode, although they were prepared to take extreme measures if necessary.

For the three years since his son Lincoln disappeared from Venus Station, the *Liberty*'s crew had been on a single mission: to shut down the galaxy's child slave trade. The Acheron-Thanatos slave network was ISPP's first real breakthrough in a long succession of rumors and false leads. Cade was eager to let someone else handle the case against Acheron so he could search the information in Thanatos's log for a clue to Linc's disappearance. His senior engineer was already working with several translation programs, trying to break the encrypted code on the slaver's datapad.

While he waited for the log translation, Cade spent every waking moment working on the case. Bringing Acheron to trial was ISPP's responsibility, as was investigating the entire Central Intelligence Police department on Mars Station. Most of Cade's crew was already dirtside, interviewing hundreds of CIPs and compiling evidence. He knew it would take time, but he was impatient to get back to the star lanes to continue the search for Linc.

The com made a soft crackling sound, interrupting his thoughts. "Captain?" Cade's first officer from New

Kabul had a firm, authoritative tone which always got his attention, even when he was sound asleep.

"Go ahead, Rashid."

"Captain Danae Shepherd is here for your scheduled briefing."

"Please escort her to my office."

"Yes, sir."

A few minutes later, Nazira Rashid strode through the open doorway to his office adjoining the bridge, one pace ahead of a slender woman who appeared to be in her mid-thirties. Rashid stepped aside and gestured for the woman to approach Cade's desk. "Captain York—Captain Shepherd," Rashid announced and stepped out of the room. The door slid shut after her.

Cade stood, making an effort not to gawk at Shepherd's colorful tropical-print shirt and tight blue jeans. Only her synthleather traction boots identified her as a civilian spacer. From the knees up, she could've passed as a surfer. Shepherd had short, wavy black hair, streaked with brown, especially near her scalp, and she was tan. Only her prominent blue eyes indicated she was Caucasian, and they seemed out of place with the rest of her altered appearance.

There was also a half-healed cut on the left side of Shepherd's mouth. *Acheron's handiwork,* Cade thought. *I wish I could have five minutes alone in a dark alley with that filth.*

Shepherd faced him across the desk. She sized him up with a piercing look which made him feel as if he was intruding on *her* ship. He realized she was waiting to be invited to sit and stuck out his right hand to cover the awkward pause.

"Captain Shepherd, thank you for taking time to meet with me."

Shepherd reached across the space between them and shook his hand. She had a powerful grip for such a small woman. "I'm pleased to meet you, Captain York."

"Won't you have a seat?" Cade indicated a chair in front of his desk.

"Thank you." She sat just on the edge of the chair, and Cade surmised she was nervous, despite her calm appearance.

Cade noticed for the first time the words *Alex's Legacy* embroidered in white over the right breast pocket of her orange, red, and pink flowered shirt. Though he preferred to get straight to the point at meetings—Cade hated meetings—he thought a few minutes of small talk might help Shepherd feel more at ease.

"I don't believe I've ever seen a ship's uniform like yours." Cade made an effort to sound jovial, which wasn't his nature.

"My ship is based out of Maui, Captain York." Shepherd's reply was guarded. She looked him in the eye, as if daring him to criticize her uniform as unprofessional.

"You're Hawaiian?"

"No, I'm Martian." Her gaze was unchanged. She was giving nothing away. This was going to be a challenging interview.

"I understand that when your ship was here last month, it was called the *Ishmael*, and it had a Mars Station passenger registry."

"That's correct."

Cade paused, hoping she would offer some more information. When she didn't, he felt the familiar stirring of impatience. "You're not on trial here, Captain Shepherd. You and your crew have been cleared of all charges. You're free to return to your ship as soon as you brief me about your involvement in this case."

"You have my written report." She glanced at the stack of datapads at his elbow. "I assume you've read it?"

"Yes, but I want to hear it from you, to make sure there's no detail that might have been overlooked."

"Are you implying I deliberately left information out of my report, Captain?" She put some ice on the last word.

"No, of course not." Cade felt his temper rising. *Why is she so reluctant to talk?* He glanced at his favorite hologram on the desk of Yong Min cuddling a smiling, three-year-old Linc. *Calm down, York. This is too important. Don't lose your temper.*

An awkward silence fell between them. Cade studied her expression, and she seemed to be scrutinizing his right back. He decided to try a more personal approach. "Won't you tell me a little about yourself, Captain Shepherd? Are you married?"

She flinched and broke eye contact. He had inadvertently struck a nerve.

Cade shifted to damage control. "I didn't mean to—"

"I'm recently widowed, Captain York," Shepherd spoke over him, her calm restored in an instant, her eyes once again locked onto his. She gestured at the name of her ship on her shirt. "Alex was my husband." She hesitated a moment before adding, "Ishmael was my father."

Cade nodded and turned the hologram on his desk so Shepherd could see it. "We have something unfortunate in common. I lost my wife three years ago."

Her eyes shifted to the hologram and back to him. "You have a son?"

"Yes, Lincoln was abducted by slavers the night my wife was murdered. I had a newborn daughter too, but she was abducted the same time as Linc, probably by black market adoptions."

Shepherd's large eyes grew larger. Cade could almost envision the wall between them coming down as she sat back in the chair, her gaze softening.

"I think I owe you an apology, Captain York, and an explanation."

Cade nodded. "ISPP makes most people nervous at first, but I can assure you we aren't CIPs. We're diplomats."

"Diplomats with guns?" She smiled for the first time.

Cade thought the smile transformed her entire appearance. He was seeing Danae Shepherd through new eyes, and he liked what he saw.

It took some mental effort for Cade to drag his attention back to the conversation. "'Peace through strength'," he quoted the ISPP motto. "You know, 'Speak softly but carry a big stick'?"

Shepherd nodded. "President Theodore Roosevelt. But I do owe you an explanation for my defensiveness."

Cade nodded for her to continue.

"When you stood to greet me and I saw how tall you are," Shepherd paused and shifted her gaze a fraction so she was looking over his left shoulder, "with your dark complexion and your solid build, I realized you look a lot like my husband. Your faces are different, of course, and your personalities," she added before Cade could get a word in. "Alex was an optimist and had quite a sense of humor, and you seem to be more . . . serious, but from a distance, you could be brothers. It just caught me off guard."

Well, she sure didn't seem startled to me. Maybe I should ask her some tips on keeping a straight face. Cade wasn't sure how to respond because he couldn't tell if he was being flattered or criticized. He nodded, tried to appear sympathetic, and changed the subject.

"Please start from the beginning, Captain Shepherd. When did you first suspect Acheron was abducting homeless children?"

"I'll tell you the whole story if you'll call me Danae."

He nodded. "You're right. Let's drop the titles. Call me Cade."

"This is how I stumbled upon this mess with Acheron . . ."

Danae Shepherd spent the next half hour relating the most amazing story of courage and self-sacrifice Cade had ever heard from a civilian. He read her report—skimmed it, really—but hearing it firsthand was an eye-opener.

In her quest to replace her four dead crewmembers, including her husband, Danae had run across Acheron and Thanatos, who were plotting something together. She was able to uncover their secret with the confession of her newly hired navigator, who'd worked for Thanatos. Danae and her crew formulated a plan to rescue the children who were at risk of being abducted. She discovered allies on the station with the same goal and, with their assistance, smuggled one hundred and forty-eight homeless children aboard the *Ishmael* before Acheron's minions could get to them. In the escape, she shot Acheron, killed Thanatos, and was seriously wounded herself, along with the navigator she was protecting from Thanatos. This had all taken place in less than twenty-four hours.

She took her plan a step further by taking the children to Earth. "We were out of fuel, and I barely pulled off a glided landing on Maui. The solar engines were torched, and I almost lost my engineer in the fire."

Cade's jaw dropped. "You successfully performed a glided landing?" At her nod, he shut his mouth and urged her to continue.

Danae's estranged mother left her a sugarcane plantation, and the captain wasted no time turning the large house on the property into an orphanage. She hired a social worker who set to work finding adoptive homes for the kids. Once the solar engines were replaced, she changed the ship's registry, disguised herself and her crew, and returned to Mars Station to rescue her allies Erik and Kirsten Sorensen. The risk of being arrested by Acheron was high, but that didn't deter Danae.

"How did the rescue attempt work out?" Cade knew the answer from her report, but he was enjoying her account of the adventure.

"Not so well." Danae shook her head. "I'd make a terrible private investigator. Acheron caught me right away. He and Monsantos caught my navigator aboard the *Elmina*, but my engineer managed to escape detection and find Thanatos's log. My helmsman was shot by one of the CIPs with Monsantos, after he and my cook slipped a copy of Thanatos's log to Rosamar Delacruz. If it wasn't for the councilwoman's brave assistance, we would all still be in jail and Acheron would probably be planning his next harvest of homeless children."

She folded her hands in her lap. "So that's it. Any questions?"

"How's your helmsman?" Cade asked.

"He's in a coma, but my senior medic believes he'll recover."

"Let's hope so."

Danae nodded, but made no further comment. She waited, no doubt expecting more questions, but Cade couldn't think of any. He thought for a moment, trying to decide how to express his gratitude for her assistance without embarrassing her.

"It's courageous people like you who make my job easier. I wish there were a dozen like you on every station."

She didn't seem embarrassed at all. "Thank you, but I think you should know I was highly motivated to take action."

Cade raised his eyebrows at her. "What motivated you?"

"My crewmember Shima." Danae paused, thinking. "She's more than crew. She's like a sister to me. She has a niece who was abducted from the station seven years ago." She frowned. "And Acheron threatened me. He said he'd arrest my helmsman and impound and destroy my ship."

Cade nodded. "It sounds like he threatened the wrong person."

Danae's frown settled into a defiant scowl. "Yes, he did."

"Have you been able to determine from Thanatos's log where your crewmember's niece was taken?"

"Not from the legible text, but my engineer is running the encrypted code through a hacking program right now. I'm sure he'll have the answer soon."

Cade nodded. "I'm planning to search it myself as soon as my engineer breaks the code."

"You're hoping to find a clue to where your son was taken?"

"I know it's a long-shot because he was abducted from Venus Station, and I know there are other slavers out there, but if Thanatos was the one who took him . . "

"Then you'll find him," Danae finished with a nod of encouragement. "I'll contact you the moment Blaze breaks the code—if you'll do me the same courtesy if your engineer breaks it first."

"Of course." Cade made up his mind. He was impressed with Danae Shepherd, and it took a lot to impress him. "You know, there'll be many child slaves wherever she's being held. You'll need ISPP's help."

"Maybe, but I have a gut feeling we need to find her soon, or the opportunity will be lost forever. Seven years is a long time to go missing, and she may have been moved several times by now. If we locate Zuri"—Danae shot him a challenging look—"I won't wait around for backup."

Cade frowned. "That could be dangerous." He was careful to omit what he really wanted to say. *That might be suicide.* "What are you planning to do if her captors are armed?"

Danae shook her head. "I'm not sure yet, but there's a lot of talent and ingenuity among my crew. We'll think of something." She rose to her feet before Cade could come up with a good reason why she shouldn't embark on this rescue mission alone. "Now, if you'll excuse me, I need to return to my ship."

Cade stood too, disappointed the briefing was over. "When do you lift?"

"In five hours."

"That soon?"

"It's urgent we return to Maui as soon as possible." She hesitated a moment before offering more explanation. "There was a tragic accident at the orphanage. It affects several members of my crew."

"I understand." Cade extended his hand for her to shake, but then held on to hers a few moments longer than necessary. "I normally don't approve of armed civilians, but it's obvious you know how to handle a gun. I think it would be wise to teach your crew to shoot before you go charging into the unknown on a rescue mission."

Danae extricated her hand from his with a puzzled frown. "You're saying I should teach them all to use my gun?"

"No, I'm saying each member of your crew should carry a handgun and know how to use it."

She frowned. "I can barely afford ammunition for my Glock since I have to special order it from a museum in Wyoming."

Cade nodded. "I thought you might say that, which is why I'm loaning you some pistols from the *Liberty*'s arsenal."

"You are?" Danae stared at him as if he lost his mind.

Maybe I have lost it, Cade thought. But he went with his instincts, nevertheless. "How many are on your crew?"

"Normally eight, including myself." She frowned for a moment, and Cade was reminded she was short one helmsman.

"Com." The shipboard communicator crackled to life. "Moniesa?"

"Yes, Captain?" A prompt reply came from Cade's senior weapons officer, Wisdom Moniesa.

"Meet me in the arsenal in five." He glanced at the half-curious, half-suspicious look on Danae's face, but didn't offer her an explanation.

"I am already in the arsenal, Captain." He wasn't surprised to hear this.

"Please have eight Excalibur G30 pistols ready."

Moniesa never questioned why. Cade appreciated that about her. "Yes, Captain. How much ammunition?"

"At least two cases."

"Yes, Captain."

Cade turned his attention back to Danae. "Right this way."

Danae followed him across the unoccupied bridge to the central lift in the corridor. Once they began the rapid descent to Level 6, she asked, "Are you sure about this?"

"Not completely," he said. "But I think courage and determination deserves a fighting chance. Anywhere ISPP docks, we never know if the local CIPs will be cooperative or hostile. Too often they ignore crime, or they're bribed to ignore it. Mars Station is a prime example of CIP corruption. I feel confident you'll put these weapons to good use if the CIPs are turning a blind eye to child slavery."

She nodded but didn't reply.

The ship's arsenal was located in the center of the ship, far from the engines, which could potentially be targeted in a ship-to-ship battle, and far from the airlocks, which could potentially be infiltrated, although anyone who tried to breach a warship would be crazy or suicidal.

Cade escorted Danae down a short hallway on Level 6. They stopped in front of an unlabeled door, and he pressed his thumb to the ID lock. The extra-thick door slid aside. "One visitor, captain's authorization," he spoke to the security barricade and stepped aside so Danae could enter the room ahead of him. The door slid shut behind them, and the locks engaged.

Captain York gave her a moment to look around the four-by-four-meter room. There were a dozen meter-high cabinets which spanned the length of the room, bolted to the floor in three parallel rows. Synthvelvet counters covered the tops of the cabinets, like long red tables. The cabinets contained every state-of-the-art firearm Earth produced. Mounted behind indestructible glass on every wall were several types of rifles, swords, and bows, plus a few illegal devices like long-handled nerve prods and molecular disruption grenades. ISPP took *peace through strength* seriously.

Moniesa was standing at the back row, facing them. Eight tiny black pistols were lined up on the countertop in front of her. She glanced at Danae without even raising an eyebrow. "G30s are ready, Captain."

Cade's weapons officer had a lilting Nigerian accent most people found charming when they spoke to her on the com. But in person, Wisdom Moniesa would never pass for charming. Two meters tall, ink-black skin, shaved head covered with wild, colorful tattoos, and built like a small tank, Moniesa was a deadly weapon, even when she was unarmed. Cade had learned his lesson about challenging her to sparring practice after she dislocated *both* of his shoulders during a single session.

"Would you please demonstrate for Captain Shepherd how to assemble, load, and fire one of the Excaliburs?"

"Of course, Captain."

Cade leaned down and rested his elbows on the first countertop, watching with interest as Danae threaded her way between the rows of cabinets to Moniesa's. The two women faced each other across the counter. Captain Shepherd had to look way up to see the other's face.

Moniesa placed one of the pistols in Danae's right hand and let her take a moment to examine it. The barrel of the tiny weapon was ten centimeters in length, the grip was seven centimeters long, and the entire pistol, loaded, weighed only five hundred grams.

"This looks a lot like my Glock." Danae glanced back over her shoulder at Cade. "Only smaller and more lethal."

York nodded. He had chosen the compact Excaliburs because they were easy to use and easy to conceal.

Moniesa picked up another G30, removed the magazine, replaced it, released the lock, locked it again, and adjusted Danae's hand on the grip of her own weapon. "You can set the trigger for single shots or rapid-fire." She pointed out a tiny switch, just behind the safety. "But remember if you use the rapid-fire setting, it will unload the entire magazine in point three seconds."

Danae uttered an approving "huh" and with quick hands, disassembled and reassembled the weapon to Moniesa's satisfaction.

The weapons officer withdrew a small gun case from another cabinet, set it on the counter between them, and began arranging the Excalibur on the padding inside. "I am including a left-handed pistol, if needed, and two cases of ammo." She reached into a different cabinet and added two brick-size boxes to the case. "One with blanks, for practice. One with titanium five millimeter bullets, for shooting bad guys."

Danae corrected her. "For self-defense, and only if needed."

Moniesa smiled. "If you say so, Captain." She closed the gun case and turned it around so the ID lock was facing Danae. "Press your thumb here. You will be the only one authorized to open it."

Once secured with her DNA imprint, Danae Shepherd lifted the heavy case and turned back to face Cade with a half grin. "This is just a loan, right?"

"Yes, and I recommend you have your crew practice with targets as soon as you're back on Maui."

"I have one medic who doesn't even like guns." Her half grin vanished. "If Ting had one of these a few hours ago, he probably wouldn't be in a coma now."

Cade just nodded, unsure of what to say.

Danae made her way back to the door and looked up into Cade's face with a genuine smile. "I'm grateful for your assistance. This will make our mission much easier."

He waited for the door to slide open before replying. "Taking out Thanatos made my job easier, so I'd say we're even." He nodded to Moniesa, who was already unlocking one of the glass wall cases and taking down a meter-long Excalibur battle rifle. The weapons officer could be counted on to have every gun clean, loaded, and ready to be used at a moment's notice.

Cade escorted Danae to the lift and rode down with her to the entryway on Level 1. He thought about offering to hold the gun case for her but didn't want to offend her. Danae Shepherd seemed quite capable of handling the box's weight. *She seems capable of handling anything,* he thought.

He cycled open the *Liberty*'s airlock doors before turning to face her, reluctant to say goodbye. "Hopefully one of our engineers can break the encryption code soon so we'll have some answers. Please contact me if you locate the niece. If you can wait, it would be safer for ISPP to handle the rescue. I have four other ships that report to me, and there's a chance one would be close enough to assist you. We have the training and experience to go into dangerous situations."

Danae nodded without comment.

There was another awkward silence as the two captains scrutinized each other. Cade had already made up his mind that Danae could be trusted, but she didn't seem sold on the alliance.

Not even with the pistols as a good-faith gesture? This thought both intrigued and annoyed him. *Maybe I do remind her too much of her dead husband.*

"Good luck, Captain Shepherd," he said, more brusquely than he intended.

"I'll let you know if, and when, we locate Zuri," Danae spoke at last, her calm expression locked in place. "And we'll wait for ISPP's assistance, if we can. Goodbye, Captain York. I hope you find your son."

Before Cade could thank her for the words, she stepped through the antechamber, into the spaceport access corridor, and walked away.

Captain York sighed to himself as he cycled the doors closed. One of the bleak realities of working in space was that it was rare to meet anyone again on a different station, particularly those who lived and worked on starships, like Danae Shepherd.

***

Cade yawned, his vision growing fuzzy. He had been awake for at least forty-five hours. He wondered if he should get some sleep or put on a stim-patch.

The stim-patch won. He was determined to finish reading the last tedious report on his desk so he could work on something much more important: searching Thanatos's log for a clue to Linc's abduction. His senior engineer had assured him she was close to breaking the code, and Cade wanted to focus on the log the moment it was translated.

Lincoln would be eight years old next month. Cade tried not to think about the three years he missed of his son's short life. He missed his daughter too but was at peace with the thought that Lia was being raised by adoptive parents. They were probably decent people who had no idea she had been abducted—at least, he liked to think so. Even if by some miracle he found Lia someday, he realized it would be traumatizing to take her away from the only parents she had ever known, so Cade had let go of her, in his mind, and focused his energies on finding Linc.

Impatience gnawed at him. He shoved aside the report and took Thanatos's original log out of a desk drawer. The weathered datapad contained hundreds of pages of Thanatos's records. Cade had only been able to scroll through the unencrypted pages during the rare moments he was able to take a break from ISPP work. These legible pages contained detailed descriptions of Acheron's illegal activities, including the organized mass abductions of homeless children, but nothing specific about where the kids were taken.

Cade suspected Thanatos wrote these legible pages to incriminate Acheron if they were ever caught. *He was trying to save his own skin. No loyalty among thieves—or slavers.*

The com crackled. He grimaced at another interruption. He was tempted to ignore it, but the weight of responsibility weighed heavily on his mind. He still had a job to do.

"Captain York?" It was his first officer.

"Yes, go ahead. What's up?"

"What's up?" Rashid echoed. "Have you been drinking, Captain?"

Cade was too tired to reprimand her for the comment. "I can assure you I'm completely sober. Anything new to report?"

"Yes, Captain. Councilwoman Delacruz would like to meet with you at 0700. She and your father-in-law have compiled a new collection of witness interviews."

"Did you say 0700?" Cade stole a glance at the time. It was 2328. He reached behind his left ear and peeled off the stim-patch.

"Yes, Captain."

"Sounds like a long day ahead. I think I'll get some sleep."

"Yes, Captain, I think that would be wise." Cade could detect mirth in her tone. "Goodnight."

***

Cade was up early, his mind too busy to let him sleep past 0630. He brushed his teeth as he again scrolled through the legible entries in Thanatos's log.

He rinsed his mouth and didn't take his eyes off the datapad as he left his cabin and wandered down the corridor to the bridge.

"Good morning, Captain." Cade's senior helm officer Heath Bergen glanced up from his station where he was running scans on the ship's systems. Most of the crew was still dirtside, at CIP headquarters.

Cade glanced up for a split second, said, "'Morning, Bergen," and gave the datapad his full attention as he sank into the captain's chair.

"Any new orders, sir?" Bergen asked.

"I have a meeting on the station at 0700."

"Orders for me, sir?"

Cade forced himself to look up and focus on what Bergen was asking. "Yes, I want the ship prepped to lift the moment we wrap up this case."

"Yes, sir." Bergen turned back to the helm.

He scrolled to the next page, but the helm officer interrupted his search again after only a few minutes. "Captain York, shouldn't you be leaving now?"

"Thank you." Cade marked his place and slid the datapad into a cargo pocket on his uniform.

"You may want to let them know you'll be a few minutes late," Bergen suggested with his usual tact.

"Thank you, but I won't be late," Cade said over his shoulder. He had already reached the *Liberty*'s central lift.

Exiting the spaceport elevator dirtside, the captain unlocked his solar cycle parked at the curb. He strapped on his helmet, threw a leg over the seat, kicked the engine to life, and made fast time across the city.

Although he tried to keep his eyes on the road, Cade sometimes glanced over at the sidewalks. Everywhere he looked, he saw people sleeping on tramstop benches and children sitting on doorsteps, begging for food from any pedestrians up this early. York had witnessed some bleak conditions in post-war sites on Earth, but he'd never seen so many homeless in one city. He felt a little guilty he hadn't known how bad conditions were on Mars Station.

Wei should have mentioned something, but I guess he didn't want to divert my attention from the hunt for Linc. He felt a pang of sympathy for a young mother huddled with her three tiny children in the doorway of an abandoned shop. *It will take a long time to get people back on their feet. This station should have been purged of Acheron and his thugs years ago.*

Cade was distracted for a moment too long and had to swerve hard to avoid a vendor who was pushing her cart of scrap fabrics across Teacher Street. The woman yelled something at him, but the roar of the engine drowned out her curses.

"Sorry!" He shouted to her over his shoulder, even though he knew she couldn't hear him. He acknowledged her fist-shaking with a conciliatory backward wave but didn't slow down.

Cade arrived at city hall only five minutes late. He locked his cycle and reached Delacruz's office a scant minute later. Sometimes impatience had its advantages. He could have been a cycle racer on any Earth track.

There was no one at the assistant's desk outside the Councilwoman's office, so he knocked on the inner door.

"Come in, Captain York."

Another remarkable woman, he thought as he walked into the office. Delacruz had proven herself to be a courageous and clever old lady. "Councilwoman?"

"Have a seat." Delacruz pushed two teetering stacks of datapads to the far sides of her desk so she could see him from her chair. "How's the case coming along?"

"I'd prefer to wrap it up as soon as possible and lift out of here. We have slavers to track down and sifting through all this," he gestured to the piles on her desk, "is a waste of time."

Delacruz raised an eyebrow at Cade's frankness, but didn't disagree. "I'd be glad take over the case if I weren't so busy trying to clean up Acheron's legal messes all over the station."

Cade realized hed been rude and tried to interject some diplomacy into the conversation. "I appreciate the hard work you're doing, Councilwoman. I meant no disrespect."

She scoffed. "I'm sure you didn't."

It took some effort for Cade to suppress a chuckle. He admired Delacruz's spirit.

"Good morning, Rosamar, Cade." Judge Wei Forsetti stuck his head in the doorway of the office.

"Come on in, Wei." Delacruz waved him over. She shot Cade a mischievous look. "The captain was just telling me he'd like to make this a short meeting."

York stood and shook hands with his father-in-law. The judge and Moniesa were the only people Cade knew who were tall enough to look him in the eye. "How are you, Wei?"

When Yong Min was alive, Cade called the judge Dad, but they weren't close anymore. Yong Min's death had left a gulf between them. Cade still respected him and was grateful to have his assistance in the hunt for Linc, but Wei was no longer someone he confided in.

"I'm doing great." Wei's smile was evidence of his optimism. "We finally have a lead to Linc."

"I think we're close." Cade pulled Thanatos's log out of his pocket and resumed his seat. "I'm waiting for my engineer to break the encrypted code on this. As soon as she does, I plan to spend every waking moment reading the translation." He glanced over at a frowning Delacruz. "Figuring out where Thanatos shipped these children is more important than compiling mountains of interviews and reports."

Wei handed him yet another datapad and pulled up a chair. "I understand your concern, Cade, and I agree there's too much evidence. It could take months to sort this out."

"I don't have *months*." Cade glared at the new datapad and stuffed Thanatos's log back into his pocket for safekeeping. "Let's stop right now and give Acheron a trial. There's more than enough evidence to convict him."

Delacruz blew out a long breath. "I wish it were that simple, Captain, but we must have due process."

Cade bit back a sharp retort about due process. *Sarcasm isn't going to solve anything.* He had an idea. "Would you consider allowing my first officer to take over for me?"

Before they could both say no—and he could see it in their faces—he added, "Rashid's a paralegal." She also held degrees in education and chemistry, but Cade tried not to mention her brilliant mind outside the ship. He didn't want anyone hiring away his most talented crewmember.

Delacruz pursed her lips. "Captain York, interstellar law is clear in this matter. Internal problems on any station have to be tried by an impartial third party based outside the station."

Cade blinked. That was his answer. "I'm not impartial, Councilwoman. I should dismiss myself from the case."

This time Delacruz blinked. "You're right." She glanced at Wei. "Conflict of interest. We have to turn this over to someone else."

Yes! Cade thought, trying to keep a straight face. "If anyone can sort this out fast, it's Rashid."

Wei gave a reluctant nod. "We should have realized this earlier. Please bring Officer Rashid up to date on everything you've compiled so far."

"I will." *Nazira's going to be furious when I spring this on her.* "If she agrees to take over, I'll leave her with you until the investigation is complete."

"What do you mean, Captain?" Delacruz narrowed her eyes at him.

"I mean she'll live here on the station and work with you on the case while the *Liberty* continues the search for Lincoln—and other children who've been enslaved."

Wei frowned. "It would be great if you could leave as soon as possible to search for Linc, but you know ISPP is expected to be on hand until a verdict is reached."

Cade shook his head. "Once ISPP completes the gathering of evidence, you won't need us anymore. You just need an impartial judge, and Rashid is quite capable of handling Acheron's trial."

Forsetti and Delacruz exchanged a pained look and then turned to stare at Cade for a few moments. He gave them what he hoped was a reassuring smile, although he suspected it was more like a snarl, and wondered how fast he could get his ship off the station.

"Very well," Delacruz said. "Please have Officer Rashid meet with me as soon as possible."

"Is this afternoon soon enough?" Cade got to his feet. "I need to get back to the *Liberty* and record some transmissions for the other ISPP captains. We have children to rescue, and we'll know where they are as soon as the log is translated. Thank you both for your help."

"Happy star trails," Wei said.

Cade just nodded and was out the door without another word.

***

To say Nazira Rashid was upset to hear her new assignment would be an understatement, but she didn't get angry, to Cade's relief. His first officer had a temper to rival his own.

Cade recalled the time when a new junior officer leered at Rashid a few times too many. She invited him to sparring practice, and when she was through with him, he had a nose that resembled a potato. He was reassigned to a different ISPP ship for his own safety.

"*What?*" Rashid's voice went up an octave. "You want me to take over the investigation? You want to *leave* me here, Captain?"

"I promise we'll be back for you in a few months."

"*A few months!*" She pressed her hands to the sides of her head, her full lips twisting into a grimace. Cade wondered for a moment if she was going to tear her headscarf or punch him, or both. Instead, she said something which almost made him laugh.

"What have I done to deserve this, Captain?"

"This isn't punishment." Cade tried to appeal to her logic. "You're the only one on the crew who's capable of filling this assignment. You know more about the law than I do. You're organized, smart, and can work independently. Consider this a promotion—"

"A *promotion?* It feels like I'm being *sacked!*" Rashid began pacing the floor of Cade's office.

He watched her pace, allowing her time to work through the shock. After a few minutes she stopped and turned to face him with a less panicked expression.

"When do you lift?"

Cade breathed an internal sigh of relief. She already accepted the assignment. He knew he could count on her. "We'll lift as soon as Delacruz thinks we've collected all the evidence." He frowned. "Actually, I want to lift as soon as Thanatos's log is translated. I'll probably get reprimanded, but there's so much to compile, we could be stuck here a long time."

"So you're giving all the headaches to me?"

He shrugged. "Yes, I guess that's what I meant."

Rashid nodded. She was still frowning but much calmer. "Where will I stay dirtside?"

"You can choose a hotel or the Councilwoman's guest room."

She sighed. "I guess I'll stay with Delacruz if it means we can get the case finished quicker."

Cade smiled. "I'll let her know you're on your way." He glanced over at the pile of datapads on his desk. "Download all of that onto a mainframe and take it with you."

"Yes, Captain."

"Good luck, and keep me advised on your progress."

"Yes, Captain." Rashid left his office.

Moments later, Cade heard, "Captain York?" It was his senior engineer, Annalise Tse, on the com.

"Yes?" He held his breath, hoping it was good news.

"I've broken the encrypted code, Captain."

"Good work, Tse! How soon can you send me the translated text?"

"Ten minutes."

"Good! Do it."

"Yes, Captain."

"Com officer?"

"Yes, sir?" One of his junior officers, Roland Diaz, responded.

"I need to speak to *Alex's Legacy* on ship-to-ship com."

There was a pause, and Diaz said, "That ship is out of com range."

Cade had expected this. "Understood. Tse?"

"Yes, Captain?"

"Send a copy of the translated text to the com. Diaz, send the file in a transmission to Captain Danae Shepherd of the *Alex*."

"Yes, Captain," both said.

York attempted to lounge back in his chair, but he couldn't relax. His heart was pounding with anticipation. The monitor on his desk soon made a chirping sound, and he opened the file. He scrolled through the pages, stopping only when he found what he was looking for. There was a section organized into chart form.

Date of harvest . . . Spaceport . . . Number of livestock . . . City or port of delivery . . . Price paid for each animal.

The only animal was you, Thanatos. Cade couldn't think of a word bad enough to describe the slaver. He typed *Venus Station* into the search box. Dozens of entries filled the screen.

So the demon did do business on Venus!

It took only two minutes for Cade to find the entry he was looking for. He sat up straight in his desk chair as he focused on re-reading the single line of text again: Venus Station—and the date was correct. *I found him!* And the next line held the answer he desperately hoped to find: port of delivery.

"Com!" Cade barked. "Bergen!"

"Yes, Captain?"

"We're lifting as soon as I speak to Councilwoman Delacruz tomorrow morning."

"Tomorrow, Captain?"

"Yes. I'm turning the investigation over to her and Rashid. Contact everyone dirtside and tell them to finish up whatever they're working on. And I want a navigation officer in my office in ten minutes."

"Yes, Captain," Bergen said. "Destination, sir?"

"We're going to someplace called Hat Yai, in Malaysia."

THIRTEEN
SLAVE

"THERE'S A WARDEN stationed in the shower room tonight, Zuri."

Zuri Oketta acknowledged Ekaterina's warning with a weary nod. She stretched out on her bunk, resigning herself to another night without a shower, even though she itched from the dried sweat of her grueling fourteen-hour shift at the factory.

Ekaterina leaned over Zuri, whispering as she towel-dried her auburn crew cut. "I think it would be safe to wash up in the sink room."

Zuri gave her friend a sad smile. "The warden sometimes checks both bathrooms. I cannot take that chance."

Ekaterina sat on the edge of Zuri's bunk. She glanced around to make sure none of the other girls in the room could overhear. "Where do you think they took them? The older girls who left today?"

Zuri bit her lip. She didn't want to think about what happened to the slaves who reached puberty. One day they were working the assembly line, perhaps taking more than the usual number of bathroom breaks, and the next day they were gone.

She shook her head and refused to answer Ekaterina. Zuri had witnessed human trafficking in the chaotic war-torn streets of Kampala, Uganda, when she was a small child. Teenage girls were lured away with lies of glamorous work and good pay. Girls who didn't come willingly were often abducted. Zuri never left the house without an adult family member at her side.

Abducted, she thought, *just like I was seven years ago. Snatched right off a park bench on Mars Station.*

Zuri knew what happened to the older girls, which was why she tried not to think about it. Ekaterina was lucky, she was only twelve and still had a stick-straight figure. She was safe for at least another year.

But Zuri was fourteen, and she knew it was just a matter of time before her body betrayed her. She was careful not to shower when a warden was stationed in the communal bathroom. She ate very little to keep herself thin in a desperate attempt to delay menarche. Zuri wore her work tunics loose, asking for a larger size when clean clothes were distributed once a week. So far she managed to escape detection by the ever-watchful wardens, but she lived in fear of the day she would have to request an extra bathroom break in the factory.

Some things cannot stay hidden forever. What will I do when the change comes?

"Goodnight, Ekaterina, *rafiki.*"

"Goodnight, Zuri, *prieten.*"

The slaves in the girls' dormitory were of many different nationalities and spoke many different languages, so their common communication was a collection of single words they learned from the wardens, some English, and lots of hand gestures. Zuri understood some of Ekaterina's Romanian, and the younger girl understood a few words of Zuri's Swahili. After seven years, Zuri had learned a smattering of many languages, including Spanish, English, Chinese, Arabic, and French.

Ekaterina climbed into the bunk bed above Zuri's and fell asleep as soon as her head hit the pillow. The other girls in the crowded bunk room settled down for the night. Exhaustion was a condition they all shared. The work in the factory was physically demanding and mind-numbingly dull. Seven days a week they worked an assembly line, putting androids together. After seven years of this drudgery, Zuri still didn't know what happened to the completed mechanicals. She had worked every station on the line, and as near as she could guess, the androids were sold to wealthy countries like the United States. But she didn't know for certain. As a slave, she wasn't privy to any information except what was required for her work.

It was a harsh life for children, but Zuri knew it could be much worse. She tried not to give up hope, no matter how despondent her fellow slaves became. The other girls ranged in age from five to thirteen. Zuri was fortunate none of the wardens kept track of how long she'd been at the factory.

Slaves were an investment, so they were kept healthy. Their living conditions were Spartan, but sanitary. They were given ample time to sleep, shower, and eat their meals. The food was bland but filling. It consisted of rice, root vegetables, tofu, and an occasional piece of fruit. The girls were vaccinated against every known disease, and if one fell sick, she was quarantined in a clean infirmary until she was well enough to return to work.

Zuri had bronchitis once and enjoyed her first day off from work in the infirmary, but she had nearly gone mad from boredom because there was nothing to do lying in bed for three days. There were no holo-vids, no books, no visitors. She couldn't even look out a window—none of the rooms in the factory or dormitory had windows. She looked forward to getting back to the assembly line when her illness was over.

The slaves were allowed to see a dentist if their teeth hurt and were allowed medicine if they had a chronic condition such as type-six malaria. Their heads were shaved once a month to prevent lice, and they were allowed to have their own toothbrushes. It wasn't quite a prison, but it was close enough.

What slaves were not allowed to do was ask questions, have any contact with the boys in the factory next door, or talk back to the wardens. The new slaves always talked back, but they soon learned it was better to keep their mouths shut than be disciplined by the cruel women who kept constant watch over them with fists and nerve prods. In her first week at the factory, Zuri resisted the demands of the wardens. She was knocked to the floor once, slapped across the face for refusing to clean up another girl's vomit.

Zuri also felt the agonizing sting of a nerve prod once, when she got behind in her work and held up the line. The pain from a nerve prod was worse than anything she ever experienced. Every cell in her body felt as if it were on fire when it touched her shoulder for a moment. It left her paralyzed and trembling for an hour afterwards. The cruel device left no physical mark, but it left an unforgettable impression. It wasn't an experience a slave risked repeating. Zuri learned to work faster and to do exactly what was expected of her. She couldn't bear to witness other girls punished with nerve prods, so she learned to close her eyes and ears to the torture in order to preserve her own sanity.

Twice a day the girls got fresh air as they walked through a high-walled grass courtyard from the dormitory to the android factory, and back again at the end of the day. The weather was always warm, sometimes raining, sometimes blistering hot, but never cold. The grass always felt soothing beneath Zuri's bare feet after spending thirteen hours standing on concrete. Thirty minutes to sit down for lunch and two fifteen minute bathroom breaks during a shift wasn't enough of a rest, but Zuri knew better than to complain about the pain in her knees. A visit to the doctor was a risk she wasn't willing to take.

Zuri rolled onto her side and faced the wall. She was tired but couldn't seem to fall asleep. She massaged her sore knees and thought back to the last time she had been outside the factory walls.

Leaving her mother, brother, grandparents, aunts, and cousins behind in war-torn Kampala had been devastating. Starvation was ravaging the city, and Zuri knew her family wouldn't survive. It seemed cruel only two family members were chosen to escape certain death: Zuri and her sixteen-year-old aunt Heshima, her mother's youngest sister.

Shima tried to wear a brave face as they made the long trip to Mars Station with the money their grandfather managed to raise by selling everything the family owned. But Zuri could tell Shima was hurting too.

Shima was able to find a job on the station, cleaning rooms at a rest home, but it wasn't enough to pay for any type of housing. They spent their nights in McConnell Park, along with thousands of other homeless people who came to Mars to start a new life. The irony of their refugee status wasn't lost on young Zuri—she was familiar with African history.

They lived in the park for four months, until the night when they both became ill after eating free oranges offered to them by the CIPs. Zuri remembered being tired and too weak to move. She had fallen asleep on a park bench with Shima stretched out on the grass near her.

That was the last time she saw Shima.

Zuri had been groggy and confused when she awoke from the drug-induced sleep. She found herself strapped to a thin cot in a tiny, windowless room with no other furnishings and a strong smell of urine. The straps didn't confine her hands, and she was able to easily remove them.

She soon realized she was in some type of starship, traveling with other children who'd also been in the park. She saw them when she was allowed out of the room twice a day by armed guards. The children could use the bathroom during these short breaks, but then they were taken right back to their cells.

Zuri began to suspect the food was drugged, just like the oranges in McConnell Park. Nothing else could explain her persistent grogginess. She must have slept eighteen hours a day, lying on the bare cot with only the crook of her arm as a pillow.

A few days passed before Zuri was awakened by the guards, who strapped her to the cot with the padded cords and warned her not to get up. Shortly afterwards, Zuri experienced several minutes of violent turbulence which left her feeling nauseated and dazed. When the turbulence ended, the guards returned and dragged her from the cell, blindfolded her, and herded her off the ship with the other captive passengers. They were separated by gender and loaded onto two buses, and then driven a short distance to the factory.

Once inside, the children were allowed to remove their blindfolds. Zuri remembered looking around at her new prison with tears in her eyes. That had been seven long years ago. New slaves joined the work crew only when older girls were taken away.

Zuri thought about Shima as she nodded off to sleep. She wondered if her aunt was a slave too. *Or is she free and searching for me?*

Shima is the only person alive who remembers I exist.

FOURTEEN
PROMOTIONS

THE GRAYISH-GREEN WATER lapped Shima's ankles, leaving behind trails of iridescent foam on the sugar-white sand. She watched the waves crash over the huge clusters of rocks which jutted out of the ocean. A fine mist caressed her face as the breeze caught a breaker. The beach was deserted; the ocean seemed to beckon. Shima walked forward into the surf.

The next wave rolled in, coming up to her knees. She felt the undertow trying to yank her off her feet. *I cannot swim!* She ignored the voice of reason. She couldn't resist the cool embrace of the ocean. The next wave reached her waist.

A tall wave crashed over the nearest rock. This time the resulting spray left her face damp. Shima knew she should be afraid, but she wasn't. *How can something so beautiful be dangerous?* She waded deeper, until she could no longer stay on her feet in the current's powerful grasp.

She lost her balance when a huge wave broke over her, propelling her to the bottom so fast, she scraped her chin on the rough sand. She clawed her way to the surface, fighting the undertow with all her strength. The moment she was able to seize a breath of air, she spotted something in the water, not far from the rocks.

A lone figure struggled in the surf, frantic to keep her head above the waves. "Help!"

It was Beth Murphy.

She did not drown! Shima felt a rush of relief. *I can still rescue her!*

"What should I do?" she shouted, watching in frustration as a wave swept Beth a few meters closer, but still too far away for Shima to reach.

Before Beth could reply, another massive wave slammed into Shima, forcing her to battle the undertow again. Her need for air became desperate, but she was able to reach the surface and fill her aching lungs.

She heard, "Help!" again, but it wasn't Beth's voice shouting to her. This voice was different, masculine and hauntingly familiar. Someone else struggled in the water where Beth had been moments before.

It was Hugh Zimmerman.

He did not die? Shima's courage faltered. She felt fear for the first time since wading into the ocean.

She recalled the terrible moment in the *Ishmael*'s post-op, when her fiancé's final breath stilled the seizures, releasing his feverish, comatose body from the torture of Zenithian Flu. Hugh's hand grew cold in her own as she stood at his bedside, unable to fathom the depths of this loss.

She stared at the young man fighting to keep his head above water. "Shima, help me!"

I cannot swim! She didn't know what to do. Another wave broke over her head.

It was much harder to find the surface this time. Anguish seemed to drain her last remnants of strength. When she was able to take a desperate gulp of air, she heard another cry for help. Once again, it was a different voice shouting to her.

"Shima!" Hugh was gone, and in his place was a woman Shima hadn't seen in a long time. The woman's beautiful face had become lost in the murky depths of Shima's painful memories, and it took a few moments to recognize her.

"Ngoma?" The woman was Shima's second oldest sister. Like Shima, Ngoma couldn't swim. Her arms flailed, helpless, beating at the cruel waves.

Shima felt her fear turn to despair as she watched Ngoma's dark ringlets disappear beneath a breaker. The brief moment she glimpsed her sister's face was enough to etch it into her memory again, even as the faces of her other family members remained elusive, their features blurred by time and grief.

She opened her mouth to shout to Ngoma just as another wave engulfed her, filling her lungs with water. She could feel her life slipping away as she was caught by the undertow and drawn downward into the eerie, suffocating silence of the ocean's deadly embrace.

How can something so beautiful be dangerous?

Shima awoke with a start, her heart pounding against her ribs. She wiped the tears from her face. *It was just a nightmare, Shima. Let it go.* She took some deep breaths, grateful she didn't have to fight for air, and tried to calm down.

She reflected for a moment on the images still fresh in her mind. She could understand why Beth and Hugh had been a part of her nightmare, since she witnessed their deaths, but she couldn't fathom why Ngoma, Zuri's mother, made an appearance. Shima was fortunate to have been spared the agony of witnessing the deaths of her family in Kampala, so she had no idea how Ngoma appeared in her final moments. *I wish I could have seen Mama instead.*

Let it go, she advised herself. *It does not make sense because it was just a dream.*

Shima felt more exhausted than when she went to bed the night before. The reason for her poor sleep couldn't be helped. She had a bunkmate.

Niyati's tiny body was burrowed against Shima's side on the narrow bed. The child often had nightmares and would cry out in her sleep. It made for a lot of interrupted rest, but Niyati needed comforting twenty-four/seven. She had been Shima's constant companion since the tragic outing to the beach.

"PTSD," was Grey's informal diagnosis. He had seen it before in other abandoned children.

"What is that?" Shima asked.

"Post-traumatic stress disorder," Grey said.

"What can we do for her?"

Grey observed Niyati hugging Shima's legs, her small brown face hidden in the folds of Shima's skirt. "You're already doing it."

Shima resigned herself to being Niyati's substitute mother until Lorina returned. The child didn't even let her use the bathroom or shower alone, but Shima tolerated the lack of privacy because she felt responsible for Beth Murphy's death. *Taking care of her is a small price to pay for my careless mistake.*

Beth's body had been discovered two days after the accident, washed up on a beach nearly six kilometers from the area where she'd disappeared. Following the instructions of Jake's father, Shima sent the body to a crematorium and shipped the ashes to the O'Brien homestead in Wilmington, Delaware.

As for The Lost Sheep, a dark cloud had settled over the orphanage. The children still played outside during the day, but they didn't laugh as much. At meals and bedtime, they were quiet. The only happy moments came when a child left with Grey to join his or her adoptive parents, but then the house was silent again as soon as his car drove away. Shima didn't know what to do or say to comfort these kids who already lost everything familiar in their lives. She prayed their natural resilience would soon return.

Shima needed to find that resilience herself. She wondered if there would ever be an end to the losses. So many important people in her life were now dead. She felt alone in her grief, weighed down by burdens she kept inside because she had no one to confide in. Normally she would take time to meditate when she felt overwhelmed, but with Niyati as her constant companion, she hadn't been able to find a moment of solitude to restore her inner peace.

She tried to set the gloomy thoughts aside as she sat up and stretched to work the stiffness out of her back. Her movement caused Niyati to wake, an alarmed look in her eyes. "Auntie?"

Niyati had given her the title the day before. Shima didn't mind if it helped Niyati feel more secure, but the word was a painful reminder of another child who once called her auntie—Zuri.

"I am here." Shima held out her arms and let Niyati climb onto her lap, which was their usual routine. She allowed the little girl a few moments to cuddle, although to Shima it felt more like desperate clinging than affection, and then set her on her feet. "We should get dressed."

Niyati just nodded and pulled her clean clothes out of the nightstand, never taking her eyes off Shima as she slipped them on.

She was pulling on her own T-shirt when she heard a distinct *ping* from the interstellar receiver, which Grey set up on one of the empty bookshelves.

"That is a transmission!" Please let it be good news!

The last communication on the receiver had been a short, rather terse message from Jake's father. "I just thought you should know we received the urn. We'll have a memorial service for my sister tomorrow. Give our best to Jake and Lorina. And Blaze and Niyati," he added, as an afterthought.

Shima felt overwhelmed with guilt to witness the grief-stricken expression on Jacob O'Brien's face. She didn't think she had the strength for another transmission like that one. She walked over to the shelf and picked up the monitor. She glanced down at Niyati, who was watching her with a puzzled frown. "It is a message from Captain Shepherd."

The cords wouldn't reach far, so Shima tapped the code into the keypad on the receiver base and sat on the floor with the monitor in front of her. Niyati plopped down next to her, and they viewed the transmission together.

Danae appeared quite pleased with herself. "This transmission is intended for Heshima Oryang, director of The Lost Sheep, Lahaina, Maui, and was recorded on November twenty second."

Danae smiled. "Mission accomplished, Shima! We were able to put Acheron in jail and get the Sorensens out, with a lot of help from an unexpected ally. I'll tell you all about it when we land. You can expect *Alex's Legacy* in three days. Kirsten Sorensen decided to stay on the station, so we have Erik and thirty-three more orphans with us." She paused, frowning. "Vipul and I will be taking turns at the helm because Ting was shot in the head. He's in a coma."

"What?" Shima gasped.

"*Amma?*" Niyati gripped Shima's elbow.

"*Amma* is fine, I think." She kept her eyes on the screen.

"Oh, and there's one more thing . . ." Danae peered into the camera, her large blue eyes both serious and excited. "Blaze found Thanatos's log aboard the *Elmina*. A lot of the information on it was encrypted, but another unexpected ally was able to break the code for us. Shima, we know where he took Zuri!"

Shima gasped again, covering her mouth with her hands as her eyes filled with tears.

Now Niyati was worried. "Auntie?"

"Shhh—listen." Shima wiped her eyes on the hem of her T-shirt.

Danae was saying, "We'll see you in a few days. Oh, and there's one more message after mine, so stay tuned."

There was a blank screen for a moment, then Lorina and Blaze appeared, provoking a happy squeal from Niyati. "*Amma! Baba!*"

Shima shushed her again because they started to speak.

"Niyati, we'll be home in a few days," Lorina said. "Be a good girl for Shima. We miss you and love you."

"See you soon, Niyati," Blaze added. "Smith out."

The screen went blank. The transmission had been short and sweet.

Shima felt the glow of optimism for the first time since the accident. She also felt a pang of sympathy for Ting's condition. *I wonder how Danae is coping.*

She set Niyati on her feet and got up from the floor. "Come on, we have a lot of work to do. *Amma* and *baba* get here tomorrow."

Niyati giggled. Shima saw a real smile on the child's face for the first time since Lorina's departure.

***

The *Alex*'s landing was much smoother than the first time the ship descended on Maui. Shima had all the kids stay in the backyard to watch the 3:00 p.m. landing. The ship set down on the original site where the grass was still crushed and burnt to a crisp.

The engine noise subsided from a roar, to an irritating hum, to complete silence. The airlock opened at the belly of the ship and the collapsible staircase descended to the ground. The children broke into loud cheers as the crew began to emerge. The grief was forgotten in an instant, swept away by the excitement of *Alex's Legacy*'s return.

Shima gave up trying to keep the children corralled and allowed them run over to greet Danae, Vipul, Phailin, and Dr. Sorensen. Lorina was only a few steps behind her shipmates. Niyati tore across the field and was in her mother's arms as soon as her feet touched the ground.

Shima watched the reunion with a heavy heart. *Lorina will never be reunited with her mother in this life.* She thought of her own mother and had to blink hard to hold back the tears.

Blaze exited the ship next, picked up Niyati in a one-armed hug, and put his other arm around Lorina's shoulders. The little family turned, as one, and looked at Shima.

She slowly started walking toward them. She couldn't look Lorina in the eye. She didn't know what she would say to her friend. An apology seemed pathetic.

The newcomer orphans emerged from the ship, several at a time. They were laughing, looking around, and blinking at the bright sunshine. The Lost Sheep kids swarmed around them, jumping up and down with excitement. Lorina shouted something to the group, and they all started toward the house.

Shima paused as the kids hurried by her. She felt confident Olivia and the McLeod twins would take care of evaluating their needs, so she didn't say anything to them.

She did note the new children were older, maybe twelve to sixteen, and wondered for a moment how their presence would disrupt the daily routine of the orphanage. *How will they treat the younger kids?* Right now they seemed to be enjoying the attention, but Shima knew this was all new to them and braced herself mentally for a challenging transition once the newness and excitement wore off.

Shima had almost reached the ship, where the Smiths were waiting for her, but Danae reached her first, enveloping her in a firm hug.

"I'm so sorry, Shima."

Shima tried to speak, but couldn't. She burst into tears. "I let you down!" she managed to choke between sobs. "I let everyone down! I was careless, and now Beth is dead! It is all my fault!"

Danae released her, held her at arm's length, and looked her in the eye. "This isn't your fault, Shima. It was an accident."

"I'll second that." Lorina reached Shima in a few strides and took Danae's place, wrapping her arms around

Shima's shaking shoulders. "It was an accident. I don't blame you, so please stop blaming yourself."

Shima couldn't stop the tears. She had been holding them in for a week, trying to be strong for Niyati and everyone else she was responsible for. Now she felt like the floodgates opened as she found herself grieving harder than she ever had in her life. She shook with sobs, exhausted and overwhelmed by the weight of so many losses.

She was aware of others surrounding her, but she couldn't hear their words of comfort. She felt as if she were falling down a deep well with people standing around the rim above, watching her plummet, their voices growing fainter as the distance between them grew. Her head began to ache. She could hear the blood pounding in her ears as she struggled to quell the hysteria, but it was as if the grief had taken possession of her.

"Shima!" A stern voice tried to break through to her, but she couldn't respond.

Then she felt a sting on her forearm and was swept into the silent, weightless abyss of space.

***

Shima awoke to the bright lights of a familiar room—the post-op of the *Alex*'s infirmary. A concerned face was peering down at her. "Jake?"

"Good, you're awake." Jake had shaved off his sideburns and goatee, but his skin was still an unnatural golden brown. "How are you feeling?"

Shima tried to sit up, was hit with an instant migraine, and lay back against the pillow. "Terrible."

"I'm not surprised. We thought you were having a nervous breakdown, so Erik sedated you." Using both hands, Jake gently turned Shima's head to one side. He moved aside her braids and placed a patch on the back of her neck. "That should help."

Shima felt the headache fading. In a few minutes, she was able to talk. "How long have I been unconscious?"

"About twelve hours."

Shima winced. "I need to get up. I should help Paul prepare breakfast for the extra children."

"Sorry, but you're not going anywhere today." Jake added, "Captain's orders," when Shima began to protest.

"But there is so much to do. My help is needed."

"I think we can manage while you take a well-deserved rest." Jake passed his scanner over her, concentrating it on her forehead.

She didn't want to ask what was going on inside her brain. "Can you tell me how the new children are adjusting?"

"No, I can't. Also the captain's orders. She said you weren't allowed to worry about anything."

"But, I—"

"Not a single thing," Jake spoke over her. "You need to stay right here until Erik or I say you're strong enough to get up."

Shima bit her lip. "I need to know what is going on."

"You can pester your visitors for information—I'm sure you'll have plenty. Now, if you'll excuse me, my presence is required at target practice." Jake squeezed her shoulder and turned away.

Suddenly Shima had many questions that needed answering. "What do you mean by target practice?"

"I can't tell you," Jake said over his shoulder. "Get some rest."

Shima tried one more time. "But what about—?"

"Relax. You're off duty," he interrupted again. "Erik is in the ICU with Ting"—he pointed to the door of the surgical room—"so just yell if you need anything." He waved and stepped into the corridor. The door slid shut behind him.

Shima lay still for a few minutes, thinking. She didn't like the idea of being stuck in the infirmary all day. *I feel fine. I just needed a good rest, and I got it last night.*

She was reluctant to admit she felt drained, too exhausted in both mind and body to attempt cutting short her impromptu vacation. She took a sip from her drinking tube, which she could reach with her right hand, and thought, *I am hungry.*

As if on cue, the door slid open, and Phailin Kim walked in, bearing a tray of food. "Breakfast, Shima?"

"Yes, thank you." Shima had never been an invalid, except for her three-day bout with Zenithian Flu, so it felt strange to be waited on.

"I'll help you sit up." Phailin set the tray on the bedside table, raised the head of Shima's bed, adjusted her pillows, and handed her a plate of scrambled eggs. "Do you need help?"

"I do not need you to feed me, if that is what you mean." Shima picked up a fork and poked at the eggs while Phailin looked on.

She managed to get two bites into her mouth and quite a bit on her shirt. Her hand was unsteady, like an elderly woman's. Embarrassed, she glanced up at Phailin. "I guess I could use a little help."

Without a word, Phailin took the fork from her and patiently fed her the rest of the eggs, offering her sips of mango juice between mouthfuls. She brushed off the front of Shima's shirt and began feeding her spoonfuls of oatmeal.

Shima shook her head and closed her mouth against the last spoonful, well aware that she probably resembled a toddler ready to spew. "Thank you, but I am full."

Phailin wiped Shima's chin with a napkin and set the bowl back on the tray. "I'll let you rest."

As the cook bent to pick up the tray, Shima noticed a glint of something black tucked into the waistband of her jeans, near her right hip. "Is that . . . a gun?"

Phailin left the tray on the table, gave Shima a thoughtful look, and drew the weapon out for her to see. It was tiny, black, and innocuous-looking, like a child's toy, but appeared to be made of metal. Phailin held it out to Shima, grip first.

She shook her head. "No, I do not want to touch it."

"I recommend getting used to the idea of handling a gun," Phailin said. "The captain has one for each of us."

Shima frowned but still wouldn't take the proffered weapon. "Jake said something about target practice."

Phailin chuckled. "If Jake can get over his distaste for guns, it should be no problem for you."

Shima shook her head again, her mind in a whirl. "You can show me later."

The cook flipped the gun around so the grip was in her palm and tucked it back into her waistband in one fluid movement. She tugged on the hem of her T-shirt until she was satisfied the gun was hidden.

"Where did the captain get them?"

"They're on loan to us, from ISPP," Phailin said.

"What is *isp*?"

"Interstellar Peacekeepers Patrol—they're a police organization, but independent of the CIPs. They're also hunting for slavers. The ISPP captain thought we should be able to defend ourselves if we're going on a rescue mission."

"To find Zuri." Shima focused on that thought for a moment. It helped her feel calmer.

Phailin picked up the tray and turned to leave. She stared at the door to the surgery for a moment, and then turned back to Shima with a forced smile. "Feel better soon."

"Thank you."

After the cook departed, Shima sat and thought. She rarely had the luxury of solitude and silence, so she decided to use the time to relax, as Jake instructed.

"How are you feeling?" Danae's sudden appearance at the doorway was like a breath of fresh air in the room.

"I am better. I am well enough to hear about your adventures on the station."

The captain grinned and crossed the room to Shima's bedside. "Well, that's good, because I have a lot to tell you." She drew up a chair.

"And do not leave out a single detail," Shima said.

***

"I think you could use at least one more day to recuperate," Danae answered Shima's query about how much longer she needed to stay in the infirmary.

"But—"

"No." Danae was on her feet, leaning over Shima so she could look her right in the eye. "I need you fully recovered if we're going to rescue Zuri. Do you have a problem with that?"

Shima tried once more. "I feel fine."

"Physically, maybe, but not emotionally." Danae placed a warm, soothing palm on Shima's forehead.

"You need to let it go—all of it. The stress, the guilt, the grief—everything that's weighed you down since you left Kampala."

Tears began to sting the corners of Shima's eyes. "I do not want to cry anymore."

Danae studied her face with a thoughtful expression. "You're the strongest person I've ever known. You've managed to carry very heavy burdens without a word of complaint."

Shima started to protest, but the captain spoke over her. "You'll rise above this, as you always do. I can see it in your eyes, the peace that gives you your amazing inner strength . . . I see it coming back, just a little."

Shima shut her eyes and allowed the tears to flow. She was grateful there weren't many this time. "You are right. You are right most of the time."

"Are you implying I've been wrong before?" Danae teased.

"Yes." Shima opened her eyes and gave Danae a stern look. "The guns you have given the crew—that is a mistake."

The captain frowned. "We may need them where we're headed. Guns can save lives."

Shima had a vivid recollection of the night Danae shot that horrible man, Wade Jackson. She could still feel his big rough hand on her jaw, gripping it tight, ready to break her neck.

She shivered. "Yes, that is true. You were able to save my life, and Vipul's, but guns also take lives." She exchanged a meaningful glance with Danae. The name Thanatos was left unspoken between them. "I do not feel comfortable shooting anyone."

"Hopefully, you won't have to. But I think we should be prepared for anything. If we don't have to use them, fine, but if we need weapons and don't have them—"

Shima was grateful Danae didn't finish the thought. "Jake mentioned target practice."

Danae nodded. "We've set up a shooting range out in the cane field, about a kilometer from the house. Everyone needs to know how to handle the pistols, or they won't do us much good."

"I will practice," Shima promised, though with some reluctance, "and I will resume my duties as ship's housekeeper."

"I'm glad you brought that up, because I've given it some thought and think you should hold a more distinctive position on the *Alex*. Housekeeper doesn't suit you anymore. You deserve a promotion."

"I do not understand."

"You're an indispensable member of the crew, and I think your title should reflect that fact. When I met with the ISPP captain . . ." Danae looked embarrassed for a moment and cleared her throat. "Captain York has a first officer. She's his second in command and runs the ship in his absence. The crew follows her directions just as they would the captain's."

Shima tried to envision what Danae was suggesting. "First officer? But *Alex's Legacy* is not a military ship."

"Makes no difference to me. I want to make you my first officer, effective immediately."

Shima wasn't sure how to respond to this announcement. "It sounds like more responsibility."

"It is. Because you've proven time and again that you can handle huge responsibilities—"

Shima wanted to protest. She thought of Beth and felt undeserving of Danae's praise.

"—and there's no one more capable of taking care of the details of running the ship." Danae grinned. "I should've done this a long time ago. I apologize for taking your talents for granted."

Shima still wasn't sure what she thought of this promotion, but she said, "I guess I accept," and decided to save her questions for later, after she had time to think.

Just then Erik Sorensen stuck his head out of the surgery/ICU. "Good morning, ladies." He wore blue scrubs which strained at the seams to accommodate his large frame. The doctor's fair skin couldn't hide the assortment of purplish-green bruises on his clean-shaven face, but he seemed to be recovered from whatever accident had befallen him.

Acheron, Shima recalled. *Dr. Sorensen's injuries were no accident.*

In the awkward pause that followed Sorensen's greeting, Shima realized the doctor had a strong interest in Danae. She could see it in his eyes and in the way his smile seemed to stretch from ear to ear.

"Shima, you seem to be feeling better."

"I am, thank you." Shima smiled at him but observed Danae's reaction from the corner of her eye.

The captain seemed flustered. She briefly returned the smile but switched back to her calm expression. "Any improvement in Ting's condition?"

Do not hide your feelings behind that mask, Danae. Shima was aware she also kept her own emotions on a tight rein and decided right then to be more honest with herself and those she cared about. *It would be better for my health,* she thought, glancing down at her hospital bed.

"He's still stable," the doctor answered Danae's question, "but no change. Do you want to see him?"

"Can I see him?" Shima pushed the covers back and swung her legs over the side of the bed before Danae could object.

"Don't—" Sorensen started to say, but he reached Shima's bedside before she had both feet on the floor. He grasped her forearm just in time.

Shima's knees buckled the moment she tried to stand. "What—?" Erik steadied her, and Danae took her other arm.

"And where do you think you're going?" the captain asked.

Shima was surprised by how weak she felt. Her legs were trembling. "I was—" she floundered for an excuse. "I need to visit the head."

"I'll help you." Danae slipped her free arm around Shima's waist and half-carried her across the room to the patients' head.

Shima had to use the sink counter to steady herself in the tiny bathroom. *What is wrong with me?*

A few minutes later, she opened the door and meekly allowed Danae to help her across the room to her bed.

"Let's make that two days before you can leave the infirmary." The captain tucked the blanket around her legs. From her tone, Shima knew better than to argue.

"Bed rest is the best cure for a simple case of stress-induced exhaustion," Dr. Sorensen said, "but if you still feel jittery this evening, I'll start you on an anti-anxiety medication."

"I will be fine," Shima said.

"You can prove it by getting some rest." Danae gave her a half smile and crossed to the surgery/ICU to join Sorensen. They both stepped inside the room and the door slid shut.

Shima lowered the head of her bed and closed her eyes. Convinced now that she needed to rest her body as well as her mind, she turned her focus inward and meditated, searching for the peace which eluded her for too long.

***

Shima flinched the first time she touched the trigger on her handgun. Even with earplugs, the weapon's discharge surprised her; it was loud.

"Whoa!" Lorina set her own pistol on the ground and reached over to lower the barrel of Shima's. "We're not trying to knock coconuts out of the tree! You've got to keep your eye on the ball!"

"What ball?" Shima peered across the field of weeds at the row of empty plastic water bottles lined up on a wooden board. "I do not see a ball."

Lorina laughed. "No, no, it's just an old expression. I mean you have to keep your eyes open and hold it steady. Watch."

She was more than willing to obey her volunteer instructor. The two women were alone at the makeshift shooting range in the sugarcane field. They knelt side by side on the black volcanic soil, twenty-five meters from their targets. Shima switched on the safety, as she had been drilled, and set her gun on the ground. Then she sat back and watched as Lorina extended her right arm, supported the base of the grip with her left hand, squinted down the barrel of her pistol, and fired off several shots.

Three bottles vanished into the weeds in rapid succession.

"Your turn."

Shima tried her best to imitate Lorina's performance, but her aim was terrible. The four remaining bottles were in their original positions, mocking her pitiful marksmanship. "This is harder than it looks."

"It just takes practice." Lorina ejected the empty magazine from her own pistol and inserted a new one.

"You have used guns before?"

Lorina nodded and concentrated on blasting another bottle. "I've been hunting since I was big enough to handle a shotgun."

"But Jake does not seem to like guns. Did he not learn to hunt with you?"

"Jake refused to hunt." Lorina switched on the safety and turned to give Shima her full attention. "He hated to see animals hurt or bleeding. He was always bringing home baby birds that fell from their nests, trying to nurse them back to health."

"Is that why he decided to become a doctor?"

Lorina nodded.

"Jake does have a wonderful gift for healing." Shima reluctantly turned her attention back to target practice. "So, how can I improve my aim?"

Lorina traded pistols so Shima held the one with a full magazine. "I think you need to put some feeling into it."

"What do you mean?" Both arms extended, Shima squinted down the sight of the short barrel and thumbed off the safety.

"I mean get mad at it. Picture Acheron on one of those targets."

Shima thought the advice was absurd but decided to humor her crewmate. She concentrated on scowling at one of the bottles. "Take that, you monster!" This time she didn't flinch when she touched the trigger.

The bottle disappeared behind the board.

Her mouth fell open in shock. "It does work!"

Lorina nodded. "Keep going."

Shima adjusted her aim. "And this is for you, Wade Jackson!"

The bottle bounced into the air and landed several meters away in the tall grass.

"And this is for you, Thanatos!"

The bullet ricocheted off the wood just beneath the last bottle, but Lorina said, "Close enough!" She got to her feet. "Be sure the safety is on, and I'll set them up for another round."

Lorina lined up the seven pierced and dilapidated bottles and returned to Shima's side. "Let 'er rip."

Shima relished the heady feeling of confidence as she used the Excalibur to release some pent-up frustrations. "This is for the Zenithian Flu that robbed me of my friends!" She blasted four bottles in a row as she shouted, "Dr. Martschenko! Alex! Vanni!" A sudden lump in her throat made her hesitate on the last one, but only for a moment. "And this one is for Hugh!"

Shima blinked back a few tears as she focused on the next target, but her enthusiasm was gone. She switched on the safety instead. "I have run out of reasons to be angry. I cannot be mad at the ocean for taking Beth away."

Lorina drew in a sharp breath, and Shima realized she shouldn't have given voice to the thought. She turned to face her friend, an apology already poised on her lips. "I should not have said—"

"It's fine," Lorina spoke over her. "And you're right. It's pointless to get angry at things we can't control. For instance, I could be angry at you—"

Shima felt a flutter of fear but decided to accept whatever Lorina needed to say, or do, to her.

"—or I could be angry at Ting for telling me about his premonition, or at the unfairness of life, or at God, or

. . . at anything—even the ocean, like you said." Lorina looked past Shima, at the lush green hills in the distance. "But Mom wouldn't want me to be angry . . . about what happened. She wouldn't want me to waste my time wrapped up in grief and self-pity, blaming others for my misfortunes. She'd want me to be happy."

When Lorina focused again on Shima's face, there wasn't a trace of grief in her hazel eyes. "And I *am* happy. I have so much to be grateful for. I have a family, with a wonderful husband and daughter, and Jake. I have an opportunity to help make a difference in some children's lives." She mustered a small smile. "I have good friends I can count on. One of my friends did her best to save my mother's life, and then took care of my daughter like she was her own."

Shima was impressed by Lorina's maturity. "I do not deserve such kindness."

Lorina's smile twisted into a smirk. "Well, I don't usually dispense much kindness—as Ting can attest, whenever he wakes up."

"In that case, I am honored to be your friend." Shima added with a smirk of her own, "And I am grateful your gun is not loaded."

***

"I want to lift as soon as possible." Danae stood next to the long counter to address the staff of The Lost Sheep and the crew of *Alex's Legacy* assembled in the galley. "But we need to discuss logistics first, so I want to hear your suggestions." She turned to look at Shima. "I'm going to need a new orphanage director."

"Gordon Grey," Shima said.

The social worker chuckled. "I'm flattered you think so highly of me, Shima, but I'm too busy with the adoptions to take on another job." He looked at his wife, who was seated next to him. "How about Olivia?"

"No, thank you." Olivia shot Grey a flustered look. "You know I don't handle pressure well, and the new kids are"—she frowned, searching for a tactful word—"challenging."

"Exhausting," Paul Ly added. There were nods of agreement from the others.

"We need a firm disciplinarian to be in charge of The Lost Sheep," Grey said, "at least until I can find placements for some of the teens."

Shima glanced around the room, trying to decide who was best qualified to run the orphanage. "What about Dr. Sorensen?"

The captain and Dr. Sorensen exchanged a meaningful glance. Many unspoken words seemed to pass between them. Shima decided to reserve judgment until one of them responded to the question.

"That would depend on which medic wants to stay and which wants to head into the unknown," Danae said, glancing back and forth between Jake and the doctor, who were sitting on opposite sides of the galley.

Jake made the decision for them. "I'm staying."

"And I can't lift without a medic on board." Danae glanced at the doctor again. "So Erik can't direct the orphanage."

"What about Lorina?" Abish piped up. "She's great at keeping the kids in line."

Lorina shook her head. "Sorry, but my family needs to stay together. Niyati's been through too much already. She needs both her parents on the ship."

Danae harrumphed. "Well, *I* can't stay because I need to pilot the *Alex*. And I don't have time to advertise and interview for a new director, so it has to be someone in this room."

Shima glanced over at Jake. *Process of elimination,* she thought, *but I think he could handle it.* She turned back to Danae, who was also staring at Jake with a thoughtful expression.

The room was quiet for a few moments as Jake returned the captain's stare. "Me? You're kidding, right? How can I be the orphanage director if I'm also the medic?"

"You only have to be the medic when someone is sick," Danae said. "And Shima tells me there hasn't been anything more serious than a few cases of head lice and a scraped knee since The Lost Sheep opened."

A drowning was rather serious, Shima thought with a fresh pang of guilt, but she remained silent.

All eyes were on Jake. His mouth opened and closed a few times, but he couldn't seem to find his voice. His defiant scowl softened into reluctant acceptance, and he nodded.

"Thank you, Jake." Danae smiled at him. "You have an experienced staff ready to assist you." She turned to Shima. "I'll give you four hours to train Jake to take over for you, and then we'll lift."

"You lift in four hours?" Jake said, "But I thought you said we needed to discuss logistics."

"We just did." Danae took out a datapad, glanced at the screen, and began firing off instructions to the rest of the staff and crew.

"Blaze, order the fuel truck."

"Erik, make sure you have all the medical supplies you'll need to keep Ting stable."

"Lorina, you and Phailin purchase anything we need for the galley."

"Vipul, run scans on all ship's systems."

"I'll take care of the water, septic, and port fees. Does everyone on the ship have a gun?"

There were nods all around.

"Good. I'll distribute the live ammo when we dock."

"What about mine?" Jake asked.

"I'll take it."

Jake handed his pistol over to Danae with a look of relief on his face.

"Ting might need it when he wakes up," the captain said.

Shima felt another pang of guilt, even though she had nothing to do with Ting's condition.

Danae had one more instruction. "The Lost Sheep staff, keep doing what you're doing, although I want to hear some plans for educating the kids when we return." She scanned the faces in the room. "Let's get to work!"

***

Shima sat down with Jake at the small kitchen table. The dinnertime chaos was over and Jake seemed to be recovering from the shock of witnessing his first meal at The Lost Sheep.

"I'm not sure I can do this, Shima."

"Yes, you can." She slid a datapad across the table to him. "I wrote down the daily schedule." She tapped the screen to bring up another page. "Here is all the financial information and the to-do list."

Jake's frown deepened. "That's a pretty long list."

"The staff keeps things running well most of the time. I take care of the basics." She waited a moment for him to look up from the screen. "So far we have focused only on food, shelter, clothing, and adoptions.

"Paul takes care of ordering the food; I just pay the delivery people. The house has renovations in progress—they are listed here. I just pay the contractors. Clothing is a constant chore, but Olivia has a system for sorting donations and a laundry schedule—it is listed here. Grey takes care of the adoptions. Olivia and the twins supervise the children. I just fill in wherever I am needed."

"There's got to be more to it than that." Jake was still frowning.

"There is a little more, but it changes from day to day."

"What changes?"

Shima hesitated but decided he really needed to know about the headaches that came with the job. "The problems change every day. They often come without warning, and I must make quick decisions. There have been some fights between the older kids—"

"I noticed some of that this evening."

She nodded and continued without missing a beat. "Visits from prospective parents can become awkward if they have their hearts set on a child who has already been chosen by another family. They often become emotional when that happens."

Jake grimaced. "I'm not good with weepy women."

Shima wondered how many problems she should bring up. She didn't want to overwhelm Jake with a daunting list. "Finding ways to keep the children occupied during the day—"

"The captain wants a plan to educate them," Jake interrupted again.

"Add it to your list," Shima said. "That means hiring a teacher—or teachers—finding a place to use as a classroom, purchasing school supplies—"

"There's no way we can afford a datapad for every kid!" Jake shook his head.

"Then you may have to teach them in rotations." Shima was already thinking ahead, but she could tell from Jake's furrowed brow that he wasn't quite grasping the organizational efforts needed to run The Lost Sheep. "Maybe the younger kids could attend school—the classroom—in the morning, the older kids in the afternoon. You could ask prospective parents to donate datapads."

"Parents . . . donate stuff?"

Shima nodded. "Yes, parents and people in the community bring donations every day. One big donation is the chicken coop. It is almost finished. You should assign a few of the children to feed the chickens and collect the eggs."

Jake was confused. "What chickens?"

"We will have twenty-five hens in the backyard."

She could see a glimmer of relief in Jake's face. "Chickens—that's something I understand. I grew up on a farm."

"Then maybe you could plant a vegetable garden with the children's assistance."

Jake nodded, picked up a stylus, and started adding notes to his to-do list.

Shima watched him write for a few moments before deciding to indulge her curiosity. "Jake, do you really want to stay?"

He glanced at her with a suspicious frown. "You know I don't like space travel."

"We are not going into space. It is just a short flight across the ocean."

Jake's expression turned mulish. "You don't think I can handle the responsibility?"

"I did not say that. I just want to understand why you volunteered for this when you know Dr. Sorensen would have agreed to stay. He has experience with children and charity organizations. Why did you decide to take his place?"

"You think I have an ulterior motive?"

Shima was frank. "Yes, I do." She went on before he could protest. His mouth was already in motion to issue a rebuttal. "If you are doing this as a noble gesture—"

"I don't know what you're talking about." But she could tell by the way he shifted in his chair and lowered his gaze that he knew exactly what she meant.

"Captain Shepherd and Dr. Sorensen can now be together on the ship."

"I'm not doing this to play matchmaker," Jake said, looking more uncomfortable at the suggestion.

Shima suspected Jake had a crush on Danae, but she spared him the embarrassment by not asking. *Staying here was a difficult choice, whether he wants to admit it or not.*

"I am glad to hear you are not doing this as a favor to them," Shima said, "because if you were, you would not have given this job much thought." She waited until Jake made eye contact again. "Running The Lost Sheep is the most difficult thing I have ever done."

"Difficult? Are you referring to . . . the accident?" Jake asked.

"It was a difficult job *before* your aunt drowned." She glanced down at the table, shame washing over her. *Why did he have to bring this up?* She couldn't bear to see the grief in Jake's eyes, just like his father's.

"Shima?"

She bit her lip, fighting back tears.

"Shima, look at me."

She raised her chin until their eyes were level.

"I know about the captain and Erik, but I volunteered to do this for you. You need more time to recuperate—"

"I am better." Shima knew she didn't sound convincing.

"Physically, yes; emotionally, no."

"You sound like Captain Shepherd."

"Good!" Jake said. "Because I think you need to hear it again. It was an accident. There's nothing you could've done to save Beth." He leaned closer, his face a mixture of grief and concern. "The ship is your real home, and I'd have to be blind not to see the bond you share with the captain. You need to be on board the *Alex* with her. You two are like family."

Shima nodded. "Yes, we are."

"You need to be away from this place, away from the memory of"—Jake took a deep breath—"of that day . . . at the beach."

Shima felt a catch in her throat. *He does not know.* She forced a smile. "Jake, you are kind, but I cannot escape the past, no matter where I am. *Alex's Legacy* holds painful memories too."

Jake looked confused again.

"Hugh Zimmerman was the steward aboard the *Ishmael* . . . and he was my fiancé."

Comprehension dawned in Jake's eyes, but Shima pressed on before he could start asking painful questions. "We were planning to be married on Mars Station in October, but the Zenithian Flu changed those plans."

"I'm sorry," Jake whispered. "I didn't know."

Shima forced a smile again. "Of course you did not know, but it was kind of you to think of my welfare."

"Not too kind. I'm like a bull in a china shop."

This time Shima was confused. "Why would someone take a bull into a china shop?"

Jake surprised her by laughing. "It's an expression, Shima. A tired old cliché."

She nodded, forcing herself to set painful memories aside and focus on what she needed to do to prepare Jake for his promotion to orphanage director. "Let me show you how to use the credit flash bank transfer for the bills and the payroll. You will need to memorize the codes."

Jake nodded. He seemed relieved to change the subject. "Lead the way."

***

"How much time did you spend at target practice?" Danae asked. They were strapping down on the bridge, preparing to lift. Shima was at the com, Vipul on navigation, and the captain at the helm.

Shima felt the hard shape of the pistol tucked into a hand-sewn holster—just a pocket, really—at the small of her back. "Enough time to know I still do not like guns."

"Probably not long enough, then." Danae swiveled in her chair to face the helm controls. "Liftoff in ten minutes! Status, Blaze?"

"We're good to go, Captain."

Danae glanced to her left. "Vipul?"

"Skies are clear, Captain. Once we reach cruising altitude, we'll be there in two hours."

"Where, again, in Asia are we going, Captain?" Shima asked.

"We're going to Bangkok, Thailand—or what's left of it."

FIFTEEN
WATER HAZARDS

ERIK REPLACED TING'S empty IV of Quickheal fluids and checked all the monitors again. There was no change in the helmsman's condition. The doctor wasn't enthused about bringing Ting along for the ride, but he knew moving him to a hospital would be expensive and pointless. The treatment Ting would receive at Lahaina Community Hospital would be the exact same treatment he was already receiving under Erik's care.

Eventually, Ting would wake up. His brain scans looked good. He was breathing on his own. He could sense what was going on in his environment. For example, he would wince whenever Erik changed his bandages. Twice, Ting opened his eyes for a few seconds, and he muttered a few words in Mandarin yesterday, but he was still unconscious.

The lights are on, but we're waiting for someone to answer the door, Erik thought. *Ting seems to have forgotten where the door is.*

Even with advances in neurobiology and medical technology, the brain still didn't follow a predictable pattern for recovering from injuries. A single damaged nerve in just the right spot could keep a patient in a coma indefinitely. This seemed to be the reason for Ting's prolonged condition.

A few hospitals on Earth owned an expensive medical device called the Wang-Ortiz Neuromelder, or WON, which could re-connect severed neural pathways in a patient's brain. The King Bhumibol Memorial Hospital in Bangkok owned one of only a dozen WONs in existence. Erik hoped the Bhumibol was still in business, and that there wasn't a year-long waiting list for treatment.

"Final approach in fifteen," Danae announced over the com. "Please strap down."

Erik secured the padded restraints across Ting's knees, waist, and shoulders, and made sure the head brace properly cradled his neck and skull.

The doctor folded down the medic's chair from the wall where it was nestled between the crash cart and the micro-pharmacy refrigerator. The seat was undersized, but he wedged himself between the arm rests, let the straps out as far as they would go, and secured the belts over his shoulders and around his waist. Then he shut his eyes and tried without much success to relax.

Erik's adoptive parents had been killed in an airplane crash-landing twelve years ago. A giant sinkhole opened up on the runway moments before their plane touched down, so it wasn't piloting error that caused the tragedy. The sinkhole was just a remnant of the war, a weak spot created by one of the many bombs that fell on Stockholm.

The doctor wasn't in an airplane, but the thought of any type of landing made him feel like there was a block of ice where his stomach used to be. He was grateful Danae wasn't there to see him dripping with perspiration and gripping the arms of the chair with white knuckles.

Sinkholes were never a concern at Earth spaceports because the ships didn't touch the ground, but that knowledge did little to soothe Erik's nerves. The landing platforms were erected half a kilometer or more above the soil, similar to the grid-style parking of the station spaceports, only without the airlocks. Instead, the platforms were connected by open breezeways horizontally and elevator shafts vertically. Only the ancient NASA shuttles required separate platforms and landing strips. The more modern McConnell-class starships could land and lift off without all the extra work, fuel, and expense.

"Five minutes." Danae's voice over the com sounded confident, as always. Erik wished he could channel a portion of that confidence into his psyche. *At least try not to puke this time.* He felt for the Banspace patch behind his right ear and rubbed it like a lucky rabbit's foot. He hoped there was enough medicine left in it to get him through the next few minutes.

The thought of being dirtside at The Lost Sheep held a lot of appeal. Erik was surprised when Jake volunteered to stay at the orphanage. The doctor assumed that with his experience at the Outreach Clinic, the position would be his. Still, he knew Jake would adapt quickly to his new role. *He was setting broken bones and doing minor surgery just a few days after starting work at the clinic. Eight months later, he's treating gunshot wounds and performing major surgery. Yes, Jake will do just fine.*

I'm not so sure how well I'll do taking over his *job.* Erik felt a trickle of sweat run down his back.

Danae Shepherd seemed pleased Jake volunteered. Erik knew it was an indication she was warming up to the idea of being more than friends, but he didn't want to get his hopes up too soon. He had learned from painful experience that he wasn't adept at navigating the emotional minefields of serious relationships.

Both of Erik's serious relationships ended for the same reason—his work. Both women tried to convince him to join a hospital staff and stop wasting his time treating people who had no way of paying him, but he wouldn't be swayed. Even now that Erik was the ripe old age of thirty-eight, the idea of going into private practice like a normal family practitioner still didn't appeal to him.

It was just a few weeks after serious girlfriend number two stormed out of Erik's life that Mars Community Hospital approved his request to open the Outreach Clinic. This endeavor finally helped him start to make a real difference in the homeless community. The thought of going out on a date hadn't crossed his mind since opening the clinic three years ago.

He would still be at the clinic, working eighteen hours a day, if it hadn't been for a fateful confrontation with Danae on the sidewalk outside the juvenile shelter Kirsten had established. Now, a month later, Erik was still focused on aiding homeless children, but he was going at it from a different angle with this makeshift search and rescue mission.

He signed a contract to work for Danae. For the first time in a decade he had a real job, and an attractive boss who made him blush like a prepubescent teenager whenever she smiled at him.

Dr. Sorensen was jolted from his reverie by the ominous sounds of metal scraping concrete.

"Tripods down." Blaze's announcement was followed by a sharp lurch that would have thrown Erik forward, but the safety harnesses held him in his chair.

"That's it," Danae said. "We're docked. Welcome to Bangkok."

Erik waited until his breathing was back to normal before releasing the straps and getting to his feet. He checked all of Ting's IVs and monitors to make certain nothing came loose during the landing.

"All crewmembers report to the bridge in five minutes."

Erik was grateful for the five minutes. It gave him enough time to take a two-minute shower and change into clean scrubs. Feeling his stress level was now within the range of normal, he checked on Ting again before exiting the infirmary and walking eight meters to the doorway of the bridge.

His jaw dropped as he was confronted by the sight of four shapely backsides, all clad in blue jeans. Danae, Phailin, Shima, and Lorina were crowded together, leaning over the helm control board, noses pressed to the small window. They were peering out at the cityscape of Bangkok on the window's magnified setting.

Erik's gaze shifted to Danae. Bent at the waist, her shirt rode up a few centimeters, exposing a sliver of her back. It was enough for him to note the difference between her normal skin tone and the darker pink synthflesh repair on her left side.

Jake wanted me to take a look at her side, Erik reminded himself, but then it occurred to him, *That'll be awkward.*

There were ethical and psychological boundaries all doctors had to navigate with certain patients. Examining a regular patient—a stranger—was straightforward, compared to examining a close friend or family member, particularly a member of the opposite sex. The latter required a level of detachment which could only be honed through years of practice. Erik was embarrassed to admit to himself he was nowhere near that level. *No, I won't be giving Danae Shepherd any medical exams on this trip, not unless it's a real emergency.*

Erik didn't realize he was blocking the doorway until Niyati squeezed by him and dashed over to join her mother at the helm.

"How's it look?" Blaze also slipped by him as he walked in after Niyati.

When Vipul arrived a moment later, the bridge was filled to capacity.

The four women turned away from the helm window. "You can tell it's still flooded," Phailin reported. "The wats are crumbling."

"What's a wat?" Blaze asked.

"A Buddhist temple," Phailin said. "They're usually painted gold. They were beautiful before the war— ostentatious, but beautiful."

Erik took Phailin's place at the window. He squinted at the urban jungle not far from the spaceport. "I can't see anything but gray buildings and smog."

The cook made an impatient noise. "You have to know what you're looking for." She pointed off to the right. "I can see the Chao Phraya River over there."

"The information in Thanatos's log stated that most of the factories are near the river." Shima's face shone with excitement and determination. "We just need to figure out which factory Zuri is in."

"So let's get started." Danae caught Erik's eye for a moment as she squeezed past her crew to reach the com control board. "We have a lot of ground to cover, so we'll venture out in pairs."

Pairs? Erik didn't have to guess who he would be paired with as Danae glanced at him again. *Should I be flattered or nervous about this arrangement?*

The crew huddled around the captain's chair as much as space would allow so they could all see the map of Bangkok on the right-hand com monitor.

"Phailin speaks Thai," Danae said, "so we have an interpreter."

"I speak a little bit," Phailin said. "I can understand a lot more than I can articulate. I lived in Chiang Mai for a few months, but that was a long time ago. My Thai is rusty. And I've only been to Bangkok once on a short vacation, so I'm not that familiar with the city."

"Relax, Miss Kim. The database can help fill any gaps in your memory." Danae tapped a keypad near her left hand. "Just download the translation program to your earcom."

"Yes, Captain." Phailin had already dropped the defensive attitude, and now she was embarrassed. "Sorry."

Danae just raised her eyebrows at the cook before turning her attention back to the map.

"What's the local time, Captain?" Vipul asked.

"Five p.m. Why?"

"It's not safe to roam the streets at night," Phailin answered for him. "We'd be foolish to attempt it, even armed."

Shima's face fell. "We must wait until morning?"

"Afraid so," Danae leaned back in her seat. "Safety first." She gave Shima a sympathetic glance. "But let's use this evening to map out a real strategy so we don't waste time wandering around the city like a bunch of—what's the word for tourist, Phailin?"

"*Falang.*"

"Yes, let's try not to act like bunch of *falang*s."

***

Alex's crew and Niyati gathered in the entryway at 0800. Each pair had been assigned a different area near the Chao Phraya to search. They loaded their Excaliburs under Danae's supervision.

Erik slid the magazine into the hollow chamber of his pistol grip. When he heard it click, he checked to make certain the safety was still on, and the gun was set for single fire. He glanced at Danae for a nod of approval, and then tucked the gun and an additional magazine into the right front pocket of his jeans.

As someone who took an oath to preserve life, the doctor wasn't happy about carrying an instrument of death on his person, but he assumed he wouldn't need to use it since he would be protected by a skilled markswoman who had no reservations about pulling the trigger.

"Earcoms?" Danae spoke to the group. "Passports?"

Erik checked both and took a minute to organize his small backpack, filled with bottled water, protein bars, and emergency medical supplies.

"Erik and I will return in four hours because he shouldn't leave Ting unmonitored for long, but the rest of you search until dusk, if you can. Are there any questions?"

"Could Lorina and I trade off at 1400?" Blaze asked.

Erik noted the exasperated scowl Lorina shot Blaze, but Danae spoke up before the engineer could get an earful from his wife. "No, it will be your turn tomorrow. Just be a good dad and monitor the com."

"Yes, Captain." Blaze shot Lorina a look filled with concern, but he had nothing else to say. He reached down and took Niyati's small hand.

The child didn't know what was going on, but she figured out *amma* was leaving. She threw herself facedown on the floor and started to throw a tantrum. "Nooooo! *Amma*, take me wiv you!"

Blaze picked up Niyati, leaned over and kissed Lorina goodbye, and whisked their hysterical daughter to the starboard lift.

Now Lorina looked concerned, but she avoided eye contact with everyone until they could no longer hear Niyati's screams. "Sorry," she muttered.

"Nothing to be sorry about," Erik said. "Let's hope the kids Thanatos shipped here have as much volume as she does. It will make it easier to find them."

Lorina flashed him a grateful smile.

"I've worked with thousands of street children," he added, "and, trust me, Niyati behaves better than most."

"Let's get moving." Danae cycled open both airlock doors. The crew followed her through the antechamber and descended the stairs to the landing platform.

Stepping outside the ship was like walking into a furnace. A wave of sticky tropical heat seemed to smack Erik right in the face. An involuntary "ugh!" escaped his lips, and he began to sweat beneath his heavy blue jeans. He questioned Phailin earlier about what they should wear into the city, and she surprised him by saying, "As much clothing as possible. You'll never see Thais in shorts."

I hope Danae doesn't mind the stench. By the time their lift reached the surface, Erik felt as if he'd gone swimming fully dressed. He wiped his forehead on a shoulder of his shirt so sweat wouldn't drip into his eyes.

The crew walked for half a kilometer across an ancient parking lot of cracked, pockmarked concrete to the tramstop, where about a dozen spacers from other ships were waiting for the next shuttle. The other travelers were dressed in shorts and appeared much more comfortable in the heat than the *Alex*'s crew.

"They'll stand out like *falang*s," Phailin whispered loud enough for her five crewmates to hear. "They'll be magnets for thieves."

Most of the *Alex*'s crew would blend in somewhat with their natural, or altered, dark skin and hair color, with the exception of Danae, whose hair was back to its natural brown, and Lorina, who was showing some strawberry-blond mixed in with her black strands.

Phailin decided Lorina's hair might attract unwanted attention. "Here." She took a flexible sun hat out of her backpack and helped Lorina bundle her long hair under it. "That's better."

The cook cast Erik a sheepish grin. "Sorry I can't do anything to help you look less conspicuous, Dr. Sorensen."

He shrugged. "That's all right. I'm used to it." He stood out anywhere he went because he was larger than most men, but here he would also stand out due to his white-blond hair and pale complexion.

"Your size might be an advantage," Phailin said. "Most Thais are short and small, so I'm sure no one will try to mug you."

Too late to worry about being mugged. My first concern should be avoiding heatstroke. He wiped his forehead again on a shoulder of his shirt.

Phailin explained the tram schedule to everyone. The sign on the lamp post was written in both Thai and English. "Green line goes across the river to the Wat Prayoon, that's where Shima and I need to search. Purple line makes a stop at the Grand Palace ruins on this side of the river, that's your area, captain and doctor. Blue line heads southeast, so Lorina, you and Vipul should just get off when you're close enough to see the river."

Erik caught sight of an approaching tram. "Purple line."

"Check in with Blaze at least once an hour," Danae told the others as she and Erik moved forward to board the tram.

The Bangkok trolleys were the standard, mass-produced models, but more colorful than the ones on Mars Station. The Purple line tram was bright purple, inside and out, with the profile of a golden elephant painted beneath each window.

Erik tried not to gawk like a tourist as he climbed aboard after Danae. He swiped his left thumbnail through the credit flash slot next to the android driver's seat and sat with Danae near the back, where it was less crowded.

Thais on the tram stared at the doctor with unabashed curiosity. He ignored them and gazed out the window as the vehicle made its way to the outskirts of Thailand's capital.

Bangkok was a dirty, crowded city, not quite modern and not quite decrepit, but somewhere in-between. Empty shells of crumbling brick apartment buildings sagged next to towering new buildings with bright pink stucco siding and gleaming tinted windows. The shops and businesses which lined the streets were either brightly painted, neat and inviting, or they were looted hovels with smashed windows, dark and neglected.

The street vendors did a thriving business, their push-carts and kiosks lined the sidewalks bordering the curbs or next to the buildings, leaving barely enough room for people to walk between them. Erik noted the variety of items being sold. Fresh fruits and vegetables, old dishes, ancient electronics, colorful silk blouses and ties, flowers, and roasted octopus tentacles skewered on sticks. *Like gross shish-kebobs,* he thought with a grimace.

The first wat they passed was in ruins, as Phailin mentioned, but scores of people surrounded it, reverently touching the exterior walls, leaving garlands of small white flowers on the blue tiled steps, and rubbing the toes of the large golden Buddha statue next to the caved-in entranceway. Erik noticed the Buddha was missing an arm and half of its smiling face.

"Why are they rubbing the feet?" Danae muttered.

"No idea."

"I'll ask Phailin when we get back to the ship."

The tram made a stop at the wat and traveled on. It made a right turn and began to drive through standing water. Erik could see the flood wasn't more than a decimeter in depth, but here the street vendors sold their wares from small narrow boats. People splashed along the submerged sidewalks in brackish water up to their knees, going about their business the same way they did on the dry streets, although the crowds were much thinner here.

"The Venice of Southeast Asia," Danae said.

"Venice sank eighty years ago."

"Bangkok will too, someday. The Chao Phraya is taking over."

"I assume the factories were built on higher ground."

Danae shrugged. "I won't make any assumptions about this place."

The android driver announced the next stop in both Thai and broken English, "Gland Pa-lice."

"Sounds like a new disease." Erik got to his feet. "This is our stop."

He went ahead of Danae, but hesitated at the open doorway, looking down at the green, foul-smelling water which was almost level with the lowest step of the tram. "I guess we should've brought hip-waders."

She poked him in the back. "Go ahead. It can't be any worse than a clogged toilet."

"I can't say I've ever stuck my feet in a clogged toilet." Erik suppressed a grimace and disembarked. The water felt warm, but as it soaked through his shoes, socks, and jeans, it turned cold and clammy. He turned and offered Danae a hand down. She gave him a dubious look—he wasn't sure if the expression was directed at him or the water—but she accepted his assistance and joined him on the street-turned-canal. They waded away from the tram so it wouldn't drench them when it drove on.

Hiking through shin-deep water, where bits of trash and things Erik didn't want to examine too close floated on the surface, was a lot harder than he expected. He grabbed Danae's arm whenever she seemed to be losing her balance, and she did the same for him. After ten minutes of this comic routine, Danae grasped his left arm with both hands and held on tight.

"I could give you a piggy-back ride," Erik said, half kidding, half serious.

Danae gave him a wary glance again, then started to laugh. She pointed out a dead rat drifting nearby, half submerged in what appeared to be a cow pie. "If I see anything more disgusting than that, I'll take you up on the offer."

Erik grimaced. "More disgusting than that, and you'll have to carry me."

They both laughed for a minute. Then they passed another waterlogged rat and started laughing again. Erik couldn't explain why something so revolting struck them as hilarious. It was just one of those moments when it was impossible to be serious.

He forced himself to sober up so he could catch his breath. He took time to study their surroundings and noticed there were few people around. The doctor felt a nudge of concern, but the mold-encrusted outer wall of the Grand Palace ruins captured his full attention.

The cracked stucco exterior wall was in better condition than the buildings it surrounded. The soaring conical roof of a golden wat—a once-famous landmark Erik recognized from old holograms—was now bent over at a weird angle, like a birthday party hat that fell off a child's head. Near the deformed wat, a massive building sported an ornate green-tiled roof with so many gaping holes, it resembled moldy Swiss cheese. Vines curled around every part of the Grand Palace ruins, as if the jungle was determined to take up residency.

"In fifty years, this will look like the Angkor Wat in Cambodia," Danae said. "But let's keep moving."

Erik agreed. "Since no one's around, I'm guessing the locals think this place is haunted. Maybe we should backtrack to the main street."

"No, according to the map, this way is faster."

"Yes, Captain." He said it without a hint of irony, but still received another curious glance from her.

"What would you like me to call you? You're my boss now."

"Danae works fine." She paused for a moment and focused on raising her left foot out of the water. It was entangled in a large clump of muddy weeds.

"Need some help?"

"Just keep me from falling in." She leaned on his arm and reached down with one hand to clear off her boot.

"And I don't think of you or Shima as employees," she said, choosing her words with care, and deliberately averting her face as she focused on pulling weeds. "More like . . . equals."

Erik didn't think *equals* was the word Danae was searching for, but before he could ask for clarification, he caught a glimpse of a long thin shape, just below the surface, gliding toward them in a sinuous side-to-side motion which could only be made by one type of creature.

Snake? He didn't intend to let it get close enough to find out.

"Time to go!" He scooped up an astonished Danae in both arms and ran.

"*What are you doing?*" she shrieked.

"Just hang on!" Erik glanced over his shoulder and saw the snake was gaining on them. It was just a meter away from his legs. He tried to put on speed, but his soaked jeans made it impossible to lengthen his stride.

Facing forward again, he discovered that the snake was chasing him toward a pair of shabbily dressed Thai men standing beneath the canopy of a large Banyan tree. *I smell trouble.*

As Erik got closer, he could see both men wore unfriendly smiles, and one of them had something in his hands that resembled a remote control. Erik realized what was happening. *It's not a real snake!*

Danae spotted the danger too. "Quick, put me down!" She was already reaching for her right hip pocket, but Erik's arm was in the way.

He realized too late he should've stopped running before trying to set Danae on her feet, but he was subconsciously fleeing the snake right behind them. He overbalanced and pitched forward. They both went down, sending waves in every direction.

Erik's knees hit pavement and water drenched his face, temporarily blurring his vision, but he struggled to his feet as fast as he could. He heard an explosion of splashes a few meters ahead of him, along with a choked gasp of either fear or pain.

"*Danae!*" He stumbled forward, wiping the water from his eyes, but was brought up short by a sharp command in broken English.

"*Stop! Doon move!*"

Dr. Sorensen froze and stared at the scene in front of him, fear washing over him faster than the floodwater which soaked him from head to foot.

The men from the Banyan tree had overpowered Danae and were flaunting that fact in Erik's face. One of the men, who was grinning maniacally, showing off crooked yellow teeth, was holding her arms behind her back. The other, who had on a pair of mirrored sunglasses with one cracked lens, clutched a fistful of her hair in one hand, forcing her head back. The other hand held what looked like a small machete beneath her chin.

Erik locked eyes with Danae, hoping to glean a little advice from something in her expression. She appeared more angry than scared. He hoped she was formulating a plan since *he* had no idea what to do.

"*Ba-gh!*" Yellow Teeth inclined his head toward Erik.

"What?" It hadn't occurred to him until this moment that the men intended to rob them.

"Your backpack," Danae said, earning herself a sharp yank on her hair from Broken Sunglasses. She gasped. A smoldering rage replaced any trace of fear on her face.

Despite the precariousness of the situation, Erik felt a stirring of admiration for Danae's temper. It had a powerful calming effect. Now he knew what to do.

He stripped off his backpack and tossed it toward them. "Let her go!" He pointed to his left thumbnail. "We don't have any money! See? It's all on here!"

Broken Sunglasses shot Erik a threatening scowl before reaching with his knife to hook one of the bag's straps before it could sink.

The instant the knife was away from Danae's throat, Erik pounced. He closed the space between them in two strides, bringing his foot down hard on Broken Sunglasses' knife hand. The man let out a howl of pain and let go of her hair.

Yellow Teeth released Danae in a panic, turned, and ran away as fast as the filthy water would allow.

Erik seized Broken Sunglasses by the collar and hoisted him out of the water so high his feet dangled in midair. "Do something *useful* with your life!" he shouted in the thug's terrified face.

The doctor shoved the Thai away from him. Broken Sunglasses hit the water spread-eagle with a huge splash, then scrambled to his feet, and took off after Yellow Teeth.

"You know he doesn't have a clue what you said." Danae was the picture of calm as she stretched her arms and rubbed each shoulder alternately. "What were you running from anyway?"

It took Erik a minute to calm down. He wanted to ask Danae, "Are you hurt?" but it was obvious she was fine. *Or at least, she does a great job of appearing fine.* He gave her a sheepish grin, turned around, and scanned the water.

"This was chasing us." He reached down and retrieved the meter-long, black, mechanical device. "Remote control snake."

"Used to chase unsuspecting *falang*s into ambushes." Danae waded over and took a moment to examine the fake snake. "I knew there was a good reason you took off like I was a heart attack patient you needed to rush to the hospital."

"Heart attack would be a good description of what I just experienced."

Danae chuckled and then surprised Erik by giving him a hug. "Thanks for the rescue, doctor."

Despite the fact that they were both dripping wet in putrid water, Erik wanted the hug to last as long as possible. But he resolved to be a gentleman and released her when she pulled away. *Well, a three-second hug is better than no hug at all.*

"I think we should get moving. The next muggers we run into might have guns." Danae turned away from Erik as she said this and glanced back at the Grand Palace ruins. She rubbed the top of her head where Broken Sunglasses had gripped her hair.

"Do you want me to take a look at your scalp?"

Danae's momentary hesitation convinced him she was in pain, but predictably, she said, "No, I'm fine," and started moving again, trudging through the water in the direction of the river.

Erik put his backpack on, tossed the mechanical snake away, and caught up to her in a few strides.

***

"That looks like an illegal factory," Danae said.

An arduous hour of hiking several flooded side streets brought them to the banks of the Chao Phraya. A nondescript, windowless brown stucco building stood at a higher elevation, on dry ground. A tall razor-wire fence encircled the boxy structure, which appeared to be four stories high.

No signs were posted anywhere. "No paved roads," Erik noted. "I guess they use the river for transporting goods in and out."

He could see dozens of boats moving up and down the river. Small, fast-moving, banana-shaped boats with outboard motors louder than jet engines; house boats which looked as if they were being held together with super-tape and prayer; long, flat barges drifting slowly along, moving garbage and construction waste out of Bangkok; a fancy, gleaming yacht; and a few handmade canoes.

"Maybe for transporting people in and out too." Danae tilted her head, indicating a copse of trees partway up the incline. "Let's move closer."

It was a relief for Erik to have his feet on dry ground, although his soggy shoes felt like lead weights as they climbed the steep bank. He kept his eyes moving, searching for any signs of trouble. There were a few Thais in the vicinity, but they paid no attention to Danae and Erik. The natives were focused on reaching the busy floating boat docks on the lower part of the riverbank.

There were no other pedestrians on the elevated bank leading up to the factory, and Erik took that as an ominous sign. He was relieved when they reached the trees. The low-hanging palm leaves made it a good hiding spot. They both leaned against tree trunks and rested.

"Dr. Sorensen? Captain Shepherd?" Blaze's voice was in Erik's ear. A concerned glance from Danae reminded Erik they hadn't checked in with the ship for a while.

He tapped his earlobe. "We're safe, Blaze. We've just arrived at what looks to be a private factory."

"How are the others?" Danae asked.

"That's why I called. I need to connect you with Shima—" Blaze's voice was replaced with Phailin's.

"Captain, we have a problem. Some of the local CIPs—"

"What happened?" Danae asked. "Are you all right?"

Phailin tried to reassure her, but her tone wasn't convincing. "It's nothing serious. Shima was stopped and the CIPs asked to see her passport—"

"Why did they single her out?" Erik asked.

"I'm not sure, maybe just to harass us. Maybe Shima's the first African they've ever seen."

"What's happening now?" Danae asked.

"They studied her passport, but they keep giving her suspicious looks, and I'm afraid they'll try to search her."

"No!" Danae snapped. "You have to convince them not to do that! They'll find the gun and arrest her—and maybe you too!"

Phailin sounded really distressed now. "What do I say to them?"

"Tell them you're on your way back to the ship." Erik ignored Danae's warning glance. "Tell them you're just visiting for the day. You're tourists—a struggling city like Bangkok doesn't want to turn away tourist money."

"Do it," Danae agreed, biting her lip.

There was a pause, and Erik could hear Phailin in the background of his com, speaking to the CIPs in halting Thai.

He exchanged a worried glance with Danae.

"If anything happens to Shima . . ." There was a tremor in the captain's voice.

It was the first time Erik had seen Danae lose her nerve. Without taking time to think about what would be the most appropriate gesture, he put an arm around her shoulders and drew her close. Her eyes widened in surprise, but she didn't pull away. Together they listened to Phailin's conversation with the CIPs.

After what seemed like an interminably long time, Shima spoke up. "They are letting me go."

Danae let out a long breath. "That was *too* close," she whispered to Erik.

"But they insist on escorting us back to the ship, Captain," Phailin said. "They want to confirm my story."

"Do it," Danae said. "Just don't let them on board."

"Yes, Captain," Phailin said.

"Check in with me when you're free of your escorts," Danae said. "Shepherd out."

Erik half-expected her to move away from him, now that the crisis was over, but she surprised him by reaching up to grasp his hand on her shoulder. He rotated his palm so their fingers could intertwine.

Danae averted her gaze as she tapped her earcom with her free hand. "Blaze, what about Vipul and Lorina?"

"They have a lead, but Lorina wants to tell you about it herself. Hang on—"

Lorina's voice filled their earcoms. "Captain, I think we found something—an entire row of factories."

"You're sure?" Danae asked. "Describe them."

"Large buildings with no windows, about four stories tall, surrounded by razor-wire fences."

Erik and Danae glanced at the factory a few meters uphill from their location.

"Do they have any signs on the fences or near the entranceways?" Erik asked.

"No signs of any kind," Vipul reported. "But the armed guard patrolling the grounds inside the fence is definitely a keep-out sign."

Erik caught Danae's eye. "Armed guard?" he whispered.

"Instructions, Captain?" Lorina sounded nervous.

"Take some holograms, have Blaze note the location on the map, and return to the ship," Danae said.

"But how will we know if Zuri's in one of these factories?" Lorina asked. "We need to get a closer look."

"If you can see an armed guard, that's close enough. Let's meet back at the ship and plan our next move. Do you have a problem with that?"

"No, Captain." Erik noted the reluctance in Lorina's reply.

"Shepherd out." She lifted her chin to look at Erik with the serious gaze he was becoming well-acquainted with. "We need to see if there's a guard patrolling this place."

Erik looked up the hill. "There's nowhere else to hide if we try to move closer."

Danae frowned. "We'll just have to pretend we're lost tourists if we're stopped."

She started to move away, but he hooked her elbow and turned her on the spot to face him. He ignored her irate scowl. "I don't think we should risk getting caught—or shot."

"We need to know if this factory is using slave labor." Danae looked determined. She had already made up her mind. Erik was just beginning to appreciate how much effort Jake had to exert to ensure her recovery after Thanatos shot her.

But she has no idea how stubborn I can be too. "Take your own advice, Danae. Let's assume it's a slave factory and go back to the ship."

"It's my call," she said, "and I say it's a justified risk."

Erik stared at her for a moment, incredulous. "Your call? What happened to that nice little speech about equals?"

Her determination faded. "I . . ." She had no answer prepared, as Erik suspected.

"What would you say to Shima if she recommended retreating?"

Danae looked as if she swallowed a lemon, whole. "I'd . . . take her advice."

He couldn't help grinning. "Well, just imagine I have as much common sense as Shima."

"Are you saying I *don't* have any common sense?" Danae slowly returned the grin.

Erik was reluctant to release her arm. "I think you've got more common sense . . . and courage than anyone I've ever met." There was so much more he wanted to say, but he knew this wasn't the time or place.

He saw a flush of pink dot her cheeks, but she turned away, looking back down the hill. "It's a long hike, so let's head back to the ship, doctor."

"Yes, Captain."

SIXTEEN
STAKEOUT

"WE SHOULD REACH the spaceport in forty-five minutes, Captain." Heath Bergen didn't look up from the helm controls.

Cade noted with approval Bergen's experienced hands on the accelerator and decelerator levers. "Bring up an image of Hat Yai, Diaz."

"Yes, Captain."

A bird's eye view of the Malaysian city came up on Cade's left-hand monitor. He felt a stab of fear. "Magnify image."

The picture zoomed in, and Cade's jaw dropped. *No! That can't be right!* "What is this? Diaz, is the holo-satellite imaging the right city?"

"Yes, sir." Diaz's reply was squeaky. Cade was accustomed to nervous junior officers, particularly when his volume began to escalate, but he didn't give the young man a second thought.

"Did the spaceport give you clearance, Bergen?" Cade got to his feet, moving to stand behind his calm and composed helm officer.

"It was an automated reply, Captain."

"Let's hear it," Cade said.

"Yes, sir." Diaz was beginning to perspire as his hands flew over the controls.

A mechanical female voice came over the bridge's com speakers. "Hat Yai port master's office is temporarily out of service. All ships please proceed with care to the nearest landing platform of your choice. Thank you for visiting Hat Yai."

"*Out of service!*" Cade roared. "Bergen, have you ever heard of such a thing?"

"Yes, for smaller spaceports—" Bergen began in a reasonable tone.

"Hat Yai *isn't* a *small* spaceport!"

"Is there a problem, Captain?" Wisdom Moniesa spoke up from her seat next to the navigation officer.

Cade glanced over at her stern expression, which had *calm down* written all over it. "Yes, there's a problem. Diaz, bring up the magnified image on everyone's screens."

"Yes, Captain."

The captain folded his arms. He only had to wait a few seconds for the reactions.

"It is not there, Captain!" Moniesa gasped.

"Looks like it's been bombed," Bergen said. "How long ago, I can't tell."

Cade felt as if there was a huge weight pressing down on his chest, making it difficult for him to breathe. "Another false lead." He wanted to retreat to the privacy of his office so he could punch something, but he returned to his chair and tried to keep a leash on his emotions long enough to issue new instructions to his crew. He brought up the list of Thanatos's delivery ports on his monitor and chose one he hadn't assigned the other ISPP ships.

"Let's head for Singapore. Bergen?"

"It should only take half an hour from here, Captain."

"Good." Captain York could feel all eyes on him as he rose again. Only Bergen knew Hat Yai had been Linc's last known destination, but Cade suspected that everyone on the bridge could see the shock and disappointment on his face. *I need to learn how to wear a calm mask, like Danae.* "I'll be in my office if anyone needs me. Carry on."

He made sure the door to his office was closed before he stepped into the head and closed that door too. He glimpsed his reflection in the mirror but shut his eyes so he wouldn't have to see the pain he could no longer contain.

"*Linc!*" Cade howled at the top of his lungs, pounding his fists on the sink counter until he managed to crack it. He cursed Thanatos, and Acheron, and the faceless monsters who robbed him of his beautiful family.

He cursed himself for being a failure with nothing to show for three years of chasing false leads from one end of the galaxy to the other, wasting time and resources, and eroding the confidence of his crew.

York didn't realize he was crying until he opened his eyes and saw the tears streaming down his face. He hadn't wept since Yong Min's funeral. He didn't want anyone on the crew to see him this way and made an effort to get his emotions under control. He filled the sink with warm water and scrubbed his face, trying to wash away any last remnants of self-loathing.

When Cade peered in the mirror again to dry his face, only the redness in his eyes betrayed his emotional breakdown. He could take care of them with a few eye drops.

He stepped out of the head and slouched into the chair at his desk. He felt drained, both physically and emotionally.

"Approaching Singapore, Captain York," Bergen announced over the com. "We land in fifteen minutes."

Cade made some kind of affirmative sound and put his head down on the desk.

"Captain York?" It was Diaz, and he sounded nervous.

"What is it?"

"Transmission just received for you, Captain."

He chafed at the thought of dealing with yet another problem from one of the ISPP captains under his command. "Who sent it?"

"It's from Captain Danae Shepherd, sir. It was forwarded from Mars by Judge Forsetti."

Cade sat up. "Put it through to my office."

"Yes, sir." Diaz sounded relieved. He had probably been expecting a harangue for disturbing the captain.

Cade brought up his screen. "Play Shepherd transmission."

He was pleased to see that Danae Shepherd's short wavy hair was all one color now—brown. Her tan had faded, leaving some freckles behind. Her intense blue eyes seemed to bore right through him, as usual, and her calm expression lifted his spirits.

"This transmission is intended for Captain Cade York of the Interstellar Peacekeepers Patrol warship, the *Title of Liberty*, docked at Mars Station, and was recorded on November twenty-eighth.

"Cade, thank you for sending us the encryption translation. We were able to determine from it where we needed to search. We're in Bangkok, and we've discovered several factories that appear to be slave run.

We don't know which one is holding Shima's niece, but I thought I should let you know what we found, as you requested. There are armed guards around these factories, so getting inside might be difficult for us to attempt."

A map of Bangkok appeared on his monitor with the target areas circled in red. The map was followed by several holograms of the factories, photographed from different angles. Cade couldn't deny they appeared to be factories—or prisons. *Or both,* he thought.

Danae came back on screen. *"Alex's Legacy* is docked at the Bangkok Spaceport, Level 7, Platform 18. We're trying to decide how to proceed. Please let me know if there are any ISPP ships nearby that can aid us."

She paused, her expression turning serious. "Cade, I have a strong feeling we need to do something *right now*. I can't explain it, but I think you understand sometimes captains have to trust their intuition. I'll wait twenty-four hours for a response from ISPP, then we're going in alone. Shepherd out."

"Com—Bergen?"

"Yes, Captain?"

"We're delaying the Singapore mission. Change course for Bangkok."

"Yes, Captain."

"We are enjoying this tour of Asia, Captain," Moniesa chimed in. Cade figured he deserved the barb.

"We need each crewmember to stop by the arsenal before we reach Bangkok."

He could hear his weapons officer laughing. "Shall I distribute poison-tipped chopsticks, Captain?"

"They don't use chopsticks in Thailand," Cade replied with mock sternness. "Just handguns, please."

"Yes, Captain."

***

The flight to Bangkok took less than an hour. Cade used the time to pore over Thanatos's log again. *What did I miss? Did he intend to take Linc to Hat Yai but made a detour when he saw it was destroyed?* The datapad yielded no new clues.

Cade had to consider another possibility, one that twisted his stomach into a knot. *Was Hat Yai destroyed after Linc was taken there?* He closed his eyes, trying not to think about it. *Please, God, let Linc be safe somewhere else. Please let me find him.*

"Fifteen minutes from Bangkok, Captain."

Cade rose from his desk and walked out to the bridge. "See if you can land close to Level 7, Platform 18. Diaz, contact the port master."

"Yes, sir." After some back and forth discussion, Diaz said, "We have permission to dock at Level 8, Platform 18."

"Well done." Cade nodded to him. "We'll make a senior officer out of you yet."

"Thank you, sir." Diaz puffed out his chest, looking pleased with himself.

"Now see if anyone on the crew speaks Thai."

Diaz deflated. "Yes, Captain."

"I'll need ship-to-ship com to *Alex's Legacy* as soon as we dock, in my office."

"Yes, sir."

Cade returned to his office, strapped in for the landing, and tried to get his thoughts in order. The *Liberty* shuddered for a few moments before settling into an eight-point landing, coming to an abrupt halt which would have injured anyone unsecured.

Bergen announced, "We're docked at Bangkok."

"Com to *Alex's Legacy* is open, Captain," Diaz reported.

"This is Captain Cade York of the ISPP warship the *Title of Liberty*, requesting to speak to Captain Danae Shepherd of the passenger ship *Alex's Legacy*."

"Good evening, Captain York. We aren't quite so formal here aboard the *Alex*." There was a trace of a European accent in the voice. "I can't put Captain Shepherd on the com right now because she's dirtside, doing some surveillance."

"What?" Cade turned around and stared out his office window. It was dark outside. "She went into Bangkok—at night?"

"That's right." The speaker sounded defensive but remained calm.

"Alone?" Cade knew Danae was headstrong, but was she foolish too?

"No. She's with her first officer, engineer, and cook."

"Her *cook*?" The captain wasn't sure if he was hearing right.

"The cook speaks Thai. In fact, she is Thai." The defensiveness switched to thinly veiled impatience. "So, is there anything I can do for you until she returns?"

Cade frowned and leaned back in his chair. "You could tell me who I'm addressing."

"Ship's medic, Erik Sorensen."

Ah, the ally Danae went back to rescue from Mars Station. "You could give me an update on your helmsman, Dr. Sorensen. Has he recovered?"

"Marco Ting is still comatose."

"Sorry to hear that. What's the plan for him?"

"We're not going to space him, if that's what you mean."

Cade grinned. He didn't expect to strike a nerve so early in the conversation. "I meant his treatment plan."

"I'm hoping to get him into the Bhumibol Memorial for neuromeld, just as soon as we locate and free Zuri Oketta."

"Yes, the crewmember's niece. Danae told me about her, which is why ISPP is here now—to assist with the rescue." Cade heard the doctor mutter something under his breath. "Is there a problem?"

"*Captain* Shepherd left me instructions to give you her com code."

"Thank you. Could you also provide me with Danae's current location?"

Now the muttering wasn't so subdued. "*Captain* Shepherd isn't ready for the Marines just yet, Captain York."

Cade shook his head, amused the medic was running intervention like an overprotective father. "Fine, I'll just get her com code, then, Dr. Sorensen."

"Transmitting." As soon as Cade received the code, the doctor signed off.

He didn't give the temperamental Sorensen a second thought. "Diaz, connect me with Captain Shepherd on ship-to-shore."

"Yes, sir."

There was a soft burst of static, and a clear contralto said, "This is Shepherd."

"This is York. The *Liberty* is at your service, Captain."

There was a moment of surprised sputtering before she replied. "Cade! You're in Bangkok already? I just sent the transmission yesterday."

"And I received it an hour ago, just as we were flying over Singapore." Cade decided to voice his first concern without preamble. "So tell me why you felt compelled to visit Bangkok at night. Trying to get yourself killed?"

"We've been here since 1700, hiding in some bushes overlooking one of the factories. It seemed wiser to stay put and keep watch than try to return to the ship after nightfall. From here we can just make out a courtyard between the two main buildings with a four-story wall on either side, connecting them. The walls make it look like one large building, but it's actually shaped like a fort."

"So you're planning to stakeout this fort all night?"

"It's not fun, but since I've already had a knife to my throat once—"

"*What?*"

She spoke over him. "—I thought we should lie low, until dawn."

"Where are you?" Cade asked. "I'll send a squad over right now to give you an armed escort back to your ship."

Danae's tone conveyed a hint of exasperation. "We're fine, Cade. Thank you for the offer, but it's not necessary."

"But—" Cade tried to get a word in, but she spoke over him again.

"There's too much going on to abandon this post right now. We've learned all the importing and exporting goes on after midnight."

"Captain!" interrupted an excited female voice in the background of Danae's com. "Look!"

"What is it?" Cade was bouncing on his heels, impatient to see what they were seeing.

"Kids! Girls, I think! Their heads are covered, but they have girls' figures," Danae reported. "They're being taken outside the fence and loaded into a van!"

"How many?" York asked.

"There's four," reported a deep masculine voice, also in the background.

Danae told Cade, "One of them is putting up quite a struggle."

There was a collective gasp from Danae's group.

"What? What happened?" Cade asked.

"They hit her with a nerve prod, twice." Danae's voice was choked with rage. "Now she's on the ground . . . and she's not moving . . . They're picking her up . . . and shoving her in the van with the other girls. . . Now the van is driving away."

"We must do something." This came from a different female voice than the first. "We must follow the van, Captain."

"You can't," Cade said, at the exact same moment Danae said, "We can't."

"Where are you?" he asked. "This is all the evidence we need to raid the factory."

There was a long pause as Danae consulted with her crew. Cade was only getting bits and pieces of the conversation, but he continued to listen intently. One of the women with Danae was starting to sound upset.

Where is she? I should've tagged her with a personal transmitter when she was in my office. Cade smirked. *Of course, she would've felt the tag and probably punched me in the nose, but it would be convenient to have a way to locate her right now.*

Cade recalled one of the stories his Israeli grandfather shared with him about his childhood. Satellites circled the Earth back in his grandfather's day, making it easy to locate anyone, anywhere, in an instant. During the war, every single satellite was blown up or disabled by electromagnetic pulses, throwing Earth's communications into chaos and setting technology back at least fifty years. Without satellites, making a local dirtside com call was more of a challenge than sending a message millions of kilometers into space via an interstellar transmitter.

Danae's impromptu staff meeting seemed to be taking a long time. Cade was about to signal Diaz to call the *Alex* again to request Danae's location when she spoke up.

"Shima is concerned, and I agree, that if ISPP raids this area tonight, the other factories might move their slaves somewhere else, and we'll lose the chance to rescue them. We need to find Zuri before ISPP gets involved."

"You summoned us, Danae. ISPP wants to free these kids just as much as you do. All of them, not just Zuri. We're involved whether you're ready or not. Do you have a plan?"

Danae hesitated. There was silence from the other three with her.

Cade counted to ten in his head to give her a chance to respond. When she didn't, he began outlining his own plan. "I'll send in small covert teams to survey the factories. We'll need to analyze every detail so ISPP can move in on all of them at the same time."

Danae started to protest, but he spoke over her. "We'll cover every exit so none of the kids can be smuggled out."

"But—"

"Trust me, Danae. I know what I'm doing." He paused a moment, but when she didn't reply, he felt a fresh stirring of impatience. "My ship has a crew of forty, but I'll send a message to the other ISPP ships."

"We can't wait a week for reinforcements."

Cade frowned at her sharp response. "I'll see if any ships are within a day's flight. If not, my crew will handle it alone."

"That sounds reasonable."

He felt better about this response, but there was still some uncertainty in her tone. *She still doesn't trust me.* This fact bothered him more than he cared to admit. "I'll send a surveillance team to each of the factories at daybreak."

"We'll be here. Shepherd out."

Cade paced his office for a few minutes, lost in thought. Then he walked out to the bridge and announced, "I want all crewmembers, both shifts, assembled in the galley in ten minutes. We're going into Bangkok at first light."

***

"Are you ready for ISPP to take over surveillance, Danae?"

Cade waited at the spaceport tramstop in the muted light of early dawn. Thirty-one members of his crew stood on the platform behind him, eight teams of four, including himself. They were all clad in plainclothes and waterproof boots. Each carried a backpack containing enough supplies to last for several days, and they were heavily armed. Bangkok was a gun-free city, which meant law-abiding citizens were fair game for armed criminals. Cade thought it was a stupid law, but since he wanted to avoid any confrontations with the local CIPs, their weapons were concealed.

Danae sounded exhausted. "Did Erik send you the map with the factory locations?"

"Yes, we have it." Cade made a face, recalling how reluctant the doctor had been to share the information.

"You'll see we've numbered each factory, although there may be others we haven't located yet."

"Eight factories, and I have eight teams with me, ready for surveillance. Which one have you been observing?"

"Number six." She made an exhaling noise he thought was a yawn. "We'll wait for you to take over this post before we return to the ship."

"Good." Cade checked the map on his datapad. "We should be there within the hour."

"Don't count on it," Danae said. "The flooded streets will slow you down."

He decided not to argue the point. "See you shortly. York out."

"Blue line tram, Captain," Moniesa reported, standing just behind Cade.

Cade nodded. "Let's get moving."

***

It was nearing 0800 when Cade's team reached the riverbank and factory number six, which was one of four he could see in this area. The factories had been constructed on a high plateau overlooking the Chao Phraya. A field of weeds sloped downward from the razor-wire fences for one hundred meters, until it dropped off from a ledge high above the brownish-gray water. Because of the steep bank, it appeared this area never flooded. Dozens of Thais kept their feet dry by traversing the weeded slope, walking to and from the boat docks farther downstream.

Cade could already tell from the foot traffic on the slope and the absence of trees on the plateau that finding secluded sites to spy on the four factories was going to be difficult. He instructed Moniesa, Diaz, and Tse to survey the perimeter of factory number six while he went to find Danae.

There was a rise on the north side the factory, about fifteen meters high, which flattened out at the top and was covered with tall flowering bushes. This seemed like the only logical place for a stakeout. He walked around to the back side of the slope so he could climb up without being seen by anyone on the factory grounds.

The hill was steep, and Cade was drenched with sweat by the time he reached the bushes. "Danae?" He ducked down and made his way into the foliage.

"Here." Captain Shepherd and her three crewmembers were sitting on the ground in a small clearing near the center of the overgrown bushes, sharing a breakfast of protein bars and bottled water. "Won't you join us?"

Cade didn't have much choice because it was impossible to stand upright without getting entangled in the densely woven canopy of branches. He squatted down next to Danae and nodded to her silent crew. They were each covered in dirt, and their eyelids were at half-mast.

Danae made introductions. "Captain York, this is Blaze Smith, my engineer, Phailin Kim, my cook and—in this setting—our interpreter, and Shima Oryang, my first officer."

"My team can take over now," Cade said. "I just need to know if you observed anything else last night after the four girls were taken away."

"Yes," Oryang spoke up. Cade turned to face the thin black woman. She was agitated. "Four girls were brought in last night in a different van. They all had their heads covered, and they were sobbing."

"They were much smaller than the four girls who were taken away," Kim added.

Cade glanced at the attractive Thai cook and ventured a guess. "New slaves?"

"We need to find out where the older girls were taken." Oryang's face reflected grim determination. "Zuri is fourteen now. She may not be a factory slave any longer."

"What do you mean?" Cade knew what Oryang meant but felt her concern needed to be aired.

She returned his frown. "I was born in Uganda, Captain York. I have witnessed human trafficking in all its forms. I just hope we are not too late to find Zuri."

"I hope so too," Cade said.

Moniesa's voice was in his earcom. "We have been spotted!" Then the unmistakable *crack* of gunfire reached his ears.

"What's happening? Report!" Cade crawled over to the edge of the plateau to an opening between two bushes. He stretched out flat on the ground and looked down at the factory. No one was in sight.

"The guard!" This reply came from Diaz. "He shouted something—a warning—and fired at us!"

"Anyone hurt?" Cade asked.

Danae stretched out on her belly next to York and handed him the oldest pair of field binoculars he'd ever seen.

"We are safe. I do not think his aim is good," Moniesa said. "We have retreated downhill, toward the river."

Cade put the binoculars to his eyes and searched for his team. They must have been on the opposite side of the factory because he couldn't see anyone. "You were supposed to stay out of sight."

Moniesa huffed. "We thought we were until he started shooting, Captain."

"Sarcasm aside." He tried not to snap at his weapons officer in front of Danae. "What kind of surveillance are they using?"

"Just the guard, as far as we can tell," Tse answered this time. "No holo-cams. Maybe hidden audio sensors."

"Audio would explain how the guard found you," Cade said. "Did you notice anything else?"

"The building has a single door on each side, no windows, and the fence seems to have only one gate, which is on the side facing the river," Tse said. "The scanner can't penetrate the exterior walls, so we know they're willing to spend a fortune on lead-lined titanium to hide whatever's going on inside. There's one gravel access road to the gate, but I can't see where it originates. One guard, obviously armed."

"Could you hear anything inside the building?" Cade asked.

"No, sir. We didn't get close enough to the fence to use the audio scanner before the guard started shooting."

Danae nudged him with her elbow. "Look left."

Cade shifted the binoculars in the direction she indicated and caught sight of a man dressed in green fatigues, coming around the corner of the building, inside the fence, with a heavy military-grade battle rifle in his hands. "You're sure, Tse? Just one guard?"

"Yes, sir."

He turned to Danae, noticing for the first time how close they were in the confined space, pressed shoulder to shoulder. When she tilted her head to look at him, their faces were only a few centimeters apart.

Cade forced himself to shift his gaze a fraction so he was looking into Danae's left ear instead of her mesmerizing blue eyes. *Focus, York, focus.* "If each factory has only one guard on duty, it should be easy to get inside without raising the alarm."

"As soon as your teams report back what they've observed at the other factories, we should plan the raid," Danae said.

"Not *we*, Captain. *Me*. ISPP will plan and carry out this mission."

Her calm expression morphed into a defensive scowl. "You're leaving us out?"

"I'm keeping you safe. I can't risk anyone on your crew getting hurt—or killed."

"I think we've proven we can take care of ourselves!" Danae rose to her knees and crawled backward away from the ledge.

He swore under his breath and crawled after her. He rejoined her crew in the clearing and glanced from face to face, searching for an ally but finding none in their skeptical and worried faces. Despite the aggravation, Cade admired their loyalty to Danae.

He turned again to the stubborn Captain Shepherd, who was sitting cross-legged in the dirt, not looking at him as she shoved loose items into a small backpack. "I know you want to help, but your crew has no military training. It's too dangerous for you to take part in the rescue."

She crammed a stray water bottle into her bag and turned to Cade with a look on her face which startled him with its ferocity. "If you *think*"— she cinched the backpack closed—"we're just going to *sit back*"—she slipped her arms through the straps—"and *do nothing!*"

"Captain!" Moniesa's voice was in Cade's ear. "Take cover!"

He heard the first *crack* of a rifle shot, and a branch just above his head quivered.

"Get down! Get down!" He was already hugging the ground before he finished giving the order. Danae and her crew scrambled to follow his example.

The branches above them cracked, popped, and splintered. Shredded leaves and bits of bark floated down as bullets peppered their hiding place.

"Your position has been compromised, Captain!" Diaz wailed.

"No kidding!" Cade snapped. "Take out the gunman!"

He heard the heavier *crack* of Moniesa's custom G50 pistol. She fired three times and then there was silence.

"The guard is down, Captain," she reported. "I suggest we retreat before the CIPs come to investigate."

"Meet us at the base of the hill in five minutes." Cade rose to his elbows and looked over at Danae, who rose to her knees and was brushing at the fresh layer of dirt on her formerly navy-blue T-shirt.

Her attitude was subdued as she made eye contact with him again. "Maybe it would be a good idea for ISPP to handle this mission without us."

Cade sat up and wiped the dirt from his hands onto the legs of his cargo pants. "I was about to say," he paused a moment to filter the accusation from his tone, "before you started shouting at me, that the area around this factory has audio surveillance."

Danae grimaced but didn't apologize. Her attention was diverted to her first officer.

Oryang was close to hysterics as she rose from her prone position. "Now they know someone is spying on the factory! They might move the slaves to another location!"

"My crew will keep watch twenty-four/seven to make sure that doesn't happen," Cade tried to assure her.

Oryang didn't look convinced, but Cade was more concerned with Danae's opinion. He glanced at her, hoping she would say something supportive.

"We should head back to the *Alex*." She crawled over to the back side of the plateau and started down the slope. Oryang, Kim, and Smith were right behind her. None of them gave Cade a second glance.

Captain York fumed in silence as he descended the hill after the *Alex*'s crew. He knew he should be grateful Danae agreed to stay out of the way so ISPP could do their job, but it had taken getting shot at to convince her. *She still doesn't trust me,* was the only explanation he could come up with, but he didn't have time to dwell on that particular frustration.

There was a lot of work to be done, and fast, because factory number six might alert the other factories to the security breach and the dead guard. Cade's crew would have little time to plan and coordinate a simultaneous raid on all eight factories. He wouldn't be able to wait for reinforcements from the other ISPP ships.

There was the remote possibility the factories functioned independent of each other, but this seemed unlikely if they all used slave labor. Cade had learned not to underestimate the organizational skills of criminals. They always seemed to be one step ahead of ISPP.

They might be making arrangements to move the girls from this factory right now, which means ISPP needs to be prepared for this raid tonight.

Now that their stakeout location had been discovered, his only option for discreet surveillance was the high-tech camouflage uniform each crewmember carried in his or her backpack. The thick, Chameleon fabric of the suits covered every centimeter of the body, which could be dangerous in this heat. They would have to use the suits' air conditioning systems, which were quiet but not silent. Yet another problem. How sensitive was the factory's audio surveillance?

Cade stifled a growl of frustration as he grasped an exposed tree root to scale a steep section of the slope. He didn't like being rushed into a mission his crew wasn't ready for. As an officer in the Earth Marines, he'd witnessed the tragic results of plans which came unraveled when too many details were unknown. When Cade was recruited to captain ISPP's flagship, he decided never to risk the lives of those under his command by sending them blind into dangerous situations. His cautious attitude had paid off—he'd never lost a member of his crew.

Now Cade was forced to throw caution to the wind if he wanted to liberate the children being held in these factories. He tried to clear his mind of the what-if scenarios and focus on the why. *Is it worth risking our lives to do this tonight?*

A loose stone slipped out from beneath Cade's left boot, and he was forced to scramble for a foothold so he wouldn't fall. He steadied himself and glanced downhill at Danae and her crew, who were watching him, waiting for him to finish the descent. Oryang's determined expression caught his eye for a moment, and he recalled why she was so motivated to take action.

How would I respond to the challenge if I knew Linc was in one of these factories? The thought renewed Cade's own determination, even if it was painful to consider the bleak reality that Linc wouldn't be among the rescued slaves in Bangkok.

Cade reached the base of the hill, where his officers had joined Danae's crew. He gave instructions to Moniesa, Diaz, and Tse. "Don your camo suits, and we'll find a new stakeout site." He then tapped his earcom twice. "Team leaders, I want status reports in five."

He made eye contact with Danae. "Go back to your ship, and get some sleep, Captain. We'll keep you informed of the situation with regular updates."

"Yes, Captain." For a moment she looked as if she wanted to say something else, but she just nodded and turned away.

SEVENTEEN
TATTOO

ZURI COULDN'T STOP shaking. She remained in her bunk long after the other girls went to breakfast. She dismissed Ekaterina's concerned query with a simple excuse. "I am not feeling well," which was the truth. However, Zuri added, "I will ask one of the wardens to take me to the infirmary," which was a lie, but she didn't want to worry her friend.

Ekaterina looked scared, but she nodded to Zuri and left the bunk room behind the other girls so she wouldn't be punished for being late to breakfast.

Zuri debated what to do, but she had no answers. She'd thought about this day for years, knowing when it arrived, her somewhat safe and predictable life as a slave would be over.

In Uganda, families held celebrations when a girl became a woman, as was the case in many other nations and cultures—reaching adulthood was a joyous time. As a slave, this transition would only bring joy to her captors. She knew her life was about to become a nightmare.

Tears blurred her vision as she crawled out of bed and hurried to the communal bathroom, hoping to avoid the wardens for as long as possible. A washcloth strategically placed might hide her secret for an hour or so, but she knew by this time someone would be looking for her. The human traffickers would take her away from the factory tonight, the only home she'd known for the past seven years.

She sat on the cold tiles and wept. She heard the warden's shout from the doorway, but she was too scared to move. Zuri knew she was risking the nerve prod, but it didn't seem to matter anymore.

"Get—up!" The warden hauled Zuri to her feet by the collar of her tunic and slapped her hard across the face. "What—wrong—with you?"

The girl ignored her throbbing cheek and shook her head, refusing to answer. She knew this particular guard only by the nickname the other girls had given her, Crooked Nose.

Crooked Nose looked down at the tiles where Zuri had been sitting and saw the evidence for herself. "Ha! We get—good price—for you, pretty face!"

The warden seized Zuri's right arm and twisted it behind her back, forcing the teen to walk ahead of her. They exited the bathroom, descended several flights of stairs, and walked down a long hallway to an area of the factory off-limits to slaves. A vault-like door swung open at Crooked Nose's verbal command and slammed shut once they were through.

Zuri's destination was a small, windowless examination room which seemed better suited for animals than humans. There were steel shackles attached to each corner of the small rectangular table in the center of the room.

The sight of the table sent a thrill of terror through Zuri. *They are going to torture me!* She dug in her heels and tried to stop the warden from forcing her onto the table, but someone else, someone very strong, seized Zuri from behind and slammed her facedown onto the stainless steel surface.

Her chin hit the table hard, and she tasted blood. It took less than a minute for Crooked Nose to secure her wrists and ankles to the corners of the table.

"We get—good price—for you!" Crooked Nose repeated with a cackle.

Zuri turned her head from side to side, desperate to see what was happening, but Crooked Nose and the stranger who forced her onto the table remained out of her range of vision. All Zuri could see were the bare walls of the room and her immobilized wrists in the shackles.

Crooked Nose spoke to the stranger. Zuri heard a deep masculine voice reply. The conversation was short and curt, the words spoken too fast to translate, but she did understand the word for pain.

What kind of pain? A nerve prod—or something worse?

When her captors finished talking, she heard one of them leave the room. The one who remained moved about, opening and closing drawers on the exam table. Zuri heard the clatter of metal items, like cutlery, and felt a fresh jolt of fear.

"What is happening—*what are you doing to me?*"

"*Silence!*" The man bellowed at her.

A powerful hand seized the back of Zuri's right calf. She heard a strange, low-pitched buzzing noise and, without warning, something sharp punctured her skin.

Zuri screamed, but she could do nothing to defend herself. The buzzing sound and the pain continued, slowly extending along the tender skin on the underside of her right knee, like the edge of a razor. All she could do was scream as she felt the blood from the incision trickle around to her kneecap and drip onto the table.

Her captor made no move to blot her bleeding leg but continued to extend the incision. Down, up, a short loop, and then down again.

Zuri was breathless from screaming. The back of her leg began to sting like a dozen hornets had attacked it. She clamped her lips together and wept in silence as the wound was slowly enlarged.

She realized the man was carving a pattern or design into her leg. The humming noise was coming from a tattoo needle. *A tattoo—so the traffickers can identify me or find me again if I ever escape.*

Finally the buzzing noise ceased, and the torture was over. Zuri felt an icy blast of moist air on her leg, and the bleeding stopped. Her handler blotted her leg and the table with an absorbent cloth, and then released his hold on her calf.

Is that it? Is it over? Zuri tried to breathe again.

Her relief was short-lived.

Her captor seized her left arm, just above the elbow, and her skin was punctured again. Zuri was too exhausted to scream, even though the incision felt deeper this time. The cut was extended only a few centimeters. The cutting tool was removed, and she felt something hard and small inserted into the wound.

Zuri had no idea what was being placed under her skin, and that thought was more frightening than the identifying tattoo.

The blast of cold air was repeated, and this incision was bandaged.

She waited, trembling, wondering if more pain awaited her. She was surprised to feel the shackle removed from her left ankle, then her right.

Her captor walked around to the head of the table and released her wrists. "Get up."

Zuri rolled over and shifted her legs over to the edge of the table, hissing in pain as the raw wound from her leg brushed the surface. She stood with care, holding on to the edge of the table to steady herself.

Crooked Nose threw the door open and came into the room. The warden shoved a towel wrapped around a bundle of clothes at Zuri. "This way."

The teen followed Crooked Nose out of the room. The throbbing pain on the back of her leg made it difficult to walk without limping.

"In here."

Zuri went through the doorway indicated, and the door was shut and locked behind her. She found herself alone in a small bathroom with a shower.

Standing under the warm water, Zuri turned her leg so she could examine the tattoo for the first time. It was some type of message, written in a dozen unfamiliar characters. She didn't know which language the characters came from. Scabs were forming where her skin had been etched, although she could see the ink was neon-yellow, which would stand out from her dark skin.

She raised her left arm and examined the bandaged area. *Some kind of implant to keep track of me?* She thought about trying to remove it, but the area was so small, she would need tweezers or even a probe android. *No, I have been through enough pain for one day.*

Zuri towel-dried her crew cut and slipped into the clean clothes, which consisted of silky new underwear and a wraparound dress which was so skimpy, she considered putting her dirty slave tunic back on.

She sighed in defeat and sat on the toilet lid. There was no question in her mind what the human traffickers intended to do with her. Zuri found it ironic the reason she was here was no longer an issue. She suspected the item implanted under her arm stopped her menstruation.

What a cruel reward for becoming a woman today.

Crooked Nose banged on the door and let herself in. Zuri was taken to yet another small, windowless, dimly lit room, which contained an unmade cot and a flimsy table. On the table was a cup of water and a bowl of lukewarm rice—no spoon. Crooked Nose left Zuri alone, locking the door behind her.

Zuri sat down and ate, scooping the rice into her mouth with trembling fingers. She couldn't stop the tears this time, and she didn't even try.

***

Zuri didn't know how many hours had passed. She heard the key in the lock and stood to face the inevitable. She squinted at the sudden illumination from the hallway outside as the door was thrown open.

Two women she never saw before came in and tied her arms behind her back with ruthless efficiency. A large cloth bag was placed over her head, and her captors escorted her down hallways and one staircase, shoving her if she stumbled or tried to limp slower. Zuri stubbed her bare toes many times, but she was determined not to cry out.

"Ruan shot," one of her guards informed the other. "Dead."

Zuri had to translate some of the words in her mind to be certain she heard right. She wanted to ask, "Who is Ruan?" but knew that would earn her some abuse. It was safer to remain silent.

"CIP?" the other guard asked.

"Don't know. Early morning. Three people outside fence."

Her escorts stopped, and she heard another door being unlocked and opened. Zuri could smell fresh air and sense the lower humidity; it was nighttime. There was the sound of a motor running nearby. Her escorts shoved her forward, and she felt gravel beneath her feet. *I am outside the factory!*

Zuri had a sudden and desperate urge to *see*. She didn't care what her punishment would be, she knew this would be her only chance to see anything outside the factory walls. She dropped her chin and shook her head to get the loose hood to fall off.

"Stop!" One of the guards shoved her so hard, she fell to her knees.

Zuri ignored the sharp gravel that bit into her bare legs. Free of the hood, she brought her head up and looked around, determined to have this precious moment to see the beautiful night sky and the soft moonlit glow of a river in the distance.

She was just a few steps from the open gate of a tall, razor-wire fence. A black solar van idled just outside the fence. The side cargo door was already open and waiting for her.

The hood was again forced over Zuri's head, and her factory guards hauled her to her feet, but at the same moment she heard a woman's shout in the distance.

"*Zuri!*"

The night exploded with screams and gunfire.

EIGHTEEN
FEARLESS

SHIMA APPROACHED DANAE first, catching her during a quiet moment when the captain was alone in the galley, sitting at her favorite table and drinking a cup of chamomile tea.

She took a seat across from Danae and said what she needed to say before she lost her nerve. "I want to go back to factory number six tonight."

Danae set her cup down with a sigh of frustration. "We've been over this, Shima. Cade needs us to stay here so we don't get in the way."

"Not *we—me*. I will go alone."

The captain's mouth fell open. "*No*. Even if it was a good idea—which it's not—it's too dangerous for anyone to go into Bangkok at night. Going alone is out of the question."

"I am not afraid."

"Well, I am," Danae shot back. "ISPP will raid the factories tonight. There's no reason for you to risk your life just so you can watch the spectacle. It's crazy."

"Is it?" Shima hated arguing with her best friend like this, but she had to make Danae understand. "You think I am crazy?"

"We don't even know if Zuri is in factory number six."

"We know there are *girls* in number six. We must find out where the older girls were taken last night. It may be our only chance to find Zuri."

"Cade said he'd handle it. We have to trust him. He'll find Zuri."

"He does not even know what Zuri looks like. How can you expect me to trust Captain York when you do not trust him yourself?"

Danae was speechless for a moment. "Of course I trust—" she stammered.

"He looks like Alex." She hated to voice her theory, but she needed to be honest with Danae. "You do not want to trust Captain York because, if you did, you would have no reason to avoid him. He reminds you of your husband."

Shima felt a pang of regret at the grief which swept Danae's features. "They may look alike, but Cade is nothing like Alex."

"I know." She reached across the table and grasped Danae's hand. "I am sure Captain York knows what he is doing, but once they raid the factories and arrest the slavers, it may be impossible to find out where the van took the older girls."

Danae bit her lip. "I understand how helpless you must feel, Shima." She held up her teacup with a sad smile. "This is my fourth cup of chamomile, and it's not even taking the edge off my anxiety. I feel like there's something *more* we need to do, but after being shot at this morning, I had to face reality." She shook her head. "This is too dangerous for us to meddle in. ISPP plans to storm the factories at 0230, and then it'll be over."

"The van with the older girls left at 0130," Shima said.

"I could call the *Liberty*," Danae offered without much conviction. "I could ask Cade to have someone follow the van."

"Captain York told us he does not have enough crewmembers to track down anyone who leaves before the raid." Shima's voice rose in frustration. "He was very clear on that point."

Danae's shoulders slumped. She set down her empty cup. "We don't have any way to follow a vehicle that leaves in the middle of the night. Even if we did, it's still too dangerous to go into Bangkok alone."

"I am not afraid," Shima said again.

"I'm sorry," Danae looked her in the eye, "but my final answer is no. It's too dangerous to attempt. All we can do is pray Zuri's among the rescued slaves."

Shima's heart sank. She hadn't realized how much it would hurt to hear the words she'd been expecting. "Yes . . . Captain." She stood and left the galley.

"I'm sorry, Shima!" Danae called after her.

The first officer didn't look back. She wiped her eyes on her sleeve as she climbed the ladder down to the basement. She'd considered who else on the crew she could approach and only one name came to mind.

She poked her head in the open doorway of the engine room. "Blaze?"

"Just finishin' up here," came a muffled reply.

Shima spotted the engineer's long legs sticking out from beneath one of the many control panels stationed around the large room, which was a labyrinth of machinery.

After a few moments, Blaze scooted out from the small space and sat up, wiping dust from his face. "Did you need somethin', Shima?"

She walked over and offered Blaze a hand up from the floor. "Yes, I need your advice."

Shima was grateful Blaze was a good listener. He concentrated on her words without interrupting to offer reasonable objections—or doubts about her sanity.

When she was done explaining, Blaze folded his arms and stared at the ceiling for a minute, thoughtful. "Well . . . the only thing I can't figure out is what to tell Lorina."

Shima gave him a perplexed look, but Blaze offered no further explanation. He glanced at his watch. "It'll be dark in an hour."

"I do not understand."

"If we're gonna get to factory six before dark, we'll need to move fast."

"We?" Shima wasn't sure if she heard right.

"Got your gun?" Blaze patted his right cargo pocket, checking for his own weapon.

She shook her head. "I have not worn it since I was stopped by the CIPs yesterday. It is against the law to have a gun here, and I do not want to risk being caught with it."

"Suit yourself," Blaze said. "I guess we'll be safe with just mine." He walked over to the alcove where there was a cot he used while the ship was in Velocity flight. He returned with a small backpack. "There's already two bottles of water and some basic supplies in here— handlight, binoculars, earcom. Ready to go?"

Shima felt a rush of gratitude for the engineer, who came to her aid before without hesitation, despite the danger. "Lorina is a very lucky woman."

Blaze led the way to the ladder but let Shima climb up first. "I just hope she's a forgivin' woman. I'd better wait until we're in the city to call her because I don't think she'll be too happy about this excursion." He paused a moment, his foot on the first rung. "Someone's probably gonna hear us leave and try to stop us."

Shima stopped climbing and glanced down at Blaze. "Could you mute the shipboard com?"

He flashed a lopsided grin. "Good idea, Miss First Officer." He hurried back to the engine room.

She waited on the ladder, halfway to the entry level, and tried not to worry about being caught leaving the ship. She felt a little guilty, as if she and Blaze were trying to pull off a bank robbery.

The engineer returned to the ladder in less than a minute. "All set."

In the entryway, Blaze typed in a code on the keypad next to the interior airlock door. "Let's move."

Both airlock doors cycled open, and Shima and Blaze raced down the stairs and over to the docking pad lift. They were descending in the elevator before the outer door of the airlock finished cycling closed behind them.

"I think I'll leave the earcom in the backpack for now," Blaze said, still grinning.

"Thank you, *rafiki.*"

"Don't thank me yet. We still have to make it to the factory without gettin' mugged."

***

It was dark by the time Shima and Blaze reached the raised riverbank and factory number six.

Their only delay on the way over had been a brief confrontation with a child-thug, who jumped out of an alleyway, brandishing a long knife at them. Blaze drew his gun, the boy's mouth fell open in shock, and he turned and fled back into the alley. Shima was grateful there were no CIPs around to notice Blaze's pistol. They made the rest of the trek unscathed.

"Let's climb back up to the bushes," he whispered.

"They know we hid there before."

"We've scoped the entire area, and there's no other place to hide if we wanna see what's goin' on."

Shima nodded, and they crept as quietly as possible around to the back side of the slope where they wouldn't be seen by the factory guard. Blaze headed up first, but Shima took a moment to find her footing in the darkness.

She didn't hear a thing. A large hand was clamped over her mouth, and her right arm was pinned behind her back.

"What are you doing here, Oryang?" Captain York's voice in her ear was soft, but there was no mistaking the dangerous edge in his tone.

"Smith?" York hissed to Blaze, who was already scrambling down the slope to aid her. The ISPP captain kept a tight grip on Shima until Blaze was standing in front of her before removing his hand from her mouth and giving her a shove toward the engineer.

Shima stumbled, but Blaze had his arms out to catch her. He helped her regain her balance. Furious, she spun to face York.

Only York wasn't there, just his voice. "I thought I told you to stay aboard your ship. You're jeopardizing the safety of my crew and the success of this entire mission."

Shima's immediate thought was, *A ghost!* She put her own hand over her mouth so she wouldn't scream. "I cannot see you."

"That's good," York said, "but I *can* see you, which means so can anybody else. Danae sent you?"

"No, sir." Blaze matched York's volume, which was just above a whisper. "We came on our own. Captain Shepherd's gonna be just as angry as you are when she finds out where we are. I'm sure she knows we're missin' by now. Chameleon suit, Captain?"

"Yes, but it won't do my team any good if you're seen, so get your scrawny butts back to the spaceport."

Shima squinted, trying to discover the source of the disembodied voice. She could just make out the faint outline of a large man-sized shape standing a meter in front of her. The shape blended in with the grassy slope behind him. *It is not a ghost.* She forced the childish fear to the back of her mind. "We are not leaving, Captain York."

York swore. "I don't have time for this foolishness, Oryang, and I can't spare anyone to haul you idiots back to the spaceport right now. Do us all a favor and *leave,* before I get *really* angry."

"You said you do not have the manpower to send someone to follow the van that took the older girls away. That is why we are here. Blaze and I will follow it if it comes back tonight."

"Are you planning to follow it on foot?" York demanded.

"If we must." Shima tried to remain civil, despite her rising frustration. "You do not understand, Captain—"

"I understand a lot more than you know."

Shima felt a tremor of fear at the abrupt shift in York's tone, from sarcasm to contempt. She took a wary step back but bumped into Blaze, who also tensed at York's words. Before Shima could decide what to do, the blurred outline was in motion, and she felt a powerful hand seize her right shoulder.

Blaze made a startled noise as York maneuvered past her and seized the engineer's left shoulder. The ISPP captain kept a paralyzing grip on Shima's trapezius muscle, making it impossible for her to squirm free.

York steered them away from the factory and forced them to walk for several minutes. They descended the embankment, moving toward the Chao Phraya. Though the weeded slope had been busy with foot traffic during the day, there wasn't a soul around after dark.

York was a silent, invisible presence between them, tension radiating from him like a smoldering fire. Shima was afraid, but she was also angry York was treating them like common criminals. She tried to think of something else to say in their defense, but as angry as the captain was, she decided it would be safer to remain silent.

York marched them to a lone Banyan tree, just a few meters from the steep drop-off to the river. The thick, intertwined trunks created multiple shadows in the weak moonlight, casting the bower into total darkness.

"Sit." York didn't give them the option of refusing. He pressed down hard on Shima's shoulder, forcing her to the grass. Blaze got the same treatment and wound up right next to her, rubbing his own shoulder.

"Listen to me." Again, the ISPP captain didn't give them a chance to object. "Since you refuse to leave, I'll give you three choices. I can handcuff you to this tree, I can have my medical officer give you an injection that'll knock you out for about ten hours, or you can do as I say and *sit here* until the raid is over. It's your choice."

"I vote for sittin'," Blaze grumbled.

Shima just harrumphed, seething with resentment.

"Wise choice, Smith."

She heard fabric rustling for a moment, and then something sharp and small, like a thumbtack, pierced the exposed skin of her upper right arm. She let out a muffled yelp. "You said you were not going to knock us out!"

"It's not an injection," York said.

Blaze said, "Ouch!" and Shima assumed he had also been stuck.

"What is it?" she asked.

"It's a personal transmitter," York said. "It allows my people to locate each other in the dark and in camo. Fewer accidents that way."

Shima frowned, realizing what he meant by accidents—*so they do not shoot each other.*

York continued, "If you remove the transmitter or try to leave this immediate area, I'll know." He paused, the sharp edge now missing from his tone. "Look, we've got a job to do here. I know you want to find your niece, Oryang, but this raid could potentially turn ugly, and you could get killed—or get someone else killed—and I can't let that happen. I don't have enough officers to send someone to babysit you, so I'll say this one last time— *stay here* and *keep quiet.*"

Captain York's departure was just as silent as his approach. Shima was embarrassed the big man had been able to sneak up behind her so easily. *I would make a terrible spy,* she thought.

Everything was quiet, except for the cheerful chirping of crickets and the distant puttering of outboard motors on the river.

"I am sorry I got you into this, Blaze."

The engineer shifted his position until their elbows were touching. "I'm just sorry we got caught." He took off his backpack, opened it, and dumped the contents onto the ground between them, searching for something. "Here's the earcom. I'm sure we have some interestin' messages on it."

"Do you want me to explain to Captain Shepherd?"

"Nah, I'm bettin' the first message on here is from Lorina, and it'll probably be kinda loud."

Shima winced. "Please tell her it is my fault. I forced you to come with me."

Blaze chuckled. "I think she knows me better than that." He patted Shima on the back. "It'll be fine. Trust me."

She wished she had a portion of Blaze's optimism. She felt around in the grass for another item from the backpack. When she located the binoculars, she raised them to her eyes and turned her face in the direction of factory number six.

Shima could see the moonlight reflected off the highest loop of the razor-wire fence, plus the top floor of the building behind it. Lowering the glasses, she tried to judge the distance to the factory from where they were sitting, but the moonlight wasn't bright enough to help. There were too many shadows. She thought about searching for the handlight but realized even a tiny light might attract unwanted attention.

She sat quietly and tried not to eavesdrop on Blaze's conversation with Lorina, but it was difficult not to since he was sitting right next to her. It didn't sound like he was in too much trouble. He only apologized twice and spent more time listening than explaining.

At last he said, "I promise we won't move from this spot, sugar," and blew out a long breath. To Shima, he said, "Well, that's one down, one to go."

"I should explain to the captain," she said again.

"Nope." Blaze chuckled. "I've been on the receivin' end of her wrath before. I can handle it."

She was impressed Blaze handled the call to Danae with diplomacy, listening for long intervals with only an occasional, "yes, Captain," to break the silence.

"Yes, ma'am. We won't move from this spot." Another long exhale, and Blaze unclipped the earcom. "Well, that's it, Shima. We'll face some kind of punishment when we get back to the *Alex* in the mornin'."

"We will be here until morning? What time is it now?"

"It's 2015."

Shima grimaced. "It is going to be a long night."

"And since I was up all night, last night, I think I'll get some sleep." Blaze stretched out on the ground about a meter away from her. "Goodnight."

"Sleep well, *rafiki.*"

In five minutes, Blaze was snoring softly. Shima felt a twinge of envy at his ability to fall asleep so easily. The pleasant temperature and lower humidity were ideal for camping out, but she wasn't in Bangkok for outdoor recreation. A long night of solitude lay before her, although she knew it wouldn't be quiet when ISPP raided the factories at 0230.

I cannot believe I risked so much to get here—made so many people angry—and for nothing. I was a fool to think I could do something to help those girls. She blinked back a few stubborn tears. *Zuri must be here, in one of these factories. She has to be here. Please, God, help me find her.*

Shima touched the tiny personal transmitter York jammed into her right bicep. It didn't hurt anymore, but it seemed to be firmly attached to her arm, like a man-made leech. She wanted to remove it, but the thought of facing York's temper made her abandon the idea.

Danae is right. Cade York is nothing like Alex Shepherd.

The first officer realized her stress level was too high, and she needed to restore some inner calm. In the *Alex*'s post-op, after her near brush with a nervous breakdown, she was able to purge her mind and body of stress using meditation. Now with time and quiet at her disposal, she found a comfortable position, closed her eyes, and turned her focus inward.

Shima lost track of time. When she felt stiff, she changed positions. When she felt thirsty, she found a water bottle and drained it.

When Blaze startled her by making a soft, snorting sound and rolling over in his sleep, she opened her eyes and turned her focus outward. She felt renewed in spirit but knew nothing changed in reality.

Shima's eyesight had adjusted to the darkness. She looked around and noticed the moon was higher in the sky. She searched the items in the grass around her, located the earcom, and checked the time. 0118. *It is almost time for the van!*

Whether it was the extended meditation or divine intervention, Shima couldn't be entirely sure, but a powerful feeling washed over her, flooding every cell in her body with determination and courage.

Beth drowned because of me—because I was afraid. I will not allow fear to stop me from saving someone else! Shima found the binoculars and sprang to her feet, focusing on the sliver of factory number six she saw earlier on the higher part of the riverbank.

The razor wire glowed brightly, in stark contrast to the dark building behind it, just as it had the night before, right before the van arrived. Someone had turned on the fence's floodlights.

Shima gripped the binoculars in one hand and ran. She ascended the riverbank as fast as she could, trying to stay within the shadowy areas. She expected to be ambushed again by the stealthy ISPP captain at any moment, but she didn't care.

She reached the peak of the riverbank, where the land leveled out, and dropped to the weeds on her stomach, trying to stay out of sight of the handful of people she spotted inside the fence near the only gate, which faced the river.

Shima brought the binoculars to her eyes again to see what was happening. The gate was open, a van was waiting just outside the razor wire, and someone with a bag over her head was being escorted out of the factory.

Someone with dark brown skin, like her own.

She held her breath as unanswerable questions raced through her mind. *What should I do? What can I do? Why did I leave my gun on the ship?*

As Shima watched, the prisoner suddenly bent down and shook her head so the bag fell away. The guards shouted something and shoved her. The girl fell to her knees, unable to break her fall due to her hands being bound behind her back. The fall must have hurt, but she didn't cry out. Shima realized the girl just wanted to see what was around her, turning her head in every direction.

For a split second, the prisoner's full face was in her sights. Shima gasped and dropped the binoculars.

It was the face from her dream, the face of her older sister, Ngoma—Zuri's mother.

Shima was on her feet and racing the perimeter of the fence, straight toward the gate, her body and mind united in a single purpose: to stop Zuri from getting in that van.

"Zuri!"

Shima didn't realize she screamed the name until she saw the people inside the fence turning to face her with startled expressions. Guns appeared in their hands.

For a fleeting moment, Shima wondered what it would feel like to die, but she didn't intend to hesitate long enough to become a target; she ran faster.

The night seemed to explode with the *crack crack* of gunfire. Shima heard screams, saw Zuri's escorts jerk reflexively and fall to the ground, first one, and then the other. The other people inside the fence joined them on the ground in quick succession, but Zuri was still standing, frozen in place, just a few steps from the open gate and the waiting van.

Shima closed her mind to the deafening crackle of gunfire all around her. Her lungs burned and shooting pains laced through her shins, but she didn't care, she had almost reached the gate.

The bag covered Zuri's head again, so she couldn't see the man reaching out from the van to grab her.

"No!" Shima screamed. She hadn't risked her life—risked everything—only to watch her niece disappear again.

Zuri resisted the man's efforts to yank her inside the van. Shima saw him touch her with a nerve prod. She was so close, Zuri's piercing scream hurt her ears.

Shima put on a final burst of speed and reached the van a split second before the man could pull Zuri inside the open cargo door. She threw her arms around Zuri, causing him to lose his grip on the girl. He shouted something at Shima in Thai and swung the nerve prod at her.

Shima pivoted on one heel, turning her back to the van so she was between the nerve prod and Zuri, who was shaking uncontrollably.

An explosion of pain ripped through Shima like a raging fire. Every cell in her body felt consumed by its heat. She heard herself scream, but she kept her arms around Zuri, determined to protect her.

The pain stopped, but the effects of the prod continued to torture her. Shima's muscles seized up, sending her entire body into spasms. Her vision blurred, and her stomach contracted with dry heaves. She lost her hold on Zuri, and they both fell onto the gravel road.

Shima felt strong hands seizing her, lifting her, hoisting her inside the van. She couldn't control her arms or legs to fight back. She couldn't even make a sound to cry for help.

She was dumped onto a hard metal floor, and she felt a small shivering body land next to her. Strange words were shouted, echoing in the confined space, and the van was in motion, speeding away into the night.

Author's Note

What man of you, having an hundred sheep, if he lose one of them, doth not leave the ninety and nine in the wilderness, and go after that which is lost, until he find it? ~Luke 15:4

This story is set in the future, but the horrors of human trafficking is a reality of our day. No country is exempt from this atrocity of abducting innocent people, particularly young children, and forcing them to be soldiers, slaves, and prostitutes. I felt prompted to write *The Lost Sheep* to shed some light on missing children like Zuri. Though she is a fictional character, she represents the millions of children who are the innocent victims of human trafficking.

There are many organizations that are working to end human trafficking. Consider donating or volunteering with one of these groups to help rescue those who are enslaved and to prevent others from suffering the same terrible fate.

SterlingRWalker.com

Acknowledgments

Once again I need to offer a heartfelt thanks to my family for supporting me. I know I'm not as available to them as I should be when I'm immersed in my writing, so I appreciate their patience and understanding. I'm grateful to the members of my writing critique group, authors Tamara Ward and Jandy Salguero, who served as my beta readers. I also appreciate the sage advice of author J. Lloyd Morgan, and my editor Kayla Echols.

Thanks to my cousin, author Lisa Rector, for doing final updated edits and formatting my books and ebooks for publication.

An excerpt from
The Last Orphan,
Book 3 of
The Orphan Ship trilogy

Shima muffled a cry of pain as she was dropped onto a hard tile floor near the room's only window. One of her captors shoved her back against the wall, forcing her to sit upright.

Zuri landed on the floor beside her. One man removed the hood covering Zuri's head and untied her hands. Before either of them had a moment to recover, Shima heard the unmistakable rattle of metal chains.

She could only watch with mounting fear as her wrists were secured in front of her in thick metal bracelets. A titanium chain about two decimeters in length connected the shackles to each other, and another short chain extended outward from each of her restraints. Zuri was handcuffed the same way, and Shima was chained to Zuri on her right and another teenage girl on her left.

A loud whisper warned. "Quiet!" And their captors left the room, pulling the door shut behind them, and plunging the room into darkness. The only light came from the crack at the bottom of the door. Shima heard a key in a lock, and then it was quiet.

"Auntie, auntie," Zuri said in Swahili, "you found me."

"I have been searching for you since the night you disappeared from Mars Station."

"Don't let them hear you, or they'll punish all of us!" A scared female voice whispered in English from the other side of the room.

Shima's eyes adjusted to the gloom of the unfurnished three-by-three-meter space. It smelled like a locker room which hadn't been aired out in years. She could dimly make out the scared and tearful faces of the dozen multinational teenage girls who shared the stifling space with her and Zuri. They all sat with their backs to the filthy walls, each wrist connected to the ones on either side by a short length of chain. A squeaky ceiling fan set on low moved the air just enough to keep them from suffocating.

She responded to the prisoner across the room. "How long have you been here?"

"Two days."

"She is from my factory," Zuri murmured. "I recognize her voice."

"Did you all come from factories?"

A few *yes*'s from those who understood English.

"I haven't had any food since I was brought here three days ago," another girl said. "We're only allowed to use the toilet three times a day, so I hope you have a strong bladder."

"They give us just enough water to keep us alive," complained a young woman with a Spanish accent.

"They weaken us so we'll be more . . . cooperative," the Asian girl on Shima's left spoke up, her tone a mixture of bitterness and fear.

Shima realized she was the only prisoner who wasn't dressed in a skimpy, form-fitting shift. *Dressed for work,* she thought with a shudder of revulsion. *These girls are just children!*

"Auntie, you are bleeding," Zuri whispered.

The first officer was able to turn her head enough to see a trickle of blood oozing from a tiny wound near her right shoulder. She bit her lip to hold back a cry of dismay. "No—it is gone."

"What is gone?" Zuri turned her head to look at her aunt with her big brown eyes.

Shima felt a lump in her throat as she got a good look at her niece for the first time. Even with the poor lighting, she could see Zuri looked exactly the way she remembered Ngoma. Shima's second oldest sister had been Zuri's mother. Ngoma had died many years ago in Kampala, along with all the other members of the Oryang family.

It was hard to believe Zuri was fourteen. She was so small and thin. Shima couldn't imagine the hardships the teen must have endured as a slave for half her life.

She forced herself to focus. *I cannot become emotional.* She explained to Zuri, "I was wearing a tracking device when we were taken away in the van. My friends might be able to trace it and rescue us."

"But where is it now?"

"It must have come off when they dragged me from the van. But it may be close enough that we can still be found."

Zuri looked hopeful, but she turned her face away and leaned her head against the wall. Shima could sense her niece was trying hard not to cry.

She tried to distract Zuri from the overwhelming feeling of despair which permeated the room. "Why did you risk punishment by taking the bag off your head?"

"I do not know how to explain it." Zuri sniffled. "I just wanted to see outside the factory. I knew it might be my last chance to see anything beautiful."

"It was good you took the risk," Shima said. "I would not have known it was you if I had not seen your face."

"How did you find me?"

"That is a long story, and I promise I will tell you everything once we are free."

"What if we are not found by your friends?" Zuri asked with a tremor in her voice.

"We will be. I will think of a plan if they do not come soon," Shima said.

The room grew quiet again as the whispers between the other prisoners faded and stopped. No more advice was offered to the newcomers.

Shima was physically and emotionally exhausted. She leaned her head back against the wall and managed to doze off.

***

The sound of the door being unlocked awoke Shima. She blinked at the sudden illumination from the hallway when the door was thrown open. The two girls sitting closest to it were forced to move toward the center of the room to get out of the way. Everyone sitting near them had to shift their positions to minimize the strain on their wrists from the shackles.

None of the captives made a sound as two people stepped inside the room—a man clad in military fatigues and armed with a heavy rifle and a woman in a sleeveless, Chinese-style, red silk dress and stiletto heels. The armed guard spoke something to the well-dressed woman and pointed at Shima.

Shima felt cold, despite the sweltering heat of the prison room. The woman crossed the small room and crouched in front of her, their faces only a decimeter apart.

The first officer didn't know what to expect so she remained silent as the woman scrutinized her face. Shima guessed her scowling captor was Asian, but not Thai. Her eyes were more like Marco Ting's. She assumed the woman was a *madam*—the only word she could think of to describe a female slaver.

The madam wore heavy makeup and a floral perfume so overpowering, the scent made Shima queasy. Her black hair was pulled up into an elaborate chignon, and she wore a lot of expensive-looking jewelry. She finished staring at Shima and got to her feet, turning to speak to the armed man in a tone of authority. His response was deferential and brief.

That does not sound like Thai. I think it is Chinese.

The woman barked something at the man and snapped her fingers in the universal signal for *hurry up*. He stepped out of the room and returned in a minute with another Asian man who was built like a Sumo wrestler.

Shima had a brief flashback to the terrifying night aboard the *Ishmael* when a brute named Wade Jackson had tried to overpower her. She realized this time there would be no Blaze or Danae to come to her rescue.

The madam stepped aside so the huge man could reach down to unlock Shima's shackles. He seized her wrists and yanked her to her feet, and then immobilized her by turning her back to his chest and looping one massive arm around her waist, pinning her arms to her side. She was lifted off the floor and carried from the room. He paused in the hallway, waiting for the others.

"Auntie! Do not leave me!" Zuri's voice rose to a hysterical scream. "Auntie!"

Shima heard the unmistakable sound of a slap, and Zuri was silent. "Leave her alone!" She struggled, trying without success to kick her Sumo guard.

"Quiet!" The madam pulled the door to the prison room shut and spun the key in the lock. She then marched over to Shima and slapped her hard across the face.

Shima's cheek burned. She stopped struggling and closed her mouth but gave her captor a defiant look.

With the improved lighting in the hallway, Shima noticed for the first time a small tattoo on the woman's neck, just below her left ear. It appeared to be a symbol or trademark: a red letter B was surrounded by a circle of black barbed-wire. The rustic initial seemed out of place on the flashy courtesan.

"You spek Engrish?" Her English was so bad, Shima could barely understand her. "Thet goot! Get bic money fo you!" She snapped her fingers at the men and gave them some orders.

The madam remained at the door, watching with a satisfied sneer as Shima was carried down the hallway by her guard with the armed man close behind. She was hauled up a staircase and down another well-lit hallway. Her captor stopped at one door and pounded on it with his big fist.

The *Alex*'s first officer couldn't see who opened the door. She listened in helpless frustration at the rapid-fire conversation between her handler and the female door opener. She did hear one phrase, "*bai hu*," several times, but she had no idea what it meant since her knowledge of Mandarin was limited to *ni hao*—hello—and *xie xie*—thank you.

The man standing behind her with the rifle listened to the exchange with an ugly smile on his face, nodding with vapid approval. Shima wished she could kick him in the nose, but the muzzle of the rifle pointed at her face was a strong deterrent.

The conversation ended, and she was taken inside the brightly lit room.

No! Shima panicked and tried again to break free. She didn't want to be alone in a room with these disgusting criminals who treated women like property, like cattle.

No, cattle are treated better than trafficked humans. She managed to swing her heel back and strike her handler's kneecap, but this only made him angry.

The fist that connected with the side of Shima's head made the lights flicker and the room spin. She squeezed her eyes shut against the pain and swallowed against the bile rising in her throat.

Her handler dropped her, facedown, onto a cold horizontal surface.

A table? What is happening?